Michele Renae is the ps[...] award-winning author M[...] has published over ninety novels in historical, paranormal and contemporary romance and fantasy, as well as writing action/adventure as Alex Archer. Instead of writing 'what she knows' she prefers to write 'what she would love to know and do'. And, yes, that includes being a jewel thief and/or a brain surgeon! You can email Michele at toastfaery@gmail.com, and find her on Instagram: @MicheleHauf and Pinterest: @toastfaery.

Justine Lewis writes uplifting, heart-warming contemporary romances. She lives in Australia with her hero husband, two teenagers, and an outgoing puppy. When she isn't writing she loves to walk her dog in the bush near her house, attempt to keep her garden alive, and search for the perfect frock. She loves hearing from readers and you can visit her at justinelewis.com.

Also by Michele Renae

Cinderella's Second Chance in Paris
The CEO and the Single Dad
Parisian Escape with the Billionaire

Also by Justine Lewis

Billionaire's Snowbound Marriage Reunion
Fiji Escape with Her Boss
Back in the Greek Tycoon's World

Discover more at millsandboon.co.uk.

CINDERELLA'S BILLION-DOLLAR INVITATION

MICHELE RENAE

BEAUTY AND THE PLAYBOY PRINCE

JUSTINE LEWIS

MILLS & BOON

All rights reserved including the right of reproduction in whole or in part in any form. This edition is published by arrangement with Harlequin Enterprises ULC.

This is a work of fiction. Names, characters, places, locations and incidents are purely fictional and bear no relationship to any real life individuals, living or dead, or to any actual places, business establishments, locations, events or incidents. Any resemblance is entirely coincidental.

This book is sold subject to the condition that it shall not, by way of trade or otherwise, be lent, resold, hired out or otherwise circulated without the prior consent of the publisher in any form of binding or cover other than that in which it is published and without a similar condition including this condition being imposed on the subsequent purchaser.

® and TM are trademarks owned and used by the trademark owner and/or its licensee. Trademarks marked with ® are registered with the United Kingdom Patent Office and/or the Office for Harmonisation in the Internal Market and in other countries.

First published in Great Britain 2024
by Mills & Boon, an imprint of HarperCollins*Publishers* Ltd,
1 London Bridge Street, London, SE1 9GF

www.harpercollins.co.uk

HarperCollins*Publishers*, Macken House, 39/40 Mayor Street Upper, Dublin 1, D01 C9W8, Ireland

Cinderella's Billion-Dollar Invitation © 2024 Michele Hauf

Beauty and the Playboy Prince © 2024 Justine Lewis

ISBN: 978-0-263-32123-4

01/24

This book is produced from independently certified FSC™ paper to ensure responsible forest management.
For more information visit: www.harpercollins.co.uk/green.

Printed and Bound in the UK using 100% Renewable Electricity at CPI Group (UK) Ltd, Croydon, CR0 4YY

CINDERELLA'S BILLION-DOLLAR INVITATION

MICHELE RENAE

MILLS & BOON

To all the backyard entomologists
who love watching dragonflies, beetles,
butterflies, and other bugs.
It's a fascinating world we all share!

CHAPTER ONE

THE CLATTER OF plastic on the worn wood desktop prompted Wolf to shift his sight from the computer screen, effectively surfacing from his mental foray through the python computer code that occupied his early mornings. The director of operations of Concierge, his best friend Skyr Svedahl, stood on the other side of the desk, hands on his skinny hips, curly blond hair always falling over one eye.

Wolf plucked up the daily desk calendar Skyr had set down and shrugged. "What's this?"

"It's a challenge calendar," the man announced with declarative gestures.

Wolf crimped a brow. "You know this company does have an app for that?"

"Really?" Skyr mocked uncertainty. "A calendar, sure. But not with challenges for each day."

Wolf had created the Concierge app years earlier. It organized all apps on a person's phone into one central hub. Everything from your grocery order, dinner deliveries, gas mileage, texts, alerts for monthly payments, medical info, household appliance reminders, fertility cycles for women, workouts, and all things baby related. If a person had an app on their phone, it could be incorporated into Concierge in one way or another. It had gone viral in the first week of its release. Last year Concierge had hit the billion-dollar sales mark. And since, Wolf's life had not been the same.

"Maybe you need to add this particular calendar format to Concierge," Skyr said. "See." He peeled off the top page that featured yesterday's May date. His actions were demonstrative and over the top. A showman during company meetings, the guy knew how to get a point across. "This is how low-tech items work. You gently tear the page. Feel the paper. Read the page…"

Wolf leaned back in the ultra-comfy high-tech office chair that could give him a massage, measure his heart rate, and remind him to get up and move every twenty minutes. "Not funny, Svedahl. Is this your way of apologizing for leaving Concierge next week?"

Skyr shrugged. "You know I'm in love. I would follow Melanie to the ends of the world. And Sweden is my home."

Wolf had met Skyr seven years earlier at a tech conference in Stockholm. They'd bonded over shared interests in the future of decentralization and craft beer. "We can make this work remotely, you know."

"I know. But I'm happy, Wolf. Thanks to Concierge, I've earned more than enough to live comfortably. Now I want to make a family."

"Yes, yes." Wolf gestured dismissively. "The simple life."

He'd never reveal how he completely agreed with Skyr's decision to leave the corporate rat race behind and settle into a low-tech, much more relaxed life with a beautiful woman and the hopes of family glinting in his eyes. All that living-off-the-grid jazz. He just needed space! Yet Wolf's chances of finding a woman who could truly love him had dropped off the charts. In fact, that miserable statistic had been the catalyst to his current dating sabbatical.

"I'll miss you, buddy."

"We'll Zoom. But here." Skyr nudged the calendar closer to Wolf. "Each day issues a challenge to try something new or do a normal task differently. You need this. It'll get you out of your rut."

"I'm not in a rut."

Skyr wobbled his hand before him and winced. "You come into the office every morning at five. You code until ten. You head to the coffee shop to fill up on octane. Spend twenty minutes sitting in the shop ogling the barista with the ponytail—"

"I do not ogle her," Wolf protested. His surveillance of the bright-eyed barista was more subtle than that.

"She's cute. I've checked her out. You should go for it. But I know you won't, because you are scared."

"Just cautious of my privacy."

"I get it. The paparazzi. But back to your rut of a schedule. Business meetings until two when you have a late lunch delivered right to your desk. Then work until it's dark. Sleep. Rinse. Repeat."

Wolf winced. When Skyr listed his routine like that it did seem mechanical and, very well, like a rut. He'd never been so focused on the job, determined, moving as if on autopilot. Unconcerned about having a social life. And what had happened to his libido? It was still there, but the relentless paparazzi—and a million-dollar lawsuit—really knew how to cool a guy's sex drive. But while the Concierge app had gifted him the ease of not having to worry about money, it had bracketed his world down to a tightly confined diorama of rote actions and daily grind.

On the other hand, his dull routine did keep the paparazzi away. Make a move in a new direction? Those curious camera hounds lurked, drooling for a salacious lede. Much like his office mates who gossiped behind his back. Could a man exist without the world wanting to know his every move?

"For your information," he said, "I'm not scared of the barista. I'm just…"

Cautious about dating. Especially when he never seemed to attract a woman he could trust with his fragile heart. "This calendar is half used." Changing the subject was much easier than talking about his nonexistent dating life.

"Because I've been using it. It's what made me decide to quit."

"Well, in that case…" Wolf picked it up and made like he would dump it in the trash bin.

"Do it for me," Skyr said. "I know you trust my opinions. Together we've grown Concierge into a company at which people dream to work. And don't I always have your back in Halo?"

They didn't spend much time online gaming anymore, but true enough, Skyr was a man who always had his partner's back. Virtual or otherwise.

"That calendar will change your life."

Wolf grunted dismissively. Then set the calendar on the desk. For now.

"I've got my replacement narrowed down to two candidates," Skyr said. "I'll give you my choice by the afternoon. Before I make my grand exit, do you want me to quell the office rumor that women are avoiding dating you because you're maybe gay?"

"What?"

Skyr shrugged. "Kidding."

"I haven't dated since before Christmas. Do they still gossip about my terrible dating life behind my back?"

Skyr nodded. "Janice set up a betting pool on how long before you do date. And how much the resultant lawsuit will cost you. Sorry, man. You just have bad luck with women."

It wasn't him. Was it? Wolf felt sure it was all the hundreds of millions that had suddenly befallen him. His last dissatisfied girlfriend had taken him to court for emotional distress brought on by a quarter-million-dollar diamond ring!

Thus, a sabbatical from dating.

"You know why I don't date," Wolf muttered.

"According to Page Six, it's because you don't like getting sued. But I know you, man. That last one was crazy. Just because you gave her a ring she thought that meant you were going to marry her?"

"I said nothing about marriage when I gave it to her. It was just a bauble she saw in a jewelry store, and I wanted to make her happy." Wolf raked his fingers through his thick hair. Buying things for others was the easiest way to ensure he held a place in their lives. "Is it too much to ask for someone real?"

Skyr swept his hand in Vanna White fashion beside the calendar. "This will help."

"I seriously doubt that, but I'll take it off your hands just to keep from seeing more of your Vanna impersonation. We done here?"

"We are." Skyr gave him a salute and left the glass-walled office.

Wolf owned the entire building. He'd thought by choosing something in the Chelsea area, better known for being the center of the art world, away from the financial and the techie Flatiron districts, that would promote a calmer atmosphere for his work life. Concierge was his safe space.

Becoming a billionaire had made him a celebrity, and that had flipped his calm, quiet world upside down. He hadn't even known what Page Six was until he'd started dating models and actresses. Initially he'd thought he'd hit the jackpot. Poor kid from a small village in Germany, once scrawny, who wore thick glasses, always beat on by the bullies, grows up to create an app that the world couldn't get enough of, thus making him strangely attractive to some of the most beautiful women he'd ever laid eyes on.

But none of those women had been capable of *seeing* him. The real Wolfgang Zeigler still sometimes felt like that bullied boy with the thick glasses and had a penchant for avoiding crowds because he preferred to isolate himself in the wondrous world of computer code. Coding was what made him happy.

Wolf leaned back in the chair and closed his eyes. With the one friend he was always able to talk to leaving, would he now fall deeper into the apparent rut Skyr had said he was in?

He opened one eye and read the sentence on the calendar page for the day. Stupid.

With a sigh, he shook his head. Skyr knew him too well. Wolfgang Zeigler was not a man to resist a challenge.

"Your turn, Ivy." Estelle Clement replaced the bean hopper on the espresso machine and then swiped her hands down her apron that bore the But First... logo for the coffee shop she'd owned for fifteen years. "I gave you my list of items required to make the perfect man. What about yours?"

Estelle had watched *Practical Magic* last night—for about the fortieth time—and she'd told Ivy about her favorite scene where the young Owens sisters make a wish for their perfect man. Estelle's list included blue eyes, the ability to mambo at the drop of a hat, and various bodily expectations that Ivy could wholeheartedly get behind.

They had become good friends in the three weeks Ivy had been working the morning shift as a barista. She was thankful for Estelle's kindness and that they got along. Otherwise, this soul-sucking menial job would annihilate her will to live.

"The perfect man, eh?" Sliding a soft-bristled cleaning brush along the stainless-steel machine components, Ivy focused on getting into the crevices. "Well, he has to be smart. Give me a real conversation over texting, please."

"Hallelujah to that one. I am so over emojis and hashtags. My boyfriend is a physicist. He can talk me between the sheets with the theory of quantum physics any day."

"Wow. You are not easy. I like that." She and Estelle bumped fists. "What else? He has to be strong. I like a man who can pick me up and carry me away."

"Oh, so you're into fairy tales, eh?"

Ivy imagined a man carrying a woman up a long stretch of stairs. Without dropping her or knocking her head against a wall. Yeah, probably fairy-tale stuff.

"I guess I am. Though ixnay on the glass slippers. I'm not much for pulling glass shards from my soles. He's gotta be protective, too. That goes along with the sweeping-me-away part."

"So, you are definitely into muscles."

Was she? She'd never devised a list of attributes for the perfect man. This was just a game, right? Well, if there was one thing she did require in a man…

"And he has to believe in love," she declared as she set the cleaned portafilter on the mat beside the espresso machine. The sudden jab of an elbow into her rib made her chirp. "Ouch!"

"Shh." Estelle leaned in and whispered. "He's back! Don't look. You know he comes in every morning just to see you."

Ivy rolled her eyes. Then she managed a glance out the corner of her eye while maintaining her attention on her cleaning task. "It's just his routine."

He was back. Wolfgang Zeigler. The man who owned the art deco building in which the But First... coffee shop occupied the bottom floor, alongside a twenty-four-seven gym. Assorted businesses filled the ten floors above them, mostly office space. The top two floors were dedicated to Concierge. Zeigler was punctual, always arriving at ten o'clock. And his order never changed. Black coffee. Slice of chocolate chip cake. Estelle had filled Ivy in that he was the creator of the wildly famous Concierge app. And he was a billionaire. Apparently, though, since his dating life had taken a dive, the street had cleared of paparazzi. Something Estelle cheered because the photogs had a tendency to scare away the customers in their frenzy to snap a shot of Zeigler's every move.

Was that all it took nowadays to garner celebrity? A fat wallet? Ivy supposed being a billionaire did make one a celebrity, but she much preferred her celebs to display talents that lifted her mood. Like Lucille Ball or Michael Bublé. From the little she'd heard about Zeigler on the news, he was a savant when it came to programming. He had a reputation for dating gorgeous women. And then dumping them less than a month, or even a week, later. Celebrity rags called him the rogue billionaire.

But what Ivy saw when he strolled into the shop was a ruggedly handsome man with thick black hair and a black beard and moustache. He looked like a lumberjack who had been caught by a styling team, pomaded, groomed, and released back into the wild. His uniform was a white business shirt, the top two buttons undone to reveal a peek of black chest hair, and the cuffs were usually shoved to his elbows, not neatly rolled. His trousers were perfectly fitted, yet the way they stretched across his backside revealed the fact the man must work out. He was built and beefy. Yet curiously reserved.

That was the part about him that intrigued Ivy. For a man who must have the world at his grasp and had dated famous people, he was guarded, even a little shy. She'd always thought those in the limelight shone brightest when given attention, so his quiet demeanor fascinated her.

Alas, she was a simple barista. At least for the moment. Certainly not a stunning model or actress capable of capturing the sexy man's attention. Nor did she consider dating a celebrity a sane move. Of course, that didn't stop her from daydreaming about him. How else to make the day go by?

Lifting her shoulders and smoothing a hand to tuck in the loose strand of hair that had fallen from her ponytail, Ivy forced on her "I'm a retail worker and must be nice to customers" smile and turned to greet the man who occupied her daydreams.

"Good morning, Mr. Zeigler." Who was she kidding? Her smile was natural and oh so easy when directed at him.

He nodded. She'd never been a woman to fawn over a handsome face, but this man had some serious bedroom eyes and that beard looked so soft she wouldn't mind getting lost in it. And if that meant their lips had to collide? Do not send out the rescue crew.

"The usual?" she asked, fending off wandering thoughts of five-alarm fires and kisses.

"Black coffee," he said, "and…" As Ivy bent behind the counter to reach for his usual snack, she paused when he announced, "A slice of lemon cake. Please."

She snapped upright, peering over the glass display case at the man who had stuffed his hands in the front of his trouser pockets. "What?"

He nodded. "Lemon cake, please."

"But…"

He took a moment to study her expression then shrugged. "I know. Thought I'd change things up today. And…" he pulled a folded piece of paper from one of his pockets "… my calendar told me to do it."

Ivy narrowed her gaze onto the paper he held for her to read. It had today's date on a little desk-calendar-size note. The logo *Challenge Yourself* was flourished across the bottom. And the sentence printed in the center read: *Try a new-to-you food today.*

This billionaire who could have anything he desired—and anyone, for that matter—took directions from a corny desk calendar?

"Well, okay then." She pulled out a slice of the lemon cake, frosted with a tart lemon glaze, and set it on the counter. Black coffee in a small cup, no cover, she set beside it. "Good luck with your culinary adventure."

A smirk revealed his reluctance at the change. "I'll need it." And then he peered at her chest for a moment. "Thanks, Ivy."

"You're welcome, Mr. Zeigler," she managed in a calm tone while her insides burst into a festive dance.

He settled into his usual seat by the front window, attention on his phone, and took a sip.

Meanwhile, Ivy was jerked around behind the stock shelves by Estelle. The woman's gold hoops jangled madly as she clutched her fists in glee before her. "Did you hear that?"

She had heard that. "He ordered lemon instead of chocolate chip," Ivy whispered, not wanting any of the patrons to hear them.

"No!" Estelle whispered enthusiastically. "He called you Ivy."

"That is my name."

"Don't be smart with me. I can sense your insides jittering with glee. That man has never called you by name, or anyone else in the café. He likes you." Estelle fluttered her lashes. "And he does qualify for both the strong and smart items on your list."

"Whatever. I need to finish cleaning the espresso machine."

Ivy picked up the cleaning cloth and went back to work, and acknowledged her insides were indeed doing the gleeful dance Estelle had discerned. The man with the intense yet softly searching brown eyes had called her Ivy. That had been the most personal thing he'd said to her in the three weeks she'd been serving him daily.

Drifting back into the fantasy of a soft beard and hard, tight muscles, she dared a glance over the top of the machine. She caught Zeigler in the middle of a bite. That wince did not signal approval. She hadn't expected he'd like the tart lemon. He was more of a constant, comfortable chocolate chip guy.

Tossing aside the cleaning cloth, she slid a plate out from the display case and then wandered around to the dining area. "How's that lemon cake working for you, Mr. Zeigler?"

He offered her another of those brief but captivating smiles. "I think it requires a certain palate."

"It's a bit tart." She set the plate with a slice of chocolate chip cake on his table. "Trade?"

He pulled the plate to him. "Hell, yes."

Retrieving the lemon cake, she was about to leave him to himself when he touched her wrist. "Hang on. I'll get my card to pay for it."

"It's on me," she hastened. "Seriously, Mr. Zeigler, you're

our most consistent customer. Every day at exactly ten o'clock. I can set my watch by you."

He swiped a hand over his jaw and beard. "You think I'm in a rut, Ivy?"

The question was so out of the blue she could but mutter, "Uh…"

"I know I am. This calendar is supposed to make me think out of the box. Do things differently. Not a very good start, eh?"

He liked to try new things? She mentally added that to her list for the perfect man. Why not? It was her list; she could edit at her whim.

"You did give it a try," she offered. "There's something to be said for taking a chance, especially if lemons have caused you trauma in the past."

His laughter was deep and easy. Ivy wanted to lean forward and stroke his beard. Make contact with the larger-than-life man who lifted her weary spirits each morning she saw him.

"No citrus trauma," he said. "Though, now that I think about it, there was that one time me and a buddy robbed a lemonade stand."

"You did not!"

"I was seven. And I needed the change for some new shoes." This time his wince seemed to take him unawares and he straightened, shifting his body to a less easy posture. "Ancient history. Thank you for rescuing me from that sour yellow cake."

"No problem, Mr. Zeigler. See you tomorrow at the same time?"

He thought about it a moment. "Maybe I should surprise you with a different time?"

"Now that would be stepping out of a rut," she teased.

"Yes, it would." He lifted his coffee cup in a toast. "Here's to trying new things."

"Hear, hear!" Ivy called as she strolled back to the counter where a customer waited. While she filled the complicated latte order, her focus kept drifting to the man who devoured the cake.

Trying new things? And he'd called her by name. This day was already better than any of them had been since she'd had to suddenly move to New York to take care of her brother. She'd had to refuse an excellent job offer for a position in Switzerland and find something close to where her brother was staying, thus the coffee shop. These past weeks had been a challenge. But she wasn't complaining. That never got a person anywhere. Besides, she'd get a chance at her life after she ensured her brother was on the right path.

And now she had something to add to her *Things to Be Thankful For* list. He'd called her Ivy. And had actually spoken a few sentences to her.

Nodding with satisfaction, she peeked around the espresso machine to watch as Zeigler left the shop. A rogue billionaire? To her, he was more like an exotic insect perched on the edge of a jungle leaf, just out of her reach. Where he should stay. A mental reminder that he was a celebrity and she didn't need that drama in her life prodded.

Yet she'd never been able to resist the allure of the rarest of the species. Continued observance was required.

CHAPTER TWO

ON TUESDAY, Mr. Zeigler ordered the usual, went to his usual table, pulled out his phone, and began his usual—whatever it was he usually did for the twenty minutes he sat there.

Standing behind the counter, still taken aback, Ivy glanced to the clock on the wall behind her. Nine fifty-five. He'd come in ten minutes early. Wonders did not cease!

Picking up the coffeepot, she decided to also switch things up. He never requested a refill. But her ability to resist curiosity was weak. And mental field notes on his rare species were a necessity.

Arriving by Zeigler's table, she held up the pot in offer. "Refill?"

The man's focus switched from phone screen to the pot and then to her. His mouth softened into a genuine smile. It made her core swirl with a sensual heat. "Sure."

She filled his cup without losing her gaze in his deep brown eyes. A feat, actually. "What does today's calendar page demand of you?"

"An easy one." He dug out the folded page from his pocket and handed it to her.

She read the unfolded square. "'Take a five-minute cold shower at the beginning of every day.' Easy?" She mocked a shiver. "Don't tell me you already do that?"

"It's good for the circulation. And a bunch of other health stuff. You don't do cold showers?"

"I'm not big on shock. Especially at five in the morning. And I'm pretty sure my scream would be heard by the neighbors in the brownstone next door. I'll pass."

"It's exhilarating. Kind of like when I walk in the door to But First…"

"Oh? This dorky little café gives you a lift?"

He nodded with a shy bow of his head. Then a shrug. It was as if he'd reverted from a confident billionaire to a small kid right before her eyes. A kid who didn't know how to express his feelings but had accidentally blurted out a private detail. Or more likely, an adult man checking his personal boundaries.

"Glad to hear it," she said. "I'll see you tomorrow, Mr. Zeigler. Whenever time that may be."

The touch of his hand on her arm paused her. A sensuous heat moved from her wrist where his hand made contact with her bare skin and wavered up to her shoulders then spilled to her breasts. Such a visceral thrill! She was suddenly glad she wore a dark T-shirt and the heavy canvas apron because her nipples peaked tightly. So much for personal boundaries.

"My name is Wolfgang," he said. "Call me Wolf?"

Her entire body swam in the ocean of desire that his deep voice conjured. And if she looked at him one moment longer she would definitely fall into his eyes. Ivy rescued herself from an embarrassing plunge. "Wolf. The guy who owns the building, right?"

"I do. My office is on the top floor."

"That's Concierge," she said. "I have the app."

His smile was, curiously, much closer to a smirk. "Most everyone does."

"It's a life changer."

"Really? For the good or the worse?" he asked.

An unexpected question from the creator of the famous app.

"For the good, of course," she said. "Streamlines my life. Reminds me of things I need to remember. Collates all the assorted other apps into one quick look in the morning. It's all good."

"Fair enough." He leaned back in the chair. "But…it doesn't make you feel like you're in a rut? I mean, the app does everything for you. You don't even have to think about things. Your phone pings. You check it and respond."

"Are you suggesting a person *shouldn't* use your app?"

He shrugged. "Never. I've just been thinking differently lately."

"Because of your calendar. Well, I'm pretty sure five minutes under cold water isn't going to change a person's life."

"You'd be surprised, Ivy." He stood and gathered his coffee cup and tucked a twenty-dollar bill under the plate. His usual tip. "Thanks. And, uh, don't forget. It's Wolf."

"I could never for—uh, yep. Wolf." She waved as he strolled out of the café. Only when he was clear of the front windows did Ivy exhale and shake her head. "Oh, my God, I'm such an idiot. I almost said I could never forget you, Wolf. Yikes!"

And yet, he may never realize he was the one bright spot in her day.

On Wednesday, Wolf strolled into But First… around ten-thirty. He'd just finished a workout at the gym next door. Not his usual evening workout time, so his entrance had made the receptionist do a double take.

He'd only been following the pages a few days and,

weirdly, his brain had started to hit him with questions before he did things. Can it be done a different way? Would changing a tried-and-true method or routine make him pay closer attention? Even the few paparazzi who lurked in the neighborhood had been taken off-guard with Wolf's mixing things up. And that was a kick!

He knew this sudden need to pay closer attention to the details wasn't because of some stupid calendar. Because he'd finally talked to the pretty barista. He'd spoken her name. A name he'd read on her nametag in his head every day he'd gone in for coffee. And by finally speaking it out loud, it was as if he'd released a clasp on that shy young boy inside him who was always unsure about talking to the pretty girl. Hell, he'd touched her wrist!

Wolf met all kinds of women, all the time, and in every situation. It always started out friendly, then moved to flirtation, then most of the time his libido charged in and they hooked up, sometimes even for a few weeks.

But because of his innate desire to trust and be loved, he'd been burned by those women. They always wanted something from the man who had been branded with the mark of billionaire. It felt like a red letter on his chest. The app, and the brand he was growing around Concierge, attracted money like a magnet. Pretty damned crazy for a guy who had grown up in the foster system and had never had a bed to call his own until he'd rented his first apartment at eighteen.

"Good morning, Mr.—er… Wolf."

Ivy's voice was dulcet. But with a solid firm edge. When he thought about her—which he did as he sat nursing his coffee, pretending to skim his emails—it seemed as though she didn't quite fit in this cozy coffee shop, brewing lattes and skinny mochas. She carried herself tall and proud. Her sleek brown ponytail was always tight and neat. He sensed the coffee shop's textured gray walls and white marble counters studded with neon lamps was not her natural habitat. And he wanted to discover more about her. Because really, he'd not developed a coffee habit until a few weeks ago when he'd spied the beautiful woman behind the espresso machine. He hadn't missed a morning since.

"The usual?" she prompted him with a smile that glittered from her bright blue eyes. Hex code 74D4E7. He knew the chart programmers used for colors like the back of his hand. When he nodded, she gestured to the empty table by the front window. "I'll bring it out to you."

Wolf turned to face his table. *His table?* Really? *Yep, you are in a rut.* Turning, he eyed the table in the corner. Why not?

When Ivy arrived with coffee and a slice of chocolate chip cake, he thanked her. "I know," he offered, with a gesture to take in his new digs. "Mixing things up."

"The corner table. It is prime real estate. Just don't let your knees nudge up under the table."

"Why?"

"Gum," she said. "I don't get paid enough to do that dirty job."

"Thanks for the warning, Ivy." Her name felt like candy on his tongue. He wanted to have a real conversation with her, something that went beyond pleasantries. And today he had his chance. But it could only happen if he shoved aside the shy boy and put on his big boy cap.

Wolf pulled out the calendar page from a pocket and handed it to her.

"Okay, let's see what today brings," she said. "Take a walk in the middle of the day. So how did that go?"

"I'm not sure. I was going to ask when you get a break. Would you go on a walk with me, Ivy?"

"Me?"

She looked around. The café hummed with the sounds of the espresso machine. No one paid them mind.

Please don't say no...please don't say no.

"I...uh...well, I do get off at two."

That was a yes! "Great. Will you walk with me? Just around the neighborhood. I promise I won't keep you long."

"I'd like that."

"It's a date then. Er, well, I mean, it's a..." He fidgeted with the calendar page. Dates were off-limits!

"I know what you mean. It's another challenge! I'm happy to help you with it. I'll see you in a few hours."

Another barista called for Ivy's help, so she swung around and back behind the counter. Wolf followed her walk. Tall, shoulders proudly back, sexy sway at the hips. She was one beautiful woman.

Not in the right place, though. He couldn't shake that feeling about her. Interesting.

And he had not a date with her—but a challenge.

Hmm, he didn't like the sound of that. However he labeled the walk, he would finally get to talk to the woman who had the power to stir him from his desk every morning to take a break.

There was something about Ivy he couldn't get enough of.

Wishing she had worn something prettier than a T-shirt and jeans, Ivy reminded herself she was not on a date with the sexiest man she'd ever served coffee to. This was just a challenge he was completing. And she was helping. That made it much easier for her heart to manage as well. She didn't have the emotional energy for a relationship right now, but friendships were always welcome.

So it didn't matter that her shirt advertised that *Bugs Are Beautiful*, or that there was a hole in her jeans just above her knee—usually covered by the work apron. The day was bright and warm, and the route he'd suggested took them down a quiet street that led them to a small park. A yoga class currently occupied most of the park, so they strolled around the area beneath pear trees that had recently bloomed. Spent white blossoms gently snowed down on them. It felt magical.

But Wolf seemed nervous. He'd only asked how long she'd lived in the city—about a month and a half—and what she liked about working at But First… Not much, but she did enjoy the conversations with customers.

"Spiders," he suddenly said. He smiled at her double-take and then made an expert toss of his cup, landing it in the garbage can.

"What?"

"I paged back to the previous day that my friend had left on the calendar just to read it. It said to reveal a fear to someone. I'm afraid of spiders."

"Oh, well, arachnophobia is shared by most. Personally, I love the furry little critters."

"I get that from your shirt. That's why I brought up spiders." A flower petal landed on his sleeve and he observed curiously before brushing it away. "What's beautiful about a hairy, eight-legged creature that crawls over your hair in the middle of the night and bites your legs?"

"They don't all bite. And really, if I were a spider I'd go immediately for your hair, too. Oh." Ivy bit her lower lip.

"Because it's a good place to hide?" he asked.

No, because it looked soft enough to nuzzle her face into.

And it probably smelled like leather or steel or some manly scent that she wanted to inhale and get drunk on.

"Arachnids are attracted to dark, confined places." Whew! Way to make the save. "But not all insects stir dread in your heart, I hope?"

"Just spiders." They rounded a corner where the sunlight was no longer blocked by the tree canopy. Wolf pulled out a pair of sunglasses and put them on. "Tell me what you're afraid of?"

Fair enough. Anything to make this conversation last.

"Fears?" Never getting back the life she'd almost held in her hands? Watching her brother be decimated by a malicious disease? "I'm not a big fan of horror movies or serial killers. I don't watch a lot of TV, actually, because I don't like to put that sort of stuff into my brain."

"I agree. I can't remember when I last flicked on the screen. I have one in my penthouse, but I'm pretty sure the dust has grown so thick…"

"That spiders have moved in?" she teased.

"Don't say that!" With a laugh he paused and leaned against the wrought-iron fencing that corralled the park. "This little park is nice. There's so much concrete and tarmac in New York. It was a major adjustment after I moved here from Germany." He thumbed a couple more flower petals on his shirt sleeve then offered her a warm smile. "I can't remember when I last took a few minutes out of the day to shift my focus from coding and business."

She had read something about him being a coding savant. "So you're the coding genius behind the app? That's cool."

He pushed the glasses up to the top of his head. Ivy was thankful for the move; she liked looking into his eyes. "I love coding. It's like a second language to me. Maybe even my native language. I'm a geek. What can I say?"

The last time she had seen such a muscled, sexy geek was never. He certainly didn't fit the geek model. "Geekery is good. And there's nothing wrong with avoiding media and all the sensational images that suck away your soul. So what do you do with your free time? That is, if you have free time."

"That's just it. I work a lot." He blew out a breath. "Doesn't really seem to move the scale much either."

"How do you mean?"

"Like, is all this work improving my life?"

"I seem to recall reading that you earned a bit of cash from the app."

He chuckled. "I did. But money doesn't make a guy happy or move the scale."

She might argue differently. The medical bills stacked on the table at home certainly would, too. She and Ivan, her brother, had not yet reached financial panic mode. But it would arrive soon enough.

"I think I'm at an inflection point," he said. "I'm standing in the middle. I can go one way. The usual way. Keep doing what I'm doing, making more money that I don't need, pushing apps on the masses that they don't need, and life goes on. Or…"

"Or?" She leaned against the fence beside him, propping her hands on the iron rail behind her. Standing so close to him, she could smell his—well, it wasn't cologne. More like a sweetness and spice. Was it his hair product? Whatever it was, she could almost taste it, it smelled so good. Aphrodisiac pheromone attractor, she scribbled in her mental field notes.

"That's the thing. I'm not sure what the *or* is. What could I have if I wasn't so focused, so stuck in this rut that feels so deep I'm drowning?" He straightened abruptly, gesturing before him. "Sorry. That was… Too personal."

But an excellent addition to her notes.

"It's okay. I like talking to you, Wolf. And even though this is just a challenge to you, I appreciate the chance to get to know you better. You're an interesting man."

"I can say the same about you. Bugs, eh?"

She shrugged. No reason to reveal her purpose for the T-shirt. She was, after all, just another page on his calendar.

All of a sudden, a shower of white petals rained over their heads. Ivy tilted back her head and closed her eyes. She could have been enjoying nature, working outside right now had Ivan not called her two months earlier with his devastating news. She was not a woman who could maintain her sanity for long confined in a little shop, pressing coffee grounds for a living.

When Wolf took her hand with both his, and the warmth of his touch traveled like fire up her arm, she sucked in a breath.

"Thanks," he said. "This means more to me than you'll ever know. I mean, you took time out of your day to give me your attention. I appreciate you going along with my silly calendar page."

"Always happy to help a man of discernment."

He lifted a brow.

"The chocolate chip cake. It's amazing," she said.

He chuckled. "That it is. You've a petal on your lashes. Can I?"

She nodded. As he carefully plucked it away Ivy took in his determined brown gaze, the tip of his tongue as it slipped out of the corner of his mouth. And that hair. So touchable. But she didn't see any petals on him that would require a subtle brush.

"Thanks," she said shyly.

Who had she become? She wasn't shy or mincing. She'd

dated some amazing men and most of them had been handsome, prone toward the scientific arts, and always quite kind. She knew how to talk to and relate to a man. Not that any of her lovers had ever stuck around for more than a few weeks. That was her choice. She'd always been focused on school.

But there was just something so…intimidating about Wolf. Not in a scary way. But rather, in a manner that warned if she was not cautious she might succumb to his pheromones and—

"Should we head back?" he asked.

Wrenched from the image of falling into the man's arms, Ivy nodded. She didn't want the walk to end. And she was off from work. But she did need to get home to her brother. Back to reality. Observation of her knight in rugged armor would have to wait for another day.

At that moment a dragonfly fluttered before them and she held out her finger. The insect landed, flapped its wings, and settled there, content.

"Wow," Wolf said. "You have some kind of bug mojo." He peered closely at the insect and his breath on her hand made her imagine his breath elsewhere on her body.

Really, Ivy? *Yes.*

But whether or not to net this particular man perplexed her. Because she wasn't just the person who shared an interest in his calendar pages, but rather, she was the woman who wanted to peel back his shy armor and see if his insides were as interesting as his outsides. Yet, with caring for her brother, she hadn't the emotional headspace to open up to him and allow him into her life on a relationship term.

Did she? Or, more honestly, *dare* she?

CHAPTER THREE

ON THURSDAY, Wolf sat down at a table on the opposite side of But First…, near a bushy plant that he flicked aside so it wouldn't tickle his neck. Ivy brought him black coffee and chocolate chip cake, and then waited for him to reveal his next assignment.

He handed her the page as she said, "Ten-thirty today. How do you exist on such a wild and crazy schedule?"

He initially took that as a dig but then realized she was joking with him. The last time he had been able to sit and chat with a woman and not have a trail of paparazzi stalk them or have to try to impress her with his money was, well, he'd given up on meeting that ridiculous standard months ago.

To simply enjoy talking to Ivy without her expecting a thing from him was refreshing.

She read the calendar square, "Read a book in a genre you would normally avoid. So, what's that? Mystery? Science fiction? Self-help?"

"None of the above." He dug out the tattered paperback he'd purchased at the secondhand shop down the street and set it on the table.

Her gasp made him look around to ensure no one was watching them. Seriously, the cover was lurid peach and purple.

"Are you kidding me?" She picked up the book and fanned the pages. "Romance? And Loretta Chase? I love this story!"

The book title had called to him: *Lord of Scoundrels*. And while he'd been sheepish about selecting it, the clerk, an elder woman with bright violet hair—hex code B618CB—and half spectacles, had given him an enthusiastic recommendation.

"I read the first two chapters in the store, and I have to admit, it is good. I like how the author shows the hero as a kid in the beginning, so you know what it was like for him growing up."

He also related to that neglected, battered, and desperate child in the story. But that was a story Wolf kept close to his vest. No woman wanted to hear about his tough past. They preferred him in expensive suits, freely swiping his black credit card.

"You read two chapters in the store? How long were you there?"

"I'm a speed reader. It'll take me about an hour to finish the story. Figure I'll put away a few more chapters while I'm here."

"You really are switching things up. And a romance."

"Guys can read romance," he added defensively.

"Oh, I know they can. You just don't seem the type…" She shook her head. "Sorry. I wouldn't want anyone to presume anything about me, either. I am not what I appear on the surface."

He suspected as much about her. But how to really delve beneath her exterior? Because he wanted to learn more about Ivy, but without having to emotionally commit or fend off a court case. Was that asking too much? Probably. He'd never had a friendship with a woman, so navigating what was going on between them was a challenge beyond anything listed on a little calendar square.

"I'm happy you're enjoying the story," she offered. "You will fall in love with the couple, I promise."

"Thanks. And thanks again for talking to me like…"

"Like?"

"Like a normal person. I just…" Feeling his muscles tense, he wanted to close off the sudden need to express his desire for connection to her. So he did. "It's weird for me. New York is a weird city. It's so confined. And I'm either at work or at some celebrity function running away from the paparazzi."

"Estelle mentioned something about the paparazzi. She's the owner," Ivy explained. "She said there used to be days the customers could barely make it past the wall of photographers eager to get a shot of you. She's so relieved your love life has—er. Sorry."

Wolf shook his head. Even the coffee shop owner knew about his horrendous luck with women?

"I shouldn't have said that," she added. "Your private life is your business. I'm just sorry you have to endure things like crazy photographers trying to get a photo of you."

"I'm glad they've gone away. For now. But as soon as I start dating?" He shook his head. "They'll be back."

"Well, I hope it doesn't make you swear off dating forever. We humans are, by nature, in need of connection."

Connection was something he craved despite his finding it difficult to form such connections. It was the way he'd been raised. He'd learned to survive on his own, and welcoming others into his life wasn't so much a challenge as a lesson in protecting his boundaries. Feeling nothing was much easier than being vulnerable. As for romance? Caution was the key word after what he'd been through.

Ivy was suddenly summoned by Estelle's call across the café. "It's your brother."

"I have to take this. He's…not doing well lately. See you tomorrow?"

"For sure."

Her brother wasn't doing well? What was that about? And the fact that he was genuinely concerned surprised him. In a good way. He'd connected with Ivy. And that put a smile on his face for the rest of the day.

Dread curdled in Ivy's gut as she took the phone call in the back room.

"Ivan, what's up? Are you okay?"

"I don't want to scare you, Ivy, but the physical therapist wasn't able to make it in today and… I took a walk out to the park. But now…it's my eye. It's… I can't see out of it at all."

Her brother had been diagnosed with MS two months ago. His gait was unsteady and he'd begun to use a cane to get around. His doctor warned there were a litany of symptoms that may yet rise. The world had changed for him. And not in a good way.

"I'll be right there," she said.

"But you don't get off for another hour and a half. I'm sorry. I should have waited until you got home, but… I'm still in the park… I know I can make it back…"

"Ivan, it's a fifteen-minute walk home. Hang on!"

She turned to find Estelle behind her, nodding. "Go ahead, sweetie. If it's your brother, he comes first. I've got two girls coming on shift soon."

"Thanks, Estelle. I'll put in extra time tomorrow."

"I know you will." Her boss hugged her. "Take that almost-expired cherry cake home with you as a treat for your brother."

"I will. See you tomorrow."

* * *

Should he or shouldn't he? Wolf's thoughts wandered as he typed. His mind was capable of focusing on a programming task while he simultaneously processed unrelated thoughts through his cortex. And he couldn't seem to keep Ivy out of his brain.

Not a terrible distraction.

Whether or not to ask her out was the question. He'd instituted his dating sabbatical because his lawyer had suggested he didn't need any more lawsuits or the bad publicity that came along with them. Yet he'd also given Wolf the name of a private investigator should he wish to date. He'd used him once, right before the sabbatical, and that woman had not checked out.

Clicking on the Concierge app in the upper right corner of his screen, Wolf searched for the PI's info and texted him a name, business name. That was the only information he had on Ivy. Then he hit *send*.

He sighed heavily, feeling some regret. It was what he had to do to avoid a lawsuit.

"I'm so sorry, Estelle. You stay home and take care of that flu. It's not fun being sick in the summertime."

Estelle sighed over the phone. She'd just let Ivy know she wouldn't be in today. They had four employees scheduled for the day so she wouldn't be missed. But First… would be fine without her.

"I'll work an hour later to cover until Valerie comes in," Ivy said.

"Thanks, sweetie. Is your brother doing okay?"

"He's got an appointment tomorrow with an ophthalmologist. He panicked yesterday, but it is something we need to address."

"I'm praying for him. Uh, there's one other thing. It's killing me, but my boyfriend is thrilled."

Ivy could not imagine what her boss would next say, so she listened.

"We were supposed to see the New York Philharmonic tonight. Mandalbrot is the featured violinist. Tony hates classical music, but you know I like to try new things. Anyway, do you want the tickets?"

"Oh? Uh…" Did she? Ivy had never been a fan of classical, yet she also didn't hate it. And wouldn't a night out be a nice vacation from her life? "I think I'd love to take them off your hands. Not sure who I can bring along with me, though."

"What about Ivan? You did say he gets around well enough with the cane. Might take his mind off the eye issue?"

Ivy chuckled. "Yes, he can get around, but I'm pretty sure hell can't get cold enough before Ivan would step inside an orchestral hall. He's heavy metal and alternative, all the way. I'll find someone. Maybe Valerie will want to go."

"Great. The concert starts at eight. It's at the Lincoln Center. It's not super fancy, but if you have a dress, wear that. I'll have a courier bring the tickets to the café right away. Call me if there are any problems."

"We'll be fine without you, Estelle. And checking the schedule, you have the weekend off, so that means you're all about snuggling up on the couch and watching *Practical Magic* for the next few days."

"Sounds kind of dreamy. Except the part where I can't look at food without getting sick. Too much information, sorry. Thanks, Ivy!"

Ivy hung up and Becky's shout alerted her the front counter had a line waiting, so she hurried out to meet the early-morning rush.

* * *

Just as Ivy was getting ready to punch out on break, Wolf walked through the door and looked for a table. Twelve-thirty? Really? She'd almost thought she wouldn't see him today. That thought had put her in a grumpy mood and caused her to nearly spill a mango coconut smoothie on a customer's lap.

The lunch rush had settled but still there were no available tables, which left Wolf standing in line, looking perplexed. When he reached the counter, Ivy pushed in front of Valerie and told him she'd pack his chocolate chip cake to go.

"Thanks. I guess I should stick to the earlier hours. It's crowded in here."

"That's how the lunch rush goes! I have a break now, so I'll bring it out to you. I'll meet you outside?"

He gave her a grateful nod. "Sounds good."

She punched out, hung her apron, then grabbed Wolf's order and met him out front.

"You want to walk?" he asked. "I'll share my cake with you."

"Definitely—wait!" She remembered the call from Estelle. "I think I'd better stick around the shop front. My boss sent a courier, and I need to receive it when it arrives."

"How about across the street?"

They settled on the bench under a maple tree with wide leaves that frothed halfway across the street. Ivy gleefully accepted the bigger half from Wolf when he divided the cake. She hadn't eaten since an early breakfast of burnt toast smeared with peanut butter with blueberries.

With crumbs licked from her fingers, and a sip of Wolf's coffee to wash it down, she then asked, "What's today's challenge?"

"Say yes to everything."

"Oh? That covers a lot. What have you said yes to so far?"

He cleared his throat and recited, marking off on his fingers as he did, "Next week off for Carol because her parents are in town visiting."

"Kind of you."

"We'll manage for a few days without her tendency to sing show tunes at the top of her lungs. Then I said yes to a round of boxing with the brute who occasionally comes into the gym."

"Oh, yeah? Who won?"

"Let's just say my bruises are covered by my clothes. But I did give him a good fight."

"Wow. I'm so impressed. Handsome and a skilled fighter. Uh… I mean…"

"I think you just called me handsome." His smile was liquid seduction. A blush warmed her ears. "I'll take it. And I just said yes to a pretty woman who asked me to meet her outside for a snack. That was a nice surprise."

Likewise. "Unexpected surprises are always fun."

"Really? You like surprises? I like knowing what's coming. To be prepared."

"No spontaneity for you?"

"Probably not." He offered her the last corner of his cake and she took it. "How long is your break?"

"I'm going to hang here to wait for the courier. Oh."

She was all about helping him with his calendar challenges. Dare she? It would be sneaky, since he had committed to the yes.

"Oh?" he prompted.

"I was just thinking about if I should dare go for another yes from you. Even despite your fear of spontaneity."

He turned to completely face her, resting an elbow on the

back of the bench. Bemusement was an interesting emotion on him. But also charming. His virile intensity made her want to run her fingers through his thick beard—and tug him in for a kiss.

"Are you taking advantage of my inability to say no today?"

Was she? Maybe a little? It wasn't as if they were anything more than friends. It would mean nothing to him, and she needn't think of it as a date because she did not want to become tabloid fodder. Yet, Valerie was busy tonight, so...

All right, she dared!

"Estelle is sick and so gave me two tickets to a concert tonight. It's an orchestral performance at the Lincoln Center. I wonder if... Would you like to go with me?" And then she quickly added, "Just as friends, of course. Because I know you have the dating sabbatical going on."

He nodded quickly. "Friends. Of course, that's...us."

Was that reluctance for the invitation or something deeper in his pause? Ivy did not regret the ask, but she would be disappointed if she earned his first no of the day.

"You don't have to say yes if the idea of listening to violins and cellos sounds super boring."

"Actually, I do have to say yes. But also, it's not killing me to say it. I listen to all kinds of music. What time is it?"

"At eight. I can meet you out front of the Lincoln Center around seven-thirty?"

"I can pick you up."

"No, I don't want to ask too much of you. And besides, well..."

Besides what? His picking her up would definitely feel like a date. Going Dutch was the only way she could do it and make it work for her strangely pining heart.

"It's how I want to do it."

"Sounds workable. Tonight! What should I wear? Is this a fancy shindig?"

"Not super fancy, but maybe a suit?"

"I can do that." He tossed his cup and it landed in the nearby trash bin.

At that moment the bike courier parked before But First…

"I think that's the tickets." Ivy stood and rushed across the street, calling back, "See you later!"

CHAPTER FOUR

HAVING LIVED IN New York City four years, Wolf had gotten invited to many events at famous buildings and venues, but he'd never been inside the Lincoln Center. The outer façade, a travertine and glass box, was brilliantly lit at night, inviting all who passed to gaze at the building that looked like a fallen star among the surrounding stuffy brick and limestone buildings. Inside, the David Geffen Hall had been recently gutted and remodeled, and he loved the warm, natural wood interior. Their balcony seats directly overlooked the orchestra. It felt cozy and not too pretentious. He could relax here. And he needed to do that. Because this was a new experience for him.

That experience being attending a concert that played music he'd rarely listened to, but more importantly, attending it with a woman who was not a girlfriend. He wasn't sure how to parse it all. Because Ivy felt like someone with whom he wanted to be more than a friend.

Should he stop looking at her, inhaling her, wondering how soft her skin might be should they kiss? Of course. Because his instincts warned: *Beware. Don't let her in. Remain cautious.*

And yet... Just how gorgeous could a woman, who seemed to be wearing barely a hint of makeup save some mascara, be? She wore a sleek white knee-length dress that revealed shoulders and a diamond of her bare back. Her hair was up in a tight, smooth ponytail. *De rigueur* for her. Higher on her head than she usually wore it at But First… It looked classy. But also controlled. Like she wasn't comfortable with letting down her hair. He could imagine her full, lush hair spilling to mid-back. Tickling her bare skin. And she smelled like those treats he should have cut out of his diet for the calendar challenge.

He leaned in, taking a moment to inhale and linger in her aura. Her scent was so soft, forcing him to be still and crowd out all other sensations. *There*. Like a warm summer day near a garden. But as well, sultry, teasing of moans of satisfying sex.

Don't do it, man. Keep your distance.

Right. Because letting a woman into his life never ended well.

He muttered, "I've never done this before."

"What's that?" She leaned closer, their heads nearly touching.

She smells like a garden, not the promise of sex. And don't forget it!

"Listened to a live orchestra performance."

"They'll be performing Beethoven's *Fifth* tonight. You'll recognize that one."

"Will I?"

She slid a hand over his and patted it. Such an easy, natural move. Her skin was soft and warm. "You will. Trust me, this could be fun."

"I'm game for anything."

She turned to study his face. Eyes like blue icebergs were cool yet so full of life. He could stare into her eyes all day and forget all about the bits and bytes that made up his world.

"You know the color of your eyes is 74D4E7?" he blurted out.

"I—what?"

"It's a hex code for programming colors." He repeated the code.

"I didn't know my eyes could be labeled with a code. Kind of cool," she whispered as the lights suddenly dimmed. "I know tonight is just a means to help you with your challenge, but I haven't had a night out in so long. I appreciate you doing me this favor."

"No problem." A favor sounded safer than a date. Yet, why did his self-imposed boundaries suddenly feel so confining?

As the musicians took their seats on the stage and the house lights went down, Wolf's brain chastised him for missing an opportunity. Could this have been a real date? He shouldn't have to close off his life from others just because the press hounded him.

Thing was, all he wanted was for someone to see him. To value him. And that had never happened. Ever.

Crossing his arms, Wolf nodded. Just a challenge, this night. It could never be anything more.

After the concert, they took an Uber to a restaurant a few blocks away from Ivy's brownstone. They ordered dessert and shared a lush chocolate caramel bomb cake. Ivy was aware of her white dress with every bite she quickly maneuvered to her mouth. No spills. Points for her! Wolf got some caramel in his beard but before she could reach for it, he swiped it with a napkin. No points for him. Just as well. She felt off-balance, unsure how to act toward him. He was a friend, sure, but—did she want this to become more?

Of course you do. And stop using the excuse that you're observing him as if he's an insect under the microscope. You're attracted to him. You want to know if he can tick off all the items on your perfect man list.

Guilty as charged.

The restaurant was crowded, and it was difficult to hear each other so when they finished eating they immediately left. With her place so close, they strolled down the sidewalk, shoulder to shoulder. The night was warm and the air humid with scents of tarmac and newly unfurled spring leaves. Walking alongside Wolf felt like where she wanted to be.

His outer actions lent to some kind of date-ness going on. Did friends walk down the street nudging each other's shoulders? Catching each other's gaze across a bite of cake? Telling her what code her eyes were? He confused her. And she didn't like to be strung along if his only goal was to use her to better his life via some daily challenge.

But who was she fooling? He'd been clear about not wanting to date. And why did she need this night to be more than friends? She was reaching for stars. Trying to fit Wolf into the parameters of that silly list she'd made with Estelle was just a fairy tale. And fairy tales were for children and hopeless romantics. Of which, she was not.

If she wanted to date and have a sex life, she could attract a willing man. She didn't have the time for it right now. Or the emotional heart space. All attention had to be focused on her brother.

And yet at the moment, all attention veered toward the overwhelming presence walking alongside her. He filled the air and she felt protected, as if he wrapped himself around her and occupied the air she breathed. It felt immense. Promising.

Just friends, she reminded herself inwardly.

They arrived in front of the brownstone Ivan was housesitting. Across the street, a small park with a dog area and a few benches beckoned. Ivy veered toward the green lawn, and they sat on a bench. Not far from them a streetlight glowed. Somewhere crickets chirped. It was almost midnight, and there were no walkers. They had the park to themselves.

"That's your brother's place?" Wolf asked.

"Yes. It's really nice inside. Very modern and minimalist. He has it until the beginning of January."

"Has it? It's…not his?"

"Oh, no. That place would cost a fortune to rent. Ivan, well, he's created his own profession. He's always been a nomad, a guy who likes to adventure and see new places. He figured out a way to do it as inexpensively as possible. Also, he likes to push his boundaries, challenge himself to live on as little as possible, make a small dent in the environment."

"Noble. But what's the profession he created?"

"He's an international house sitter. He'll watch someone's house for a week or even months when they go on vacation. In this case, it's nearly a year. I understand the owners are traveling the world via sailboat. So Ivan gets free rent, a place to stay, and usually only has to pay utilities. And he's a master at finding short-term work in the area to cover those expenses. He even does volunteer work. He's been house-sitting probably five years."

"That's resourceful. What's his current job?"

"Well." Ivy dropped her shoulders.

"Does he have one? Or is he doing volunteer work?"

"It's complicated."

He leaned against the back of the bench, bringing up an ankle to rest across his opposite knee. "I recall you saying something about caring for your brother? Is it okay to ask about that?"

Ivy inhaled, fortifying herself for the information that she rarely told anyone. Estelle knew her situation. The interesting friendship that had formed between her and Wolf felt trustworthy. At the very least, he was expressing interest, and that made her feel safe. So why not tell him?

"I was intending to move to Switzerland two months ago."

"For a job?"

"Yes, I got accepted by the Mercer Institute to join their research team on Insect Systematics."

"Okay, wait." He turned to face her. With the streetlight beaming across his face, Ivy memorized the exact shade of his eyes. "I thought I attended a concert with a barista tonight. But you're talking about bugs and research. So that's not just your weird T-shirt obsession? Who *are* you?"

Ivy chuckled. In a moment of villainous teasing she said, "Wouldn't you like to know."

He caught the levity and countered with a, "It'll go a lot easier for you if you spill the beans now."

A waggle of his brow reminded her how easily she could succumb to any suggestion he might make regarding intimacy between them.

Just friends, remember. He said yes to you tonight because he had to. That's all there is to this. Stick to field observations.

"It's nothing so interesting as a supervillain," she said. "I'm an entomologist. I studied environmental biologics. I'd love to secure a position studying the population biology of, well, any endangered species. I adore a fuzzy bee or dragonfly, and don't get me started on the order *coleoptera*. That's beetles."

He smoothed a hand along his jaw, mirth evident in his eyes. But he didn't say anything, so she rambled on some more. Because right now her nerves translated to talking.

"After I finished college, I got a job working for the Maine forestry service. Eighty percent of the work was outdoors, which I love. I traveled around the state tracking invasive species, tagging moths, and talking at events for kids, but I've always wanted to venture to new places. Across the ocean, to rain forests, deserts, wherever bugs can be found. I'd had the Mercer Institute on my list since walking into college. After three long but successful Zoom interviews, I was offered the job. It was a dream come true."

"A dream that you're...not living right now?"

Another sigh rippled down her spine, settling uneasily in her gut. "My brother, Ivan, has been feeling odd for years. Low energy, sleeping more than his usual five or six hours a night, muscles kinking up on him. Some days he couldn't even get out of bed. And that was strange because he's an athlete. He had plans to ride his cycle across the United States until—well."

Ivy realized her story was complicated. She had never told anyone the full version. It was all still so fresh and happening to her day by day. Yet with two glasses of wine swirling in her brain, she decided to go for it.

"Okay, here's the full history of Ivy Quinn. Shortened because I don't want the audience to fall asleep."

"I would never fall asleep listening to you," he said quickly. "Read to me from one of your dry college textbooks? I'm there."

"I'll remember that. Anyway, my parents died in a boating accident when I was twelve. Ivan was eighteen. He was one month away from beginning that bike ride. He intended to zigzag across the US, hitting every state, and then take Canada back to Maine, where we grew up. But after we lost our parents, that plan had to be shelved. Ivan stepped up to become the head of the household. He took care of me. Got a real job so he could pay the bills. We inherited the house and land. Selling some of the land kept us going until I graduated. I thought then that Ivan would go on that ride, but instead he suggested we sell the house and use the money to really start our lives. And pay for my college. Ivan put most of his share in savings and started doing his house-sitting thing, and I finished college. Flash forward years later and I got the job offer. And Ivan was finally diagnosed with MS."

Wolf blew out a breath. "I'm sorry. That's rough. I know a guy who has that. He...well, he's in a wheelchair."

"Some can have mild cases and function quite well. Others are not so lucky. I'm learning there are so many versions and varying stages of the diagnosis. Ivan is at an early stage where doctors believe he may be able to function quite well with it, but he could also take an extreme left turn and—" She bowed her head.

Wolf clasped her hand. The heat of his touch startled her. A gentle squeeze made her swallow back a tear. She wasn't a tearful woman. And she would not be so in front of this man.

"Ivan is currently moving about with the help of a cane. His vision in one eye has blurred recently. I moved from Maine to stay with him. It was the least I could do after all he had sacrificed for me after our parents' deaths. I feel like I owe him that much. I want to make sure he gets good health insurance, finds the right doctors, doesn't have to—do it all on his own. So we're taking it one day at a time now."

"You're a very good little sister. Sounds like you two take care of your own. I'm proud of you."

That statement loosened a tear in her eye, and before she could stop it, it spilled. Ivy caught it with her fingertip. "Thank you."

It had been a long time since anyone had affirmed anything she had done. No parents to congratulate her at high school or college graduation. It felt good to hear it from Wolf. But in a bittersweet way.

"Sorry," she said. "I never cry. This is silly."

"Don't be ashamed. You're one strong woman, Ivy. I'm glad you trusted me to tell me that. It means a lot. And I don't say that lightly."

"Enough of the sob story. I'm doing just fine. Ivan is the one who needs the support right now. We were able to hire a physical therapist to help him navigate the progression of his condition. She stops by a few times a week. But since Ivan doesn't have a real job, he doesn't have health insurance. We need to plan for that future when the last of our parents' house sale money is gone. I just want him to get the help he requires to live and function, you know? I have work that's, well, it doesn't pay as much as the Mercer Institute, but it puts food on the table and pays for some of his medications. As well, it gets me out in the community. I need the interaction. I like talking to people."

"But you'd be much happier studying bugs."

"Much." Now she laughed softly. "So I'm the crazy bug lady. I know I'll get back to doing what I love someday. But for now, I'm content to help my brother any way I can. I just hope we can get his life on a track that works for him before he has to give up this fabulous brownstone. And if he can eventually return to traveling, that would be amazing. I'm not sure how that's possible, though."

"Maybe if he had a traveling partner? A health professional accompanying him?"

"Sounds perfect, but also expensive. We'll see. I try not to worry too much about things. I like to stay positive for Ivan's sake."

"Your positivity is catchy. There's a reason I've stopped

in at But First… every morning since you started working there. I wasn't much of a coffee man before that."

She turned to study his face now. "Really?"

He shrugged. "What can I say? I guess I can't keep away from you. And look at us? We've become friends."

Friends. Coming out of his mouth, it sounded like a dirty word to her. When everything about Wolf made her senses stand up and take notice. It would be so easy to lean against him, tilt her head onto his shoulder, and just…see what might happen next. He was a sexy man, handsome and smart and…he checked off a lot of the items on that list she'd made. Surely, he believed in love.

Oh, why did her heart have to struggle so with her common sense?

Best to avoid asking him about his belief in love. It wasn't an appropriate question for their friendly evening.

"What about you?" she asked. "What strange or horrible history are you keeping close to the vest?"

"You don't want to know."

"I think you owe me."

"Maybe?" He did that straight shoulders thing that clued her in to something inside him shutting down or changing. Becoming less open. "Let's focus on your stuff tonight. Caring for your brother is a lot to handle. And if you ever need a hand to hold or an ear to listen, I'm there."

"That means a lot. Thank you. It is late. I should probably get inside and check on Ivan. Thanks for coming along with me tonight. For saying yes."

"Honestly? Forget about the stupid calendar. I'd go anywhere with you, Ivy."

"I'll keep that in mind next time I want to escape my life for an evening."

He grasped her hand and kissed the back of it. A surprising move that stuttered her breaths. "Please do. Let me walk you to the door."

At the top of the brick stair before the brownstone door, Ivy paused and turned to him. She stuck her hand out to shake, thinking how much she'd rather lift her head and close her eyes. Wait for a kiss. To know the touch of his mouth on hers. Their breaths mingling. Bodies melding...

The sudden firm squeeze of her hand brought her back to reality with the sad exhale of a deflating balloon.

"Goodnight, Ivy," he said. "See you tomorrow."

"Of course."

He took the steps swiftly, and as he walked along the sidewalk, he turned once to wave. She waved back. A heavy sigh deflated her shoulders.

"What are you doing wrong?" she muttered.

Of course, she knew it hadn't been a date. "Just friends" had to become her motto.

But really? Was she that unattractive to the man that he hadn't at least tried to make a move on her? Should she have been more forthright, perhaps initiating more intimate contact? It hadn't felt right at the crowded concert. And in the park the conversation about Ivan's condition hadn't been the perfect moment either.

Dare she imagine she could move beyond friends and break down Wolf's walls to capture the rogue billionaire's attention? And if she did, did she want it? Could she manage a love affair while also caring for her brother? She did not want to bring media snoops into Ivan's life merely because she had been seen with Wolf. He didn't need that stress on top of all the medical stress he was dealing with.

Besides, it seemed Wolf's relationships were accompanied by paparazzi and a fast ending.

Contrary, Ivy was all about true love and happy endings.

CHAPTER FIVE

ON SUNDAY MORNINGS, his first stop was the gym. Wolf had lifted for half an hour then did some boxing with the heavy bag. Now, following a shower, he stood in the elevator alone, riding it to the top floor. He enjoyed being in the office on weekends. The quiet allowed him to focus.

What did give his head a dizzy swirl was thoughts of Ivy in that stark white dress. All eyes had been on her as they'd walked through the concert hall to their seats. He'd dated some beautiful women. Some of them very smart. A model here and there. The choices in New York were endless. And it wasn't so much that he had to put himself out there as they seemed to be attracted to him like flies to flypaper.

He was over being sticky.

And yet.

How long *did* he intend this sabbatical from dating to continue? He'd never drawn an end date. Yes, dating was dangerous. He suspected it was so because women tended to be blinded by his dollar signs, never truly connecting to the man he was on an emotional level. Most of them, anyway. And if he were honest with himself? That little boy inside him who never got any attention growing up loved getting it from the women he dated. Yet, it never felt true, or genuine.

Should he jump back in, there was always the chance of

getting burned, no matter what rules he made regarding dating, or how long he tried to avoid relationships. He'd sighted a couple paparazzi outside the hall last night. He didn't want to do the chase anymore. And he certainly didn't want to put any woman through that craziness.

And yet, Ivy was different. Spending time with her did not feel surface or material as had his previous relationships. He'd never gone slow with a woman.

His heart craved emotional regard, the knowing comfort of a real connection.

He'd text Ivy later, see what she was up to. Thank her again for helping him out with his "yes" day. And if the moment took him, maybe he'd ask her out for real.

Because he was shaking things up, wasn't he? Trying new challenges? Trusting new experiences? Ivy didn't seem the least interested in his money. She had been the one to ask him to the concert. A bold move, if he considered it.

Or was that simply her plot to snag him? Get him interested. Then, wham! What can you do for me, Zeigler? You've got money. Show me how much you want to keep me in your life.

Wolf hated to think in those terms. But he'd lived those terms. So he'd be cautious where things went with Ivy. Yet, he had to start trusting his judgment sooner or later.

He strolled into his office and tossed his workout duffel onto the floor then picked up the calendar to read the day's challenge.

"Seriously?"

He rubbed a hand over the back of his head. Well, that certainly would be a challenge. Guess he wouldn't be seeing Ivy after all.

Instead, he took out his phone and snapped a photo of the calendar page.

* * *

Ivy wandered into the kitchen in her two-piece silky pajamas. A rim of marabou sewn around the ankle hems had worn away long ago. So she liked to do the glamour thing once in a while. Despite her love for bugs, she was a girly girl at heart.

Ivan was still asleep, so she'd start breakfast. Using the shiny copper cookware that hung from a rack over the center island was fun. The sleek, modern kitchen made her feel as though she were on a cooking show, creating savory dishes for so many watching.

After breakfast she'd use her day off to continue the search for affordable insurance. For a man who thrived on physical activity and never slowing down, this diagnosis had been particularly hard on Ivan. Even with his symptoms aside, he wasn't designed to sit still. And while the physical therapist did accompany him on walks in the park across the street, that may not last forever. Ivy hoped it did. Perhaps even that the exercise would help him to improve. She'd done a little reading on the disease and some websites where fellow MS patients chatted and posted diets and exercise routines that actually improved their symptoms.

Wolf's mention of finding a traveling professional health assistant intrigued her. Did something like that exist? If Ivan was able to travel, that could prove to be his best bet to have as close to normal a life as possible. She added that to her list of things to check out.

There were studies he might qualify for that would offer him free medical treatment—experimental, of course. She had created a list over the weeks she'd been here and would start filling out applications for Ivan's acceptance. It was a move in the right direction.

But as she cracked some eggs over the frying pan, her thoughts segued from Ivan's dire future to last night. It had felt good to get dressed up and sit beside Wolf. The music and the company had energized her. Touched the woman inside her that loved being seen by a man. And it had made her forget about Ivan and his troubles, if only for an evening.

And while guilt prodded at her, a part of her did a little happy dance because she'd allowed herself to enjoy last night. Until Wolf had asked about Ivan. Really, when did she cry? In that quiet moment on the park bench, it had felt as if she'd unloaded a heavy weight. She'd needed to tell someone. And that he'd held her hand meant the world to her.

Now, would he call? He had no reason to. Last night had been a transaction. Alas, they were just friends. Just another man in the wild she must observe and learn about.

"No emotional energy for a relationship, remember?" she quietly reminded.

Her phone pinged with a text message. Ivy scrambled the eggs with a spatula while checking the screen. Wolf had sent a photo of... She laughed when she read the calendar page for today. *Spend the day alone. Go within. Listen to what's inside.*

And he had added:

Great to spend time with you last night. See you Monday morning?

She texted back:

For sure.

Spending the day alone seemed like something Wolf might find easy to do. But she also knew he did like to be out in the world, not necessarily face-to-face with others, but beside them, especially when it related to business. No wonder it had bothered him so much what the office thought about his past romances. He put a lot of weight in what others thought of him.

Whereas Ivy cared little if a person liked her. So long as they were not hateful or falsely accommodating. Perhaps Wolf's past relationships had pushed him too far into the noise and busyness of social media, entertainment, status, and…well, he'd mentioned the money.

What she could do with the money Wolf had would be phenomenal. First, she'd get Ivan the best medical care. Then, she'd move to Switzerland and take the job. Though, she knew that job was no longer available. Then? She'd buy herself a small but cozy place to live. Or maybe she'd get a backpack and travel the world, seeking insects in the rainforest and accepting jobs where she could find them, following in her brother's nomadic footsteps. Yes, money would change her life. But it wouldn't necessarily make it easy.

She wondered what Wolf did with all his money. News media and tabloids liked to write about the rich and famous. But when she had the idea to look into him a little more, she shook her head. She liked the Wolf she knew right now. And whatever she learned about him would be what he wanted her to know.

Though she was curious about his eye color. After sliding the eggs onto a plate, she searched online for hex codes.

On Monday, Wolf's calendar challenged him to expose a mistake to a friend. So while on a walk along the pier with Ivy during his lunch hour, he bought her a corndog and they shared a large cherry frosty that she insisted she could never finish, but she did make a concerted effort at consuming her share.

"A mistake?" she asked when he told her about the challenge. "It should be not too devastating, but not too simple. Something middle ground."

He leaned back on the bench, his shoulder hugging hers. Before them the Hudson's bean soup waters wavered and crashed against the docks. Beyond the pungent scent he picked up coffee beans. Did she notice that he took a few seconds to inhale her with an unobtrusive tilt of his head to the side? If she did, she didn't say anything.

"I've made plenty of mistakes," he said. Like swearing off dating. Because really? Gorgeous woman sitting so close he wanted to kiss her. "But one I do regret was when I was fifteen. Me and a couple guys from the foster home snuck out to the shed and gave one another tattoos. With a hot needle, not a tattoo gun."

"That sounds like something a teenage boy would do. Where is it? Show it to me?"

He propped an ankle over his knee and lifted his pant leg to expose it. In blurred blue ink a makeshift hand with the middle finger lifted.

Ivy touched his ankle as she inspected. Wolf sucked in a breath. Her skin against his was the conduit to something so intense. Every time she touched him he felt an erotic thrill.

"That's hilarious," she said.

"More like stupid. I haven't had the desire to get inked since."

"I don't know, I could see you with a wild animal or tribal something or other. Or how about your namesake?" She shrugged when he shook his head. "I have a couple tattoos."

"Do you?"

"One is on the back of my shoulder." She scooted forward on the bench and tugged down the sleeve of her T-shirt. "Can you see?"

He spread his hand across her back and tugged the shirt

down to expose a beautifully rendered metallic green and shimmery copper tattoo of what looked like… "A beetle?"

"*Chrysochroa aurora*," she said. "It's one of my favorites. I also have a *calopterygidea*, which is a jewelwing damselfly, on my hip. I think it would be awesome to be covered with fluttering insects."

"You really do love your bugs. What inspired you to entomology?"

"I've chased and studied them since I was a kid. They are nature's works of art. Also, my dad was a wildlife biologist. You know we have only classified and discovered less than thirty percent of the entire insect species? I want to travel to the rainforest someday to hunt for butterflies. Finding the blushing phantom butterfly is my dream. It has the most incredible rose-red coloring on its mostly transparent wings." She tilted her head down and smiled up at him through her lashes. "I have big dreams."

"About little things," he added. "I hope you get to do all of that, Ivy. And send me the pictures when you do."

"I will. I'm also polishing my photography skills. Have you seen close-up macro shots of bugs? They are amazing. They capture all the microscopic details like the *ommatidium* and detailed mouthparts. A fine jungle of hairs on a carapace. I could stare at them for hours. But I'd never catch and kill an insect just to take its picture."

"Don't entomologists kill bugs for research?"

She winced. "We try not to. Sometimes it is necessary. Especially in a big netting situation."

At that pronouncement her eyes took him in. As if wondering how large a net she might need for him? The thought made him smile.

"You'll get your chance to do everything you dream about." He clasped her hand. "Your brother will get the help he needs and become self-sufficient, then you'll be off to the wilds of Brazil to photograph butterflies."

"Ivan is so positive it sometimes freaks me out. There are days I find this all so overwhelming. And he just sits there with a smile. I know this is devastating for him, but he'll never say that to me."

"He sounds like a strong person. Like you. If you need anything, you must let me know."

"Thank you. You said something about you and some guys from a foster home. Did you…live in a foster home?"

Wolf slouched against the bench and stretched out his legs. No woman had ever seemed to care enough about him to ask about his history. He would never completely trust any woman, but Ivy came close to opening his heart for a careful peek into his past. And he wanted to tell her. He needed to share that part of himself with someone. Perhaps as a feeler to see if she really could be trusted. Dare he?

"You don't have to tell me," she said. "I understand you are guarded. You must have to be with the world wanting to photograph your every move."

She understood that part of his life. Bless her.

"I lived in foster care since birth." He glanced to see her expression. A calm, interested pair of 74D4E7s. He'd never felt more seen than when Ivy was with him.

"My parents, I was told, were killed in a plane crash. My mother was nine months pregnant. After she had been pulled from the crash, they performed an emergency caesarean and rescued me."

She took his hand and held it without saying anything. In that moment something tugged at the back of Wolf's throat and the corners of his eyes. Crybabies got bullied and beat up. The smart kid worked hard to earn a few bucks' allowance and then paid the bullies to stay away from him.

"I lived in a total of nine foster homes," he said. "Once a kid gets older, their chances of adoption go way down. I was always a kid who lived inside his head too, so I hadn't the talent to put on a show when a potential permanent family came to visit. I left the CPS system when I was seventeen. Found a couch to sleep on at a friend's house. Spent my days with my nose to the screen. Still doing that." He laughed.

"How did you develop an interest in coding?"

Ah, now there was a topic he enjoyed talking about. And that she'd not lingered on the worst part of his history? Another point for Ivy Quinn.

"I used to help my foster moms with their passwords and computer problems. That would earn me some time on the computer. I discovered the hacker boards and the private net. I instantly understood. I caught a math teacher coding one afternoon while he was on a lunch break. He allowed me to look over his shoulder and I pointed out a mistake he had made. From there he allowed me to spend time programming after school. Taught me a lot. He was the only person who ever made me feel as though I could accomplish something."

Wolf laughed nervously. "I mean, well, I don't want it to sound like my life was so terrible…" Even though it hadn't been all that great.

"I love that a teacher took you under his wing," she said. "That's so important. Teachers can shape the trajectory of a child's life. So you really are a coding savant?"

"Yes, it's served me well. I created my own tech empire. But in the process, I learned not to trust people. Well, I guess you could say I've always been that way. Never had an opportunity to learn what trust really meant."

"Because of the way you grew up, you have boundaries. I respect that."

Wolf felt that comment deep in his chest. A validation

of sorts. And issued without pretense or an ulterior desire to get on his good side.

"What gave you the idea for Concierge?"

"Just trying to keep my life together, the few bits I could carry from couch to couch. I wanted a means to always know what I had and where it was. I guess that was the kid in me that was used to guarding the few things he owned. I actually coded a few apps by the time I was seventeen when I was still couch surfing. I got my first apartment when I was eighteen and had an offer for my first app on the table. That app was Zang."

"I remember that one. It didn't seem to last very long, though."

"It wasn't designed to. It was a data collection app. Data is king. Companies pay big bucks to know everything about the consumer, even things you probably don't know yourself."

"Really? Like what things does a company know about me that I don't know?"

"Your interests. Your dreams. Your goals."

"That's unbelievable."

"It is, but not unattainable if you have some ones and zeros programmed to access how long you pause when you're scrolling through social media apps and how you respond to those silly quizzes and rampant advertising."

"Oh, my God, I'm never filling out one of those quizzes again."

"Good call. Protect your data." He shook his head and chuckled. "Sorry. I could talk tech all day. So, I told you one of my mistakes. An ugly one, for sure. Will you tell me one of yours?"

"A mistake? Hmm..."

Everyone made mistakes, but Wolf found it hard to believe this perfect woman could make any serious transgression beyond a screwed-up latte recipe.

A burst of wind off the Hudson warmed his face and tickled his ear, until he realized it was Ivy's hair brushing his skin. He closed his eyes, savoring the sensation.

Just kiss her already!

Dare he? It felt…not right. The moment needed to be bigger, yes? Maybe? Hell, he wanted to do things right with Ivy. Not have a replay of every relationship that had exploded in his face since moving to New York. She was not a woman to be rushed.

Finally, she said, "I'm not sure I made the right choice in refusing the offer to work at Mercer."

"But you wanted to be with your brother, to help him."

"I did, and I do. But my finances took a hit with that choice. Would it have been better had I gone to Switzerland and arranged for Ivan to receive the care long distance? I don't know. I feel as if it was a good decision, but then some days I think it was a mistake. I passed up a well-paying position."

"Is your brother in such a place that he needs twenty-four-seven care?"

"No. And actually, he's been on his own up until I arrived. But with his vision giving him trouble—well, I want to help him navigate this diagnosis. He's spent his life on his own, defying challenges. He really deserves some compassion and assistance right now."

"I get that. What if…someone were to offer to pay for your brother's medical care?"

"Oh, I don't think that will ever happen," she started and then she paused, looking quickly to him.

Wolf raised a brow and pointed at his chest.

She shook her head furiously and stood. "No, absolutely not."

"But—"

"I don't want to discuss it. Between the two of us, Ivan and I have enough for a year or so. And by then I'll have figured things out, perhaps gotten the perfect job."

"Sure, but until then…"

"Wolf, I…" She tugged out her phone and checked the screen. "I should get back to work." She turned and started walking quickly back toward the building.

Wolf managed to toss the drink cup in the garbage but the corndog wrapper missed, so he doubled back to pick it up and make the can, but that gave her a head start. "Ivy!"

He had opened up to her about growing up. Had bared his soul. And he'd felt as though she had listened without judgment. So how could she switch her emotions so quickly and storm off like that? Couldn't they have a simple conversation regarding his desire to help? The money meant nothing to him.

That thought made him stop, while Ivy crossed the street ahead of him. If the money meant so little, then why was he still here in New York, a city that seemed to press in on his very skeletal structure with immense force, squeezing out his privacy and self-confidence?

You're in a rut.

And he needed to do more than tearing pages off a calendar. He needed to step up and take control of his life. Walk toward the life that would make him happy.

He let Ivy go. He'd talk to her later. Apologize for trying to help. Which seemed counterintuitive. But he understood. She was a proud woman. It would be difficult for her to accept charitable assistance.

Just as it was difficult for him to surrender his fears and open his heart again to a relationship?

CHAPTER SIX

IVY HAD PUNCHED out before her walk with Wolf. She didn't need to return to But First… But her anger had clouded her senses, so now she veered toward her brother's home and, before going inside, decided to sit on the front steps and cool down.

She rarely got angry. And if so, usually she hid it with a cool demeanor. But Wolf's offer to pay for Ivan's medical bills had hit her in the gut. It had felt solicitous. Though, now that she considered it, Wolf may not have meant it in such a manner. Had he been genuinely trying to help?

She did not need the man's money. She and Ivan were perfectly capable of handling his medical expenses on their own. They'd not taken the million dollars offered to them by the boat manufacturer after their parents' death because, after discussing it, both she and Ivan had felt it was hush money. Don't tell anyone there had been a delayed recall on that part that could have very well been the result of the accident. They'd walked away from that deal with their heads held high.

And Ivy wanted to feel the same now, having refused the offer from Wolf. But for some reason, she was torn. Sure, they had money remaining from the house sale, but that wouldn't last longer than a year or two. Yet, damn it, both she and Ivan were smart. They could handle this. Many people handled worse medical diagnoses. As soon as she could find Ivan the proper medical insurance, that would help immensely.

It had been a spur-of-the-moment offer from Wolf. He'd think about it and realize it had been offensive.

She checked her phone. No text from Wolf. Did she expect one? It wasn't as though they were a couple.

You want him to be more than a friend, and you know it!

Was it possible to juggle Ivan's care with her own self-care? Which suggested having a relationship with a man who excited and interested her. Beyond just friends. Of course, anything was possible. But she'd moved to New York specifically to help Ivan. Would it be fair to him to divide her time? For that matter, would it be fair to Wolf?

Not like she had any chance with the man anyway.

Leaning forward and catching her chin in hand, Ivy zoned out on the park greenery across the street. Just when she'd thought he'd begun to let down his emotional walls—telling her about growing up in the foster system—suddenly he'd closed up.

Rather, she had closed up. Why had she acted that way after he'd opened up to her? She didn't want to ruin what they had created between them. She couldn't imagine what it would be like to have never known a real family. At the very least, she had enjoyed twelve wonderful years with her parents. They had taught her much, and she had emulated her wildlife biologist father's work ethic aimed toward curiosity mixed with a fascination for nature. How many times had they gone on butterfly hunts with nets in hand and notebooks to sketch their finds? Her dad had always returned any caught insect back to the wild. The times they had found a dead bug nestled in fallen leaves they had taken it home, pinned it, and he had taught her how to look up information on the species online or in his small library.

As a kindergarten teacher, Ivy's mother had been the more studious of the pair. Teaching her how to cook, be practical with her buying decisions, and not to succumb to the teenage angst that demanded social submission. When most kids had been staring at their cell phones, Ivy and Ivan had been staring at nature or running through the woods. The rule had been no phone until you could pay the bill yourself. Ivy had proudly walked her own path through high school and had always felt her parents' angels on her shoulder as she did so.

"I miss you," she whispered to her parents. "I wish you were here to help Ivan through this now."

Had her brother wished for the same thing immediately following their deaths when he had no choice but to step up and become the parent figure in her life? Probably. Ivy had always been cognizant of his sacrifice for her. Which is why staying with him while he figured out this MS diagnosis had been a no-brainer for her.

She looked at her phone again. Wolf may have been perplexed at her sudden need to rush away from him. It had been a stupid move. She should have talked to him, calmly explained that she did not need his charity. End of it. Move on.

Opening the message app, she started to text him…

I'm sorry…

Ivy tapped delete. Texting was no way to apologize. It had to be in person. And not in the coffee shop, either. She wrote another text.

Could we meet later for something to eat?

Waiting, she saw the three dots pop up as he replied.

Meet me at the Korean barbecue down the street from you at seven?

Yes, she texted back.

And with a smile, she stood, and saw a pretty young woman with tasteful pink dreads and a nose ring, wearing violet scrubs, approach the brownstone.

"Heather?"

"Hi, Ivy."

Heather was an occupational therapist. Ivan had met her the day of his diagnosis. She'd suggested she could help him adjust to his declining health. She stopped by three days a week and spent about three or four hours with him. A big part of it was just providing companionship. But she did also assist him with things he had difficulty with like bathing and shaving.

"I don't believe you are scheduled for Mondays?"

"I'm not." She stopped on the bottom step. "My shift ended early and it's so close, I thought I'd stop by. I don't think Ivan will mind."

"Probably not. But we can't pay you for unscheduled visits."

"No problem, Ivy. I wouldn't expect it. I just like spending time with your brother."

Well. That was…exactly how she felt about Wolf. And Ivy wouldn't argue a friendship for her brother. She stood and opened the door and gestured that Heather enter. "Let's see what we can put together for lunch."

"I'm sorry," Wolf said after a sip of wine.

"No, I'm sorry," Ivy insisted from across the intimate table lit by flickering candlelight.

The waiter arrived to take their order. The restaurant was

small, elegant, and located four steps below street level. It served amazing Korean barbecue that Wolf could eat by the bulk. But he'd rein in his voracious appetite because he didn't want Ivy to think him an oaf. Especially after their tense conversation earlier had resulted in her racing away from him.

The waiter left them with refills on their red wine.

When he was about to negate her need to apologize, Ivy put up a palm. So Wolf sat back. He wasn't a master at arguing with women. And he had the real scars to prove it. Best to hear her out.

"I reacted," Ivy said. "Your offer made me feel…like you were trying to step in and take control."

"I would never—"

"I know. You're not that guy. So please, accept my apology. I don't often get in such a snit that I storm off from a conversation. I guess the unexpected offer caught me off guard."

He nodded. "Apology accepted."

"Never mention such an offer again."

He opened his mouth but then shut it. Never again? When his money might help them? And it would be like mere pennies to him. What was wrong with his money?

"Agreed?" she prompted.

Her sharp tone pinged at something inside Wolf. A stern warning about going against the rules. Or he would be overlooked. Forgotten. Forced into yet another home to be ruled over by yet another uncaring family that was only in it for the monthly support checks. Dispensable.

Wolf nodded silently, bowing his head. He didn't like to feel reprimanded. But he wasn't going to lash out at Ivy. She could have no idea how it made him feel. And he didn't want to make this little tiff even messier. Besides, he had begun to trust her, and that was a delicate thing he wanted to guard.

With an inhale, he set back his shoulders. "Then let's move forward. How was your day?"

"It was productive, actually. I found a possible insurance company and downloaded their information to read over the weekend. I also filled out an application for a medical research study that Ivan might qualify for."

"That's excellent. Is the research for a cure?"

"I don't know that a cure is so close on any medical front. It's for drugs that can arrest the disease from progressing."

"I don't know much about MS. Will you tell me about it?"

"I'm still learning myself. It's a central nervous system disease that disrupts blood flow and communication between the brain and the body. It can affect each person quite differently. Some can function in the real world without too many issues. Those in the middle are plagued by any number of symptoms like Ivan's fatigue, cognition issues, and muscle weakness. They can have periods of remission, then have sudden flare-ups. It's unpredictable. The worst, well, you'd mentioned you have a friend in a wheelchair. But it doesn't have to be a death sentence, by any means. Ivan just has to incorporate it into his life."

"That's gotta be tough for a man you said was intending to bike across the United States."

"Yes. Ivan has never not been active. He has good days and then there are days his hips hurt so badly he can't even get out of bed. I have hopes he won't digress to the level where he can't move on his own. Since I've moved in with him, he's been about the same. But that same is devastatingly inactive compared to his norm. It's quite humbling, actually."

"I know you don't want to hear this, Ivy." He wouldn't blow it again, but his heart wouldn't allow him to remain silent. "But I also need you to know…" He put his hand over hers. "I'm here for you. And your brother. It doesn't have to be monetary. Whatever you need, you've only to ask."

"That's kind of you." She clasped his hand. "Just having a friend who I can talk to means more than you can know."

"We are...friends." And how to change that? Did he want to? Things felt a little too unsure right now with Ivy. They clashed in ways that surprised him.

"Yes, but..."

"But?" Wolf looked up with hope prodding at his carefully protected heart. Perhaps he could prove a bit more indispensable to her than she thought?

At that moment the waiter arrived with their food.

Ivy quickly said, "Doesn't matter," then dove into her dinner.

Wolf wanted to know what that *but* had been about. Was the friend thing not working for her? Did she want something more? She must understand that he needed to take it slowly with a woman. And yet, even as he had that thought, he knew what he had with Ivy had become more than a friendship. And that frightened him.

He cared about Ivy Quinn. And his heart was already deep in the thick of it.

Dare he make the leap and start to trust his own judgment? Did he really have to wait for the results of a background check? Even if something terrible were documented, he'd ignore it for the sake of his own needy want to be with her.

Was that it? He was needy when it came to love and affection. He'd a tendency to overlook a bad situation in hopes it might change. A welcome embrace was all he really needed. And it could happen with Ivy. If he took his time.

He raised his fork and said, "To the best damn barbecue in all of America."

"I'll give you that." She ate another bite and nodded in agreement. A hearty eater, she never shied from anything he offered her. About time he met a woman who didn't subsist on lettuce and diet soda. "You're originally from Germany?"

"Yes, Burghausen. In the western part of the country, not far from the Austrian border." At least, that's the only place he wanted to claim as his own. Heaven knew, he'd lived in too many places for any kid's sanity. "We're known for having the longest castle in the world. And there's the chemical factory. It's a pretty little village. You'd like it. Once you wander into the forested areas, there are plenty of bugs."

"I think I'd like any quaint little village. I'm all about traveling as soon as Ivan finds some stability. Then I hope to relocate overseas. Anywhere, really."

"It'll happen." He winked at her. "You are a smart woman, and I feel like nothing will stop you for long. You're just on a detour right now."

"A detour? In a coffee shop." Her shoulders dropped. "I am so not a barista."

"Yeah? But you make a mean cup of coffee. And I mean that literally. That stuff is so black it could wake a coma patient."

Ivy laughed. "That's about the only thing I can make. All those fancy lattes and frappes and espressos are silly. I still have to use the recipe cards to make some of them." She sighed. "People are really fierce about their drinks."

They shared tastes of their meals and Ivy liked his so he forked her a couple more pieces on the edge of her plate.

"I added a few classical songs to my playlist this morning on the walk to work," she said. "Did you like the concert?"

"I did! And I did the same. Working out to Beethoven's *Fifth* keeps the adrenaline pumping."

"Now if I see you in the gym when I walk by, I will immediately envision you lifting to Beethoven."

"I forget the gym is walled with windows. They used to have paper up on them. To keep the paparazzi from flocking."

"You must enjoy being able to walk around without having a camera snap your every move."

He shrugged.

"You like to be photographed?"

"I hate that. I snuck out of my place tonight and took a circuitous route here. Old habits. But what made them follow me was because I was dating someone. And… I guess I miss it."

"I thought you'd sworn off dating?"

"Yeah, but for the wrong reason. I do like the communication and companionship. Like what we have. I'm so glad you don't mind spending time with me, Ivy."

"Yes, well…" She shook her head and returned to eating. "It's not a hardship spending time with you. You're an interesting man. Despite our differences, we seem to work well together."

"We're not that different. We're both trying to survive in this crazy, busy world, dealing with whatever the universe decides to toss at us."

"Well, but you get to do that with a hefty bank account. I'm not discounting that you earned it. I mean, you get tons of credit for building the Concierge empire from the ground up."

"I did have some excellent angel investors for the first few years."

"Because they knew you were worthy of such a risk. You're a true and genuine person, Wolf. I can only aspire to be like you someday."

Wolf winced. He didn't like to be put on a pedestal. Especially since he was not aspiration worthy. He'd led a tough life and had made plenty of mistakes along the way. The last one costing him a million dollars.

"Don't say that, Ivy. You'd never get taken to court for emotional distress."

She gaped at him. "Someone sued you?"

"My last girlfriend," he said. "Apparently, when a guy buys a diamond ring for a woman because she was swooning over the thing for ten minutes while we were shopping in Dubai, she takes it as a marriage proposal. I didn't even say the M word."

Ivy's jaw dropped open.

"I mean…" He studied her shock, unsure if it was because of what he'd done or what she would have expected. "Did I do the wrong thing? How would you have taken such a move?"

"I would have never begged for a diamond in the first place."

"Exactly. You're too classy. I got off easy, though. She started by asking for ten million. We settled for one."

"Just because she assumed the ring meant…? I can't believe some people. How long had you been dating?"

"Four weeks."

"Four— Did you love her?"

Had he been in love? Wolf wasn't sure what love felt like. He knew material things and sex did not equate to love. And yet, he had been soft on his last girlfriend. Perhaps even his heart had been open to a future with her.

"You must have been," Ivy decided. "I mean, to spend that much on a ring for her?"

He shrugged. "It was just a bauble. I like to give people things. It makes them happy."

He thought of his offer to pay for her brother's medical

expenses. Damn. Maybe he had been trying to win her over with his money. Idiot.

"Doesn't matter because she got an even bigger payout with the lawsuit. She got to keep the ring, as well."

"Incredible. Now I really understand your reluctance to put yourself out on the dating scene again."

Wolf nodded, prodded at his food. It felt good to have spilled that to her. And yet, it also bothered him. Was he putting up another blockade to keep her from getting too close? Of course, he was! Yet, he wanted more with Ivy. Hell, he'd settle for a kiss. But he was skittish. And why did he have to be like that? He was a strong, capable man who had built his own empire.

Why the hell couldn't he just kiss the girl?

The waiter stopped by their table with the bill. He signed the receipt and added a fifty percent tip. Because the waiter had been courteous, and why the hell not?

Ivy sipped her wine and eyed him curiously.

"What? Do I have sauce on my beard?" He rubbed his chin. "You have to tell me if that happens. I can be a real ogre sometimes."

"I like the ogre in you. I looked something up last night."

"Yeah?"

"724717."

His genuine surprise manifested in a nodding grin as he swiped a hand over his beard. "That's *my* eye color?"

She nodded and waggled her shoulders, obviously proud of her sleuthing.

"Nice," he said. And about the most romantic thing a woman had ever done for him. Wow. Just, wow. "I'll have you speaking in code in no time."

"I like learning new things. What code is my shirt to-night?"

He studied the soft purple and said, "D9D2E9. It looks great on you. Goes well with your 74D4E7 eyes."

"Has anyone told you how romantic you are?" She batted her lashes at him. "Hey, that reminds me of that romance you are reading. Did you finish it?"

"I did, and I went back to the store for another one."

She leaned forward, this time her gape more wondrous. "Do tell."

"The author was Nora Roberts. The bookstore owner told me everyone reads her. It's about witches. I'm liking it."

Ivy sat back, her smile so delicious when she did that thing where she nodded her head and made her ponytail swing. That set his thoughts to pondering how he could accidentally unloose her hair and watch it spill over her shoulders. The guys in the romance novels did it all the time. Best to start taking notes as he read.

"I like you more every time we get together," she said. "I'm thankful for that calendar of yours."

"Me too. It was given to me by my best friend who is leaving for Sweden tomorrow. Used to be my director of operations."

"What's in Sweden?"

"A pretty woman with whom he wants to make a simple life. Much as he's been a backbone of Concierge, I didn't argue too much when he gave his notice."

"A simple life." She sipped her wine and wobbled the empty goblet before her. "That appeals to me. A little house in the country. A nice position with a solid research lab. Maybe a few kids later on in my thirties or even forties. A handsome husband who is happy with his work and..."

"And?"

She compressed her lips and he sensed she didn't want to say the next part out loud.

"Well," she offered with a conspiratorial lean across the table, "he has to believe in love. I don't think that's too much to ask."

No, it wasn't. Wolf wasn't sure he did believe in love. He had no idea how to define it. He was quite sure he'd never heard the words "I love you" in any of the foster homes in which he had grown up. And the few women he'd dated usually blurted it while he was handing them expensive gifts, so he'd never felt it a genuine statement of affection.

"What about you?" she prompted.

He couldn't tell her that he didn't believe in love.

"What kind of life do you enjoy?" she asked. "I suppose you thrive on the bustle of the big city and the techie job?"

Whew! He wouldn't have to reveal his cynical side tonight.

"Not at all. Confession? I moved to New York City because this was the place where I could grow Concierge. But now that it's established and we've got the next phase ready for release? I've begun thinking about what my next move is. I want to return to Germany."

"Interesting. I remember you saying something about too much concrete. The greenery in New York is rare, save for Central Park. So that village in Germany would make you happy? Was it the last place you were fostered?"

"No, it was the first place I moved after getting out of the foster care system. It's also where I started coding Concierge. It holds a lot of good memories for me. But I want to do it the right way."

Which, to Wolf, meant not going back alone. His idea of having made it? The wife and family. A fantasy he'd had since he was a kid who used to watch ancient reruns of family sitcoms.

"Space," Ivy idly said. "That's what you crave."

He could but nod in awe that she had accurately assessed his most basic and desperate desire. He really did crave a simple life. Space. It would come to him. But only if he had a supportive partner at his side.

Yet, that would never happen if he did not believe in love.

CHAPTER SEVEN

ON WEDNESDAY, Wolf had to examine his diet and make a positive change. He showed Ivy the calendar page. They both glanced to the slice of chocolate chip cake sitting before him. Both shook their heads.

"Absolutely not," he agreed with her laughter.

"Try drinking more water," she suggested. "It's supposed to be good for everything."

"Sounds much easier than sacrificing this," he said and took a big bite of the cake.

And yet, he knew the cake, while tasty, wasn't the reason he came to But First… every morning. And no calendar was going to stop that visit.

On Friday, Wolf stared at the calendar entry: *Do something unexpected.*

Following a quiet ping on his phone, he glanced to the text reminder on the Concierge app: Saturday office party.

Once a year, he threw a fancy black tie ball for his employees, which included flying in the crew who worked remotely across the United States and France and a couple coders who lived in Germany. Everyone had a good time. Including himself.

Last year he'd brought a model who had been introduced to him at a tech conference. She'd seemed normal those first few dates. But following the Concierge party, the fireworks had exploded. And not the good kind of fireworks. She had left him with a literal scar on his bicep. He'd not dodged fast enough to avoid the knife she'd thrown at him. She'd been upset when he wouldn't agree to fund her shopping trip to Paris. He owed her after she'd spent a fortune on her gown for the party! When he'd laid down cash to cover the gown, she'd grabbed it, called him an asshole, and left, never to darken his threshold again.

Those disastrous relationships had scuttled his inner common sense. Could he ever trust his judgment if and when he actually found a genuine and real girlfriend?

When he'd given up on women six months ago, he'd only told Skyr. He hadn't suspected Skyr would gossip to the rest of the office, so he figured it had been Janice with her bionic ear. She occupied the office across the hallway from his.

This year, the entire office expected he'd show up to the party alone. Janice couldn't hide the betting chart she had posted on what she thought was a secret online board. All office communications were monitored. Were they that naïve?

Flicking a glance to the desk calendar, he wondered what he could do that was unexpected. Everything he'd done since starting the calendar had been new and unexpected. Except the cold shower.

Janice popped her head into the office and waved the engraved invite for tomorrow's shindig. "I'm bringing a friend instead of my husband to the party. Is that okay?"

"Of course, it is. Plus-ones can be anybody, Janice."

"Thanks. Me and the hubby are not on good terms lately."

"I'm sorry to hear that." And really, stop there, he thought. Janice did like to unpack her personal stuff. To anyone who would listen.

"I think he's having an affair—"

He held up a hand to stop her. "I'm sorry, Janice. Take the friend. We'll be happy to have you both there."

"No plus-one for you, eh?" She winked.

Wolf controlled the wince and kept his mouth straight.

"Well, you know…" she started. With a dismissive wave of her hand, she then offered, "Nothing to worry about. We wouldn't expect our fearless leader to have to divide his time between master of ceremonies and a date. Bye!"

She quickly left.

And Wolf curled his fingers into fists. There was nothing wrong with showing up at his own party dateless. He was the fearless leader. A man who had to work the room, offer small talk with all the employees, smile at the plus-ones and seem interested in it all. It was a monumental task for a guy who preferred the solace of programming. But he understood the social side of business, and also genuinely liked to see his employees happy. It made for a successful work atmosphere.

He could bring a woman if he wanted to. She didn't have to be a girlfriend. She could just be a friend. Laugh, have a few drinks, take her home. Nothing like a date.

But why the hell *not* ask a woman out on a date? Hadn't he sacrificed long enough? He was seriously itching for a night with a woman, yes, laughing, having a few drinks, and then…maybe there would be more beyond that. Like sex. He loved sex. No-strings sex, especially.

He flicked a finger at the calendar and then leaned back in his chair. He could break his sabbatical. And it could be good. No fear of flying kitchen utensils. And wouldn't the office drop their jaws if he walked in with a woman? Janice would never reap the betting rewards.

He smirked. And then, nodded.

Wolfgang Zeigler could do whatever he damn well pleased. And he wanted to take a beautiful woman to the party.

Wolf walked into But First… with a big smile on his face. He laid the calendar page on the counter while Ivy filled his order. She picked it up and read it: "Do something unexpected?"

"Meet me at my corner table when you have a break?"

"Five minutes," she said.

Turning, Ivy walked right into Estelle, who wore the biggest grin on her face. "What?"

"You and that man finally getting cozy?"

"He's…" A very slow move. Her field journal had discovered his strengths and weaknesses. Dating was not a strength. "…just a friend, Estelle."

"Not according to that dreamy look you get in your eyes every time he sets foot in the café. Be careful, Ivy. If he's intent on playing the friend card, you will get hurt."

"I'm a big girl. I know what I'm doing. It's just…" Field notes? Please.

"All right. Carry on with your break. But I'll be watching him. You know I will."

"Wouldn't have it any other way." She grabbed the coffeepot and sailed over to Wolf's table. "Refill?"

"Half." He shoved his cup toward her and she filled half.

"So what's the unexpected?"

Setting his elbows on the table, he clasped his hands together and looked over them at her. Oh, those 724717s. "I have something to ask of you."

Sounded promising.

"Concierge is having our annual office party tomorrow night. It's black tie. At the Waldorf Astoria."

"I've heard about that place. It's a New York treasure."

"It is. And I was wondering if…you would like to go with me? On…a date?" he asked with a wincing lift of his shoulders.

"Seriously?" Yes! Calling all fire crews, the flames were getting higher! And yet… "What happened to taking a dating sabbatical?"

"Don't you want to go out with me?"

"Yes, I'd love to—I mean…" What had happened to focusing on Ivan? She lifted her chin. "Answer my question first. What's up?"

"Isn't asking you out unexpected?"

"It is. But if this is a real date, I don't want it to be a challenge date."

"I get that. I wanted to ask a beautiful woman to the party, so I am. And I don't want it to be a friends thing. This is real. Can you deal with that?"

"I can deal." Ivan would be just fine for one night. "Can *you* deal?"

He smirked.

"I mean, what if I insist on sucking your bank account dry?"

"You wouldn't do that. But if you want to try, you can go for it."

"I would never."

"I know that about you." He winked. "So. What do you think? Are we…ready to move beyond friends?"

"More ready than you know," she said quickly before her common sense wrestled her inner romantic to the ground. "And it is very unexpected. Romantically burned bachelor asks temporary barista to a fancy party? Sounds like a romance novel."

"I do enjoy reading those. Another plus to this date is that it would also defeat Janice's betting pool about me showing up to the party dateless."

"Ah." Ivy set down the coffeepot. "We arrive at the real impetus behind your evil plan."

"It's—no. I mean, that's just a bonus. I'm not plotting anything evil—Ivy, I want to take you out. Show you a good time. Introduce you to the people I work with. Do date things. Like…kiss you?"

She raised a brow. All of the above sounded excellent. But she had to be sure this was more than just another challenge. Because her heart could not withstand any more teasing.

"Do you want me to beg?" he asked.

"Promise it will be a real date? Including the kiss?"

"Hell, yes."

"All right then. I would love to go on a date with you, Wolf. Tomorrow night?"

"Yes. This time, though, it's glamorous. You get to dress up. I'll do a black tie and fancy cuff links."

She owned nothing that would allow her to fit in with a black-tie crowd. But that wouldn't stop her from trying.

"I'll pick you up at eight," he said. "You're the only one I want to go to this party with me."

"I'll see you tomorrow night."

He thanked her and just when he spread his arms and it looked like he might move in for a hug, he adjusted his position and instead took her hand and shook it. "Thanks."

"Of course. So. Back to the grind. Literally!"

Ivy veered back behind the counter. She wanted to spill the details to Estelle, but the lunch crowd pouring in kept her busy for the next two hours. Only when the tables were wiped and the afternoon slump began was she able to punch out.

Estelle cornered her in the break room. "You've grown an inch since talking to Mr. Zeigler. What's going on with you two? And don't spare any of the salacious details."

"It's not salacious. It's…"

Dare she believe this was it, a real date? There were too many side factors that polluted the genuine date-ness of it. The office betting pool. The calendar challenge. The fact she'd not wanted to date a celebrity. Reservations abounded.

"I'm not going to explain. Suffice, he invited me to a fancy party tomorrow night and I have nothing to wear!"

"How fancy?"

"Waldorf Astoria fancy."

"Oh, sweetie, you need some help. And that hair."

"What about my hair?"

"It's always so…tight. You've got a day to get fancy party ready. You need a fairy godmother."

"Do you know where I can find one?"

Estelle called out Valerie's name and the slender Nigerian woman poked her head into the break room. "What up?"

Estelle studied Valerie, then switched her preening gaze to Ivy. Back and forth. "Valerie has a side job as a costume handler for a modeling agency, isn't that right?"

"It is. What do you need? Business suit? Afternoon tea dress with flounces and fascinator? Thigh boots and leather bodysuit?"

"A ball gown," Estelle declared, with a flourishing gesture toward Ivy.

Valerie eyed up Ivy, who now felt like a piece of meat on display at the grocer. Then she nodded. "I have something perfect. But what about her hair?"

"Exactly." Estelle put her hands akimbo and said to Ivy, "One fairy godmother coming right up!"

A manila envelope lay on Wolf's desk. His name was typed on a white sticker affixed to the upper right corner. A scan of the QR code below indicated it was from the private investigator.

He turned the envelope over and pushed his forefinger under the flap, then…stopped. Frowning, he decided to open a drawer and drop the envelope inside. Whatever the PI had learned about Ivy could wait. He'd already asked her to the party. If there was damning info inside the envelope, it was too late to cancel.

And he didn't want to cancel. He wanted to take Ivy out on a real date. For himself.

He'd open it later. Maybe.

CHAPTER EIGHT

IVY COULD NOT believe her luck. The gush of frothy red fabric that billowed out of the dress bag made her do a little dance, hands to her mouth. And she actually squealed.

"Are you serious?" she asked Valerie, who fluffed out the gorgeous creation she'd just revealed.

Estelle walked around the dress, nodding in appreciation. "This one belongs on a princess." She glanced at Ivy. "I guess I really am your fairy godmother."

"I can't believe this. Are you sure it's okay to borrow it? It's so fabulous. And it looks spendy."

Valerie laid the dress across Ivy's white comforter. The bedroom was ultra-modern, all white and pale pine so the red screamed. "It is spendy. And it is fabulous. We used this on a Vogue shoot. It's due back at the designer on Monday. That means I need it back tomorrow."

"Or you'll turn into a pumpkin," Estelle added with a laugh.

"Do you have glass slippers, too?" Ivy asked as she ran her palm over the soft, floaty material.

"Will Louboutins do?" Valerie pulled out a shoe box from her bag.

"Are you kidding me?" Ivy sat and took it in, gliding a hand over the tulle fabric. Never in her wildest dreams had she imagined Valerie would bring something so beautiful.

And expensive. And, yes, worthy of a princess. "I can't wear it. What if I spill on it?"

"You will not spill on it," Valerie admonished tersely. "Or I will get stuck with the cleaning bill. It's okay, Ivy. This dress was made for your figure. It looks fluffy but it's sturdy. Don't you want to try it on?"

"Yes!"

"I'll get the curling iron," Estelle said, heading toward the makeup bag she'd toted along. "We're going to make a princess out of you tonight!"

Wolf adjusted his tie before the mirror. Suits were uncomfortable. He rarely wore them. But the black-tie party made the event more special. Anticipation always shimmered through the office. An excuse to buy a new dress for some. And hell, the men liked to look dapper, too.

"Dapper?" He peered suspiciously at his reflection. "How old are you? Keep it together, man. Tonight will be fun."

And that Ivy had said yes to a date that wasn't between friends? Score! But caution must be wielded. She didn't look at him with dollar bills in her eyes. Hell, she'd been upset by his spur-of-the-moment offer to help pay her brother's medical bills. But a guy just never knew. The armor that wrapped his heart was solid.

As well, everyone would see he had a girlfriend and they could all stop gossiping behind his back. And they would also stop trying to fix him up. If Ellen in sales stopped by one more time to show him a photo of her cousin or niece or long-lost sister…

He flicked off the lights and tucked his phone in a pocket before heading down the hallway to the elevator.

Twenty minutes later, the limo pulled up before Ivy's building. It was an older brownstone walk-up with masses of climbing greenery covering the façade and a gothic iron fence. Ivan had scored well with this house-sitting job. And he got to stay in the place for almost a year? The guy was industrious, as well as smart.

"I'll head up," Wolf said to the driver. "Shouldn't take long."

He got out of the back seat just as an incredible vision floated through the front door to stand at the top of the steps. A princess in candy red. A fitted bodice accentuated her gorgeous bust and slender waist. From there the skirt blossomed out in waves of red, dusting the steps in froths of ruffle. It was as if a lush treat stood waiting for him to dive in, swim and lose himself. And her hair, no longer tidied in a ponytail, spilled over a shoulder and down her arm in sleek curves.

But that wasn't what took his breath away. Her lips matched her dress. Perfect bow lips that parted slightly when she noticed him standing before the limo.

"F80825," he whispered. He could practically smell the bright, delicious color. And taste her kiss.

All of a sudden her eyes brightened and her smile felt like a warm beam of happiness to his heart.

Wolf exhaled. He'd not expected a date with a princess this evening. Hell, he should have spent more time with his grooming rather than finger-combing his hair after a shower and smacking on a bit of beard oil. And had he remembered deodorant? He'd forgotten cologne! Would she notice? Would she flinch when she felt the touch of his sweaty hands?

Get it together, man!

"Hey!" She waved, then gathered up her skirt to carefully ascend the few steps. When she landed on the sidewalk, she twirled, swishing the skirt out in a wide, billowing circle. "What do you think? Good enough for the Waldorf?"

Good enough? Ivy Quinn was beyond. The Waldorf was not good enough for her. This woman belonged on a pedestal so that others could gaze up and adore her like the princess she was.

"Wolf?" She peered at him carefully. "Is everything okay? It's too much, isn't it? Oh, I—"

"It's perfect." He caught her hand in a clasp and pulled her closer to him. She smelled like flowers and her eyelids glinted with sparkles. Her mouth pursed. And he wanted to touch every part of her, taste her...

What do you think you're going to do, Zeigler? Kiss the girl?

If he was lucky? Yes. Tonight was a beginning. *To everything.* He hoped it would go well.

"A friend lent it to me." She slipped her hand from his and fluffed at the skirt. "Because seriously? I don't have something so fabulous as this just hanging in my closet. You look very handsome. Dapper."

Wolf laughed at the word she used.

"What? You don't think so?"

He leaned in and kissed her cheek. A reaction. He'd kissed the princess! Now, to not mess up the rest of the night so he could earn a real kiss on her lips.

"You look incredible, Ivy. I can't believe I get to escort such a beautiful woman tonight. All eyes will be on you." He hooked his arm for her to take. "Let's do this."

As the limo cruised through Manhattan, slowly making its way to the Waldorf Astoria, Ivy got a handle on her nerves and was able to relax against the seat. Until she thought of something. Her shoulders tightened.

"What's our story?" she suddenly asked Wolf.

"Our story?"

"I know this is all for your challenge calendar, but for your employees' sake, is this our first date? What does the office think? You mentioned something about quelling some rumors, so I feel like I have to be on my toes. Have we been dating? How long?"

"Ivy, chill. It's our first date. Of a sort. I kind of count the orchestra as a date too."

So he did consider this a real date? But also a challenge.

"I...do, too." But there hadn't been a kiss, so... Not a real first date by her standards. "Right then." She smoothed her palms over the red fabric, using the motion to focus and deflect her annoying nerves. "Just chill. And yet...all the people will be staring at us because the boss who swore off dating is there with someone."

He chuckled in that deep tone that snapped at her nerves and teased up a soft, sensual relaxation of her muscles. "They have a habit of keeping an eye on me."

"That's sweet in a weird stalker-ish way."

"Are you nervous?"

"Of course!"

"I am, too."

"You are? Why?"

"Because look at you. You're...everything."

The hush on the word *everything* settled at the base of her throat and felt as much like a kiss as she could imagine. Ivy closed her eyes and nodded. This really was a fantasy night. And she intended to enjoy every moment of it.

"You don't think I'm overwhelmed to be sitting in a limo with the handsomest man I've ever fed cake to?" she asked.

He turned on the seat to face her and she tried not to make direct eye contact. Too intense. Most importantly, she didn't want to sweat in this dress!

Focus on enjoying yourself!

"Relax, Ivy. Everyone is going to love you."

With an accepting nod, she looked out the window at the passing shop fronts. He saw her as different from the other women he'd dated, and whom he had decided were terrible. That was good, right?

Ivy wasn't sure, exactly, what sort of woman would appeal to Wolfgang Zeigler. And much as this was a date, this was also just another page to tick off for his calendar challenge. It was a weird situation to be wearing a fantasy gown and walking into a fabulous party on the arm of a man who had already conjured many a late-night sex dream.

Then again, who didn't dream about a man before their official date? It was a prelude to what she hoped would come true. Tonight? She wanted to get that kiss for sure.

"We are here, Mr. Zeigler," the driver announced.

"Thanks, Charles." Wolf grinned at Ivy. Touched her lower lip with his thumb.

"How's my lipstick?" she asked.

"Perfect. F80825." His eyes wandered over her lips, and then finally up to her eyes, as if he'd gotten lost. He blew out a breath. "I really want to kiss you."

Yes! Heartbeat racing, she managed, "Same."

He clasped her hand and kissed the side of it. "But not right here. Are you ready?"

For the forthcoming kiss? Hell, yes! But she knew he meant to walk inside on his arm. To fully commit to the fantasy.

"Ready as I'll ever be."

The Waldorf Astoria on Park Avenue was *the* place in New York for glamour, riches, and celebrations. Sure, it was a bit old-school, but Wolf tended toward the less modern and trendy. Some of his best memories of Germany were while living in a town known for its castles; of course, he preferred the grandeur and pomp of things.

The grand ballroom had been recently remodeled. The Art Deco space had been restored to its early splendor. Wolf's eyes slid along the elegant gilded ceiling reliefs and the walls. Two tiers of balconies overlooked the dance floor and a couple employees in them waved as they sighted him. Concierge employed about three hundred people worldwide. And tonight he intended to treat them to a sumptuous party.

"Wolf!"

He waved to a couple who acknowledged him with a lift of their champagne goblets. Ivy held his hand a little tighter. The woman certainly had daring to walk into this situation. Three paparazzi had manned the curb as they'd arrived. They'd snapped some shots, much to Ivy's surprise. He'd quickly guided her inside, fighting the urge to yell at them to get the hell away. How did they know when to seek him out? Only an employee could have given them info about tonight's party. Or a hotel employee. He'd thought he'd paid enough for privacy, but apparently not. But the press weren't allowed access to the ballroom, so this was a safe zone.

"How you doing?" he asked Ivy.

"Overwhelmed after our exit from the car but now...excited. Let's get some champagne in me and make things a little easier."

"I like how you think."

Ivy had been introduced to dozens of people. All shook her hand and commented on her dress. They were friendly, all seemed in awe of their fearless leader, and most whispered as she walked away on Wolf's arm. Wondering if the boss's new fling would hurt him as so many others had before her?

Ivy had no intention of hurting Wolf. And she couldn't

understand the mindset of a person who would demand things and expect money from a person just because they had so much.

Earlier, Wolf had whispered a warning not to talk too long to Janice because she'd learn her life story. So when she approached now, Ivy braced herself. Instead of shaking Ivy's hand, the woman leaned in for a buss of both cheeks. Weirdly awkward, and she pulled back with a greedy smile on her face. "You're so beautiful. And quite…unexpected."

Ivy flashed a smile to Wolf at the use of that word. He shrugged and then took her hand. "We need to make the rounds," he said apologetically to Janice, then whisked her away.

"Catch you later!" Janice called with a wave and a discerning cast of what felt to Ivy like the evil eye.

"Was I right?" Wolf asked.

"She does give me a weird stalker vibe."

"She's not that extreme, but there are days when I wonder if there's a listening device from her office directly to mine. There's a couple employees from the overseas offices. Let's go say hi."

As they did, the band kicked into an anthem rock song and the crowd applauded. Champagne glasses were raised. The dance floor filled. And Ivy floated through the dream alongside her Prince Charming.

A few hours into the party, Ivy and Wolf had drifted apart, which was fine with her. He needed to work the room, and she had stolen a moment to slip into the bathroom and inspect her hair and lipstick.

The lip stain Valerie had lent her really did stay on. What was the code for it? She couldn't recall, but she marveled that Wolf must see colors as numbers. A weird bit of synesthesia brought on by his years of coding? It was a quirk that made her feel as if she were privy to a secret part of him that others may never understand.

"Oh, Ivy." A woman in a glittery white gown cut low to reveal a star tattoo on one of her breasts sidled up alongside Ivy before the marble vanity. She seemed about Ivy's age, perhaps even late twenties. The glitter in her hair was subtle, glamourous. "I'm Sandra. We haven't met but everyone is whispering your name. The gorgeous model on Wolf's arm."

"Oh, I'm not a—"

"I know. An entomologist? Janice told me. She's been gathering intel about you."

Ivy cautioned herself from rolling her eyes at that information.

"Where did the two of you ever find each other?"

"At the coffee shop on the first floor of his building."

"But First...? Oh. Huh." The woman studied Ivy's reflection more carefully. "Maybe I have seen you before... So, you're just a barista?"

The last thing she wanted was for the office gossip to whisper that Wolf was dating a barista. Not cool for a man of his clout.

"It's a temporary job until I begin work with an institute later this year," she lied. Wishful thinking? More like a form of protection for Wolf's reputation. "That dress is beautiful."

"Oh, thanks. I love this party! It's the only opportunity I get to dress up and play at princess."

"I can relate. My fairy godmother fixed me up with this dress."

"She certainly knows your color. That red. Well, you're gorgeous. You just be nice to our Wolf, okay?"

"I...uh...of course. I wouldn't be anything but."

"Well." Ivy felt the woman's gaze switch to judgmental in a snap. "He's a good man. Too good. We'll be keeping an eye on you." With that, the woman left the bathroom.

"They really care about their boss," she muttered.

A good thing. More often than not, employees tended to despise their boss. Wolf was a kind man. Who had obviously been hurt in his relationships.

Did she actually think she could be the woman to change that?

"Not if I can't break through his emotional barriers."

And hers as well. She'd been shocked by the paparazzi flashes upon entering. Had cringed. And for a moment had felt like climbing back into the limo and hiding. She'd thought dating a celebrity was not for her. And having gotten a taste of it, did she really believe she could manage the loss of privacy? And what if they learned about her brother? She had to protect Ivan from it all. He did not need that added stress right now.

This couldn't go on. She had too much to protect. Perhaps tonight was merely meant to be one fantasy night to remember. A treat. And then back to real life.

CHAPTER NINE

WOLF CLOSED HIS eyes and leaned against the wall. He'd found a cove away from the main ballroom. He'd schmoozed and laughed, and smiled, and chatted. An escape was necessary to recharge his battery. He was thankful this was a once-yearly party. But he was glad to see all his employees so happy. And he'd not met a few of the international associates, beyond Zoom, so that had been great to finally shake hands and chat.

With an empty beer mug dangling from one hand, he remembered Ivy had spoken the word *space*, and it made him smile. Yes, she understood that part of him he guarded so fiercely.

Everyone had come up to him and told him they liked Ivy, that she was beautiful, and interesting. He'd found a good one. Now the office gossip would cease. Or would it only get fueled? Surely the paparazzi would label her his girlfriend in whatever media they posted those photos. This was a date, after all. And yet... Could he do that to Ivy? Thrust her in the path of the hungry photogs merely because he enjoyed spending time with her?

Ivy was incredible. Not only was she gorgeous, outgoing, and so easy to be with, she seemed to sense when he was open to her being at his side and also when he needed a squeeze from her hand.

He'd kissed that hand a few times as they'd navigated from small chat to small chat. Man, he wanted to give her a real kiss. To linger in the discovery of her soft mouth, her scent, the lithe and responsive curves of her body. He could take her home with him... No, he couldn't expect her to go beyond a kiss on the first date. Could he? Happened all the time with his previous girlfriends.

Maybe there was something to that. If he'd gone slower with those women, gotten to know them before moving right to sex, would the course of those relationships have gone differently? Been more trusting?

He did enjoy the companionship. And he did enjoy sex. And he did enjoy Ivy. Dare he tell her as much? Would that ruin her expectations of him? This was supposed to be a fun evening, just another challenge presented by that stupid calendar. That it gave him such conflicting emotions about everything was enough to make him want to toss the thing in the trash when he got back to the office.

"Hey, there you are." Ivy walked up and put her back to the wall to stand beside him. "Mind if I hide out with you? They've turned up the music and everyone is shaking their booties."

"You don't shake your booty?"

"I do, but I'm afraid this dress is a little too delicate for that hip-hop action going on out there."

"Then do join me. I needed to escape. It's an introvert thing."

"I get it."

"You do. Which is surprising to me. Usually extroverts can't comprehend our brains."

"I'll give you that. But I did date an introvert a few years ago. That taught me some people are not wired for exuberant conversations. They need to recharge their batteries.

I'm good with it. Even we extroverts need the occasional recharge."

"Bless you."

She tilted her head onto his shoulder. "Thank you for inviting me tonight. It's been a lot of fun. A much-needed release from life's worries."

"How is your brother?"

"He invited Heather over to watch a movie with him. I had intended to not think about him tonight. You know, just try to enjoy the evening."

"Sorry, I shouldn't have brought it up."

"It's fine. I know you care."

"I do, Ivy. I really do." He clasped her hand and kissed the back of it. "You know there will be more paparazzi waiting for us to leave?"

"I suspect so. That was…eye-opening. I can't imagine living a life where you have to always be concerned about others intruding on your every moment."

"It's why my dating life is a shambles. But I think the reward is worth the risk. At least, with you."

"Really? You'd forge through hordes of reporters just for me?"

"I would. But I really shouldn't ask the same of you. It's tough for someone who has never experienced it before."

"It is interesting. I hope I don't make Page Six."

"Are you regretting going out with me tonight?"

"Honestly? Yes and no. Yes, to the photogs. No, to spending time with you."

"So…uh…" He leaned forward, his eyes dancing with hers. "We are alone."

Ivy bowed her head, looking up through her lashes at Wolf.

He slipped his hand along her neck. The electric connection skittered down her spine, opening her like a flower. As his hand glided up through her hair, feeding that vibrant shock of desire, she closed her eyes as his lips touched hers.

Heat. Power. Passion. It mingled, creating an intense moment of connection. Wolf's breath danced with hers. Her skin shimmied in a tingling sensation. Champagne and body heat and a certain masculine perfume surrounded her.

Ivy could have never anticipated this moment. Standing in a fancy ballroom, wearing a princess dress, being kissed by the man who held a place in her dreams. And, oh, what a kiss.

Body curving forward, her bones went liquid, seeking Wolf's brute physicality. Melding against him, she gave him every sigh, every wish that she'd had about him. His mouth explored hers, knowing exactly how to touch, with firm pressure yet a soft teasing tongue. Fingers twined into her hair, holding her to him, keeping her. Making her his.

I am yours. For tonight.

With heartbeats racing, she gripped at his suit lapels, twisting, taking from him. The dress hem was so fluffy their feet didn't meet, but their hips did. He wanted her. She wanted him. Could she climb inside him and live there? Away from the world? Away from everything that could ever challenge or give her pain? What a dream.

Ending the kiss with a slow parting, they bowed their foreheads together. Ivy had never felt a kiss so perfectly easy and yet electrically exciting. She wanted another.

Dipping her head, she kissed his mouth, hot from their connection. He tasted salty and calm. Sparks of champagne mingled with the masculine heat of him. The brush of his beard and mustache teased her nipples to peaks.

His eyes danced over her face. "I've never felt a kiss like I just did."

"Same."

He kissed her cheek and thumbed her jaw before brushing the hair from her face. "You told me you felt like a princess tonight."

"Well, come on, I've got the dress, the shoes, a fairy godmother who sent me off. I'm not sure if I'll turn into a pile of rags before the stroke of midnight, though. We should be very careful the limo doesn't shapeshift into a pumpkin on the ride home."

He laughed and kissed her forehead. "I'll protect my princess. But why is it the women always get the fairy-tale dreams? We aspiring princes have our fantasies, too."

"White stallions and vanquishing swords?"

He smirked and bowed his head before looking up into her eyes. "I was thinking more along the lines of being seen and accepted."

Those simple dreams grabbed Ivy by the heart and squeezed, gently, but enough to make her mush from the tips of her lashes to her toes.

"I see you," she said.

"I know that you do. It's…humbling."

She hugged him. And he hugged her back. If that was all it took for the man's dreams to be fulfilled then her part was easy.

Never had she hugged a person for so long. Really let her body melt against his, feel his presence, his warmth, his very being. It felt beyond good. And not even in a sexual way. They connected on a DNA level that she had once read about in college. When humans touched they actually shared vulnerabilities, respect, and could even promote healing. Actual RNA was also shared. It was amazing.

Wolf was the one to pull away and kiss her quickly before saying, "That's the best hug I've ever had."

"Almost better than the kiss."

"Promise me that wasn't our last?"

Could she make such a promise? The paparazzi's insistent flashes had warned her to be more cautious. What to say that wouldn't disappoint him?

"Wolf!"

They turned to find someone waving his drink high and gesturing toward the ballroom. "Speech?"

"I'd better go and thank them all," Wolf said. He kissed her hand. "This has been the best night."

The limo parked before Ivy's building. She'd had a night! It was sad that it had come to an end, but she was thoroughly exhausted and almost glad for the finale. Almost. Leaving Wolf's embrace felt unimaginable. Yet, the stumble through a barrage of paparazzi to the limo had further cemented her determination to make this a one-night experience.

"Thank you," he said, clasping her hand.

"Anything to help you out with your challenges," she offered, trying to make light of something she'd fallen deep into and wasn't sure how to climb out of.

"Ivy, don't do that. Do you think tonight was just for the calendar? It wasn't. Please tell me you know that."

The desperation in his tone chided her. Why did she have to insist on keeping them at a distance even after that kiss? Oh, that kiss!

"Of course, I know it was a real date. I was just teasing." But if she was truthful with herself, it had been a form of protection against her already challenged emotional reserves. Amazing kiss or not, she had to draw a line. "Don't even tell me if my face shows up on the socials tomorrow, okay?"

"I won't. Promise." He kissed her hand. "Did you have a good time?"

"I did. It was like a fairy tale." A once-in-a-lifetime adventure. "And speaking of tales of wonder, I have to get this dress back to my friend tomorrow or else she'll send the cavalry after me."

Wolf laughed. Then he stroked her hair. "I like your hair down. It's so soft."

"Being a barista is not glamorous. If I don't tie my hair back, it'll end up in someone's coffee. But it was fun to go glamorous tonight. Now, as soon as I leave this coach, it will turn into a pumpkin." She opened the back door, pushed to get out, and then turned to smile at him.

The kiss was unavoidable. Her field note journal abandoned for real experience. Had she thought to capture this man in her net? Because really, there were thousands of butterflies fluttering throughout her system with his kiss. And they were captured within, free to react to Wolf's every sensual touch. She had to escape his net before it was too late.

He bowed his forehead to hers. "I'd ask to come inside, but I wouldn't be at all surprised if your brother was waiting by the door. Do you have a curfew?"

"Nope. But I won't invite you in. The place is very open. There's not a lot of privacy."

"I get it. We could have gone to my place…"

Was he intimating they might have ended the night in bed? Ivy could certainly get behind that. Or rather, in between those sheets.

And yet, with her official dating badge so shiny and new, she was reluctant to crawl into bed with Wolf. Sex meant something to her. She didn't have flings or share her body with just anyone. Emotions were involved and she required, at the very least, the suggestion of a commitment before she got naked with a man. And above all, no paparazzi to record the event.

"Maybe," she said in response to the open-ended sort of suggestion. "But I really should be getting inside. I don't like to leave Ivan alone too long. He has trouble getting into bed sometimes. I should go in and check on him."

And avoid the gorilla sitting on the trunk behind them? The will-they-won't-they? Their kiss seemed to want to lead somewhere, but not into bed.

"I get it," he said.

No, he really didn't, because even she couldn't get things straight in her brain right now.

"I've got an early morning at the office."

He always did. Why couldn't she just grab him by the collar and shake some honesty out of him? Make him face the truth? Make him commit to either being in or out with her? Again, it was those boundaries of his. She didn't want to break them and risk him fleeing. He was too precious to her. And she knew that men could be vulnerable when pressed.

And really, what did she expect? The night had come to an end. She had to move forward, away from the drama that surrounded Wolf's life.

"To a fairy-tale night," she said, then gave him a quick kiss. "See you in the morning?"

"Always."

She left him sitting inside the limo. Once inside she saw that Ivan's bedroom light was off. A quick peek confirmed he was asleep. All was well.

Except with her heart.

Wolf blew out a breath and stretched his arms across the back of the limo. He'd almost suggested they go back to his place and have sex. Ivy had successfully dodged that unspoken prompt. He'd give her the benefit of the doubt. Her brother did need care.

What was he doing? He hadn't needed to impress anyone tonight. Hadn't needed to prove to his employees that he was happily dating to stop the rumors. So why couldn't he just step out of the role and be himself? The man who wanted Ivy more and more. A man who felt as though a piece of him were missing when she was not around.

CHAPTER TEN

IVY HANDED VALERIE the dress bag and the shoebox. She had intended to deliver the dress to her this morning but Valerie, who currently stood in the living room, said it had been no problem to stop by. Which meant, she had been nervous about its safe return.

"Thank you again," Ivy said. "It made the night like something out of a fairy tale."

"Oh, I think it was the handsome prince you were seen smooching in the limo that did that," Valerie said.

Ivy gaped.

"Page Six, my dear." The side glance Valerie gave her, accompanied with a smirk said everything Ivy needed to know. "I'll see you at work tomorrow."

Ivy's heart sank. She'd been photographed while kissing Wolf? Must have been as they'd left the party. Yes, he had given her a smooch in the back of the car. She'd been so enthralled by him, she hadn't realized the paparazzi had surrounded the car until the limo driver had apologized for his slow departure as he had to carefully navigate the throngs.

Tugging out her phone, she almost typed in Page Six, then shook her head. "Don't do it."

But curiosity prodded. The page came up, and there she and Wolf were in a huge photo in the back of the limo. They weren't kissing, but he was leaning in looking like he might be kissing her. It had really been that he'd been reaching to shield the flashes with his hand out her side of the vehicle.

The headline read: *Billionaire Rogue Romeo Seen with Mystery Woman*.

And underneath:

Creator of Concierge app back on the dating scene. Who is the mystery woman in red? And how much will she take him for?

"Really? Those assholes."

They'd taken a perfectly romantic first date and made it wrong. Already labeling her a gold digger? The nerve!

Ivy swore under her breath just as Ivan walked into the kitchen. He was quite steady and didn't use the cane any more than to direct his steps. "The woman in red," he said and winked. "Oh, sister, what have you gotten into?"

"I'm not sure. This is terrible."

"You're not dating Wolf?"

"Well, yes, it was a date. But look, this ridiculous article claims I'm going to take him for another million like his former girlfriend did. How dare they!"

"It's what those vultures do. Sensationalism sells much better than 'it's their first date and they were so precious.'"

"What a mess." She slammed her phone down on the counter. She'd not wanted to involve Ivan in any sort of gossip. He had enough stress to deal with. If she continued to see Wolf, would the paparazzi follow her home?

"Well, I think you two look great together. Don't you want it to be a thing?"

"I've got too much on my plate to think about having a relationship, Ivan."

"Are you talking about me? Because I will not be used as an excuse to avoid your own personal issues."

"Yes, but… I don't want it to affect you. You've got enough on your plate right now."

He shrugged. "We'll deal with that if it happens. From the little you've told me, Wolf seems like a nice guy. Dude is rich, too. What's not to like about him?"

"I tend to look beyond a person's financial worth. I'm surprised you'd even say such a thing."

"I'm sorry. I know you do. As do I. But how can you not entertain thoughts about all his cash? He's swimming in money."

"I like Wolf for who he is. And I hope he likes me for who I am."

"Does he know you're not a coffee slinger in real life?"

"Yes, and he's afraid of spiders."

"The horror!" Ivan sighed and shrugged. "That man will never be the one for you. If a little bug scares him…"

Ivy stuck out her tongue at him. But he wasn't wrong. Had she netted a catch that was too big even for her to handle? But where *did* she stand after their first official date? True, she should not use Ivan's health as an excuse to avoid a relationship. And he'd brushed it off as insignificant. But after she helped her brother get his life settled, she intended to find a real job, possibly not even on this continent. Where would that leave her future with Wolf?

On Monday, Wolf met Ivy outside But First… She handed him a cup of black coffee, and then gave him a bite of her chocolate-frosted donut.

"Not so big!" she protested when he took a chunk out of one side and handed it back to her. "Yeesh, it's like you've never seen food every time you see food. Have you eaten lunch?"

"Today?"

She rolled her eyes, and took a bite of the donut, then handed the rest to him. "Have at it. It was just a treat. But you need fuel to keep that brain working properly."

He downed the donut in two bites as they walked. "You think sugar is good fuel for thinking?"

"Not really. But at least the calories will go to your hips instead of mine."

He leaned in and gave her a kiss that tasted like chocolate and donut crumbs.

"I can get behind those invisible calories," she said. "Kiss me again?"

They paused and just when she was prepared to meet his mouth with hers, he took a moment to glance over her shoulder.

"What? Paparazzi?"

"Surprisingly? Not one in sight. Which makes me nervous. They could be hiding, getting long-range shots. Let's keep walking."

Disturbed that they could be followed, Ivy shifted her focus. Was she moving forward in this relationship? It felt like it. And honestly, she wanted to explore their connection. Her heart was screaming to give it a chance. Was there a way to make it happen while also protecting Ivan from the nosy press?

"I've got a meeting in half an hour so this will have to be a quick walk."

She nodded and sipped her coffee. "What does a day in Wolf Zeigler's life look like?"

"At Concierge? Boss things. Coding, for sure. But I have dozens of excellent coders on staff, here and in Europe. So

I've been able to let some of my work be divvied out to them. I oversee all the designs and tech on the new apps. We have two planned for release next year, which is what the meeting is about."

"Can you tell me what they are?"

"Sure, but then I'd have to kill you. And I don't think I'm cut out for burying a body."

"But the killing part works for you?"

Wolf laughed. "Touché. I'll give you a hint: it involves NFTs and creating an accessible marketplace."

"NFTs. Non-fungible tokens," she said. "And that's all I know about that."

"You got the acronym right. That's better than ninety percent of non-techies. I'm also teasing the idea of selling Concierge. The app, that is."

"But doesn't it make you tons of money?"

"It does. And I would probably make a cool billion selling it."

"Why sell when you can continue the income stream?"

They paused beneath a flowering tree. Wolf turned to her, crushing his empty coffee cup. She did not miss his scan of the neighborhood. Being protective? Mark another one off her list. And yet, she really wished they'd stayed indoors, away from spying cameras.

"Ivy, I don't need more money. I have more money than God. In fact, I don't think God has money. That would just be wrong. Anyway, I'm set for life. So I want to start focusing on what comes next. My life."

"Your life? You don't have one now?"

"Do you think spending sixteen hours a day at work is a life?"

"Not at all. So what's next?"

"Well—you gave me an idea."

"I did?"

"Yes, you've inspired me to start investigating charities and design a plan for distributing my income. I figure giving half away should be good for starters."

"That's a hell of a lot of money. But also, that's amazing. How did I inspire such a grand idea?"

"When you told me about your brother, I started thinking about ways I could help people. You know, people that would take the help."

She got the dig. And she still wasn't changing her mind regarding taking financial help from him. "Good for you. What focus are you going for? Humanities? Environmental? Technological?"

"All of the above? I'm not sure yet. I'm just getting this idea going. I alerted my financial advisor. And you know? It's already made me feel lighter. Like all this money will become much less of a burden than it's been to me."

"The burden landing squarely on your failed relationships?"

"Yes."

"Are you sure it's all because of your money? Maybe it's you?"

"Well, hell, I'm such a lovable guy, it's got to be the money, right?"

She caught his wink and laughed. "All right, I concede. You are a lovable guy. And any woman who can't see beyond your dollar signs is crazy."

"You've seen beyond the dollars."

"Because you let me. But seeing beyond all those camera flashes the other night was a challenge." And now would be the perfect time to tell him about her hesitancy…

"I hate that others have to suffer just because they want to spend time with me. If I could pay them all to stay away from me, I would." He made another surveillance around them. "But the money would just make them even more greedy. Blackmail involved, I'm sure. I'd hand it all back for some peace, trust me on that one. And…for a simple, quiet life."

"Really? I have to believe that you'd keep some of it. Just enough to make that simple quiet life?"

"Yeah, you're right. A little cottage out in the woods and a family are on my radar."

"Wow, that does surprise me. Do you think it's even possible?"

"Escaping the paparazzi can be done. Especially when they think they are being covert. Three o'clock in the bushes. See that lens?"

Ivy twisted her glance to the right. Sunlight flashed in the middle of a hedge. Mercy. "I have to tell you that I'm a little worried about them."

"The paps? Don't be. I'll protect you from them. Promise."

"I know you will, and that's not the part that scares me." Now that she'd seen the paparazzi, she couldn't look away. "It's Ivan. If we, well…the more we're seen together and photos are taken, then they'll probably look into me and my life. I don't want any of this craziness to carry back to my brother. He doesn't need that."

"I get it. But I can't protect your brother from what they write. Or you. That headline was nasty. You're not a gold digger. I know that. You just have to not read anything they write."

"Easier said than done. I know it's not your fault what the press prints. I just had to tell you that so you know where I stand. Because, well, I know last night was a date. But what does that mean? Are we dating now? Are we…"

"I've been thinking about that, too. Ever since I watched you walk up to the brownstone and close the door, I wanted to be inside that house with you. Not standing outside."

"Same."

"Really?"

"Yes. Wolf, I know how you feel about dating, and believe me, I respect your need to be cautious and go slow. However—"

He leaned in and kissed her. It was a kiss she had been waiting for all her life. A real one. An honest one. One that said they shared things, understood one another. But it ended too abruptly. And she followed his glance across the street to the jiggling shrubbery.

"We've gone slow," he said. "I trust you, Ivy. I know you're not interested in my money."

"I'm not."

"Are you interested in me?"

"Hell, yes. But I wouldn't have invited you in last night, brother or not. I'm not the sort who gets intimate with a man unless we're exclusive. Sex is special to me."

"I'm glad you told me that. I want you to be my girlfriend. And not because I think there will be sex sometime in the future. I want the exclusivity thing, too. We're more than friends. Do you think you can handle dating a reclusive introvert with a penchant for eating too much and with more money than he knows how to spend?"

"He sounds a little quirky," she said.

"And there is the added hindrance of spying your every intimate moment on all the socials."

"That is the weird part. Oh, Wolf, I had talked myself into not wanting to do the whole dating a celebrity thing. But I've fallen for you. And my heart is jumping up and down because it feels like a win, so...yes, I'll be your girlfriend."

"As my girlfriend, things won't change."

"They won't?" She pouted. "I was hoping that would grant me access to information about the secret apps. Darn! Foiled again. But what about the cameras?"

"Do you think you can handle the unwanted attention? It might get worse. It might not. And I won't argue if you suddenly feel you need to split. But promise me you'll be nice and not ghost me or throw things at me if you do want to break up?"

"Throw things?"

Wolf nodded, then pointed to a scar on his bicep. "Knife. She was off aim. Just a bit higher and I would have lost an eye."

"Why are people like that? That's just crazy."

"I guess I have a bad eye for picking women." He put up a hand. "Until now. I have a feeling we will work, Ivy. You want to come over after you get off?" he asked.

Did she? Yes and no. She'd already broken her staunch need to keep it at one date by agreeing to be his girlfriend. She needed to get quiet and figure out if she really wanted that or if it had been an exuberant reaction to feeling like a princess who had been claimed by a prince. She needed some space.

"Actually…" She opened the Concierge app on her phone and verified what she'd just remembered. "Ivan and I have a Zoom call with one of the research centers offering an MS study."

"I'll cross my fingers for the both of you."

She kissed him. "See you tomorrow morning." She turned to spy the photogs leaning against a street post. "And so it begins."

CHAPTER ELEVEN

DESPITE BEING TIRED after a long day on her feet, Ivy couldn't begin to touch anything but joy. Since there hadn't been a single camera-wielding paparazzi between Wolf's place and work, she'd dismissed the niggling feeling to end this relationship. How could she end something that had only just begun? If she couldn't withstand a few photographers for someone as wonderful as Wolf then she was seriously missing out on something.

Wolf had picked her up after work, greeted her with a long, delicious kiss, and handed her the calendar page. It read: *Let someone in.*

They'd both shared a knowing glance. Suddenly the calendar had gone all wise and prophetic, seeming to read them both.

Now she stood in his penthouse. It was a total man cave with stone walls and brushed black steel stylings. Massive dark wood furnishings, and a huge TV on the wall. For work, he'd explained. He'd cast his laptop to the screen. In the center of the room hung a four-tiered chandelier of more black iron. It was a two-story, open floorplan, with a black iron staircase hugging one wall. The corner space—the two connecting walls were all windows—looked over an old railyard that the city had rewilded with grass, flowers and trees.

"It's cozy here." She wandered into the kitchen to lean against the black marble countertop. "Feels weirdly homey."

"Why weirdly?" He kissed her and walked around to unpack the food that had been delivered just as they'd arrived. "I like to think I have a little style."

"You do. It's exactly what I'd expect to represent you." That kiss had been too brief. It had ignited something within her that she knew would smolder until answered. "Mm, that smells good."

"You like peanut noodles?"

"Heck, yeah. Hand me a fork. I'm starving."

After much food and wine, and laughter, Wolf said, "I've never met a woman with whom I've been able to really share food. I mean, I can make a pig out of myself and you don't care."

"You go voraciously at what tastes great. You're comfortable around me."

"I am."

"Good, because there's not a thing about me that should be intimidating."

"I think the fact that you're an entomologist is intimidating. You've got bug smarts."

"Ha! Don't even get me started on the order of *coleoptera*. I will talk your head off."

"That's beetles, right? See, I've learned a few things from you already. I've seen pictures of some beetles that look like chrome or a shiny car finish."

"You should see the *polybothrus sumptuosa gema*. It's purple with green flecks on its carapace. Very small. Found in Madagascar. It's one of my favorites."

"Seriously? Show me."

Ivy tugged out her phone and searched for an image. As she did, they moved from the counter to the massive leather couch while she pulled up more images and explained where the beetle could be found and if she'd had opportunity to see it in the wild. She gave him the rock 'n' roll tour of the beetle kingdom.

"The purple and blue ones are my favorites. Wait, I forgot about the *cyclommatus metalifer*. It's got massive pinchers. But even the plain beetles fascinate me. Oh, here I am going off on a wild and boring tour of the beetle kingdom." When she finally glanced out the window to see it was dark, she shoved his shoulder. "I told you not to get me started!"

"What? Everything you've shown me was interesting. But really, there should be an app for beetles. You know, one that identifies them with space for you to add your own images."

"That sounds useful. Make it for me."

"Don't think I won't. I sense bugs are the way to your heart."

"You're a smart man. But there are other ways to my heart." She touched him under the chin, luring him toward her so he scooched closer on the couch. The smolder had only grown heavier, more wanting. "Kiss me."

"Always and whenever you want, Ivy. I like kissing you here…" He leaned in and nuzzled his nose aside her cheek, brushing light kisses on her earlobe. That felt like every fantasy bursting free from the seams and gliding over her skin.

He breathed against her cheek and moved up to feather his lips across her lashes. Ivy twined her fingers into his beard and held him close. Their intimacy felt easy. Not demanding. Yet hungry. She kissed him deeply, wanting to dive into him, discover all that he hid. And yet, she would not touch those places he protected unless he offered her entrance.

"I want to make love to you," he said.

"Well, that's why I'm here, to help you with whatever challenge your calendar presents."

He laughed but silenced quickly. Looking up at her, his

hair tousled and his eyes glimmering in the low light, Ivy saw the little boy inside him that still hid behind the barriers.

"This is not about a calendar tonight," he said.

"I know. I was joking." She kissed him and began to unbutton his dress shirt. "This is about us. Finally saying to each other that we trust the other. Do you trust me?"

"Do you trust me?"

"I do. There's nothing about you that comes off as untrustworthy. But I know you've been burned by women, so I expect your trust might not be as easy to win."

Another kiss tasted her lips slowly and ended with a dash of his tongue. "I do trust you. But it still feels like maybe I'm just saying it because that's what you want to hear. Does that make sense?"

"I get it. Don't rush it, Wolf. I'm not going to hurt you. I'm in this for as long as you desire."

"What about the paparazzi? I can feel you tense up whenever they are near."

"Truth? I'm struggling with being a part of your celebrity life. I keep telling myself I don't want it to lead to Ivan and then give him more stress than he's already got, but... I know he's very capable. So maybe it's just an excuse?"

"Could be. Maybe it's best if you just cut and run right now?"

Ivy's jaw dropped open. Was he serious?

Wolf shrugged. "I don't want you to, but I also don't want to do anything to hurt you."

"Thank you. But I don't want to run. Especially not at this part."

"What part is that?"

She bowed her forehead to his and licked the tip of his nose. "The part where we have sex."

"Let's take this upstairs to my bedroom." He stood and held out his hand.

When Ivy stood and took his hand, he suddenly bent and lifted her over his shoulder. She whooped as he carried her up the stairs and dropped her on the bed. The thick, charcoal velvet spread caressed her body.

"See? All that weightlifting is good for something." He unbuttoned his shirt and tugged it off, tossing it aside before giving her a flex of each biceps.

Ivy preened over his incredible physique. Honed hard from his workouts and brushed with more of the soft dark hairs like his beard and moustache. His biceps flexed and his six-pack tempted her onto her knees to touch. He growled as she slid her hand over his abdomen and around to clutch his derriere.

A kiss to his chest devoured his essence. He smelled like peanut sauce and wine. Desire had reached full capacity. She had to answer it. Now.

With a tug, he pulled the cloth-wrapped tie from her ponytail and then glided his fingers through her hair.

He kneeled on the bed. Face to face, they explored one another. His hands gliding under her T-shirt and pulling it off to toss. Wolf laughed when he saw her bra. "I should have guessed!"

So she had the one bra with butterflies on it. She wasn't about to apologize for being the crazy bug lady.

When he bowed to kiss her breasts and tugged down the bra cup to tongue her nipple, Ivy clawed her nails gently but firmly down his back. "That's so good."

"You got a little wild to you?" He growled and gave her a gentle bite, which only rocketed up the giddy want swirling in her core. With another tug, he pushed down her jeans and panties and tossed them aside. He stood to remove his pants, and when he stood naked before her, Ivy leaned back on her hands and admired his physique.

"What?" He shrugged.

"I certainly hope you're not going to be shy with that."

He leaned over her, kissing down her neck and to her breasts. "You got it."

Wolf stared up at the black spot on the ceiling and frowned. It moved. A spider? Better that than a cockroach, of which he'd seen far too many times since moving to the States. He should be thankful it wasn't larger.

Beside him lay a long stretch of soft warmth. Ivy's hair spilled across his arm and shoulder. The sage scent from the potpourri thingy he'd bought on a whim mingled with her heat and skin, filling his nostrils with a heady remembrance of last night. That had been some sex. Intimate and feisty. Fiery and fast. They'd both gone at each other as if they'd known exactly what the other desired. So cool, especially since first-time sex with women usually resulted in some awkwardness, much faster climax than usual, and sometimes even the woman getting all demanding and weird or even submissive.

Wolf had never been with a woman who had known exactly what she wanted. At the same time, he'd felt an equal partner in their give-and-take. Ivy Quinn was one hell of a woman. Who knew how to pour a wicked cup of coffee.

He had to smile to think that he'd found her in the shop in his building, and it had taken him weeks before he'd rustled up the courage to talk to her. And now that he had? This beautiful woman wanted to be in his life. And without asking for his money. It didn't feel possible.

Well. She'd been right about guessing his trust wasn't completely there yet. Something could still happen that would send him reeling. It always happened. So he would be cautious. He didn't know any other way to walk through life. Keep to himself, protect his boundaries, and always be the first to walk away. Those precautions kept Wolfgang Zeigler's heart protected.

The flash drive the PI had sent him still sat in his desk drawer. A smart man would make sure he knew what he was getting into. But Ivy trusted him. And if he opened that envelope then he shattered that earned trust. Besides, she was still leery about the photogs. He had to make this as easy for her as possible.

When she stirred beside him, he turned his head to nuzzle into her hair. The princess between his sheets lifted her head. She blew at the hair tangled over her face.

"Morning," he offered.

"Sure."

Not a morning person? Maybe she needed coffee.

When her hand slid across his stomach and moved lower, all thoughts of coffee vanished.

"You think so?" he teased.

"I do."

Wolf snickered. "Good call. But can we move it off the bed? Maybe into the shower?"

"But I'm so comfy and warm right here against your big, hard—" she gave him a squeeze "—mmm."

"I'm just a little freaked that spider up there will drop on us when we're going at it."

Ivy rolled to her back and squinted to pinpoint the black spot he'd kept in his sight since opening his eyes. *"Pholcidae,"* she said on a yawn. "Just a daddy longlegs. It won't bite."

"I did not need to hear that." He sat up and pushed the covers off Ivy to reveal her curling up into a reactive ball. "Come on!"

CHAPTER TWELVE

APPARENTLY THE MAN was a morning person. Something Ivy could never relate to, but knew she had to incorporate into her life if she ever wanted to hold a decent-paying job. On the other hand, field research tended to follow the project leader's timeline, and that was her ultimate goal. Stalking through the Amazon in search of the blushing phantom butterfly? Let's get together after noon, team, because that particular insect doesn't come out until dusk.

But Wolf had gotten out of bed, muttering about the spider. And his bare derriere had lured her to follow him into the shower. The quick burst of cold water had made her yelp. She'd forgotten that was one of his kinks. He'd quickly comforted her shivers by turning her to face the wall and kissing down her shoulder. They fit perfectly. And thank that spider for the shower sex, right?

Now they stood before the marble vanity, morning sunlight beaming through a high, long window. The mirror reflected his clever grin as he cupped her breasts and thrust inside her from behind. The sight of his big hand covering her breast amped up the erotic thrill. That slightly sneaky smile—his sex smile—was something she would never get from her thoughts.

When he came, he hugged her tightly against his body and his shudders vibrated her very bones. But he wasn't greedy. Slipping his hand around and down between her legs, he masterfully brought her to a shivering climax.

"Do you have to work today?" he whispered.

"Nope."

"Then we're doing this all day. I'm going to order in some breakfast. You like eggs or pancakes?"

"Both."

He nuzzled a hard kiss against her neck, and she reached back to run her fingers up through his thick hair.

"Stay naked," he murmured, then stepped back, winked at her in the mirror, and left.

Ivy nodded at her reflection. That handsome, bearded wolf of a man was all hers? What a ride. This makeshift princess really had found a prince charming. A reluctant billionaire who sought a simple life amid the chaos of his reality. And she had been able to step beyond her cautious worries to embrace it all.

Out in the bedroom, she navigated around the tousled bed sheets that lay on the floor and a pillow that lay against the wall. She smiled to recall their lusty antics. She glanced overhead but did not spy the arachnid.

She plopped onto the bed and scanned the floor, spying her phone peeking out from under her discarded shirt. She picked it up and saw a missed call from ten minutes earlier. When she'd been in the shower? She clicked through. It was...

"Heather?"

Suddenly, the freedom she had been luxuriating in swooshed out through her pores. Her body tensed.

She called the number and Heather answered immediately. "Ivy, I'm so glad you called back. It's Ivan."

"What is it?" Her heartbeats thundered to top speed. Ivy clutched a sheet against her chest.

"He was unresponsive when I checked in on him this morning. His breathing was—I had to call the ambulance. We're at the ER. Can you get here?"

"Of course. I'm on my way right now. Is he...?"

"They were able to revive him. I haven't spoken to the doctor. Just get here, okay?"

"Yes." Ivy hung up and dove for her clothes.

"Eggs, pancakes, and—" Wolf stopped in the bedroom doorway.

He was naked and Ivy didn't take a moment to even look at him.

"What's up?"

"It's Ivan. His physical therapist tried to call ten minutes ago. He's in the ER."

Wolf swore. "You're heading there?"

"Of course. I can't believe I did this!"

"Did what? Ivy, don't blame yourself—"

"Don't tell me what to think!" she snapped. She pulled her T-shirt over her head then grabbed her shoes.

"I won't. I'm sorry. I'll call a ride for you."

"No, I can—" She stopped in the doorway. She didn't have a vehicle. And the hospital was a subway ride away. While panic set her nerves to a buzz and made her shake, she had the sense to realize her best, and quickest, route to the hospital. "Yes. I'll take that offer for a ride."

"Let me get some clothes on," he said and disappeared into the walk-in closet. Less than a minute later he appeared, zipping up his jeans and pulling on a T-shirt. "Let's go."

Ivan had taken the wrong medication, which had resulted in an overdose. The pill bottles were the same size and color and the pill shapes had been remarkably close, so it had been, unfortunately, an easy mishap. And with his vision blurry in the one eye, he may have made the mistake no matter what.

He was stable now, and the doctor told Ivy that a night in the hospital, some fluids, and careful monitoring would see him home in better shape. It hadn't been something she or Heather could have anticipated. It was just a mistake. He also suggested Heather label Ivan's pill bottles with a larger font.

Ivy thanked him then went to sit at Ivan's bedside. He was sleeping, so she let him rest. There was no place she wanted to be right now. Estelle had told her it was no problem to miss a day or two at But First… Coffee was not as important as family.

Wolf had accompanied her here and had stepped aside when the doctor had wanted to speak specifically to Ivy. She briefly wondered if he had left, then her brain wouldn't allow her to do anything more than focus on Ivan.

She clasped her shaking hands together on her lap. She had been out of the house, enjoying herself with Wolf. It was difficult to even consider how she had been so lacking in concern for her brother's safety. She was not prepared to experience the loss of a family member again.

Damn it, why had she thought she had the right to something so self-indulgent as sex? Last night had been good. Seeing fireworks explode, good. But now she was being punished for her selfishness. There was just no getting beyond that truth.

Late in the afternoon, Ivan woke. He was groggy but managed a smile. He apologized to her, and that made Ivy feel even worse. None of this was his fault. He hadn't asked for this disease. And he'd been nothing but positive since learning about it. She didn't tell him she'd been having sex with Wolf. Her brother wasn't stupid. He knew where she had been.

"You should go rest," Ivan said quietly. "You look tired."

"I'm fine." Hungry, but she'd manage. "I'm not going to leave your side."

"You can't be by my side forever, Ivy. Things will happen. It's something we have to accept."

"We don't have to accept anything, Ivan. We'll figure this life out for you. This will get better. It has to," she said on a failing tone.

All she wanted to do was cry. To bury her head against someone's shoulder and bawl. She'd failed Ivan. And she'd almost lost him. What she wouldn't give to have her parents here right now to support and hug her.

"At the very least, will you move to the sofa by the window?" Ivan asked. "You're making me nervous sitting so close. Your jaw pulses when you're tense. Just stretch out for a while. Take a nap. It'll make me feel better."

She eyed the sofa. Short, flat, not designed for comfort. Yet, it did appeal. "Maybe just ten minutes. You rest, too. The doctor comes back on shift later this evening, and I want to talk to him and see if he has any info about local studies."

"You're a trooper, sis."

She got up and her bones protested after having sat on the hard chair for half the day with only one bathroom break. Feeling older than her years, Ivy crept over to the sofa and lay down, her head landing on the armrest, and her legs bending to tuck her feet against the other end. Ivan winked at her. He was getting back some of his energy. That made her feel a minuscule better.

And with that small hope to assuage her fears, she closed her eyes.

* * *

Wolf had been at the hospital since bringing Ivy here this morning. He'd peeked in a few times but each time her body language had told him to stay away. By mid-afternoon his stomach had begun to growl. And if his was growling, he knew Ivy's would be also. He slipped out to pick up some food.

He hated that he couldn't sit beside her and hold her hand. Offer his shoulder for her head to rest on. But he didn't want to overstep her boundaries. He was familiar with personal boundaries. And even though they'd exploded those barriers last night, he suspected she might be feeling some guilt over their antics. She'd been away the one night her brother had needed someone to help him. It had been a random incident. But Wolf also felt extreme guilt.

And there wasn't any way to make it better. He couldn't throw money at the problem because what was done was done. Ivan was now recovering. But he had heard the conversation suggesting the medications could be labeled with larger fonts and color coding. And that had sparked an idea. He'd tugged out his phone and researched, finding some pharmacies did color code their bottles, but they still used the same amber-colored plastic or white containers. He made a note to investigate pharmaceutical innovations.

Now, with food in hand, he looked inside the room. Ivan sat upright in the hospital bed, a woman leaning over him and—

Ivan tilted his head to eye Wolf. The woman, with long pink dreads and a cupid bow smile, stepped back and smoothed down her scrubs. A nurse? Not if they'd been doing what Wolf had just caught them doing.

With a glance around the room, Wolf saw Ivy sleeping on the sofa.

He stepped inside and whispered, "Hey, man, I'm Wolf Zeigler. Uh, your sister's…boyfriend?"

"You don't sound very sure of that," Ivan replied in a quiet voice. They both glanced to Ivy. Still asleep.

Wolf walked inside and stopped at Ivan's bedside. "We just made the labels official."

The woman kissed Ivan on the forehead and told him she'd leave him for a bit. "I'm Heather," she said to Wolf. "Ivan's physical therapist."

"I've heard about you. Nice to meet you."

"I'll leave you two alone." She left quickly.

Wolf held up the bag. "I brought food for Ivy. She's been holding vigil."

"She feels guilty. I wish she wouldn't."

"Hard not to. I feel the same having been the one who kept your sister from your side. How are you feeling?"

"Better. It was a quirk what happened. It wasn't Ivy's fault. And even if she had been home, asleep in her room, it still would have happened and she wouldn't have found me until she woke. Don't let it bother you. What food did you bring?"

"Sandwiches. You hungry?"

"I'm starving. And if Ivy's going to sleep then I'm taking half her sandwich."

Wolf sat and quietly pulled out the sandwiches so as not to wake the sleeping beauty. He offered Ivan the ham on rye and he halved it then handed Wolf back the rest to save for Ivy.

"So," Wolf said around a bite of pastrami. "How long have you and Heather been a thing?"

Ivan paused with the sandwich before his mouth.

Wolf couldn't prevent a grin. "Just calling it like I see it."

"Don't tell her," Ivan said with a nod toward the couch.

"We haven't figured out how to do that yet. Ivy might not like the hired help getting involved with her brother."

"I don't know. She's pretty easygoing."

"Yeah, but we are paying Heather. So… Just keep it quiet for now."

"Not a problem."

"So you finally decided to make my sister an official girlfriend? Page Six and everything?"

"She seems to like hanging out with me despite the circus that follows. Uh, I hope it didn't upset you?"

Ivan shrugged. "I just want my sister to be safe. It's gotta suck, having to dodge the press."

"My entire dating history sucks, man. I'm pretty cautious around women."

"I read the reference to your past paramours. My sister is not a gold digger."

"I know that. She's good stuff. Ivy is…" Wolf blew out a breath. Brothers didn't know everything about their sisters. That file in his desk drawer haunted him. Should he read it? "Do I even deserve someone so special as her?"

"Time will tell. And a discerning brother." Ivan set the sandwich on his lap. "So I've always wanted to ask a man who has billions what he spends his money on?"

"Cutting right to the chase, eh?"

"If it's not too personal. What kind of car do you have? What's the most extravagant purchase you've made? Give me something here. I need a little fantasy to brighten my day."

"I don't drive," he offered to Ivan. "I know how to, but New York traffic makes a sane man crazy."

"I hear you. I'm a bike man myself."

"Ivy told me you planned to bike across the United States?"

"Yeah, that was a dream. Not sure I'll ever be able to sit on a bike again. It's my balance." Ivan swore.

Wolf could feel his pain. And in that moment, he knew he'd never been so devastated by life as this man had been. He may have struggled as a child, fending for himself in foster care and learning to survive, but life had not stolen his freedom.

"How about one of those fixed-position indoor bikes? A fancy one with the screen you can watch so it looks like you're biking outdoors?"

Ivan shrugged. "Let's not talk about my inability to be normal. You didn't tell me your craziest purchase."

"I haven't made any crazy purchases." Well, beyond the diamond ring that had brought on the lawsuit. "Too much money can be too much of a good thing."

"I can't believe that. There's got to be something you've always wanted?"

Indeed, but that was an intangible a man could never buy. Love and the constancy of family did not come with a price tag. Was Ivy the sort who could ever be happy living in a little village with toddlers chasing through the garden?

No, she needed to study the insects in that garden. Kids might get in her way. He shouldn't imagine too much about what she wanted from life. Nor should he expect he deserved such a woman as her.

"I do like motorcycles," he offered as a means to entertain Ivan's request. "Maybe someday, when I move home to Germany, I'll get a Ducati and cruise the Autobahn."

"Sounds wonderful. The wind blowing through your hair. Your body capable of responding to what you ask of it."

Wolf slapped a hand on Ivan's shoulder. "Just know, man, that I'm here for you. I care about your sister and want to see her happy. And that means you're coming along for that ride."

"Sounds like a bumpy one, but those are the best kind. But you better treat her well. Because if you don't…"

"I'll have to answer to you."

Ivy stirred on the sofa. Ivan shoved his half-eaten sandwich toward Wolf, who immediately figured that Ivy might be upset to see her brother noshing on non-hospital-approved food, and he gobbled it up as he walked over to the sofa. "Hey there, sleepyhead."

"Wolf. You're…still here?"

"I brought some food. You've been going all day. I knew you'd be hungry."

"Bless you."

"Got to meet your brother as well," he added with a wink toward Ivan that Ivy could not see. That sandwich sat at the base of his throat, he'd gobbled it so fast. "You two are cut from the same cloth, that's for sure."

"Stubborn, independent and assertive?" Ivan said.

"Exactly." Wolf chuckled and then grabbed the sandwich bag for Ivy.

She bypassed his offer and went to the bedside and took her brother's hand. "How are you feeling?"

"Whipped, but I'll survive. You eat something. Then you can go home with your boyfriend."

"My—" She glanced over her shoulder. "You two did have a talk, eh?"

Wolf shrugged. "Was that supposed to be a secret?"

"No." She sat beside the bed and Wolf set the food bag on the tray beside her. "I'm not going home until the doctor says you're out of the woods and signs you out."

"Ivy, I'm good now."

"Yes, but—Ivan, don't argue, please?"

"Fine. Stay. But I'm not great company."

"I've known that for twenty-some years." She opened the bag and took out a sandwich. "You should go," she said to Wolf. "I appreciate you hanging around all day. But like Ivan said, he's good. We can take it from here."

An abrupt dismissal. Wolf almost took offense. But this was a family matter. He didn't want to intrude.

"Will you give me a call before you turn in for the night?" he asked as he leaned close to her, sliding a hand across her back. He felt her melt against his palm, responding with a sigh.

"I'll make sure she does," Ivan said. "Thanks, man."

"Not a problem." Wolf kissed Ivy on the cheek. Too quick. He hated walking away. Leaving that beautiful woman behind.

In the hallway, he passed Heather, who was headed back toward Ivan's room. Weird that Ivan didn't want Ivy to know. Then again, she may be upset that her brother was—well, why couldn't he have a relationship, hell, a healthy sex life, if it was there for him?

And as for offering to help them financially, what could be so terrible about that? Ivy's defensive stance against any monetary help was like…well, it was how he acted when he wanted to control a situation. Wolf pushed everyone away.

But since meeting Ivy, all he'd been doing was pulling her closer. She had changed him. And he wouldn't argue that change. But in the process, had she become more protective of her heart?

CHAPTER THIRTEEN

IVY AGREED TO leave the hospital after the doctor told her Ivan was doing well and could be released in the morning. She was exhausted and hadn't slept much beyond the nap on the couch. Now she texted Wolf a quick "See you in a few days. Ivan coming home tomorrow. I'm staying with him for a day." Then she hit the sack and was asleep within minutes.

The next day, after Ivan arrived home, she watched him like a hawk. Heather had relabeled his medication bottles, but Ivy had insisted she had things under control and told her to leave. She spent the day filling out more study applications and helping Ivan browse for online jobs. He needed something that would appeal to his adventurous and active heart, but without requiring him to leave the home. Or located at a facility that catered to his physical needs. It was a tall order, but not impossible.

Browsing an online retail site, she eyed the stationary bike with the electronic screen that was supposed to immerse the user in a virtual experience of biking through meadows or across the country or even in Paris. It was costly, but no more expensive than some of his medical bills. But where to put it if Ivan was out of this place early next year? He couldn't travel with it. She put it on her wish list, for a future that might see her brother in a permanent home.

Ivan was the one to let out a hoot when he found a coaching job that offered virtual training for athletes. The home office was in London, but their employees were stationed all over the world. He filled out an application, then Ivy made him something to eat.

They could do this. She just needed...

One of those big bear hugs from Wolf. Because that was capable of changing her world.

"No coffee today, boss?"

Wolf didn't look up when Stacy entered his office. She set a stack of mail on his desk. He'd foregone stopping for coffee this morning, knowing his favorite barista wouldn't be there to serve him. He planned to stop at Ivan's brownstone after work.

"Busy," he muttered, without looking up from the computer screen.

"You want to do a bar hop with a bunch of us later?"

The invitation took him by surprise. No one in the office had ever invited him to any sort of extracurricular activity outside of work. Not in the three years Concierge had been in this building. He'd heard the gossip; he was a liability with the paparazzi hanging on his every move.

He narrowed his brows at Stacy.

She shrugged. "Figured you might like to join us. It's always couples. And since you and Ivy are a thing, and she's not so—well, you'll fit in now. She was nice, by the way. You surprised us all that night. Thought for sure you'd sworn off women."

"Never say never, Stacy. I'll pass on the bar hop." Much as he wouldn't mind getting to know his employees in a more casual setting. "Ivy's brother isn't well. She's taking care of him and—we're busy."

"Oh, sorry. Is he going to be okay?"

"It's a complicated situation. But thanks for the offer. Maybe next time?"

"Sure. We just got confirmation from DynaTech on the contract. I'll send the closing documents to you for a signature."

"Excellent. I'm hoping to meet in person with the CEO very soon."

That company was helping Concierge to expand to more services and insert themselves in the major socials and search engines. It was a natural alignment that made a lot of sense and would see the Concierge name everywhere, from cell phones to televisions to even household appliances. The sky was the limit.

Yet, as exciting as that future for his company was, Wolf found that with every step he moved Concierge forward, he wanted to take a step away. Completely offload the company and go off on his own? Not quite so extreme. He liked to guide the path. It was his product. He felt as though his name and reputation were on every single tap of the app and product that may eventually carry the name.

But he could do it from a different country. That little cottage in the German countryside. A wife. Kids. More and more he could imagine settling into that cottage with Ivy. Of course, she wasn't the settling type. She had a career waiting for her to explore. And he loved that.

Ivy was not so...

Not so what? Stacy hadn't finished that statement, but Wolf suspected it would have ended with something like "surface," "materialistic," or even "greedy," as would aptly label his previous girlfriends.

He opened the drawer and eyed the flash drive. The private investigator always delivered the reports on a flash drive so nothing could be traced via email. The previous time he'd gotten a report, it had detailed the woman's criminal record. He'd dodged a bullet with that one. Ivy's report could be completely blank. She had no skeletons in her closet. He knew that.

So he closed the drawer and left the office for the day.

While walking toward Ivy's neighborhood, Wolf swung inside a flower shop to pick up a dozen—Ivy didn't seem like the classic roses kind of girl. He perused the assorted bouquets and decided on a frilly purple flower the clerk called beebalm. Perfect. It had the name of a bug in it!

The jewelry boutique next to the flower shop featured an elaborate diamond necklace in the window. He paused but then shook his head. Not Ivy's style. And he could imagine her outrage should he spend so much money on her. She was the opposite of any woman he had dated in the past few years. And while he should be rejoicing that fact, it hurt his heart in a way that surprised him. By not accepting his money, it felt as though she was rejecting him.

What was wrong with him that he needed to use money as a means to validation? Maybe she should be the one ordering a background check on him instead of the other way around. Ivy Quinn was a normal woman with a normal life and some challenges. He, on the other hand, was not fit to walk alongside her. How could she see beyond his hang-ups and rules about money and dating?

He stared into the flower bouquet. Should he stick to models and money-hungry actresses? Maybe that was his lane? It was certainly the slot the world tried to jam him into.

He shook his head. Square Wolf did not fit in those circular slots. And Ivy didn't even have a shape. She was free and open. She'd already smoothed some of his sharp corners. He couldn't mess up. Losing her didn't seem feasible.

At the brownstone, Ivan greeted him at the door, standing quite steadily with the aid of a cane.

"Wolf, come in. Ivy is making cookies and her hands are covered in dough." He closed the door, then carefully turned and made a slow beeline to the sofa, where he sat.

Wolf wandered into the kitchen where he found his girlfriend elbow deep in cookie dough. It smelled like chocolate and sugar. Something white smudged her cheek. He kissed her there. "Ugh. That wasn't sugar."

"Probably flour," she said. "Have a seat. Did you bring flowers for Ivan?"

"If he likes beebalm, I guess so."

"I'm allergic," Ivan called from the living room. "Let Ivy have them."

"Well, there you go." Wolf presented the bouquet to her. "Second choice, but it'll have to do."

She bent to sniff the bouquet, dough-covered hands held near her shoulders. "Mm, I love that oregano scent."

"Oregano?" Wolf sniffed the bouquet and it did have a strange pizza scent to it. "Weird."

"You can use the leaves for some traditional remedies. Not sure what, exactly. Thank you." She kissed him. "I'll keep them in my room so they won't bother Ivan. Will you put them in something for me? There might be a vase under the sink."

Wolf found the vase while Ivy pulled a pan of steaming cookies from the oven and replaced it with another that held globs of raw dough.

"We both had a craving," she offered. "Will you commandeer that spatula and put a couple on a plate for Ivan?"

Happy to help, Wolf shoveled three huge cookies onto a plate then handed it off to her brother. He'd never known a foster mom who would bake for him. Most meals had been from a box, fast food, or leftovers.

That's the past, man. You're here. Right now. Make this a moment.

Wolf claimed a cookie for himself. "I don't think I've ever had a fresh-baked chocolate chip cookie before."

"Seriously? You must have had a poor childhood—oh." Ivy's shoulders dropped. "Sorry. You eat as many as you like. After I pull this last batch from the oven, we'll go sit in the park and devour them. How does that sound?"

"Like my best day ever."

Ivy finished her second cookie. Wolf had eaten half a dozen. She was glad because the recipe had made four dozen. Far too many for just she and Ivan.

"My domesticity is showing," she said as a biker cruised before them on the sidewalk.

"I'm thankful for it. Like I said, I've never had a fresh-baked homemade cookie. I would pay serious cash for more of this."

"Save your money. I'll make them more often and make sure you get a dozen every time I do."

He leaned in and kissed her. She tasted like chocolate. "Your brother looks like he's doing well?"

"Well as he can be. His vision is less blurry today. In some cases, the eye problem goes away after a few months. I just hope it doesn't become..." She looked away from him, unable to speak the worst thing she could imagine.

"Don't think ahead like that," Wolf said. "Take it day by day. And he's got Heather stopping in, too. That must help a lot."

"She's got to stop coming by when she's not scheduled. We can't pay for those extra hours."

Wolf took her hand and squeezed it against his chest. "I wouldn't worry about Heather and Ivan. In fact, I suspect she wouldn't mind a little extra time with your brother. Maybe a weekend alone?"

"What are you implying? She has a full-time job that keeps her busy."

He shrugged. "Have you paid attention to those two together?"

"Well, I—" Ivy gaped at him. "Are you suggesting…?"

Wolf raised a brow and shrugged.

"Ivan would tell me if they were—they can't be. What makes you think so?"

"Just a suspicion. But back to the weekend off idea. I have a proposal for you."

"Oh, yeah?"

"I have to fly to Venice this Friday. I've got a meeting with the company that is going to take Concierge to the next level. I plan to stay the weekend in my palazzo. So… I'm wondering if you would like to come along to Venice with me? I'd only leave you on your own for an afternoon while I take care of business, then I promise the rest of the time would be for touristy stuff and lots of sex."

That last part sounded wonderful. And so did the part about flying to Venice. But really, did the man not pick up on her angst? She'd just barely avoided losing her brother because she hadn't been home to help him with his medication, and now he wanted to whisk her away for an entire weekend?

"I can't leave Ivan that long. He needs to be my priority."

"Heather can stay with him. And like I said, they might enjoy the time together. Alone."

"I still don't get why you think they are having a thing. Unless Ivan said something to you?"

"Just a guess."

"Well, even if that was so, I can't afford to hire Heather for an entire weekend."

"I'll hire her. And I won't take a no from you. This is something I want, Ivy, and I'm willing to put my money where my mouth is."

"Don't you understand what I'm going through? Wolf, it's as if you don't know me at all."

"Is it what *you* are going through," he challenged, "or rather, what your brother is going through?"

"I don't—" She closed her mouth.

He had a point. And she hated that he did have a point. Because it put her in the wrong. She didn't have the emotional head space to devote to both caring for Ivan and keeping a romance with Wolf going. For one night she'd felt she could manage it, and look what had happened! Regret overwhelmed her desire for romance. She couldn't possibly enjoy herself while Ivan was home alone suffering.

"I can't do this." She stood, and when Wolf took her hand she shook it away. "I don't want your money. I never want your money. You can't buy my cooperation. Or my love! This is my problem to handle. Good night. I'll… You can text me later."

She hurried across the street and disappeared inside the brownstone.

Wolf pushed his hands over his face and leaned forward, catching his elbows on his knees. Ivy's statement about him trying to buy her cooperation—her love—knocked the wind out of him. It immediately shot him back to when he was a kid, trying to survive in the foster system. He'd been scrawny, quiet, and an easy target for the older siblings who he would never call actual brothers. They had kicked him, called him names, taken his food, and pissed on his sheets. Until finally he'd gotten smart and started using his meager paper route money to buy them off. That had quickly turned into a shakedown on their part. But as long as he handed over his money, he hadn't gotten a black eye and had clean sheets.

He was ashamed that he'd had to go to such lengths. And angry that his foster parents had not made it stop. It had been a vicious cycle. Never had he felt wanted. Easily disposed of at the whim of a family who would never love or really care for him.

Ivy had just walked away from him, leaving him alone. Overlooked. Disposed.

He swore and shook his head. Ivy couldn't know the minute details of his history. How such desperation had pushed him to offer others money to ensure his own safety. To buy a little kindness. The facsimile of love. But he hadn't offered her money to make something in his life better.

Or had he? Was he trying to keep Ivy by the same means he had utilized when younger? Was he truly buying her love?

"No." He shook his head. "Why does money always seem to jam a wedge in any relationship I have?"

It was different this time, though. Ivy wasn't insisting he pay for her dinners or clothes or even trips. She couldn't care less about his money. It was him trying to get something from another person. Something like...

He had seen the caring, loving relationship the Quinn siblings shared. *Love.* All he wanted was to feel loved. He had begun to relax and loosen his shoulders and believe that maybe it could happen with Ivy. She made his days brighter. She enjoyed spending time with him. He thought of her every moment that numbers and code did not fill his brain. She was everything he had never thought he needed.

He turned a look over his shoulder at the brownstone. He couldn't screw this up. He didn't want to lose the best thing that had ever walked into his life.

But had that just happened?

CHAPTER FOURTEEN

IVY BREWED COFFEE and scrambled eggs. Ivan had just woken and called for her to help him shave. She did not mind helping her brother do the things he was losing control over. It made her sad, though, to see him want to hold the razor, knowing he was too shaky to do so. She'd reassured him that it was early. He was usually much steadier in the afternoons.

He'd said he could dress himself, so she left him to it, but would be there to help if he called.

With a sigh, her thoughts switched to how she'd walked away from Wolf last night. That had been wrong. She didn't want to alienate him from her life by treating him as if he weren't worthy of being a part of that life. All things included. But the offer to help Ivan had, once again, put up her backbone. And yet, she knew Wolf had only offered out of kindness.

Did she really believe she couldn't juggle Ivan's care and a romance with Wolf? Some moments she did. But after sleeping on it, she realized that was an excuse to not step up and embrace the good that life was offering her.

She slid the eggs onto a plate and covered it with another plate to keep it warm, then plucked the toast from the toaster and buttered it.

Would their lives be different now if they had taken the settlement money from the boat manufacturer? What had they really gained by standing firm and refusing to be silenced? They had spoken out regarding the faulty parts on only one television interview. The company had issued a recall on the part. End of story.

That money would have been helpful now. But still. No. She shook her head. She felt good with that decision. Morally.

"You can't buy my love."

She never should have said that to Wolf. It had slipped out. She hadn't meant it. Had she?

"No." But she may have screwed up the opportunity life had given her for good.

Ivan walked into the kitchen with the use of his cane, a curve of aluminum emblazoned with red and purple flames. He had a big smile on his face. "I love scrambled eggs and toast. Thanks, sis."

"Ivan…" He sat down at the table and she set his plate and coffee before him. "Do you still feel like we made the right choice regarding the settlement money?"

"One hundred percent." He dove into the eggs with a fork. Only after many bites did he stop to meet her gaze. "Why? Are you having second thoughts?"

"That money would come in handy now."

"It would. But we didn't know that at the time. And had we known I was going to fall apart like this, would we still have made the same decision? I hope so."

"You're quite morally straight. Just like mom. Always walking the right path."

"You think I don't make mistakes?"

"Name one." She sat across the table with him and bit into the crunchy toast.

"How about that time I biked through White Mountain National Forest and should have taken a compass?"

"You survived two days and finally found your way out. You were prepared. You didn't starve or lack water. I like to believe it was meant to happen that way. Aren't you the one who is always saying there are no coincidences in life?"

"Exactly. We make the moves and decisions that are meant to be made. Not taking that money? Meant to be."

"I'm not quite so fate-based as you are."

"I'm going to make it through this, Ivy." He clasped her hand. "Promise."

"I know you will."

"Then what's with your sad face? Is it Wolf? I like the guy. He seems to be head over heels for you."

"You think so?" Then why had she walked away from him again last night? "Ivan, he…he offered to pay for your medical bills. I refused. But then, this morning I'm thinking, is it even my place to say yay or nay? It's your health. The money would help you. You should have some say in the matter."

"He didn't make the offer to me. It's your call, sis."

Ivy exhaled dramatically and set her fork down with a clang. "I don't want it to be my call. And he probably didn't make the offer to you because I've been so firm in refusing him. Tell me what you would say if he made that offer to you?"

Ivan shrugged, teased at his remaining eggs with a fork. "I don't know. I've only met the guy a couple times. But I do suspect he's really thrown for you. He is a great guy, Ivy."

"That's not the question I want you to answer."

He set down his fork and wobbled his head, something he did when he was thinking. "Maybe?"

Her heart dropped. "I knew I shouldn't have refused him. And now I can hardly go back and ask for his help. It would make me like all those other women who hurt him in previous relationships."

"Ivy." Ivan leaned in and put an elbow on the table. "Don't stress about this. I want you to enjoy what you have with Wolf. I know me and Heather are…"

"You and Heather?" Wolf had suggested there might be something going on between the two of them. "Really?"

Ivan shrugged. "I think I've fallen in love. And she feels the same."

"Wow. That was fast." But no quicker than she had fallen for Wolf. When the right people came together, things did seem to click. "I'm happy for you, Ivan. Though I wish you wouldn't have felt you had to hide it from me."

"Heather didn't think it wise. Employer-employee kind of thing, you know."

"Maybe she'll give you a discount on the home visits?" she joked.

He laughed. "I wouldn't dream of asking her such a thing."

"I know. She's worth every penny. I believe she's been a huge part in you retaining your confidence and positivity. And if she's someone you enjoy spending time with, then that makes me happy." She patted his hand. "I have to get dressed and go to work."

"I'll clean up the dishes."

"Oh, I can do—"

"Absolutely not." He grabbed her plate from her. "Let me do what I'm still able to do. It gives me some sense of accomplishment. Okay?"

With a nod, she relented. Who was she to steal any bits of independence he might still retain?

Back in her room, Ivy tugged on a T-shirt and green chinos then stood before the mirror and pulled her hair back into a neat ponytail. The woman in the mirror smiled at the news her brother had found someone he loved. And then the smile dropped. Did that mean she was no longer needed in Ivan's life? Heather could certainly care for him and make him happy.

While the prospect of returning to the life she had put on hold should make her jump for joy, it felt as if the lack of need for her presence in her brother's life hurt. Being needed had been the one thing to keep her going.

As well, it was the only argument that kept her from completely diving into the relationship with Wolf. Was that it? Was she afraid to grab that happiness? It wasn't that she didn't deserve it, it was that she couldn't enjoy it if Ivan wasn't also happy.

The thought was selfish. Ivy hated that she could think like that.

But now she wondered if Wolf had felt much the same when she'd told him she didn't need his help?

On Wednesday, Wolf's calendar read: *Invent a new business.*

So he leaned back in his office chair, closed his eyes, and thought about it. Eventually the craziest ideas spun in his gray matter.

Midnight cookie delivery—hot and with ice cream on the side.

Doggie Dating.

Rent-a-Scholar.

LawnDashers—just click on the app to arrange a lawn mowing.

It was enjoyable, and a practice in allowing his brain to shift from left to right for some creativity. But ultimately, he veered back toward his medical labeling idea. He'd made some contacts. They'd been as excited about the idea as he was.

Since Ivy had come into his life, she had inspired him to seek new ways to give away his money and he had begun to feel as if the money weight was lifting from his shoulders. It was time to stop grumbling about the bad things money brought to his life and instead of reacting, be more active. And besides new business ideas, charitable contributions were a must.

Now that, he could do.

He glanced at the clock. Ten a.m. He had to finish coding this current assignment before noon. He wasn't sure what Ivy thought of him after she'd left him alone on the park bench yesterday. He'd send someone down to collect coffee and a slice of cake.

On Thursday, Ivy wondered what Wolf's calendar asked of him. And what it had asked yesterday. He hadn't come in for coffee. She'd texted him last night before going to bed.

Miss you. See you tomorrow?

He hadn't texted back.

This was bad. He must hate her for her refusal. For treating him like his money was no good. She hadn't meant for it to come out like that, but she completely understood how he must view it. She should apologize.

"Ivy!"

Estelle's shout zapped her back to the present. Ivy saw the espresso machine overflowing and jumped. Coffee spattered her apron. The customer shook his head. And Estelle took over.

"Your head is not in the game today, sweetie." Estelle

wiped the cup and handed it to the customer. "On the house, sir." Then to Ivy she asked, "What's up? It's Mr. Sexy, isn't it?"

"Mr. Sexy? When did we give him that name?"

"Oh, I've always called him that. In my dreams. Don't worry, I don't dream about him—too much—since you two became a couple. Okay, maybe every other day."

"Dream about him all you like." She wanted to say *because he's mine*, but she wasn't sure anymore if he was. "We're just having a tiff. That's why my brain is not focusing."

"A tiff? You know your tiff cost us a coffee and cake yesterday. And I'm not so sure he'll be in this morning either."

"You're really going to lay the loss of ten dollars on my head because of a romantic setback?"

"Oh, it's a setback now? See, that's more than a tiff."

"We just… It's hard for me to parse the two of us being together. I mean, he's so rich."

"Money has nothing to do with love, sweetie."

"I know that. My brother knows that. Why am I finding it so difficult to just let Wolf be Wolf?"

"Yeah, why are you?" came a deep male voice from behind her and across the counter.

Ivy gave Estelle an admonishing face—she could have told her Wolf had walked in—and then turned to smile at him. "Good morning. Coffee and cake?"

"Always. So you don't want me to be me?"

She poured coffee while Estelle grabbed a slice of chocolate chip cake and set it on the counter before him before slipping into the back room.

"I do want you to be you." She set the coffee cup before him. "I'm sorry," she said quietly, casting a glance around the coffee shop. About half a dozen patrons, each seemingly occupied by their cell phones. "I shouldn't have walked away from you like that the other day."

"I get it. I really do. Can you spare five minutes over at the corner table?"

Estelle called out from the back room, "Yes, she can!"

Wolf winked. "Meet you there."

When Ivy arrived tableside, Wolf stood, pulled her close and kissed her. He nuzzled her cheek and said, "Had to do that. I missed it yesterday."

"I did, too. You must have been busy with work? To have missed your morning coffee?"

"I was. And… I wasn't sure you wanted to see me."

"Wolf, I always want to see you. We just…" She kissed his head then sat across from him at the small, intimate table. "I think we had our first fight the other day and I'm sorry."

"So am I. I promise that if it makes you upset when I offer money to you, I will never do it again. But, Ivy, can you trust me just a little? I'm a pretty smart guy. I know my reputation with women sucks, but—"

She leaned in to kiss him quickly, then said, "Yes. I trust you. It's been difficult for me to separate caring for my brother from having a life. But Ivan is a big boy. He's got this. And I realized that the having-a-life part is important for my mental health. And that ultimately makes me a better sister."

"Does the life you're talking about include a dorky coder with a penchant for death coffee?"

"It does. Can we kiss and make up after I get off work?"

"Deal."

Wolf's bedroom featured a massive paned window that over-looked an unkempt railyard. Lights strung along the pier beamed and flashed and twinkled like the stars Ivy missed.

"You never get to see stars when living in a big city," she said.

They'd just made love. Her body was lax and warm. Snuggled next to Wolf's warmth was the only place she wanted to be.

"You can see them in Burghausen."

"Is that where you intend to build your little cottage and raise a family?"

"There or somewhere in the vicinity. I like being close to a big city to access the things I need, but then to have the solace of a little town or village to keep my heart in place."

She turned and faced him. "Your heart belongs in Germany. Does this business thing in Venice have to do with you possibly moving back there someday?"

"It does. Concierge is moving to the next level. World domination!"

"And you plan to take over the world from a little village?"

"If I can, I will. I'm thinking of transferring control of the CEO duties to someone else and just becoming the owner who sits on the sidelines and oversees things."

"Wow. That's a huge step."

"It is, but more and more I believe it will make me happy."

"I can see that it will. I hope it all works out for you."

"It will if I can loosen my tight grip on the business reins. Now I'm going to ask you to Venice again and this time—"

"I'll go," she said simply. With a kiss and a nuzzle of her nose into his beard, she hugged up against his body. "I'd go anywhere with you, lover."

CHAPTER FIFTEEN

Venice

IVY HAD NEVER traveled out of the United States. Now, as
Wolf helped her to step off the water taxi they'd taken from
the Marco Polo Airport on the mainland over to the island of
Venice, she took in everything. It was a completely different world from the tall buildings and enclosed tight spaces
of New York. Water everywhere, and ancient buildings, and
so many tourists bustling about. Wolf had insisted they do
the tourist way of taking a taxi and walking to his palazzo
instead of a private water taxi to his place. That way she
could take in the Piazza San Marco and get a feel for the city
before he had to leave her this afternoon for his meeting.

Following him through a bustle of sightseers, Ivy spread
up her arms and tilted back her head. Everything smelled
lush and like the sea. A green saltiness that she could literally taste at the back of her throat. When she walked right
into Wolf, his grin was irrepressible.

"Penny for your thoughts? On the other hand, my money
is no good to you so…just tell me what put that gorgeous
smile on your face?"

"This place." She kissed him. And while he couldn't wrap
his arms around her because he held both their suitcases,
she pulled him in tight for a hug and another long kiss.
"Thank you for convincing me to step out of my self-im-

posed boundaries. I know Ivan will be okay with Heather to watch him. And I intend to enjoy every moment I'm here."

"You don't know how happy that makes me. Come on. Let's do the fast and furious tour through the city. My place is a ten-minute walk from here."

They strolled through the massive Piazza San Marco, Wolf pointing out the Basilica that gleamed like a gold idol in the sunlight. The tall, bronze-capped Campanile that was once a beacon for incoming ships. And pigeons flying everywhere in wait of a dropped treat. The coming and going tides shushed a quiet symphony over the city. It was beautiful and such a wonder.

As they passed luxury storefronts, Ivy's head turned at the sight of a pretty red silk dress. Once again she walked right into Wolf.

He laughed and noticed what he drawn her attention. "F80825 is definitely your color."

"A color similar to the red velvet mite."

He hugged her. "We have our own unique languages but somehow we understand each other."

"I love your color language. I know your eyes are 724717. So! I feel like I need to buy myself a treat while I'm here," she said as they continued to walk. "Something small. A reminder of my visit."

"There're plenty of tourist shops. I'm sure you'll find something. Over there. That little restaurant looks unimpressive, but it has the best carbonara in the world. I'll take you there tonight."

"I look forward to it. Do you think I'll be okay to wander around on my own while you're at work?"

"Of course. Venice is a very walkable city. Let's sync our phones so if you do get lost, I can find you." He winked then nodded to the right. "Over here's my place."

The Istrian stone front of the palazzo was simple and unimposing. Wolf punched in the digital code and pushed the door open, allowing Ivy to walk in onto the marble-tiled floor that stretched to the opposite side of the building, where a tall doorway gated with wrought-iron let in the bright sun through colored glass. An old iron chandelier hung in the center of the long hall. To each side were doorways leading to rooms and places she was eager to discover.

"This is beautiful," she said. She rushed forward to look through the far doorway. The Veneto sloshed right up to a short dock and to the right she could see the open garage where boats must park. "Can we ride a gondola?"

"Yes, to everything you desire." Wolf set down the suitcases and pulled her into a long, soul-shivering hug. "You give the best hugs. I'm glad this place makes you happy."

"Being here with you is what makes me happy. But how soon before you abandon me?"

He checked his watch. "Actually, sooner than I thought. I have to meet the client in an hour. Time enough to take a shower and get on my way."

"Can I help with…" Ivy fluttered her lashes, not even embarrassed at such a cliché flirtation "…anything?"

He grabbed her hand, then with a fast move she didn't see coming, he swept her into his arms and carried her up a stairway. And Ivy recalled the day she and Estelle had made their lists of the perfect man. Sweeping a girl off her feet and up the stairs? Check *strong* off the list. The only thing that remained was…believing in love.

And she wasn't so sure Wolf believed in that.

Ivy spent the afternoon walking the city. She strolled across bridges over canals and took in the opulent palazzos. Gondolas in all shapes, sizes and colors ferried sightseers along the waterways. Elaborate masks displayed in shop fronts drew her interest, and she watched one being crafted with feathers and rhinestones. She noshed on a Chantilly-cream-stuffed croissant, fried calamari, and tart lemon gelato. Window-shopping, she spied fabulous gowns, sky-high heels, pricey purses, and… She settled for a touristy T-shirt.

When she returned to the palazzo, she met Wolf as he was getting in. They kissed all the way across the threshold and halfway down the foyer.

"Did you have a good meeting?" she asked.

"Phenomenal. Concierge is going meta by the end of this year. It's going to be amazing, and take a lot of work, but the crew I spoke with today have already got people and projects set up to make it run smoothly. What about you? How was your day?"

"Perfect. A little lonely, but I only thought of you, hmm…a couple times an hour."

"Only a couple?"

"Well, I had to focus or walk into the Veneto! What's that you have behind your back? That pink bag does look intriguing."

"F808C4 is definitely another of your colors." He handed her the bag. "A treat for you. And I won't accept any arguments against it," he said as she pulled out the box from a clothing store.

"You won't get any." Ivy peeked in the box to see red silk. "The dress?"

"Yep. The store clerk wondered what size you wore and when I started to look around for a woman about your shape, I mentioned the dress had made you crash into me earlier. She saw that! And she said this would fit you perfectly."

"Will it be too fancy to wear out?"

"Never."

"Okay, give me ten minutes. I have to refresh from the day."

"Take all the time you like. But if you hear something rumbling down here," he called as she rushed up the stairs to the upper bedroom that overlooked the lagoon, "it's my stomach!"

Ten minutes later Ivy twisted her hair into a chignon and stuck a silver hair stick in to secure it. She stepped back and admired the dress in the floor-length mirror in the massive bathroom. The sensuous red silk landed just below her knees and swished with every move. It revealed every line, curve and indent on her body. The silk swept over one shoulder where a small gold ring connected the back to the front. The magnetic ring held a pouf of red silk at the top of her shoulder like a flower burst. It was a removable decoration. She liked it so she kept it on.

Who would have thought she'd be standing in Venice, wearing a beautiful dress given to her by her super-sexy, kind, handsome—and rich—boyfriend? Life could not get better. Well, it could, but she'd promised herself not to think about Ivan's troubles this weekend. She was in Venice! And the only dream she'd ever had of an overseas excursion had involved her dressed in khakis and wielding a mosquito net, searching for some rare insect to study.

She'd netted the best prize yet.

"Ivy!"

"I'm coming! Tell your stomach to hold on."

She hadn't a purse, so she slipped into the black heels she'd packed. An inch heel; perfect for walking. Sailing down the stairs, she saw Wolf had put on a suit coat and—oh, that dark beard and his piercing eyes always ignited her core. She landed in his arms and kissed him.

"That dress is…" He made a show of looking her over. "Not right."

"What?" Her shoulders dropped. She smoothed a hand up her stomach. "But I thought you liked me in this hex code?"

"I love you in it. There's just something not right about that thing…" He pointed at her shoulder where the flower pouf sat.

"I can take it off. It's magnetic."

"I know." He grabbed the pouf of silk and tossed it over his shoulder. Then he pulled a small box out from inside his coat. "Got you something to replace it."

"Oh, Wolf, you didn't have—" Ivy stopped herself from refusing his kindness. She knew it came from his heart. "I love surprises. What is it?" She opened the flat box to discover a gorgeous brooch.

"I saw it in a jewelry store," he said. "I knew who it belonged to right away."

"This is incredible." The box dropped to the floor as she took out the brooch. It was a beetle, and the shell was metallic violet and red and green that changed with movement. "It looks like a *coleoptera buprestidae*. A jewel beetle. It's found on a small Indonesian island," she said. "I can't believe you found something like this." She turned it over to see it did not have a pin on the back of it but rather a small metal circle. "I'm not sure how to wear it, though."

"I asked the jeweler if he could make a specific adjustment." Wolf took the brooch from her. "And he had to do it in the few hours I was in the meeting. He stepped up to the challenge. So let's see if it works." He placed the beetle over the gold circle on her shoulder and it clicked into place.

"Oh my gosh!" Ivy rushed up to the massive mirror hung over a table on the opposite wall and studied the pin sitting on her shoulder as if the beetle had landed there. "It's perfect!" A giddy wave made her spin and do a little shimmy before dancing up to Wolf and hugging him. "I…" The words *love you* stalled on her tongue. Would they frighten him away? Did they frighten her? Best to avoid that truth at the moment. "Thank you, lover."

After dinner of fresh seafood and peach Moscato, Wolf escorted Ivy on a gondola ride in the San Polo, explaining that if they chose a less touristy canal the experience would be more romantic. Then he laughed at himself as he helped her step down into the gondola. Had he actually used the word *romantic*? Yes, yes, he had. And he looked forward to this moonlit ride upon the quiet, dark waters snuggled next to his girl.

Was he turning into some kind of romance hero? Crazy. The heroes always won the girl by the last page. He had even begun to dare to dream about his future. He'd dropped his caution when with Ivy. And it felt amazing.

Ivy settled into the plush red seat and leaned over the side to trail her fingers in the water. They glided down the narrow canal lit by festive lights that wrapped the few trees and many of the palazzo facades.

"Cold?" he asked.

"No, it's actually lukewarm."

"I mean you." He put an arm around her shoulder as she sat back and flicked the water from her fingers. "So what kinds of bugs would an entomologist find here in Venice?"

"On my walk I discovered a few private and public gardens humming with insects. Of course, there's mosquitoes. They love the water. I've never been a mosquito magnet."

"Me as well. So we're safe then." He kissed her and she turned her body to snuggle against his chest, but then she suddenly pointed upward.

"Look at that architecture!"

"I think that's a church. I haven't taken much time to sightsee Venice."

"But you have a home here."

"It's a stopover for when I'm in Europe. Also, when I started to grow my bank account it was a whim buy. I liked the idea of owning a palazzo."

"I can't imagine buying something on a whim beyond some pretty shoes or a fancy chocolate bar. You could rent it out when you're not here?"

"I could but…it's mine. I don't like people touching my things. And to know strangers were actually living in my home?" He mocked a shudder.

"Does that come from you growing up in foster homes? Not having much to call your own?"

She was perceptive. "It does. I suppose I'd never make a good client for one of your brother's house-sitting jobs, eh? What do you think about that sunset?"

She tilted her head against his shoulder and slid a hand over his chest. They snuggled and watched as the boat sailed closer to the end of the canal that opened onto the Grand Canal, which Wolf had instructed the gondolier to take to his palazzo.

This was a dream. Because he'd allowed himself to drop his caution, he now sat next to a woman he cared about. Wolf wasn't sure when he'd last felt so unencumbered. His shoulders relaxed even more. So many things left his muscle memory with a sigh. To be replaced with the happiness of simply being.

"I'm glad you convinced me to come along with you to Venice," she said. "This is an experience I won't forget."

He nuzzled his nose aside her luscious locks, kissing her head. "Being with you makes me forget everything to do with the rush-rush of business. You calm me, Ivy. I've never felt this way with another person."

"Maybe it's that I bore you?" She popped up her head to meet his gaze. The fairy lights strung along the windows of the homes they passed glittered in her eyes.

"Never," he breathed and then bowed to kiss her. But it was an abrupt one.

"It feels weird to kiss with the gondolier right there."

Wolf smirked against her mouth. "He's seen it before."

"Still, let's save it for when we get to the palazzo."

She was a private person, and more power to her. So Wolf would not point out the paparazzi he spied in the gondola across the canal. How did they always find him? Probably they'd been tracking him since he'd arrived this morning. And with those long-range lenses they surely got the shot. Had they snapped one of them kissing?

The tension that had sluiced from his veins scurried back through his system, as he kept one eye on the photogs and directed the gondolier to his private dock. When they arrived, he leaped out to help Ivy from the gondola. The photographers yelled across the canal for them to pose. They also called out, asking if they were a couple.

"I didn't even see them," Ivy said as she ducked behind him.

He could feel her tremble. And that stirred his rage. He fisted a nasty gesture to the photographers and called out an oath—the only one he knew in Italian—then grabbed Ivy's hand and pulled her inside the palazzo, slamming the door behind him.

A search light from the photographer's boat flashed through the windows. His hand turned the knob, but he didn't open the door. That's what they wanted from him.

To see him react. To get salacious photos to smear all over some social media page.

So much for dropping his caution.

"I'm sorry." He leaned his head against the door and splayed out his arms. "I shouldn't have done that. I thought I was better at ignoring them."

"Don't apologize. It's rude that they think they can intrude on your life like that."

It was, and yet...

"Yes, but I just broke a rule," he said. "There's a certain social contract. A quid pro quo. It's expected that, as a celebrity, I will allow the press to report on me, take photos, and print them. And as long as I play along, they'll be kind, or at the very least, print the photos where I'm not stuffing my face with food. But when I turn on them, as I did just now, then they'll punish me with bad press. It's how the game is played."

"But when did you agree to play such a ridiculous game? It's not fair."

"It's not, but that's how it works. I'm sorry."

"Don't apologize anymore. And thank you for schooling me on the rules. It was a few seconds. Forgotten. In the past." She lifted her chin and looked at him through long, lush lashes. "I want to play a different game."

With that, she took off the magnetic bug pin from her dress and turned to walk toward the stairs. Slipping the gold ring and red fabric from her shoulder, she cast him a teasing look and a blown kiss. Then she dashed up the stairs.

Wolf caught that kiss right in his heart. It went in smooth as an arrow, but he didn't feel any pain. Only a hot explosion of desire. He flicked the lock on the door behind him, then raced up the stairs.

CHAPTER SIXTEEN

"Did you know there is a research institute on the mainland that is scheduled to do a study on damselflies?"

Ivy sat up straight from her slumped position on a bench. After a late breakfast, they'd walked for hours, then found a sunny spot in the Campo Santa Maria Formosa to rest. The bench was backed by a thick jasmine hedge, and the scent intoxicated. Wolf had been occupied with his phone for twenty minutes, which she knew was probably work, but she didn't mind.

"How do you know that?" she asked.

He turned his phone toward her. The screen showed a website for an Italian institute that listed a call for entomologists. He'd been researching jobs for her while she'd been aimlessly watching tourists? What a sweet move.

"You should apply," he said. "You'd probably get the job. It starts next year."

The project did sound interesting. And to work in Venice? And to actually hold a real job in her field and not have to sling lattes and mocha loca whatevers?

Ivy's shoulders slumped and she shook her head. "I'd love to, but Ivan still isn't in a place where he can manage on his own."

"Ivy, Ivan has help."

"We can't expect Heather to be a girlfriend and a full-time caregiver. That's asking far too much."

"So, you'll hire a different nurse for your brother. If he even requires one. And it's still half a year away. Ivy, this is a challenge I'm issuing you. Like a calendar page."

"That's a whole lot bigger than a suggestion to eat lemon cake. Ivan needs me."

Wolf sighed heavily and leaned back, their shoulders hugging. "The last time I brought this up you walked away from me so I'm a little leery, but…"

Yes, she did have a tendency to run when confronted with truths she didn't like to face. The man did not deserve that from her. It was about time she pulled up her big girl panties and faced reality. Life was difficult. Dealing with it required finesse. And she was a woman who possessed finesse and determination. Time to stop reacting.

"Say it."

With a heavy sigh, he then asked, "Is it that Ivan needs you, or that you need to *feel needed* by him?"

Was it? No, it—well, there were many other factors. She would step away and start her own life as soon as she felt confident Ivan had a handle on his situation. It would happen. And her brother would never ask her to stay longer than she was needed.

And…yes. She did like to feel needed.

But also, she'd realized he could take care of his issues on his own. So what excuses had she left?

"And I'm not going to accept the money argument," Wolf added. "There are foundations, charities, grants that Ivan can apply for. I know, because I've done the research."

"You have?"

He nodded. "I did some research on the flight here while you were sleeping. I also worked on my newest project."

She had slept six hours and didn't even feel jet lag. But she'd been unaware he had been awake the whole time. Did the man never sleep? "A new project?"

"It was inspired by your brother's condition. It's a medical labeling app that puts QR codes on all prescriptions. Users scan the code before taking the medication. They can set the app to speak the medication name out loud so they can confirm it's correct, and even use the camera to identify the pills by shape and color. It should reduce mistakes measurably. I've already tasked someone at Concierge with taking charge of the project."

"That's incredible. And sounds very usable. I wish Ivan had such a thing days ago. You really do care about people."

"Don't let anyone know. I might get a complex."

The man was a wonder. And seeing this charitable side of him made her fall even deeper in love than she already was. Yes, she loved Wolf. But she still didn't dare tell him.

"Listen, Ivy." He kissed the back of her hand. "I respect your need to take care of your brother, to ensure he gets the very best care. But you can't do for your brother unless you take care of yourself."

Her thoughts, exactly. Why did she find it easier to believe coming from him and not her own thoughts?

"You've got to make yourself happy. I'm not asking you to take my money. I'm just asking you to trust that Ivan will find his way through this."

"I understand. To be honest? I do like the feeling of being needed. Yet, I really do want to be working in my field. But that Venice study is a long way from New York."

"What if Ivan got accepted into a research study somewhere in Europe?"

"We did fill out an application for a study in Sweden. He qualifies. But if he did get accepted, his living expenses would not be paid. We've been living on the remainder of the sale from our parents' home. It may cover a stay in Sweden, but I haven't researched the expense side of it yet."

"Please reconsider my offer to pay Ivan's expenses. And…about allowing me to make that offer directly to Ivan. It is his life, after all. And you know I'm not doing this as a means to buy your love, right?"

Soft brown eyes searched hers with a glint of hope. Of course, she knew that. He wasn't the kind of person who could even think to buy her love. Albeit, he had used money to buy off bullies when he was a kid. That had been a survival reaction. A smart one, too. And his money wasn't offered to her as a means to silence her about faulty boat parts that had caused her parents' deaths. This was completely different. He just wanted to help Ivan get the best care.

"I'm just like you, Ivy." He tilted his head onto her shoulder. "I'm still that scrawny kid who is trying to navigate his way through life and be accepted by others. Somebody tossed a boatload of money at me, but it didn't change who I am inside. You have to believe that."

"I do believe that. I know you are kind and sweet and honest and… I feel as though I've been living in a fairy tale lately. I got to wear the gown to a fabulous ball. And my coach didn't even turn into a pumpkin. And now I've been taken to a kingdom of wonder by a handsome prince."

Wolf's look melted right into her heart. "You know this regular guy found a beautiful princess who wears bugs on her shoulder and beams like the sun. I'm the one who feels like a prince who won the best thing in the world."

"You won my heart the moment you said my name in But First…"

He gave her a wondering lift of brow and she nodded.

"I'll look up the application for the Venice study," she said. "And... I'll seriously consider applying."

"Yes!"

On the flight home, Wolf slipped into a snooze with the ease of closing his eyes. Ivy found that remarkable. With the time changes she'd experienced over the past few days, she was wide awake.

Fortunately, the in-flight Wi-Fi allowed her to do some surfing. She read all the details for the Venice study. It was right up her alley. It didn't begin until next March. Dare she apply for it? Surely that would allow ample time to get Ivan set on the right path and leave him feeling like he had a handle on the MS?

Why was she so determined to control Ivan's life? As Wolf had suggested, wasn't it Ivan's choice whether or not he accepted help from Wolf? It was his disease. She couldn't know his every thought, concern, or desire regarding how he wished to proceed with such a diagnosis. And she had gotten the feeling when talking to him about how he would answer if he had been offered money by Wolf that Ivan would say yes.

Perhaps it was time she surrendered to the universe and simply went along with it. Actually ask Ivan for his input instead of planning around him.

With a nod, she decided she would have a good talk with Ivan. Thanks to Wolf's influence, she was learning to relax a little, allow life to flow without feeling as though she had to stand and face it with a shield and sword. Everything was going to be okay.

Touching the insect pin made her smile. The jeweler had designed it so a magnetic piece holding a pin could be fitted into the back for when she didn't wear it on the red dress. Now it sat on the shoulder of her tee shirt just for fun.

She wanted to know more about the artist so she found the website and read up on the enameling process and how he crafted his insects based on real ones but added his own whimsical touches. With a click, her screen flashed with a bunch of obnoxious ads for celebrity sites. Finger hovering over the delete button, her vision focused on a shot of a familiar man, standing on a dock before a Venetian palazzo, giving the photographer a nasty gesture.

"Oh, dear."

The headline read: *Rogue Billionaire Shows His Ugly Side!*

Ivy quickly read the article below the image.

Tech billionaire Wolfgang Zeigler, on a trip to Venice with his latest paramour, explodes at photographers.

"He didn't explode," she muttered. "He had every right to be angry. They were using searchlights!"

The article continued.

Will this woman be like all the rest? Does Zeigler have a cool million set aside to assuage her shopping needs and head off a litigious attack?

Ivy's jaw dropped open. How dare they assume so much? It was completely untrue.

She read more.

According to an anonymous source, Zeigler now has all his dates vetted with a thorough background check. She must have passed!

Now Ivy's jaw snapped shut. She reread that line about the background check. Then she glanced to the sleeping billionaire beside her. Had Wolf had her checked out? How dare he? After their conversation about how a person should be allowed their privacy, and his fight to keep that...

She shook her head and flicked the screen off on her cell phone.

Under her breath she muttered, "Jerk."

CHAPTER SEVENTEEN

AFTER DEPLANING, and while waiting for their luggage, Wolf noticed Ivy's quiet mood. He kissed her on the forehead but didn't try to engage. She hadn't slept on the flight, so probably wanted to get home and crawl into bed.

She followed him to the curb where a limo waited and allowed him to open the back door for her and slide in beside her. But when he bent to kiss her, she turned her head and closed her eyes.

"Sorry," he said. "I get the jet lag thing. I'll have you home in no time so you can get some sleep."

She sighed and shook her head. "I'm not tired. Well, I am. I'm just…"

The limo pulled away from the curb. Ivy's hair was in a not-so-neat ponytail and her touristy T-shirt featuring a map of the Venetian lagoon was rumpled. The bug pin glinted on her shoulder. A beautiful mess. But Wolf could feel tension waver from her.

When she didn't seem to want to continue what she was saying, he leaned back and closed his eyes. The limo navigated the bustling New York expressways. Venice had been a treat. He'd never enjoyed himself with a woman so much. Not a thing about Ivy felt wrong.

Save for the chill vibes he was sensing from her now. What had he done wrong? He didn't want to do this again.

Not when he'd thought they'd come to an agreement about silly arguments over silly things.

"What is it, Ivy? Talk to me."

With a heavy sigh she finally faced him. In a weary tone, she asked, "You did a check on me?"

"What?"

"I read an article about us on the flight. It posted the photo they took of us on the dock with you flipping them off. They mentioned something about the rogue billionaire doing a background check on all his girlfriends?"

Hell. So that was the press's punishment for his fit of anger? Touché. "Ivy, it's something my lawyer suggested I do after the lawsuit."

"You think I'm going to sue you? Take you for millions? My God, you know nothing about me."

"Ivy, I do know you. And I know you would never do anything like that. But…"

"But you still had a background check done on me?"

He nodded. "It's something I need to do to protect myself. Legally. Please believe me when I say I didn't read it."

"Why not?"

"Because you're different. You're… Ivy."

She shook her head. "I can't believe you would do such a thing."

The limo pulled over. They had arrived before Ivan's brownstone. She got out and slapped a hand on the trunk. The driver opened the trunk, and before Wolf could help her, she held her suitcase in hand.

"Let me help you with that, please."

"I don't want to talk to you right now." She tugged the wheeled suitcase toward the front of the brownstone.

Wolf splayed out his arms, at a loss at what to say or do. Whenever she was confronted by something she didn't like, she fled. Pushed him away. Like he wasn't important enough to stay and work things out.

And that hurt his heart so much, he clasped a hand over his chest. Ivy made him feel unworthy of her love.

Heather greeted Ivy when she got inside. The bubbly therapist asked all sorts of questions about her trip. All Ivy wanted to do was bury her head under the sheets and cry. Wolf had betrayed her. In the cruelest manner.

Seeing her yawn, Heather said Ivan was showering and they intended to go for a walk in the park. Ivy said she needed some rest and thanked her.

It was six hours later when Ivy woke and pushed tangled hair from her face. Someone knocked on her bedroom door. Heather called softly, "Mr. Zeigler is here to see you."

She glanced to the bedside clock. Seven in the evening. Still out of it and feeling her anger rush up and warm her neck, Ivy said, "I don't want to talk to him. Tell him to go away."

After a long, restorative shower, she combed through her hair and decided her sleep schedule would force her to try and sleep again tonight if she wanted to adjust and make it to work in the morning. She was awake now and hungry. But hearing Ivan and Heather laughing out in the living room made her want to hide away. They sounded happy.

She had had such a wonderful time in Venice with Wolf. The prince had won her heart.

Only to crush it with a background check.

And while common sense prodded at her to view this from both sides, right now she was hurt and confused and… she glanced out the window overlooking the front sidewalk. She recognized the back of Wolf's head. He was sitting out on the park bench. Had he been sitting there since he'd knocked about an hour ago?

She pulled the curtain before the window. She didn't want to talk to him. Not yet.

"What are you doing?" she muttered. Hadn't she left her need to react in Venice? Wasn't she moving onward and upward, taking life at an easier pace?

Apparently not.

To distract her thoughts, she wandered out to the living room. Half a delivery pizza sat on the counter. Heather had also just popped popcorn and the rich buttery scent filled the room.

"We're going to watch *Princess Bride*," Heather said. "Want to join us?"

Ivy didn't want anything to do with fairy-tale love right now.

"He's still out there." Ivan glanced over the back of the couch out the front window. "You going to talk to him?"

She shook her head and took a big bite of pizza. Ugh. Cold pepperoni grease.

"It's not my place to ask what sort of romantic squabble the two of you are entangled in," Ivan said, "but I suspect the guy might sit out there all night. And it's starting to rain."

Ivan could ask her whatever he wished. Because she had swept in and taken charge of his life…

Ivy swallowed hard on a bite of pizza. Had she ever really asked Ivan what *he* wanted, how he wanted to proceed forward? Or had she literally moved in, made up lists of studies and doctors and taken over his life?

"I'm sorry," she said to her brother. "I really am."

He didn't hear her as the opening music for the movie started.

Outside, raindrops spattered the window. Ivy dropped the

half slice on the greasy cardboard and then went to face her demons. By the time she got to the park bench, rain beaded her hair. Her bare toes squished in the grass.

Wolf stood as she rounded the bench. "I'm sorry, Ivy."

"You shouldn't be sitting out in the rain. You'll catch a cold."

"That's an old wives' tale."

Likely. But how to start this conversation she didn't want to have but really needed to have?

"I just wanted to make sure you were okay," he said. Then with a heavy sigh, he added, "You pushed me away, Ivy. Do you know how that makes me feel?"

She did. Because he'd shared that personal part of his growing up. How cruel of her to have ignored his feelings for her own stupid anger. An anger she had once already chastised herself for allowing to react when it wasn't fair to him.

"I've lived that all my life. I won't do it anymore." He tugged a manila envelope out of his jacket and handed it to her. "The flash drive is in there. My guy never emails me info. Too easy to trace. The envelope is still sealed. I didn't open it. I…should have never done it, but it's what I've been conditioned to do. I know that's not fair to you."

She took the envelope, which was getting wetter by the second, and tucked it under her T-shirt.

"I wish I could take it back," he said. "But it's who and what I am. I protect my boundaries."

But he had let her inside those boundaries. And she had banged against them and kicked in a few holes. Politely, and…very well, those angry outbursts had been undeserved.

"I know it's going to be a barrier to me ever finding someone to love me," he said. "But I don't believe in love anyway. I want to believe in it, but I know if I do, it'll be ripped away from me. So there you go."

Ivy's heart dropped. He didn't believe in love. And yet…

Wolfgang Zeigler just didn't know what love felt like and so when he found it, he couldn't recognize it.

"I hope you'll call me after looking through the information on that drive," he said. "But if you don't, I guess I'll have to accept that."

He kissed her forehead. "I…" Another heavy sigh. What was it he wanted to say but couldn't?

With that, he walked away.

Rain blended with Ivy's teardrops. She had hurt that man as much as he had hurt her. But *had* he hurt her? He hadn't even looked at the information on the flash drive.

Why couldn't she make herself run after him, call the prince back into her life?

Because maybe this makeshift princess didn't deserve such a wonderful man.

CHAPTER EIGHTEEN

ON WEDNESDAY, Wolf's calendar suggested he learn a few words in a new language. Thirty-four hours had passed since he'd spoken to Ivy. In the rain. And his heart felt as if it still rained within. She'd not contacted him. Which meant she didn't want anything to do with him. He'd avoided going into But First... for both their sakes.

He'd been honest with her. And yet, he knew part of what he'd said had been a lie. He really did want to believe in love. And he may have found it. Was it love? He'd never felt so torn over a woman. But if this was love, now it was too late to keep it.

He grabbed the calendar and flung it across the office. It hit the wall and the plastic frame broke. Pages scattered on the floor.

Ivy filled an order for six lattes, each involving various complicated recipes, and put the cups in a cardboard carrier and handed it to the perky young accountant who came in every morning to fill her office order. With Estelle out talking to a new vendor, she and Valerie were left to manage the lunch rush.

She appreciated the busyness. Otherwise, her mind would switch to everything she'd discovered on that stupid flash drive. The envelope had indeed still been sealed. Though she had mentally argued that Wolf could have put it in a new one after opening it, she reasoned his word had always been good.

What the background check contained had startled her. Made her angry. And then made her cry. So much information! Most of it innocuous. Yet, that a private detective had found out so much about her life frightened her. It listed her addresses since childhood. All jobs, all schools and even college tuition charges. Where she shopped and how often she'd hit the fast food drive-thru in her hometown. All of it trackable with a credit card, she realized. It included various websites she had browsed, the number of calls she made to hospitals and clinics on Ivan's behalf.

But worst? It had listed the information on her parents' deaths and included the details on the settlement she and Ivan had refused. The information came from the boat company and had labeled them as insurance frauds. Seriously? As if she and her brother were the criminals!

She'd pulled the flash drive from her laptop and tossed it across the room.

"Ivy, did you get the Americano for the gentleman in the red shirt?" Valerie called.

Right. Clear her brain of that horrifying report and get to work. Focus!

She tilted a double shot of finely ground beans into the portafilter and tamped it, then slid it into the espresso machine. Looking over the top of the machine, she zoomed in on the front door. He hadn't come in on Tuesday, or today. Hadn't even sent someone down for coffee and his chocolate chip cake.

Was he avoiding her? Or was he simply done with her? She didn't want either. She probably deserved both. She had to make things right.

* * *

Around six, Ivy finally punched out. She'd been in the shop since seven a.m. Had gotten a half hour lunch break. Estelle had issues with a few vendors and hadn't been able to come in at all. Ivy hadn't minded the double shift, but now she was tired. Perhaps some jet lag still lingered. Or maybe it was that she wasn't right with the world. Things had changed between her and Wolf. But that didn't mean those changes had to tear them apart. She didn't want that. They needed to talk.

Out front of But First…, she paused and looked to the left where the main entry doors for the building were located. Most of the Concierge office had likely punched out, but Wolf tended to work until something compelled him to stand and shake out his muscles.

She turned and walked by the gym that required a membership and code to get in—she raced up to the door just as the woman she recognized as the receptionist walked out. Over her head, she could see Wolf inside, lifting weights.

"Could I…slip inside?" she asked sweetly. "My boyfriend is back there."

The woman nodded and opened the door for her. "He's a nice catch."

He was. But did she still have control of the net? She had to stop thinking in such terms. The man was free, and no one had a right to *net* him.

Ivy slipped inside and strolled past a few stationary bicycles, some rowers, and stacks of weights. A boxing ring sat at the back of the club. It smelled like a sweaty gym, but the alluring scent that drew her like a moth to a flame was just a few steps away.

As she gained his side, Wolf noticed her and set down the weights labeled with a fifty on each. "Ivy?"

"Can we talk?"

He grabbed a white towel and swiped it over his face. "Yes."

He gestured she sit on a chair near the boxing ring, but she declined, so he punched a nearby heavy bag a couple times, then swung around to face her. "Did you read the report?"

"I did. And I believe that you did not since the envelope was still sealed."

"I couldn't." He approached her and took her hands. She wanted to lunge against him and hug him forever. That good hug that only they shared. But this talk was necessary. "The day I got that report I should have tossed it. I knew then I'd never look at it."

She exhaled and nodded. "I'm not mad at you. I swear I'm not. Well, I was initially. But now that I've had some time to think about it, there's not a thing that you did wrong. You do need to protect yourself. Because of your job and your finances, it's a smart thing to do. I get that."

"Doesn't make it a good thing."

She nodded in agreement. "I'm more angry now because of all the information contained in the report. I don't understand how anyone can have so much of my personal and private information."

"Ivy, it's all data. The thing any company would pay big bucks for. Data that's gathered through every means possible. Every application you fill out. Every financial transaction. Every text, every message, every email you send."

"It's—it can't be legal."

He shook his head. "Do you ever read the terms and conditions? No one does. It's how companies cover their asses and give themselves access to anything and everything you put out there. I'm sorry."

"So a person can never have a completely private life?"

"You can if you stop using cell phones and apps."

"But I…" She took out her cell phone and stared at it. "I guess I know that nothing is secure or safe. We're all deceiving ourselves by thinking otherwise. Damn it." She opened the screen and clicked on the Concierge app. With one press of her finger she deleted it.

Wolf watched from beside her. "That's a good start."

"Seriously? You don't mind me tossing your app? You're contributing to the data mining with this app."

"I know. And again, it's all in the terms and conditions. Everyone knows they are handing over their personal information for the use of a convenience. It's a choice they make."

"That's not untrue. God, I hate this."

"If you're serious about protecting your privacy I can help you, but it'll require a tech sabbatical."

"I don't need Concierge. I just like the convenience, as you've said. I'm sure there's lots of apps I don't need. I can't think of one that is necessary. But my phone can still be tracked. They had locations on that report. It was creepy."

"Listen, this is a whole big conversation that I want to have with you. I'd love to teach you how to protect your privacy. But what I really want to know right now is…"

She kissed him. It had been almost two days since she'd last tasted him, felt his rugged physique meld against her, touched his warm skin. Entered that space that only they shared. A space so vast and yet cozy at the same time.

"Can you forgive me for the way I reacted to all this?" she asked.

"You don't need forgiveness, Ivy. I understand your reaction. I really do."

"But I hurt you. Treated you like…" He hadn't been worthy of a calm and rational approach to the information he'd given her.

"I know it wasn't malicious."

"You were just trying to protect yourself. And I want you to know there's nothing about me that I wouldn't share with you. You can have the flash drive back."

"I don't want it. Anything I learn about you I want to learn directly from you."

"Same. I don't want to believe anything about you that's been printed in a celebrity rag. I understand now why a little cottage in Germany appeals so much to you. Will you take me to Burghausen someday? I'd like to visit the place that gives you such wonderful memories."

"Really? Does that mean…?"

"What? Do you think we won't have the occasional argument? I'm still in if you are."

"Ah, hell yes."

He lifted her and as she glided lower in his embrace their mouths met and she wrapped her legs about his hips to stay there. Only his. She loved this man.

Two days later, Wolf looked up from coding as his office door opened and in walked Ivy all smiles and coffee and cake.

"Hey." He pushed back in his chair. A glance to the clock on the computer screen showed just before ten. "But First… has started delivery?"

"Only for our most handsome customers." She set the provisions on his desk then walked around to kiss him. The office walls were glass, so anyone walking by could see them. The kiss was too quick, but office compliant. "I have good news and couldn't wait to tell you about it."

"What's up?"

"Ivan got accepted into the Swedish study and it starts next month!"

He stood and pulled her into a hug. It was an easy reaction. "I'm happy for him. That's amazing."

"Yes, and he asked Heather to go along with him and she's in. And you know, it won't be as expensive as I'd expected. Well, he'll have to pay rent, but they've already sent info on rentals close to the study facility. And he'll have to cover food and other things. But the medical care is completely covered, and it includes physical and mental health checks. It sounds perfect for him."

"It does. But I suspect that'll set the two of you back, no matter how much you say it won't?"

She shrugged. "We'll deal. And we talked to the owners of the brownstone this morning. They agreed to allow me to stay on to complete Ivan's contract through January. I'll start looking for jobs this winter."

Wolf should feel buoyed by her enthusiasm. And he did. So why did he feel as though she was pushing him away by not asking him for financial assistance? Surely, the move would tax the Quinns' wallets. And Heather was going along too? A trip across the ocean, with an extended stay, would not be cheap.

"You don't seem excited?" Her shoulders wilted. "I'm bugging you, aren't I? You were probably immersed in an important project—"

Deciding a kiss was the easiest way to waylay her concerns, he pulled her close and initiated the distraction. Ivy had succeeded in what she'd come to New York to do. Help her brother move forward. And even though she would still be in the city through most of the winter, eventually she'd leave.

Would she walk away from him as well?

Ivy pulled away from the kiss and her eyes darted back and forth between his. "Something isn't right?"

He exhaled. "Sorry. No, everything is as you deserve.

I'm just…like you said, I was coding and sometimes I'm so deep in it that it just takes me a while to come back to the normal world."

"I know that about you." She kissed him on the nose. "And I'm not going to hang around any longer and give your office mates something to gossip about. Just wanted to bring you fuel and tell you the great news. Call me later?"

"Absolutely."

With one more kiss, she left, walking by his office with a wave and a bounce to her step.

Wolf leaned forward, palms to the desk. The coffee smelled strong. The cake sat inside a neatly folded packet. A beautiful, smart, funny woman loved him. Everything was perfect.

So why did he feel as though her not asking him for money had been the hardest hit he'd ever taken? He wasn't that guy anymore. The kid who had to buy off the bullies. The man who had to flash his credit card to feel validated by others. All he'd wanted was freedom from the chains of his billions. And now that he'd found that freedom, he couldn't help but toe those chains and wonder what the hell was wrong with him.

"Nothing. Maybe."

He shook his head. Why was this so difficult to just allow to happen? Ivy and Ivan had a handle on things.

You can make it easier for them.

Did he need to do what he was thinking about doing? It would upset Ivy, surely. But…he had to give it a try. Not because he wanted to buy her love. He had that. He simply wanted to show the Quinn siblings how much he cared about them. And there was only one way he knew how to do that.

It would be a risk. He could lose Ivy in the process.

"I have to try."

* * *

It was after four when Ivy punched out at But First… She swung around the corner of the building, heading for the main entrance, knowing Wolf would still be sitting behind his desk. The man worked too much. She certainly hoped, now that she had begun to solidify her future, that she could encourage him to make some changes. Perhaps even look into moving and taking a smaller role in his company so he could have more time for life. And her.

Janice held the door for her, nodding and then calling after her as she entered, "Wolf isn't in there! He left about an hour ago."

"Oh." Ivy turned and the woman still held the door open for her. He'd left early and hadn't even stopped into the shop?

"Everything okay?" Janice asked.

"Of course. I must have forgotten he had plans. Thanks for saving me a trip in the elevator. You have a good afternoon." She walked onward, sensing the woman wanted to chat. To dig up some gossip? Likely.

She walked quickly, but her pace slowed as she got closer to the brownstone. Tugging out her phone, she texted Wolf to see if he wanted to get something to eat. He didn't answer, which worried her.

Had she read him incorrectly this morning? She'd sensed something hadn't been right, that he'd not been as excited about her news as expected. Had it been more than her disturbing his work? Did he think this meant she was leaving him after the brownstone owners returned early next year?

That was half a year away. And she certainly hoped their relationship had more staying power than that. On the other hand, she knew his dating history. He was not a man who seemed to prefer settling in happily ever after.

What was she thinking? Her relationship with him was different. It had staying power. They cared about each other. Loved…

He didn't believe in love. Had never received it his entire life, so how could he really recognize it when he did receive it from her? Had she shown him her heart? Was he capable of moving beyond his emotional traumas to embrace what she wanted to wholeheartedly give him?

With tears spilling down her cheeks, she sniffed them away as she met Heather and Ivan outside the brownstone door. "Heading out for a walk?"

"We're going for dinner," Ivan said with a wave of his cane. "Celebrating."

"Of course! You're looking rather steady tonight."

"I feel incredible."

"I think the good news is a balm," Heather added. "He's been pacing and jumping. It's exciting."

"You two have fun. I'll see you later."

"Tell Wolf thanks again," Ivan said as the twosome walked down the steps, slowly, but with a steadiness that Ivy noticed.

"Thanks?" Ivy stepped inside and walked down the hall-way to the kitchen, where she found Wolf sitting at the counter nursing a lemonade. "Hi. What brings you here? And why does Ivan want me to offer you thanks?"

He patted the stool beside him and she sat. He took her hand and kissed it. "I did something."

"A good something?"

"I think it is. But you might not."

Her heart dropped. This was it. The big goodbye. She'd been wondering if he was capable of allowing her into his heart and— But really? No. There was only one thing that the two of them didn't agree on, and that was money. She drew in a breath and cautioned herself from reacting. She didn't want to do that with him. Not anymore.

"I'm sorry for the way I acted this morning," he said. "I guess some feelings and emotions are still deeply embedded inside me. It'll take a while to move beyond."

Beyond what? The need to protect his heart? "I don't want to guess at what you're implying."

"Honestly? I was hurt when you didn't ask me for money to fund your brother's adventure."

"Oh." As she'd suspected.

"And I reasoned with myself. I know I shouldn't be hurt, and that you didn't intend it that way, but that stupid little kid inside of me eventually won out. I know that the two of you have got this. I also know that you don't want to take money from me, and it's not because of pride but simply because, well…"

"It's a little bit of pride." She slid her fingers along his and lifted his hand to press aside her cheek. "But as I've realized, it's not even my choice, is it?"

"It's not. Which means… I offered Ivan a small stipend to get him through a year or so in Sweden." He winced, waiting for her reaction.

Was that it? Mercy, she'd never been more relieved. Ivy bowed her forehead to his. "Thank you."

He tilted up her face with a touch to her chin. "That's it?"

She nodded.

"No argument?"

She shook her head.

"But I thought… And you know, I know that if I'm ever going to get beyond this need to feel, well…needed, I've got to stop handing out money. But. Another part of me just wanted to help. And who better to help than a family I genuinely care about?"

"Who indeed? I completely relate to your wanting to feel needed. We both know I've struggled with the same." She kissed him. "Thank you. I'm sure Ivan is grateful. As am I."

"That was easier than I'd expected. I thought we'd have an argument."

"I don't want to argue with you, Wolf. I want to love you. But there's one thing…" She bracketed her hands aside his head to study his eyes. So kind and smart and funny. Love was easy when in his arms. "It was something you said. It was a lie. But I don't think you realize that."

"What did I say?"

"You said you didn't believe in love."

He nodded. When his smile grew, her heart pulsed tentatively.

"I'm pretty sure it wasn't a lie. At the time," he said. "I've never felt worthy of love, Ivy. But you have changed the way I think. Made it possible to step beyond what I've known and look to what is possible. Love is…trust and respect and desire and sex and talking out arguments and even sharing food and a secret color language?"

He got it. Oh, did he get it.

"I love you," Ivy rushed out, tears spilling from her eyes. "And I see you. I see the little boy who never felt he was lovable enough to be kept by a family. And I see the man who just wants to be normal and learn how to live in a world that expects so much from him. I choose you to be a part of my life and my family. I love you, Wolf."

"I love you, Ivy. And the way I feel right now? My heart is thundering and my gut is spinning, but my body is chill and like, yeah, this is what it's like. Like going on the best ride you've ever taken. So that's love, eh?"

"It is. Will you take me on that ride with you?"

"Hell, yes."

EPILOGUE

One year later...

IVY HUGGED UP against Wolf, clasped his hand, and kissed him. He looked sexy in a tuxedo. And she was wearing the red dress he'd bought for her in Venice. He'd needed to look dapper. As Ivan's best man, Wolf had stepped up.

The wedding was held in an outdoor chapel not far from the Swiss village where Ivan and Heather now lived. Petite cornflowers decorated the simple altar and the bride's bouquet. Thanks to some of the health measures Ivan had learned while in the study, he had greatly improved his condition. But he still had a journey ahead of him, incorporating the disease into the adventurous lifestyle that gave him breath and happiness. He and Heather would begin an across-the-world adventure in a few weeks. And he had planned to document his experience as it unfolded in an online memoir. Ivy felt sure he would accomplish everything he desired.

After a stint working on the research study in Venice last fall and winter, Ivy had recently been accepted to head a study on butterflies in the rainforest. That project began in a month. And she was so ready!

Wolf was excited for her, but had pushed ahead the building project for his home in Burghausen by months in order to occupy it himself while she was away for work. He intended to fly to the Amazon for visits. She wouldn't have it any other way.

"Let's walk." Wolf nodded toward a crushed stone path that edged the woods hugging the venue. He tugged at his blue tie, loosening it. "Maybe you'll catch a bug or two?"

Ivy set her champagne goblet on the tray of a passing waiter, and with a wink to her brother, she strolled off with the man of her dreams. A man who had learned over the course of their relationship that he actually did believe in love.

She'd known as much all along. And he was strong and smart and capable of carrying her through thick and thin. He was her rock. And he ticked off every item on her list. Ha! That list. She had not made it thinking it would actually come to fruition. Guess fairy tales really did come true.

As for her field notes on the species *wolfus zeiglerus*, they would never end. Always she was learning something new about him and hoped it would continue.

"I'm not sure about this trip to the Amazon," she suddenly blurted out as they strolled along the tree line.

"What?" He stopped and leaned against a rustic wooden fence post. "Are you telling me you don't want to fulfill your dream of finding the blushing phantom butterfly?"

He remembered that was one of her dreams. God, did she love this man!

"Of course, I do. It's just that we'll be away from each other for three months. I wish I could stick you in my backpack and take you along."

"I did say I'd visit every other weekend."

"I know. And I will count the days between those visits." A kiss was necessary. And another. He slid a hand along her neck and pulled her in for a deeper connection. She melted against him. No place she'd rather be. "I love you."

"I love you as much as you love butterflies."

"Wow."

"That's a lot, isn't it?" he said with a grin.

"So much."

"Wait a second…" He reached over her shoulder. "What's on this leaf? Is it some kind of bug?"

She waited for him to pull his hand down and then he held his loose fist before her. "You actually caught a bug for me? Mr. Scared of Spiders has grown quite daring."

"It's not a spider. And don't tell anyone about the spider thing or there will be consequences." He jiggled his fist. "It's moving in there. Want to see what I caught?"

"Yes. Switzerland has some amazing insects…" She gaped when he opened his palm to reveal what should have flown off immediately. But it did not. In fact, it flashed and sparkled. "Are you kidding me?"

He took her hand and slid the ring he'd had concealed in his fist onto her finger. Then he dropped to one knee. "Ivy Quinn, you've shown me that love exists and that it is special and wondrous. You've won my heart and my trust. I don't know if there's a luckier man in the world. But I could get even luckier if you'd do me the honor of becoming my wife."

A warm summer breeze curled between them. Ivy's heart melted as she swallowed back tears. Bowing her head to his, she nodded. "Nothing would make me happier. I love you, Wolf. More than bugs."

"That's a hell of a lot. Take a closer look at the ring. I had it made special."

Ivy studied the ring. She was so excited she'd just seen a ring and her heart had started to race and—who cared if it was big—and then she saw the tiny pink butterfly at one end of a rose gold twist laden with diamonds. "Oh, my God, Wolf, this is…"

"I had it designed specially for you. Can't have you wearing a ring without a bug on it."

"It's perfect. Yes. Yes, I'll marry you!"

He sprang up and lifted her into his arms, spinning her. His shout attracted the interest of some from the nearby wedding party. And to them, he declared, "She said yes!"

* * * * *

BEAUTY AND THE PLAYBOY PRINCE

JUSTINE LEWIS

MILLS & BOON

For Robby and serendipitous meetings.

PROLOGUE

The Cursed Kingdom
Florenan Fairy Tales, 1786

ONCE UPON A time there was a beautiful kingdom, high in the Alps. In the summer the valleys were green and lush. In the winter snow capped the beautiful peaks. Perched in that kingdom was a beautiful palace and in that palace lived a king.

But the King took all his subjects' money and spent it on cards, dice and horses. His wife left him, taking all the crown jewels. The kingdom was almost bankrupt.

A witch placed a curse over the kingdom saying that the kingdom would be destroyed if the King's sons followed their father and put their own base desires before their people. The witch prophesied that the kingdom could only be saved by a prince who was brave and true and who put his family and his people above himself.

The first Prince loved wine so much he ignored his wife and neglected his country. His wife died of loneliness and a giant earthquake shook the country nearly causing it to crumble into ruins.

The second Prince thought that he had evaded detection by the witch and her curse. He secretly loved many women who were not his wife until one day when he became so distracted by his lovers that the kingdom was invaded. The war ripped the country apart and the Prince had to flee.

And the third Prince? The third Prince vowed to break the

curse by always putting his duty first. By staying true to his country and not his base desires.

The third Prince vowed never to marry.

CHAPTER ONE

SIMONE SAID *AU REVOIR* to her last customer, closed the door to the bookshop and slid the steel lock across with a satisfying clunk. In the small office behind the counter, she turned on the television to check on the tennis scores and got to work reconciling the day's accounts. She needed to be quick if she was going to meet her friends, Julia and André, at the bistro down the street.

Tallying the days' takings was thankfully taking longer these days. Business had been steadily picking up over the past few months and she was back on track working towards her savings goal to enable her to, hopefully, buy the bookshop within the next few years.

The bookshop, The Last Chapter, was situated in Simone's favourite part of Paris, the Latin Quarter. Also known as the Fifth Arrondissement, the Latin Quarter was characterised by the sound of bells from churches small and large, the thick wooden doors hiding secret courtyards and the narrow laneways, all winding their way up the gentle hill to the Pantheon.

It was home to black ironwork decorating the windows, flower boxes with blooms of all colours. At street level, it was home to the tempting boulangeries, patisseries, fromageries and wine shops selling world-class wines that even students could afford.

This was a place of students, intellectuals, readers, dreamers with hundreds of years of learning. And, when you were particularly lucky, the smell of baking croissants.

Simone didn't even mind the tourists. They came from all over the world, bringing their own experiences, thoughts and dreams to Paris as they had been doing for centuries. Besides, tourists made up half of her customers.

Simone's boss was a British investor named Mr Grant. He owned the building and the business and spoke regularly about closing the bookshop and opening a convenience store instead. Simone had worked in the bookshop for nearly eight years and had managed it for five. She also lived in a studio apartment on the sixth floor of the same building.

'The bookshop is over a hundred years old,' she'd reminded Mr Grant. 'Think of all the history!'

It was the history of The Last Chapter that had convinced Mr Grant to keep the business operating for a while longer, while Simone saved enough money to be able to purchase it from him.

She glanced at the small television, looking for the tennis scores, but the headline on the ticker tape across the bottom of the screen made her suck in a sharp breath. *Mon Dieu.*

A woman was claiming to be pregnant with the King of Florena's child. The claim might have made some people express shock, but most would simply shrug. If Florena had been any other small European kingdom Simone probably would have done the same. However, Simone had spent the first sixteen years of her life not only in Florena, but in the royal residence, Castle Villeneuve, itself. She knew the King and his family. While she didn't return to Florena often, it was still her home. Her mother still lived there, working for the royal family. Simone could only imagine what they must all be going through.

King Edouard and Queen Isabella had always given the appearance of being, if not a happy couple, at least a functioning one. Their union had resulted in just one child, Prince Edouard, known to Simone as Ed, born exactly nine months after their wedding.

The marriage hadn't been arranged, but it had been beneficial to both. Isabella was the daughter and sole heir of one of the richest men in the world. The royal family of Florena had been struggling financially and reputationally after King Edouard's father, Old King Edouard, had wasted the royal family's private fortune with his reckless spending and womanising. Queen Isabella's fortune had meant the royals did not have to seek assistance from Florenan taxpayers, which had settled the republican cries from certain politicians.

Isabella gained a title and status, the country benefited from the money and connections she brought with her, and the kingdom gained peace and stability.

Young and good-looking, the King and Queen had probably hoped that love would grow.

It hadn't.

But this hadn't been merely indifference. The King had been having an affair and had fathered a child that wasn't the Queen's. Simone's thoughts went to the Queen, but her heart went out to Ed. Her childhood friend and companion.

She grabbed her phone to search for more information than the television was offering her. A twenty-six-year-old woman, Celine, claimed to be in a two-year relationship with King Edouard, who was thirty years her senior. She was now pregnant with their child. The King, or indeed any member of the royal family, was yet to comment. The Queen was reportedly in the Caribbean. The King was in Florena, but hadn't left the palace. And the Prince?

No one knew.

His last official engagement had been in New York as part of his duties as the Florenan trade envoy to North America. Ed's position as trade envoy might have seemed nepotistic, until you learnt that he spoke five languages and held degrees in economics and international relations. Few other thirty-year-olds were as qualified as he was to represent his country.

There was a knock at the door and she groaned. The *Closed* sign, written in seven languages, no less, was clearly visible. She contemplated pretending she wasn't there, but the customer knocked again, hard enough that she worried about the old glass pane shattering.

She poked her head out of her office.

The customer was a taller than average male. He was wearing a baseball cap and, despite the unseasonably warm autumn day, a coat and scarf.

She could have let him in, a customer was a customer after all, but his insistent knocking made her pause.

'Simone, it's me. Let me in.'

Simone moved around the counter and to the door. The man cupped his hands around his face to block out the streetlight and pushed his nose against the old glass to look inside. Their eyes met and she stopped. Green eyes that could still, despite much wishing otherwise, make her heart stop.

It was really him.

Ed.

'Sim, please.'

What was he doing here now? Just when her life was going smoothly. When she was doing just great, thank you very much.

She slid the lock back, but before she turned the knob she paused, took a deep breath, and repeated the mantra she had perfected over the years.

Don't fall. Don't fall.

His palms were pressed against the glass and above them his green eyes pleaded. She pulled open the door and he fell inside, almost landing on her.

'Oh, Sim. Thank goodness.'

'Ed! What on earth are you doing here? Haven't you heard?'

'Why do you think I'm here?'

Ed pulled his cap off, revealing the same mass of light brown curls that had always topped his head, now cut short at the sides and slightly tamed. She wasn't sure how she felt about that.

It's not any of your business how handsome he looks or how he's chosen to wear his hair.

Simone locked the door behind him, still confused. Befuddled. Shocked. And no less clear about what was happening. Ed clearly wasn't in a hurry to enlighten her. He looked around the bookshop.

The Last Chapter was older than any of Simone's grandparents. It covered the ground and first storeys of a narrow slice of the street. Its two floors, along with a substantial part of the narrow staircases, were covered in second-hand books written in several different languages. The previous owner had liked to tell customers that F Scott Fitzgerald, Ernest Hemingway and Gertrude Stein had visited the bookshop—claims that Simone had long ago decided never to try to verify in case they proved false.

Ed put his hands on his hips and surveyed the small room as though he were surveying his vast estates.

'So this is the famous bookshop.'

'I don't think it's famous,' she replied.

She'd made The Last Chapter thrive since she'd taken over the management, but it wasn't yet Shakespeare and Co.

'In the palace it is.'

Simone winced at the idea that they might talk about her at the palace.

'It's great to visit it at last.'

Implicit in his comment was that in the eight years she had managed the bookshop he had never bothered to drop in for a visit.

Though why would he? Even though they had grown up together they had seen very little of one another in the past decade, ever since she was sent away to school and banished from Florena.

'Ed, I don't understand. What's going on?'

'It's lovely. Cosy, rustic. And you've perfectly captured that ancient book aroma.' He picked up the closest book, an old copy of *Florenan Fairy Tales*, thumbed the pages and made a show of breathing in the scent.

An exasperated groan escaped her throat. 'Edouard. Please. What's going on?'

At the sound of his full name Ed's shoulders tensed.

Ed replaced the book from exactly where he had taken it, but still didn't speak.

He walked along the nearest shelf and ran his finger along it, as though searching for something. She didn't know what he was looking for, but doubted he would find it in her small section of German crime novels. He stopped and sighed, but still didn't turn.

Her heart swelled and broke at the same time. Ed was in her bookshop. His beautiful hands touching her books. His tall frame only just fitting under the low ceilings. He was in the same room as her, breathing in the same air, for the first time in years.

'You've heard?'

'Yes. Just then. On the news. But—'

'I expect everyone's heard.'

She might have seen the headline, but she had no idea what Celine's pregnancy would mean for Florena. The country was a small, progressive constitutional monarchy, but still. She had no idea how the royal family would navigate an illegitimate child. Apart from anything, the news must be personally devastating for the Queen. And for Ed.

'Ed, is it really true? It's really your father's child?'

A half-sibling for Ed.

'I assume so.' He shrugged. The attempt at nonchalance didn't hide the stress on his face, which in turn couldn't mask the heartbreak in his eyes.

'When did you…? I mean how long has it been going on?'

'A while.'

'You knew?'

'I knew he was seeing her, yes.'

She tried to keep her expression neutral, knew she'd failed. 'Your mother? Does she know?'

He laughed. 'Celine called her two days ago to tell her.'

'Oh.' Simone didn't even want to imagine how that phone call might have gone. 'But what does it mean? For your parents? For Florena? For Celine?' Simone was a little ashamed that Celine came as an afterthought. She didn't know her, but still.

'Who knows?' Ed threw his arms up to the low ceiling.

'That's what everyone at the palace is tearing their hair out about. If this had happened two hundred years ago Celine would've been given a house, a generous pension and the child would've been given a title. But now?'

Ed glanced out of the window. It was dark outside now and with the lights on any passer-by could see inside the bookshop.

'Is there somewhere more private we could go?' He nodded to the back room. 'I'm trying to keep a low profile.'

'Wait in my office for a moment and let me finish up. I'll be two minutes.'

Simone turned off the television and her computer, checked the alarm system and picked up her phone and keys.

She showed Ed through the storeroom and to the back door.

'It's very rambling, isn't it?' he said.

'I hope that's a compliment,' she grumbled.

'Of course. It's lovely.'

His attempt at flattery grated more than it should have because it highlighted the gulf between them. He would inherit a palace that she had merely lived in as the child of a cook.

The back door led to a staircase that took them up the five flights of stairs to her attic.

'Is there an elevator?' he asked at around the third flight.

'Yes, but I thought you'd like to work on your figure.'

She knew he'd get the joke. Ed was in as good shape as ever. No one could miss his strong, lean legs, washboard stomach, and shoulders that could rival those of a champion rower.

She wasn't in bad shape herself. After all she walked up and down these stairs several times a day. She still felt self-conscious, though, with him walking behind her, unable to miss the sight of her legs and bottom ascending the stairs, even if he'd wanted to. Not that he had ever, in the twenty-five years they had known one another, shown the slightest interest in her physically.

Once they reached the sixth floor, she slid her keys into the lock and paused before pushing open the door. She shouldn't be ashamed. She loved her apartment. It was perfectly big enough for her and her cat, Belle, and she was proud to be managing her own business.

But she couldn't help looking at her apartment through Ed's eyes. It wasn't vast or stylish. It was most definitely quaint. Too bad. If Ed couldn't see its charm then he could just leave.

She pushed open the door to her one-room apartment.

He placed his small black backpack on her sofa and looked around. One half of the room was her living quarters, with a soft, cotton-covered sofa, a table just large enough for two chairs, some plants, bright prints on the walls and a small book-shelf—because you still needed books, even if you did have an entire bookshop downstairs.

In the other half of the room, behind a gauze curtain that psychologically separated the spaces, but didn't provide much actual privacy, was her double bed.

The kitchen was basic, with only a small fridge, a single sink, an oven and small bench space. Despite being raised by a chef, or maybe because of it, Simone didn't often cook. The bathroom was large enough to fit a sink, shower and toilet, but not much else.

'Is this all? Is there another room?'

She made sure her glare was withering. 'It's an attic in the Fifth Arrondissement and I manage a second-hand bookshop. I'm doing very well to afford this.'

'I meant, isn't it charming?' he said.

'Were you expecting Versailles?'

'No, Simone. It's lovely. Truly.' He sat on her small sofa, lay back and spread out his arms, making himself quite comfortable. She looked at him, at a loss of where to begin.

Once upon a time, as the fairy tale went, they had been close friends. Friends who squabbled, but adored one another at the same time. He was a year older than she and had been in her life for nearly as long as she could remember. Simone's father had died when she was only four and she and her mother, Alea, had been invited to move into one of the small apartments in the back of the palace, where Alea worked as a cook.

Ed was the only other child who lived in the palace and, even though Ed was the Prince, and she the daughter of one of the staff, the two children had found one another. When Ed hadn't been at school, or doing what young princes did, he'd always sought her out.

Simone had attended day school, and had certainly not done any of the aristocratic activities he had, like horse riding or skiing, so she'd always been around in the palace somewhere. In the kitchen with her mother, in the garden with the dogs, or riding her bike around the beautiful grounds.

The two of them had squabbled and teased each other, but they'd always had one another for company on the weekends when he was home from school and during some of the holidays.

Being with him now was familiar, almost like going home.

She told herself her feelings for him were only platonic, because of their long friendship. Because he reminded her of simpler times. Because he'd been with her through some of the saddest times of her childhood.

Not because the sight of him made her heart race. Or because catching a breath of his scent could make her head swoon. Or because she trembled just thinking about pressing her body up against his and...

Platonic. That was all her feelings were. All they ever would be. She might have had a childish crush on Ed once upon a time, but she had well and truly moved past that. She'd had to.

'Wine?' she asked.

'I thought you'd never ask.'

'It's not fancy.'

'Thank goodness. I plan to drink it quickly.'

She hid her smile. They would be fine. Two old friends catching up over a drink. She could manage this without getting any ideas that it might be something more. She took a bottle of cheap Bordeaux from the rack and uncorked it before sitting on the sofa next to him, being careful not to brush against him.

She poured two generous glasses and let him take a few sips before saying, 'I'm so sorry again. What a shock.'

He shrugged. 'Yes, but also no. The thing I can't get my head around is that I'm going to have a half-sibling. At thirty!'

Ed was at the age where he might have been having children himself, but he was the Playboy Prince. Unmarried. Unattached. And seemingly proud of it.

'Have you spoken to your mother? How is she?'

'Furious. He's always been much more discreet.'

'What do you mean? Always?'

'About all his affairs.'

'*All* his affairs? There've been others?'

Ed gave her another quizzical look. 'You must have known.'

'I mean… I guess I didn't think he'd been faithful. But two years is a relationship.'

'I mean, *you* must have known.' He stared at her, waiting for a response.

'I've never had an affair with him!'

He burst into laughter. 'That's not I meant.'

What did he mean? What did any of it mean?

'Ed, what's going on? Why are you here?'

He put his glass down. 'I was actually hoping I might be able to stay.'

CHAPTER TWO

'STAY? HERE?' Ed watched as Simone looked around her apartment, such as it was. If he'd realised she lived in a studio he might have thought twice. But his need to see Simone had overwhelmed everything else. When he'd received the phone call from his father, telling him he was going to have a baby brother or sister, one of his first thoughts had been of Simone. Growing up, she had always been there for him. And now he needed her more than ever.

Ed had jumped on the first plane from New York to Paris as soon as he'd received his father's order to come home. But in the seven hours it had taken the plane to cross the Atlantic further developments had caused his father to call again and say, 'Stay where you are. Lie low.'

When his father had said this, Ed had thought of Simone again and how fortunate it was that he had flown into Paris. She was safety, security and home.

His parents' marriage had always been unhappy. His home not filled with love, but with tension. From his early childhood Simone and her mother, Alea, had provided the home he craved. Even though they had drifted apart over the years, Simone was still the person he trusted most in the world. The news that he would have a sibling had made that suddenly very clear to him. He'd *needed* to see her.

He realised now he'd put his own selfish feelings above any thought for her reality. The apartment, which was really just one room, was barely large enough for Simone. If she lived here with someone else then they must share a very intimate relationship. He looked at the bed, possibly the smallest double he'd ever seen. The idea of sharing a small bed with Simone sent an unexpected jolt through him. The tabloids might say that he, the Playboy Prince, was happy to share a bed with the nearest warm body, but the tabloids exaggerated. And Simone wasn't like any other woman. She was his oldest and dearest friend.

The sofa where they sat was on the same scale as the bed: cosy. He and Simone sat hip to hip on the sofa, which wasn't unpleasant, but the warmth of Simone's leg against his was certainly distracting. Two years it had been, maybe three, since they'd seen one another. And she was different, though he couldn't pinpoint why.

'I know it's sudden. Celine spoke publicly before the palace got their story straight and a plan in place. Press are camped outside the palace, with more flying into Florena each hour. Father told me to stay here and lie low. It'll probably just be one night.'

Simone drew and released a deep breath before saying, 'Yes, of course. But don't you need to be there?'

'You'd think,' he mumbled, mostly to himself.

While it would be years—decades, even—before he became King, he was still the Prince. The King's only child. He wanted to be there to help. The matter involved him too. Most of all he wanted to help his father decide on the plan of action. The King had several options, but there was one in particular Ed really didn't want him to choose.

'Maybe he wants to spare you from it?'

'It's his scandal, not mine. Doesn't it look worse if I'm not there? Like I don't support him?'

'I don't know.'

She shrugged and looked as confused as he felt. In the craziness of the past day it was such a relief to be here, with her. She lifted her feet and tucked them under her bottom. He liked her hair. It was even longer than when he'd seen her last. Dark blonde, and falling in messy waves down her back.

Her face was shaped like a heart and her eyes as brown and bright as ever.

She had been adorable as a kid, with big eyes, blonde curls and chubby cheeks. He wasn't quite used to her seeing her older. Grown up. He still sometimes saw the four-year-old he had unexpectedly stumbled across one day in his garden. He hadn't been much older. No one had told him another kid was moving in. Discovering her playing with his dog had been like magic. A friend he'd always wanted. A playmate who would play hide and seek and all sorts of games with him. A confidante who, despite their different backgrounds, still understood what it was like to live in the beautiful yet secluded palace.

He also remembered her as an uncertain teenager. The friend he'd seek out when he returned from school every holiday. Simone and Alea's apartment in the palace had been an oasis away from his cold parents. Alea's kitchen always warm and welcoming. His parents didn't even love each other enough to bicker, but Simone and her mother had always shown unconditional love and support. When someone mentioned the word 'home' his thoughts always flickered to Simone's apartment before duty focused them back on the palace proper.

Now, sitting on the sofa next to him, he saw child, teenager and woman all at once. The chubbiness of her cheeks had vanished, leaving cheekbones. Her bright blonde curls were darker and heavy with the weight of her thick, long hair. But her beautiful big brown round eyes remained the same. And they were looking at him now with concern.

'What do you think will happen? With your parents…?'

'Divorce? Probably. But then there's the issue of Mother's money. Her fortune has been paying for the running and the upkeep of the palaces and the family's expenses. Mother's father left me some money, but it is nowhere near the same amount. Besides, I don't know if she'll give Father the satisfaction of being able to marry Celine. It could get messy. I don't know if he even wants to marry Celine.'

'What about the baby?'

'I'm sure he'll look after it. He'll have to acknowledge it.'

A baby. A sibling. Twenty-four hours later he was still struggling to process the news. Ed couldn't think of another monarchy that had faced such a crisis in modern times. Sure, there were monarchs who had kids out of wedlock. But usually not when they were still married to someone else.

It would be a good enough reason, he thought, to get rid of the monarchy altogether.

The Florenans were generally proud of their independence, but there were always those who argued that the country would be better off if it were subsumed into another larger country. Like France or Italy. The current Prime Minister, Pierre Laurent, was in favour of making closer ties with France, the country of his birth. Ed had tried to raise his concerns about Laurent with his father, but the King had laughed them off.

'Nonsense. The people will never agree to that. I've seen off six Prime Ministers. Besides, the people love us. The House of Berringer has been around for five hundred years and we'll be here long after Pierre Laurent.'

Simone poured him another glass of wine and topped hers up. 'I don't have anything much to eat, I'm afraid. I could order something in.'

'Whatever you were going to have would be fine,' he said.

She looked down. 'I was going out.'

He was an idiot. He should have realised that she had a life. Plans.

'I'm sorry. A hot date?'

'No, just dinner with some friends.'

The relief he felt when she said that was almost physical, but he still said, 'You should go. I'll be fine here.'

How would he have felt if she had said she had a date? Uneasy? Sad? And that was silly. Simone was his friend.

She's probably had many boyfriends you don't know about. Look at her, she's gorgeous.

He was trying not to look at her, because each time he did his body tensed and his head became lighter.

Exhaustion. That was all it was. Nothing more. This was Simone, and he didn't get tense or lightheaded around Simone.

'No. It's okay. I see them all the time. I haven't seen you in…'

Two years.

She'd seemed to avoid Florena more and more the older she got.

'You didn't visit last Christmas.'

'Managing the bookshop…it's too hard. I open every day, except Christmas.'

'You work seven days a week?'

She shrugged. 'I'm saving up to buy this place one day.'

'Really?'

'Yes.' She sat up straight. 'What's wrong with that?'

'Nothing, it's great. This apartment?'

She nodded. 'And the bookshop. And I'm on track.'

'Wow, that's great.'

'You sound surprised.'

He was, but that was on him, not her. They hadn't spent much time together at all in the past decade, and without him realising it she'd become a grown-up. Not just a grown-up. A successful, impressive, beautiful grown-up. Who was about to own a bookshop and an apartment in the middle of Paris. She'd flourished since leaving Florena as a sixteen-year-old.

'I'm impressed, but not surprised.'

She gave him a crooked grin. Even when she made a face she was gorgeous.

Something inside him twisted. She didn't have a hot date tonight but was there someone special around? If there was he wanted to meet him.

And yet he also didn't.

'So, is it just you living here?' That sounded casual enough.

'Oh, no. My five flatmates are out.'

He stared, open-mouthed, long enough for her to laugh.

'Of course it's just me. There's barely room enough for you!'

He felt his face warm. 'I meant, is there…? That is, are you seeing anyone?'

Now it was her time to pause and study his face before answering. It was none of his business if she was seeing someone, but as her friend he wanted to know. He needed to know that she was all right. That whoever she was with was not someone like his cheating father.

She tilted her head to one side, delaying her answer even longer. With every moment the pause lasted a knot grew tighter and tighter in his stomach.

She was seeing someone. And it was serious. She was about to tell him she was engaged. Or about to be.

And he realised he didn't want that. That was…wrong. Simone married to some Parisian.

'No. There's no one.'

He exhaled. More loudly than he'd expected. Why had she taken so long to answer? More to the point, why had so much seemed to hang on her answer?

He and Simone were only friends. Besides, Ed had no plans to enter into a serious relationship—now or ever. Royal marriages were rarely happy marriages. They had even less chance than celebrity matches. Edouard Henri Guillaume, Prince of Florena, was the latest in a long line of Princes Edouard, none of whom were known for their fidelity. His father's scandal was just the latest in a long line. Ed was not going to risk his country's future on a royal marriage that would likely end the same way.

While Ed's faithfulness had never been tested—he'd never had a relationship that had lasted long enough to give it a serious stress test—he was the Playboy Prince. Everyone knew that. And Playboy Princes didn't magically change their stripes just because they were married. Genetics were not on his side. The best way to prevent another royal divorce was simply not to get married in the first place.

Which meant no wife and no children, and he was content with that. One of his cousins, or one of their many offspring, could inherit the throne. He also had no wish to bring into the world a child who would endure the same loveless, stilted childhood that he'd had. Who would watch one parent flirt with every female staff member. Watch the other slowly drink herself into oblivion.

Simone got up and moved around the small kitchen. He studied her back as she assembled a plate with some bread, cheese and hummus. Her movements were fluid, her curves hypnotising and very watchable. Though that could have been the transatlantic trip catching up with him.

She put the plate on the coffee table.

'A feast,' he said.

'Don't joke. I wasn't expecting to eat here myself, let alone entertain royalty.'

'It's great, and honestly I'm not very hungry.'

She looked at him as if she didn't believe him. She knew him too well.

'We can order something in if you like. This isn't exactly up to my mother's standard.'

Alea, an acclaimed chef, had stayed working for the King even after everything that had happened between the two of them. Ed had never been able to work out why, but he conceded there were many things he was destined never to understand about romantic relationships.

They ate the food and drank the rest of the wine. 'The bookshop is great. Truly. Why a bookshop?'

'I've always loved reading. But more than that I've always loved sharing books. A big part of my business is helping people track down out-of-print books. The bookshop is just one part of the business. Much of what I do is online.'

The certainty she had about her ambition was inspiring. He'd had no idea growing up that this was her dream. 'When did you realise this was what you wanted to do?

'Not long after I was sent away. Banished.'

'You weren't banished.'

'Yes, I was.'

'You were sent away for your own protection.'

She scoffed. 'My protection? It was a bit late for that.'

'Yes. Your protection. In case anyone found out.'

It was strange that she didn't remember, but it had been a strange and stressful time. His father had grown very close to Simone's mother gradually over the years. As their affair had developed the King, Alea and the other staff had been anxious to protect Simone from any fallout and his father had paid for Simone's boarding school fees. Ed suspected that having Simone out of the apartment had suited his father as much as his professed motive of protecting her from scandal.

Simone had jumped at the chance to leave the palace and study in Switzerland, and Ed hadn't realised at the time that it would mean that Simone would never return to live in Florena again.

'But they did find out. The video got out,' Simone said.

'What video?'

Ed's stomach dropped. It had been a day of earth-shattering scandals in his family, but he was sure he'd have remembered a video of the King and Simone's mother.

'What video? The one of me embarrassing myself in front of everyone at your seventeenth.'

Ed rubbed his eyes. It was early afternoon in New York and he'd missed a whole night's sleep. But he must be more exhausted than he realised.

He didn't remember any video from his seventeenth, but when he saw Simone's mouth fall open he stopped and, fortunately, had enough sense not to blurt out the first thing on his mind.

Was it possible that Simone didn't know about the affair his father and her mother had conducted for at least a year?

No. That would be absurd. She must have known.

Simone had been sent away to school. Not only to protect her from any fallout if the affair became known but also to hide it from her. Was it possible her mother—nor anyone else for that matter—had never told her? Was it possible she'd never figured it out?

CHAPTER THREE

WAS HE SERIOUS? How could he have forgotten about the video? *What video? The* video. The one that had ruined her life. Shaped the course of everything that had come after it. The single most embarrassing, frightening and heartbreaking moment of her life.

'This is not the time to joke,' she said.

He held up his hands. 'I'm not joking.'

'You're seriously telling me you don't know about the video of me making a fool of myself at your party?'

He looked genuinely pained with confusion, his green eyes wide and innocent.

'I honestly have no idea. What video? Please tell me.'

'I don't want to talk about it.'

She crossed her arms. If he didn't remember she didn't want to enlighten him. That would be like reliving the whole horrible experience again.

She had devised a plan. To her deluded, infatuated, teenage brain it had seemed like the perfect plan.

Ed had been about to turn seventeen and in one more year would go abroad to university. His head was beginning to be turned by the glamorous young women who had constantly been thrown into his path. He'd been growing particularly close to a girl called Morgane, the daughter of friends of his parents. Morgane had always been finding some excuse to visit him at the palace.

The world had been at Ed's feet. If he was ever going to love

Simone she had known it had to be then. Before he saw too much of the world and realised that she, provincial Simone, who had never even left Florena, was not good enough for a prince. It had been then or never.

Her dilemma had been that if she told Ed she loved him and he didn't feel the same way she'd jeopardise their friendship. So she had devised a way to let him know she loved him without actually making a declaration. Plausible deniability and all that. She'd decided she would sing to him, and if he loved her too he'd think the song was about him. He'd come to her and they would fall into each other's arms and be together for ever and ever.

Simone had helped Ed and his assistant organise the party. They'd chosen a nineteen-eighties theme, with arcade games, glo-sticks and, most importantly, karaoke.

Her plan had been much more subtle than actually coming straight out and saying, *Ed, I'm in love with you*. But if he felt the same way surely he'd understand what she was saying.

Best-laid plans and all that… The sound system hadn't been terrific. And it hadn't helped that she'd chosen a song that stretched even the best singers in the world—*I Will Always Love You*, the Dolly Parton/Whitney Houston classic.

It had turned out that Simone's voice sounded different in the summer house than it did in the shower.

There had been laughter and sniggers. Ed hadn't laughed, but he hadn't said anything either, being too busy talking to Morgane all night.

He hadn't returned her feelings. But, she'd reasoned, as she'd cried into her pillow that night, at least she hadn't come right out and told him. Heartbreak was bad enough without the other person knowing how much they'd hurt you. At least she hadn't had to face the pain of having him reject her to her face.

She had decided she would get a good night's sleep and in the morning Ed would have forgotten all about it.

But the next day it had been everywhere.

All over social media and the front page of the newspaper,

the *Daily Florenan*. She'd been made into a hashtag, for crying out loud.

And cry she had. Alone in her room. All that day and into the next.

And the things they'd written about her. The comments on the video had been merciless. All of them mean. Some dark. A few telling her to end her life.

She'd been a sixteen-year-old kid.

The next day her mother had come to her room and asked how she felt about going to school in Switzerland for a semester. Simone had never heard a plan that sounded so good. She'd known she was being sent away in disgrace, but she hadn't cared,

One semester had turned into six, and she'd never had to live in Florena again.

She swirled the stem of her wine glass, hoping Ed would change the subject.

But he pressed on. 'Do you know why you went to boarding school?'

She scoffed. 'Of course I know. Do *you* know?'

He nodded.

'Then I don't know why we're even talking about this.'

She tore off a piece of bread and loaded it up heavily with hummus. Two hours ago she'd been happily going about her life, but now Ed was making himself at home on her couch, digging up old memories and picking at her emotional wounds.

'So tell me,' she said. 'Why do you think I left?'

'No, no. You first.'

She took a swig of wine. She might as well tell the story first. Her way.

'You remember your seventeenth birthday?'

'Yes, I was there.'

The grin he gave her almost made her stop talking. He was impossible. Gorgeous and utterly, completely impossible. She looked at the spot on the wall where the paint was peeling rather than looking at his sparkly, teasing green eyes.

'There were lots of people at the party. Friends of yours. Friends of your parents.'

'And you.'

'Yeah.'

Did he remember what she'd been wearing? A red dress chosen specially that had been at the absolute top of her budget. Still not as fancy as the couture worn by some of the other guests. Did he remember how her hair had looked? Sleek and straightened and shinier than it had been before or since.

No. He did not.

Still, if he didn't remember the dress or the hair, maybe he didn't remember the singing.

'It was in the summer house…' she said.

'Nineteen-eighties theme. We hired Space Invaders machines,' he added.

He did remember. Some of it at least.

She drew a deep breath. 'And I, being a stupid sixteen-year-old, thought it would be a good idea to sing.'

He didn't speak. He just let her keep talking.

'I chose the wrong song. And I made a mess of it.'

'It wasn't that bad.'

'Thank you for saying that, but we both know it was. And I was destroyed.'

'Destroyed? By whom?'

'By the world! Everyone on social media. I was a hashtag.'

His eyes were blank, jaw slack.

'You don't remember?'

'Of course I do. I just didn't think it was that bad.'

'Not that bad?' Ed might have been oblivious to what her gesture meant, but the rest of the world hadn't. They had all deduced correctly that she'd been trying to serenade him.

'Sim, sweetheart. I had no idea you felt this way about it.'

'Well, it was awful. I was hashtag *palaceserenade*.'

'Please don't think for a second that I'm trying to diminish or dismiss what you went through, but I do understand.'

She crossed her arms.

Ed leant towards her, his green eyes holding hers in a caring gaze. For a moment she thought he might lift his hand and brush her cheek. Simone pulled her gaze away from his.

Don't fall. Don't fall.

'As someone who's been the subject of many hashtags, and more than his fair share of memes, I do understand. And what I've learnt is that the rest of the world never thinks as much about you as you think they do. I bet no one in Florena even remembers it.'

'Oh, they do.'

Each time Simone visited Florena the trolls would somehow find her. Once a photo of her in a supermarket had made it onto social media. Another time a photo of her and Alea in a café had done the rounds. With the usual number of hateful messages, comments and threats.

She wasn't a celebrity. She had been a sixteen-year-old girl at a private party. The trolls still came after her. She'd been such a liability to the palace she'd been sent away to boarding school. Ed could be blasé about it—he was always in the public eye—but he could handle it. She didn't have that kind of strength.

'Really? I'd almost forgotten.'

He had completely forgotten. Because he'd barely noticed in the first place. He'd forgotten because his life had moved on. But that video was still on the internet. With all the vile comments.

'It's different for you,' she said.

'Why? Because I'm a prince? Does that make me immune from mockery? Laughter?' He placed his wine glass down and stood. 'Maybe I should go.'

Oh, no. This wasn't what she'd meant.

She stood too and reached for his arm. 'Ed, no. Please. I'm sorry. It was insensitive of me.'

It was only then, once he was looking down at her hand gripping his, that she realised how close she was to him. And how outrageously strong his biceps felt under her grip.

'Ed, please stay.'

He nodded. 'I know you didn't mean it. I know it *is* different for me. I have the protection of the palace. I've been trained to cope. And you were only sixteen. Besides, you should've been safe in the palace. It was meant to be a private party.'

She nodded.

Growing up, he had confided in her many times about the intrusiveness of photographers. About how it felt to have his every move scrutinised. He was fortunate that his parents had made sure he had been supported, counselled and given techniques to manage the peculiar psychological stressors that came with being a prince.

'I'm sorry.' She gave his arm another gentle squeeze. Damn, it felt good. If only she could slide her hand up to his shoulder, slip it around his neck and...

Ed shook his head. 'No, I'm sorry. I didn't realise how much it had affected you.'

'Well, yes, one stupid song changed my life. But I suppose if I hadn't been filmed I wouldn't have had to leave Florena and then I wouldn't live here.'

She threw her arms wide. She loved her apartment, her bookshop and her life in Paris.

The look he returned was unreadable, but the way he twisted his body just enough to free himself from her touch spoke volumes. They were both upset but he couldn't leave. And she didn't want him to leave like this.

She poured them both another glass of wine and he sat. They settled in for an evening of chatting about his travels and work and her bookshop, the books they'd been reading, the podcasts they had been listening to. Avoiding talk of palace gossip and their teenage years.

Eventually, when her eyelids were drooping, he said, 'You should go to bed. You have to work tomorrow, I assume.'

She nodded. 'Do you want the bed? I'll take the couch.'

'I won't accept it. You're the one doing me the favour.'

'But the couch is tiny. Barely big enough for me.'

'Which is exactly why I won't let you take it.'

He could share your bed.

And what if her hands had a life of their own in the middle of the night? What if her unconscious self couldn't help sliding over to his side of the bed? How would she explain that?

'Wait a minute. Do you have any bags? Were you travelling with anyone?' Simone asked.

'I left the airport right away—as soon as I saw the message from Father. My valet took everything and went on to Florena.'

'So you have nothing?'

He looked down at his backpack. 'A toothbrush but not much else. It'll be okay. I'll have a call to return home by the morning.'

It would only be one night.

'We could share?'

The air was suddenly as thick as her voice sounded.

Her heart beat hard in her chest several times before he answered, 'Are you sure?'

'We've slept together before.'

His mouth dropped.

'When we were kids,' she said. 'Sleepovers, sleep-outs!'

'It's not quite the same thing.' He spoke slowly, carefully.

She'd gone too far. 'We're just friends. We might be a little older. But we're still just friends.'

If she kept saying it enough it might eventually become true.

He didn't speak for a very long time—so long that she was sure her cheeks must be the colour of a stop sign.

'Are you sure?' he asked.

She exhaled. 'I think I can manage to keep my hands off you,' she joked.

He leant towards her. Close enough that she could feel the heat from his body. He stared at her. Raised one eyebrow.

'What if I can't?'

He didn't smile, and a whoosh swept through her body.

The thought of Ed not being able to keep his hands off her was absurd. So why wasn't he laughing?

She looked into the depths of his eyes, so closely she could see the flecks of gold. And something else. Suddenly each breath felt as if she was dragging bricks into her lungs. There was no oxygen in the air, and something was pressing on her chest.

He turned his head and cleared his throat. 'I'm just worried your snoring will keep me awake.'

He smiled and the spell was broken.

Simone bumped his upper arm gently. 'I doubt you'll be able to hear my snoring over your own.'

She grabbed her pyjamas and changed in the bathroom. She washed her face and brushed her teeth—her usual evening routine, but it felt so strange with Ed being just outside the door. Ed Berringer was in her attic. His tall, athletic frame was sprawled on her small bed.

Oh, Ed... It was so much easier to forget him and push her feelings to one side than it was to face them. She managed when she wasn't near him. When he was simply an idea, not a living, breathing man. But tonight he was a living, breathing, beautiful man who was going to sleep in her bed.

No. She'd got over Ed once before. She was not going to put herself through that again.

Climbing carefully into bed so as not to bump him, she said, 'Will you be able to sleep?

'Eventually. I need to get back onto European time anyway. Thanks again.'

'You don't have to thank me. You're welcome any time. I'm glad you felt you could come to me.'

The smile he gave her melted every single muscle in her heart.

Don't fall. Don't fall.

It was just a childish crush and she'd made herself get over it once before.

She was about to turn and begin what would surely be a restless night when she remembered.

'Wait. Why did you think I was sent away from Florena?'

'Oh, just that... The song. The video.'

'Really? But you mentioned an affair?'

'Yes. The hashtag *palaceserenade* affair.'

She sighed. That was all he meant.

She could feel him shuffling next to her, trying to make himself comfortable. She turned out her bedside light and the room fell into darkness.

'Goodnight, Ed.'

'Goodnight, Sim. I hope the foxes don't get you.'

She smiled. They had camped out a few times in the palace garden one summer. They had put up a tent and toasted marshmallows on a small camp stove. They had made a pact to stay up all night, but they'd fallen asleep in the early hours, exhausted. They must have been nine or ten maybe.

'Do you remember when we camped in the garden?'

'Of course. We did it a few times. I was so lucky to have you growing up. And now. I know we haven't seen much of each other lately, but I really do think of you like family,' he said into the darkness.

She sighed.

He thinks of you as a sister.

Eventually his breathing became steadier and deeper. She knew he was asleep.

He wasn't in her bed by choice, only by circumstance. She didn't want something to happen between them simply because she was the nearest warm body. Besides, her and Ed was impossible. The last thing she wanted was to return to Florena and its hateful press. The last thing she wanted was to face the scrutiny that would come from dating Prince Edouard the Playboy Prince.

She chanted this to herself over and over, before she finally fell asleep.

CHAPTER FOUR

ED OPENED THE windows and the sounds of the street floated in. Snatches of conversation, cutlery clinking on plates, a television in another language and over it all the contented hum of the city. Below him the street was already bustling with Parisians going about their day. Including Simone.

He wasn't sure when she had left as he'd been in a deep, deep sleep. Exhaustion, jetlag and maybe one too many glasses of wine had thankfully, meant he'd slept soundly. Now he was awake the real nightmare began again.

There were no messages from either of his parents and neither answered his calls.

He located the coffee machine in the small kitchen, and brewed himself a cup.

He scrolled through his tablet as he drank his coffee and searched for the most recent press about his father. He'd tried calling his father's advisers, but those who answered told him they knew nothing. He should be back in Florena, showing support for his father. Being the respectable face of the monarchy.

Ha! Respectable! No wonder his father wanted him to stay away.

Ed was far from innocent. Though he was hardly as promiscuous as the tabloids would have people believe. Maybe about a tenth of their reports about him had any substance.

Still, his name was almost never printed without the words 'The Playboy Prince' preceding it. Ed enjoyed a party as much as the next single thirty-year-old, but he wasn't amoral. He'd never cheated on anyone because he'd never stayed with any woman long enough for it to be an issue. If his father couldn't stay faithful, if his grandfather couldn't stay faithful, what made Ed think he could? It was much simpler not to marry.

He wasn't the falling in love type. Just like his father and grandfather. Ed's duty was to his country first and foremost. While he was young Ed was travelling the world promoting Florena and its economic interests. A life in the air left no time for serious relationships. And in the future—hopefully many years in the future—he intended to fulfil his role as King alone.

That way he could avoid the type of scandals that had plagued his forefathers. Loveless marriages inevitably led to infidelities, unhappiness and scandal. Not to mention unhappy children who didn't understand why their parents only spoke to one another sarcastically, if they even bothered to speak to one another at all.

Apart from dating, which as far as he knew wasn't a crime, he was a respectable person. He'd studied diligently and worked hard. He treated everyone with respect and avoided trouble. He had done everything expected of him as a prince. And he'd done it well. Which was why it went against every fibre of his being to stay here and not return home to help figure out a way through this mess.

You could just leave. Get on the next flight.

He could, but his father had ordered him to stay away. His king had told him to stay where he was. So he must.

Besides, going home would mean leaving Simone. He wasn't ready to do that. His instinct to come here had been spot-on. Last night had been calm. He could relax with her. Say exactly what he was thinking and feeling. With her, the troubles and worries seemed that much further away. If he couldn't be in Florena this was where he wanted to be.

He flicked on the small television. The news channel had his father's news rotating across the ticker tape every five minutes or so, simply described as 'a disgrace'.

Ed held degrees in government and international affairs.

He spoke several languages. Why didn't his father want him in Florena?

He looked down at his clothes. The same outfit he'd been in for over twenty-four hours now. He looked up 'clothing delivery Paris'. If he bought a change of clothes and other supplies his father was bound to summon him home immediately. He ordered some clothes and pyjamas from his favourite designer and paid for an urgent delivery.

But the call from the palace didn't come.

A noise outside the window caught his attention. A black cat was on the window ledge, meowing to come in. Belle. He opened the window and the cat jumped inside. She weaved between his legs and he stroked her behind the ears.

To his mind, there were three main ways this could play out. First, his father might decide to divorce his mother and marry Celine and weather the fallout. Second, Laurent might insist he put the question of the monarchy to the people as a vote. Ed wasn't sure how that would play out. Even a narrow win for the monarchy would still feel like a loss.

But there was a third possibility. The worst possibility of all. One he didn't dare think about.

Abdication.

Ed knew he would be King—he'd been training his whole life for it and had made his peace with it. But not yet.

And not like this.

The journalist on the television was interviewing a woman who was saying that the most important person in the whole royal scandal was the unborn child. Once upon a time he'd wanted a sibling, and then Simone had come along. That little girl he'd stumbled across one morning in the garden, tossing a ball to Suzette, his dog. They had played for hours and later he had thanked his parents for getting him a sister.

They'd laughed mercilessly. 'Oh, darling. She's with the staff. She's not your sister.'

But if they'd thought she was beneath him they hadn't seemed to mind that Simone had kept him occupied. They hadn't seemed to notice the hours and hours he'd spent with her in the palace kitchens, or in Simone's apartment, eating with her, watching television, playing games, because neither of them had seemed to notice anything he did unless he got into trouble.

Ed had seen Simone irregularly since she'd gone away to school, because of his study, travels and work. He shouldn't have taken her friendship for granted. He should have visited this apartment before now. Made more of an effort to see her whenever he was in Paris.

He had been busy with his studying, his job and other official business. And other women. But it was also true that he had taken her, his oldest and dearest friend, for granted.

It was hard to shake away the guilt. While neglecting his best friend wasn't as bad as anything his father had done, it still wasn't the behaviour of the man he wanted to be.

Ed pulled out his phone and searched for the video she had claimed was the reason she'd been sent to boarding school. A video he had pretended to remember, but in reality had no recollection of.

He searched for hashtag *palaceserenade*, certain that there would be no results. But there it was. There *she* was. A sixteen-year-old Simone, belting out 'I Will Always Love You'. She didn't have a bad voice, but it was a difficult song for anyone. Let alone a kid in a room full of people whom he saw were jeering her. But she held her head high and kept going through it all.

His heart ached for the sixteen-year-old. She was gorgeous. She looked different from the way she usually had back then. Her blonde hair was straightened and sleek. The red dress showing more skin than he thought a sixteen year old should.

What had possessed her to sing that song? Other people had been singing, but he didn't recall anyone taking the karaoke as seriously as Simone had. He hadn't thought about that night in years. As far as he was concerned his seventeenth birthday had been much like his sixteenth. A palace-sanctioned party with as many of his parents' friends as his own.

He watched the video a second time and then read the comments. They were pretty horrible, and would have been devastating to read as a sixteen-year-old. But those comments and that video were not the reasons his father had paid for Simone's boarding school fees or her university tuition. Did she really think he would have done that over one video?

He watched it a third time and smiled. Sixteen-year-old Simone might have been mortified, but he'd bet if she watched it now, at twenty-nine years old, she'd marvel at the courage of that girl. At how gorgeous she looked.

He paused the video and looked at the frozen frame.

She doesn't know about the affair my father and her mother conducted. She probably thinks her mother paid her school fees.

He could understand Simone not knowing at the time, his father had been discreet, but surely at some point someone would have told her.

He looked at sixteen-year-old Simone, frozen in time. Saw the dreamy look in her beautiful eyes.

Was it his place to tell her about the affair? Probably not. It wasn't his secret to tell.

The only thing he did know was that he wanted to see her. Not the sixteen-year-old, but the beautiful twenty-nine-year-old woman downstairs, going about her day. Running her own business in one of the most beautiful parts of the world.

You could go downstairs.

And be seen? No. He pulled out his laptop. There was a day's worth of emails to catch up on. He was still the Crown Prince and Trade Envoy and had responsibilities. He set to work.

Simone didn't know what she'd expected to find when she went back upstairs that evening. But it wasn't baking.

Her apartment smelt of her mother. Of home. The source of the aroma—a plate of madeleines fresh from the oven—sat on her kitchen table.

'Are you trying to make me homesick?'

'Why? Have I?'

Simone turned her head so he wouldn't see the tears welling in her eyes. She closed her eyes and breathed in deeply. To steady herself and banish the tears. The madeleines reminded her of her mother. She missed her deeply. So much it made her ache. They spoke most days, and Alea came to Paris whenever she could. She loved it as much as Simone, and not living in the same city was hard.

'I take it you haven't heard from the palace?'

He shook his head.

'I'm sorry.'

Simone reached over and touched his shoulder. He was wearing a soft cashmere sweater and felt warm and delicious under her touch. Her hand tingled and the sensation spread up her arm. He lifted his own hand and placed it on hers, rubbing it slightly.

If only she could move closer and slip her hand all the way across his shoulders. Slide into his lap and...

'I'm sure they know you care,' she said, trying to string a sentence together even though her body was bursting with sparks.

'You're stuck with me a little longer.'

'I told you—you can stay as long as you need.'

She took her hand away with regret, because if she didn't do it now she just might slide it up to his neck, into his soft hair and...

She had to change the subject. 'I can't believe you baked. And madeleines!'

He passed her one and she took it gratefully. Sweet, with just the right amount of softness and chewiness.

'It's the only thing I know how to bake. Your mother taught me.'

Simone remembered a twelve-year-old Ed, always begging for the biscuits and watching Alea make them. Simone marvelled that Ed had actually remembered how to bake them. Just like her mother's.

You're older now. Stronger. You can do this.

He looked up, their eyes met, and her stomach swooped. This was bad. Very bad. As a kid her affection for him had been innocent. She'd adored him, but when her mind had leapt forward to what might happen if they should ever actually kiss she hadn't known what would happen next. Everything after a chaste, Disney-movie-like kiss had been unknown to her.

She hadn't experienced deep physical desire until she'd come to Paris. Since then she'd gravitated to men who looked nothing like Ed, and had several fulfilling physical relationships. She'd convinced herself she was really physically attracted to a different sort of man, and that her feelings for Ed were platonic only.

'You got some new clothes,' she remarked. 'Thank goodness. I didn't want to say anything, but the smell…' She held her nose and waved her hand.

He laughed—as well he might. Despite his wearing the same outfit for twenty-four hours, there was nothing she found offputting about his scent at all. And now, with fresh baking and a freshly showered and changed Ed, her apartment had never smelt as good.

Careful, Simone. Careful.

This was good. Banter. Teasing. Like when they were kids. Before she'd been swamped with adolescent hormones and decided she had a crush on him. If she teased him he wouldn't realise how close she was to burying her face in his neck.

'And there's more.'

Ed stepped to one side and revealed an eclectic feast. Fresh bread, cheese and a bottle of Burgundy. He lifted the lid off the casserole dish on top of the stove to reveal a simmering chicken casserole.

'You made coq au vin? How?'

'Is it still your favourite?'

'Do you expect me to believe you cooked this?'

'Why couldn't I cook this?'

She levelled him with a look.

'Okay, you've got me on the casserole. It was pre-prepared. I didn't think you'd thank me if I made it.'

She laughed.

'But I did bake.'

She nodded. That she believed.

'I wanted to thank you. For letting me impose another night.'

Another night. In the same bed as Ed. It was just as well he'd shown some appreciation for what he was putting her body through.

Before she realised what was happening, his large hand enveloped hers—warm and secure. His thumb brushed against her wrist and her body swayed.

'I'm very grateful. I know we haven't seen much of one another lately, and I know I'm putting you out. But I'm very glad I'm here with you.'

She looked into his eyes. They were earnest and serious. Deep and soulful.

Don't fall. Don't fall.

'It's been an awful few days and there is no one else who understands me quite like you do.'

Their faces were a mere foot away from one another's. If she didn't move now she'd reveal too much.

She shook her head and turned, so she didn't make a fool of herself.

As she turned she noticed the vase on the coffee table.

Flowers. The vase on her small table was filled with pink peonies.

It's a centrepiece for a table. He hasn't bought you flowers.

But it felt as if he had. And he'd baked her madeleines. And bought her wine.

Ed pulled out her chair. It hit the bookcase behind, but she didn't mind. Sitting in her cramped apartment with her prince was the only place in the world she wanted to be.

CHAPTER FIVE

BEING A PRINCE was not the endless lark everyone thought it was. On days like this it was positively tedious. Did anyone else have to worry so much about public perceptions that they would agree to be trapped in a Parisian turret for twenty-four hours?

The only communication he'd had from either of his parents in the past twenty-four hours had been a brief message from his father's private secretary thanking him for his patience and telling him his father would speak to him soon. He'd tried to get some work done, even attempted a video conference, but he hadn't been able to concentrate. His thoughts kept drifting to his father and his mother. And then Simone.

Baking was a type of procrastination that was entirely new to him, but it had worked. And, best of all, he'd made Simone happy.

Simone sat, closed her eyes and groaned as she breathed in the food. The sight did something strange to his chest. The steam from the coq au vin rose around her face, leaving a gentle glisten across her skin.

She grabbed a handful of hair from the nape of her neck and twisted it back from her face so she could eat without it falling in front of her, revealing the smooth skin behind her ears. He bit down the desire to kiss it.

How had he never noticed how gorgeous she was? They hadn't seen a lot of each other in the past few years, but even so. Now that he'd noticed it was difficult to believe he hadn't before.

Maybe it was just familiarity. She reminded him of happy times. Of childhood. Of feeling secure.

She was a best friend.

Except…not.

Now she was an independent woman, running a business in one of the world's most popular cities. The woman sitting across from him now, with her eyes half-closed, groaning gratefully as she ate the meal he'd procured.

You've actually never noticed her lips before. Pink. Plump. Perfect…

He shook his head.

'How was your afternoon?' he asked.

'Good. We had lots of traffic. And I managed to track down some sought-after first editions for some buyers.'

'Do you have any help in the bookshop?'

'A few casuals. My friend André helps out if I get really stuck.'

André. Ed's back straightened.

'His girlfriend, Julia, is my best friend.'

Ed felt his muscles relax.

'But you still work seven days? That's a lot.'

'I want to own this place, and that takes hard work.'

He drew breath, about to ask her how much money she needed, but she raised her hand before he could get half a word out.

'I need to do this by myself—and I can. Mum's offered to help, but I don't want to accept. She's done so much for me, especially putting me through school, helping me out when I first came to Paris.'

'Your mum's terrific. But did she really pay your school fees?'

He had to tread carefully. But he also had to know what she knew. While it wasn't his secret to tell, it didn't feel right that he knew something like this when Simone didn't.

Simone looked up. 'What do you mean?'

'It was an exclusive school. Your mother did well to afford it.'

'Who else would have?'

'I… That is… I wondered if my parents might have.'

The creases on Simone's gorgeous face deepened. 'Why would they?'

'Can you not think of a reason?'

She laid down her cutlery and crossed her arms.

'No. And I don't think Mum would have accepted. Besides, my father left her some money. Not a lot. But enough. We're not royalty, but she's not poor.'

He was now certain that Simone didn't know about the affair. But she was certainly suspicious.

'Ed… What do you know?'

'Nothing. I'm sorry. It was very rude of me to question you. I've had a strange and privileged life and sometimes I make assumptions I shouldn't.'

And sometimes I don't shut my mouth when I should.

Their parents' affair wasn't his secret to tell, but not telling felt as if he was betraying her. Half the palace or more knew about his father and her mother. Was it right that Simone didn't?

'My business is great. I don't need any help.'

He frowned. 'But you're working seven days a week.'

'Because I want to! I love my job,' she insisted, in a way that indicated the conversation was over.

They ate in silence a while longer. He tried to think of something else to talk about, but drew a blank.

He looked out of the window at the city lights. He hadn't expected to be staying a second night here and had assumed he'd be back in Florena by now.

'I'm sorry for imposing on you.'

'I've told you I don't mind.'

'I didn't mean to imprison myself in your apartment.'

She laughed. 'You're not a prisoner. Not really. You're free to leave any time. It's your loyalty to your father that's keeping you here.'

She smiled at him, and her compliment warmed his chest.

There were worse places to be trapped. Though it would've

been nice to be somewhere more spacious. Maybe with a pool. Or some sunshine. But at least he was trapped with Simone.

'I'm sure it won't be for much longer,' she said.

He shook his head. The silence from the palace said so many things. Was his father contemplating a press blackout or something else entirely?

A prisoner. The look on Ed's face was heartbreaking. Ed had never really struggled with his destiny or his duty. He saw it as an honour, not a burden. Simone had no idea how Ed would cope if his role were taken away from him. Some people were suited to a life of duty and Ed was one of them.

Simone was not. As a child she had adored living in the palace. Adored catching glimpses of the Queen all dressed up for a night out. Or even a night in. Young Simone had once thought it was the life she wanted. But that had been before hashtag *palaceserenade*. Before the worst of the internet had rained down on her.

'I don't know how you do it,' she said now.

'Do what?'

'Put up with everyone knowing who you are and commenting on you.'

'I wouldn't wish it on anyone.'

Her heart dropped. She knew she would never even date Ed. Let alone marry him. Her body shouldn't be reacting like this to something she'd always known was true.

Besides, apart from proving to her that Ed didn't love her, the whole hashtag *palaceserenade* nonsense had shown her that she didn't have what it took to be in the public eye anyway.

'But some people don't choose to be famous,' she said. 'It just happens because of circumstance.'

He looked at her closely and she felt her skin burn. Did he know what she was saying?

'You have to learn to get used to it,' he said. 'Or you break.'

'Yeah.'

She understood that. The few weeks when her video had

been all over the internet had been the worst of her life. Physically leaving Florena had helped, but blocking social media had been more important. The problem was every time she'd thought it might have died down she'd check to see if people were still talking about her. She'd go online to check, and all the horrible things—the really toxic comments—would come across her screen.

'You can't worry over what other people say about you. You have to have a clear sense of yourself. What is real and what is not.'

They were wise words. But easier said than done.

'Do you always manage to do that?' she asked. 'To have a clear sense of yourself?'

He pulled his 'I'm thinking' face before replying, 'Mostly. I don't go looking for clips about me. My staff tell me what I need to know. Otherwise I block it out.'

It was easy when you were a prince. And when you had staff to monitor your social media presence and advise you about it. Ed had been raised with the confidence of knowing who he was and what his role in the world was. He was also being given the support to keep doing it.

'Maybe you should too,' he suggested, leaning into her.

The words were no use to her now, but would have helped when she was sixteen.

She had been a kid. She hadn't had the training he'd had. No one had explained to her how to deal with the trolls.

How had she got through it?

The school counsellor had been amazing. A wonderful woman who'd tried to instil in Simone exactly what Ed was talking about. A clear sense of herself and a disregard for what other people thought or said.

Her best friend Julia, who was not only good at hugs, but also gave great reality checks, was wonderful too. 'He's not the one for you. And you know that.'

But looking at Ed now, reclined on her couch, twirling his wine glass, she knew a small part of her wished this was her life. Their life. Working in the bookshop in the day and sharing their evenings together. Eating, drinking, talking. And later she would take his face in her hands and....

It wasn't fair that he was still her favourite person in the entire world.

Before she realised it was almost midnight. They had been talking, laughing and reminiscing about their childhoods. As the evening wore on her thoughts became more muddied, her inhibitions lowered. She stood to get them both a drink and when she returned to the sofa her weight pushed the soft cushions closer and their hips touched. Nothing like a bit of self-torture.

But when she looked at him he was smiling. Contentedly.

'There's nowhere else I'd rather be imprisoned,' he said, and lay back.

Now their shoulders were touching. The sofa really was too small for both of them. Or she'd sat too close to him. She inhaled to clear her head, but breathed him in. He smelt of her own shampoo, and damn if it didn't smell good on him.

Even if Simone did still have feelings for Ed—which she didn't—they could never go anywhere. He thought of her as a sister. Besides, she certainly wasn't going to marry a prince. Not when she'd already experienced the kind of vitriol that was reserved for women who did.

He was finishing a story about a friend he had in New York and she was only half listening. Her thoughts were preoccupied in thinking about how close their shoulders were. The way his hair curled around the back of his ear. The light stubble that was now apparent on his cheeks.

It was lucky she was holding her glass in her hands, otherwise there would be nothing stopping her placing one of them on his knee.

Giving herself a mental shakedown, she tried looking for his flaws. His annoying habits.

He sucked on his thumb when he was thinking. He blinked

when he was lying. He often lost track of what he was saying and stopped speaking mid-sentence.

Damn. Even his flaws were adorable.

Simone came back from the bathroom after changing into her pyjamas. Ed tried not to study the loose fabric skimming gently over her curves. He ran his tongue around his mouth, which had suddenly gone dry. She eyed his new pyjamas—another of today's purchases.

'You'll be wanting your own cupboard space soon,' she said.

He was glad she kept joking. It was what they did. They *didn't* stare into one another's eyes for long, uncomfortable moments.

They climbed into their respective sides of the bed and when they were settled she reached over and switched off the bedside light. Ambient light crept in from the street but otherwise they were in darkness. They lay on their backs, looking at the ceiling.

Last night, exhausted from his trip and with more than enough wine in his stomach, he had fallen asleep easily. But tonight... He wasn't sure how he would fall asleep as long as he could feel Simone's gorgeous weight in the bed next to him. They weren't even touching, but he could feel her in his bones and in his pores.

What if he pretended to sleep and accidentally rolled in her direction? What then?

She'll push you back to your side of the bed or get up and go to the sofa.

Simone had invited him into her bed platonically. He couldn't throw himself at her.

'What if I can't keep my hands off you...?'

Last night he'd said it as a joke. Tonight it didn't feel like a joke at all.

Each time one of them moved he was careful to keep the space between them. For her sake more than his. He knew that if their bodies collided he'd be at risk of coming completely undone.

So he endured. As still as he could. Wound tighter than tight. Listening to her breathing become heavy and regular. But even then sleep evaded him.

His thoughts of Simone were confusing, to say the least. Upsetting at worst. Had she always been this beautiful and he'd just failed to see? Or had she been transformed somehow because he was trapped with her.

Excuses aside, he knew the truth. She was beautiful and always had been. He just hadn't noticed because she was his friend, and friends didn't think about friends like that. But now he had noticed the pink of her lips, the blush of colour across her cheekbones, the sound of her laugher.

It was seeing her here—in her home—in Paris. Thriving. Planning to buy her own business and apartment. He realised, with an uncomfortable lump in his chest, that she belonged here now and not in Florena. A sense of loss swept through him. He longed for her to be by his side. And not just as his friend. He longed to be even closer to her than they were now, with their bodies lying mere inches apart.

No. He told himself that he was being silly. The sensations his body was experiencing when he thought about Simone were happening just because of the immense amount of stress he was under.

The longer he lay awake and pondered, the more he realised that it didn't matter why he was seeing her differently. The better question was what he was going to do about it.

The answer, he knew, was absolutely nothing. She was his best friend. The person he was depending on. The relationship he most wanted to treasure and nurture.

Rolling over and sliding his palm over her soft curves was not even an option. Putting his arms around her and pulling her to him was out of the question. Taking her rosy lips against his and tasting their sweetness was unthinkable.

Not to mention arrogant.

What made him think she would even welcome such a move? She was happy in Paris. He was a friend from her past and had no role to play in her future.

And this was hardly the time for him to do anything that would get his private life into the public realm.

So these new feelings and desires were just a blip. An aberration. Once he was home and no longer trapped here their lives would go on as they were meant to.

Separately.

Besides, he wasn't here as Simone's prisoner, but as her guest. If anyone was keeping him prisoner it was his father.

Around two a.m. Ed carefully reached for his phone, in the vague hope there would be a message, but his home screen was blank.

Simone rolled over and a wave of her scent reached his nose. She smelt like summer in the garden at the palace and his muscles clenched even tighter.

She was comfort and home all rolled into one. That was all it was, he told himself as he lay stiffly in the dark, trying his best to keep still. He hadn't anticipated the longing he'd feel to roll over and pull her close. Hadn't anticipated how many times he'd come so close to doing so.

He contemplated getting out of bed and going back to the sofa to cool down. But his limbs were heavy and the thought of leaving Simone was even less appealing than the risk that he might roll into her.

He brought his breath in time with hers and finally fell asleep.

Ed had no idea how many hours later he woke up. The curtains were flung open and the sunlight streamed in brightly, exposing everything.

Simone handed him a cup of takeaway coffee.

'You're a goddess,' he replied, eagerly inhaling the smell of the fresh brew.

The words escaped his lips before he could think twice, but

he wasn't wrong. Her golden hair caught the morning sun and his breath with it. He couldn't read the look that passed across her face. Confusion? Annoyance? He should probably try to rein in these new strange feelings. Especially since he was already imposing so much on her. On her life. On her bed. He couldn't repay her generosity by hitting on her.

'I'm afraid you might need something stronger than a coffee,' she said. 'You need to watch this.'

Simone picked up the television remote and turned on the news.

'What is it?' he asked.

'It's better if you just see.'

It didn't take long for the report Simone was referring to to come back through the news cycle. The Prime Minister of Florena, Pierre Laurent, was giving a press conference. He was standing on the steps outside the Parliament building. While the crowd of journalists was not massive, it was big enough.

'The citizens of Florena have had enough. This is not the behaviour we expect or deserve from our monarch. This isn't the Middle Ages. This is the twenty-first century. The way in which the King has disrespected his wife, Queen Isabella, is not the way we expect our sovereign to treat women.'

Ed couldn't help snorting. Prime Minister Laurent had been divorced a few years ago after having an affair with his secretary. For him to throw allegations of inappropriate behaviour against the King was a little rich.

'But we know it isn't just the King. We know his brother left Florena several decades ago after embezzling funds from the Government. And the King's father, the former Prince Edouard, whose premature death was notorious...'

Ed groaned. His grandfather had taken a drug overdose at the age of thirty-five, before Ed had been born. He had been in a hotel in the Bahamas with two young women who were barely out of their teens.

The allegation against his uncle was fair, but Uncle Louis hadn't set foot in Florena for years.

The allegations against Ed's grandfather were, unfortunately, true, but he'd been dead for nearly forty years.

The money the Queen had brought with her to the marriage had restored the private fortune of the royal family, and Ed's father had spent the last four decades reigning over and representing Florena with success. This was his father's first indiscretion. His first public one, at least.

'The stench of this family runs deep,' Laurent continued. *'Every Florenan knows the story* The Cursed Kingdom, *but this royal family has not learnt anything from that fairy tale. They are determined to ruin us all.'*

The Cursed Kingdom! Now he was citing an old children's story. This man was the limit.

'Dignity—that's all we expect from our monarch. He's not expected to run the country. He doesn't have to make the hard decisions.'

The Prime Minister straightened his own jacket as he said this.

Ed had feared the election of Laurent as Prime Minister would be bad for the country and he was not happy to be right.

'I think it's time Florena joined the twenty-first century.' Laurent continued.

'Oh, spare me the republican speech,' Ed yelled at the television.

Simone shook her head. 'It's worse than that.'

'We could be stronger if we joined with another, larger country. We need to have a serious discussion about whether it is sensible or viable to do this. I have been having discussions with the French Government...'

'What?' Ed stood quickly, nearly spilling his coffee.

'It doesn't make economic sense to keep our nation as a microstate...'

'Microstate!' Ed yelled. 'We're nearly as big as Belgium.'

'The geopolitical reality is that we need the protection of a larger country.'

Simone stood back, her face creased with worry. Ed grabbed

his phone and pressed his father's number. To his enormous relief the King picked up right away.

'Edouard,' the King said.

'I have to come home.'

'No. Definitely not. You have to stay there. Are you somewhere safe? Somewhere private?'

'I'm with Simone. In her apartment.'

'Perfect,' replied his father.

'No! I'm no help here. I need to come home. I need to show that I support you.' He spoke too quickly and loudly, but this was the first chance he'd had to plead his case—he needed to go home.

'That's just it,' the King said. 'You need to distance yourself from me.'

'Having an affair is hardly in the same league as what Grandfather did. Or Uncle Louis.'

'That hardly matters. I don't want you getting dragged into this as well. Just stay where you are and in a few days everything will have blown over.'

Ed raked his hand through his hair. His father was in denial. What would happen with Celine? The Queen? They needed a plan.

'No, it won't blow over. Laurent clearly has a broader agenda,' Ed insisted.

He wished he were having this conversation face to face with his father, so he could see the expression on his face and his body language.

'He's all bravado. Why would he suggest joining France when he'd just be doing himself out of a job?'

'I agree it doesn't make sense, but that's his plan.'

There was silence on the other end of the phone. And then a deep, resigned sigh. 'I wish… I wish I'd planned this better.'

You should have done a lot of things better, Ed thought.

His father had been reckless, but it was hard to blame him. He was human. Ed had known for years that his parents' marriage wasn't happy. But he'd never expected his father to be indiscreet. He'd certainly never expected his father to be caught impregnating a woman who was younger than his own son.

'The last thing we need—the last thing this country needs—is you being photographed with me.'

'But—'

'Don't argue with me, Edouard. Stay where you are. This isn't about you so don't make it about you.'

With a few words the King made him feel like a teenager again. He remembered another long-ago conversation. The one where he'd begged his father not to let Simone leave Florena.

'It's for her own good. Don't argue with me. If you care about her you will let her go.'

Ed had argued then. Pleaded with him to let Simone stay. Losing her then had been a wrench. The feelings of that day came flooding back. Pleading, arguing, and then the strange emptiness he'd felt when she was gone. A feeling that would creep up on him at unpredictable times during his adult life. A feeling he was missing something, but couldn't quite figure out what it was.

Now, knowing there was little point arguing with his father, all he said was, 'Please don't make any major decisions without talking to me.'

'You have my word.'

Ed held the silent phone in his hand. He had his father's word, but what was that worth?

'Did you hear that?' he asked Simone.

'I'm sorry. It was hard not to listen.'

He looked back to Simone, looking awkward in her own home. He wanted to go to her, pull her tight, but wasn't sure if it would be for her comfort or his. He stayed sitting on the couch.

'He wants me to keep away from it all but it feels disloyal.'

'I know it goes against every instinct you have. You want to be there. You want to do something. And it's frustrating being stuck here in this shoebox.'

He did want to be doing something, but when the time came to leave Paris it would be with trepidation. And sadness.

'It's a nice shoebox,' he said.

She gave him a sad half-smile. 'I see where your father's coming from. If you go home…if you make some kind of statement supporting him…it could backfire.'

'How?'

'Because at his next press conference Laurent will say that since you support your father you can't be trusted either. And that Florena should sack the entire House of Berringer.'

'But how can I not support him? It looks worse if I don't, doesn't it? He's the King and he needs to stay being the King. For the sake of the country. Otherwise Laurent would have us become the smallest *department* in France.'

Simone turned and unpacked a shopping bag. She placed pastries, apples and strawberries on the small bench. 'Trust your father. I'm sure he has a plan.'

Ed wished he shared her optimism. If his father did have a plan, why would he not share it with Ed? He wasn't a kid any longer—he was trusted to manage Florena's trade relations with the United States. Why not the royal family's response to this crisis?

His muscles felt as if they might snap. First a sleepless night next to Simone and now feeling helpless and that his father didn't trust him.

'He's right, though. Laurent's plan to join France doesn't make any sense.'

'He was born here, wasn't he? Maybe he thinks it will give him a shot at running a bigger country. He thinks that if Florena is part of France he'd have a chance at being President of France.'

Ed buried his head in his hands. The man was ruthless and ambitious, but it hadn't occurred to Ed that Laurent would be so ruthless as to essentially destroy his own country to achieve that ambition. But Simone's theory made sense.

He turned back to Simone, who was preparing some of the fruit for her breakfast.

'That's quite perceptive of you.'

She laughed. 'You sound surprised.'

'I'm sorry if I do. It's been a long while since we spent so much time together.'

She shrugged. 'I follow the Florenan news.'

'You do?'

'My mum still lives there.' She drew a deep breath. 'And you.'

Her back was turned and for a moment he let his gaze rest on her. Her blonde hair was tied up in a messy bun. Her shirt dipped just low enough at the nape of her neck to reveal the soft creamy skin at the top of her back. He wanted to taste it. Lick it. He pressed his lips together.

'It's not the first time someone has discussed getting rid of the monarchy,' she said, not quite putting an end to his illicit thoughts.

The whole situation was strange. They were discussing the end of his country and all he could think about was what the skin on Simone's neck would feel like against his lips. He had to get a grip.

'Talking about a republic is one thing, but he's talking about getting rid of our whole country.'

Simone turned, putting an end to his opportunity to study her surreptitiously, and passed him a bowl of fresh fruit. Then she sat on the armchair, tucking her feet under herself, and hugged her coffee. He took the fruit gratefully. It wasn't what he would have chosen. Left to his own devices he might have taken a cap off a bottle of Scotch, but the breakfast was just what he needed. Sitting here with Simone was just what he needed. It was so much better than hearing this news alone.

'What do you think of Laurent?' he asked.

'Me?'

'Yes—you've been following the news.'

'Sure, but I've never met him. What do you make of him?'

'Ambitious. Slippery. Like most politicians. What do you think?'

'Ambitious, yes. And he likes to travel. He always seems to be visiting somewhere. And he's dating one of your old friends.'

'What? Who?'

'Oh, you know… What's her name?'

'No. I've no idea who you're talking about.'

'I thought…that is…maybe you dated her for a while? Morgane Lavigne.'

'Oh, her? I haven't seen her in years. Really? They're dating? Aren't you the fount of Florenan gossip.'

Simone shrugged. 'I keep in touch with people.'

'I'm impressed,' he said.

Simone continued to surprise him. The singing. The calmness and security of her flat. Her quirky bookshop. And her insight.

None of those things alone should have been surprising. What was rocking him, though, was the way he felt breathless when she brushed past him. The way his mind kept drifting to her. Just like his gaze, which now rested on her lips as she carefully sipped her coffee.

He knew he needed to get home to Florena as soon as possible, but when the time came he wasn't sure how he'd be able to tear himself away from Simone.

CHAPTER SIX

IT WAS A relief to get down to the bookshop and away from Ed.

How embarrassing to mention Morgane and know she was dating the Prime Minister when Ed didn't even know that. Simone wasn't proud of it, but she did occasionally look to see what Ed's old flames were up to. Or any woman he was currently linked to.

Morgane Lavigne had often visited the palace with her parents, and had gone on several holidays with the royal family. Like Simone, Morgane had known Ed since they were children. Unlike Simone, Morgane had shared a brief relationship with Ed in their teens. She had been the person Ed had spent most of his seventeenth birthday party with. The two of them had been wrapped up in each other. Morgane had been sultry and glamorous, even as a teenager, and each time Simone had seen her she'd been monopolising Ed and Ed had never seemed to mind.

Stalking Ed's exes on the internet was not in line with Simone's strict 'No Ed' diet, but at weak moments she did relapse. Which was how she'd known about Morgane and Laurent—from some photos Morgane had posted and her vague comments about being the 'other' first lady of Florena. Morgane owned the public relations company that completed work for the government.

If she couldn't get the Prince she'd go for the Prime Minister, Simone had thought cattily, then hated herself for it and immediately shut her laptop.

The morning started off relatively busy, with several customers, including some needing help with rare finds. A tap on her shoulder made Simone squeal in fright, stand and spin, her heart rate propelling her upward.

'Gah!'

The figure behind her was dressed in a black fedora, a red bow tie and thick-rimmed glasses.

'Are you trying to scare me to death?'

'Sorry. I was trying to be inconspicuous.'

'Looking like that?'

'I dialled 1-800-Disguise.'

'Seriously?'

'Seriously. You can get anything delivered these days. I've decided to help you out.'

'Ed…'

'It'll be fine. I need something to do. I need distracting. There were no emails waiting for me this morning. The video meetings I had today were cancelled.'

'Oh, Ed.' She didn't know what that meant but it didn't sound good.

'I'm sure there's some other explanation. The government's busy…'

Ed frowned. Something was happening in Florena's inner government circles and its trade envoy to North America was clearly not supposed to know what it was.

'There must be things you need to do. Away from the counter. Away from the bookshop, even.'

There were. She needed to shelve the new books and take some online orders to the post office, and she had no idea when she was going to manage to do that. André was due for a shift later that afternoon, but in the meantime she was alone.

'There are—thank you. I do need to go to the post office.'

'Go out for an hour or so. I'll be fine.'

'What if you're recognised?'

'Firstly, the further I am from Florena the less recognised I am. Secondly, who is going to believe that the silly man in the fake glasses and the bow tie in a Paris bookshop is me?'

'*I* don't believe the silly man in the fake glasses and the bow tie in a Paris bookshop is you.'

'See? I've fooled you, and you know me better than anyone in the world.'

His words made her heart pause. Even after all these years he still thought of her like that.

'Ed, there are plenty of people who know you. Who could recognise you.'

'It'll be fine. Besides, depending on how things go, I might need to ask you for a permanent job, and customer service experience will look good on my CV.'

Her heart broke for him. And his family. And everyone at the palace. 'It's not going to come to that.'

'There's no need for a crown prince of Florena, or even a trade envoy from Florena, if Florena doesn't exist.'

'Ed…' She slid her hand up his arm and squeezed his shoulder, but stopped just short of pulling him into a full embrace. Feeling the warmth of his body under her fingertips, she felt her heart get caught in her throat. She finally managed to say, 'Your father will take care of it. The Florenans won't stand for it. There are so many things standing in Laurent's way.'

He scoffed and she sighed. She wasn't going to be able to convince him. But he was right about one thing. He needed to be doing something other than watching the news and spiralling into despair.

'I need to go to the post office. If anyone wants something in particular that you can't find, take their details and I'll get back to them.'

'I can do this, Simone.'

This time he touched her arm. It was only to reassure her, but it felt as though he'd kissed her.

Kissed? Your heart rate couldn't handle it if he kissed you.

She gave him a quick explanation of the payment machine and gathered the parcels. As she walked along the street, dodging the tourists and breathing in the crisp autumn air, she was glad to have some space, but couldn't shake him completely from her thoughts.

Something was different about him. The casual comments. On their own they were nothing, but they were adding up.

'You're a goddess.'

'You know me better than anyone else.'

'What if I can't keep my hands off you?'

What was going on with him? He'd never been flirty like this with her before.

But the last time they'd spent this much time alone together they had been kids.

They'd seen each other since childhood, but usually there had been others around. Her mother or palace staff. They emailed one another occasionally. And he'd send her the occasional text message, usually to show her where he was in the world. Those messages would delight her and break her heart just a little as well. They only highlighted how their lives were on different paths.

This was different.

He was different.

He's stressed. He's going through a crisis and you're his oldest friend. He is relying on you and only you. He's just grateful and appreciates your friendship. That's all.

Once she'd posted the parcels and her hands were free Simone dialled her mother's number and was relieved when Alea picked up straight away.

'Darling. How are things? Did you see the press conference?'

'We did.'

'What a mess! How's Eddie?'

Simone smiled at her mother's use of her old name for him. 'Stressed.'

'Of course he is. But there's nowhere better for him to be right now.'

'He really wants to go home. I'm not sure how much longer he'll last here.'

'I honestly don't know what the King's long game is. There are rumours, but…'

'What sort of rumours?'

'Oh, just silly rumours. I'm sure things will quieten down soon.'

'Rumours about the Queen? Do you really think they'll divorce?'

'I don't see how it could be otherwise, to be honest.'

Simone stopped walking in the middle of the street, to the annoyance of the couple walking behind her. She stepped into a doorway.

'Ed hasn't even heard from his mother yet. I suppose that makes sense.'

'Don't say anything to Ed. As I said, we don't really know.'

Simone doubted she'd be telling Ed anything he hadn't already thought of. A royal divorce, a royal wedding and a royal baby seemed to all loom on the horizon.

Poor Ed. Having your parents' marriage disintegrate was bad, no matter how old you were. And having to go through it in the spotlight was even worse.

'I'd better get back to him. Let me know if you hear anything at all.'

'Of course. You too. Mwah.' Her mother blew her a kiss and ended the call.

Simone looked up at the great sky. Autumn was coming to its end and she could feel the change in the air.

Ed had spent the morning in the bookshop. He wasn't sure if he was helping or making a nuisance of himself, but it was better than staring at his phone or the four walls of Simone's apartment. Being in the bookshop, spending time with Simone, helped keep his mind off other things. When he was near Simone it felt as though everything would be all right. Somehow.

Around midday Simone went out to pick up some baguettes for lunch, and after that Ed went upstairs, to see if anyone had sent him any work. They hadn't. And the video conferences scheduled for the next day had disappeared from his calendar.

He groaned. He hated feeling useless.

The King didn't answer, but Ed was no longer surprised. He tried his father's secretary, who told him the King was in a meeting and would call as soon as he could. The King should change his voicemail message to say that and spare everyone the time.

He was used to this distance between him and his father, but still found it ridiculous that they had to communicate through a third person. If Ed ever had children they would always be able to reach him, whenever they wanted.

Not that he was going to have children. He'd told his parents as much. It was the one royal duty they couldn't ask of him. He'd do the job, but he wouldn't subject any woman to life in the fishbowl that was the palace of Villenueve. His parents had looked at one another, but not argued. How could they? They knew they were the very reason their son would never walk down the aisle.

Besides, his cousins had children, and now he was going to have a younger sibling the royal succession was hardly in danger.

Ed had no intention of marrying so he would not have children. He was always very careful about that. Unlike his father, he thought bitterly.

Besides, living a single life wasn't a problem. He'd never found someone he knew he could trust enough. Or someone he wanted to spend time with when the initial rush of seduction had worn off. He'd never been obsessed by a woman. Never been ready to chuck in his whole life for her.

Ed tried to read some reports but unsurprisingly he couldn't concentrate. He stretched and attempted some sit-ups and push-ups, the only exercise possible in the tiny apartment, though that too failed to clear his head.

What would happen to him if Laurent got his way? Presumably, his family would have to leave the palace. But could he still live in Florena or would he be an exile? He could come to Paris. Find a place—a bigger place, near to Simone. He could see her every day. They could be neighbours just like they'd used to be.

His body relaxed instantly at the thought. If Simone were fully in his life again he would be able to cope with whatever came next. The realisation was both surprising and comforting.

Would it be the end of the world to be an ordinary person? He knew other princes and princesses often longed to shake off their titles, but he never had. Apart from playing a few childhood games, he had never wanted to be anyone else.

Childhood games. The memories made him smile. Once upon a time, when they were very young, he and Simone had loved to play make-believe. They just hadn't always agreed on what to pretend to be.

'I want to play kings and queens,' she'd say.

He'd groan. 'But that's not pretending.'

'You're not King. I'm not Queen. It's still make-believe.'

'Detectives.'

'We always play that.'

'Okay, you can be a princess and I'll be a superhero.'

'I want to be a superhero too. A superhero princess.'

Simone had pretended to be a princess disguised as a superhero and they had run around the garden chasing Suzette, who had apparently robbed several banks.

He smiled. He'd have to remind her of that tonight.

But if he wasn't a prince he wasn't going to be a superhero either. Who would he be? Plain old Ed Berringer, former prince?

No. Laurent was not going to get his way. Abolishing Florena was inconceivable.

Tomorrow the news cycle will have moved on and I can go home. Everyone will forget what Laurent was saying and get on with their lives.

Yeah, that's what you thought yesterday.

Ed walked over to the bookshelf. Only a special kind of person would have two storeys of books downstairs and then have another bookshelf in their shoebox apartment. He glanced at the titles, but his eyes were drawn to the shelf with a collection of framed photographs. He picked up one that looked as though it had been taken on a night out or at a party.

Simone wore a strappy red dress, not unlike the one in that video. She wasn't looking at the camera, but at the man next to her. Her smile was magical, uninhibited. Ed felt as though he'd been punched in the stomach and put the frame down as if it was on fire.

The woman in the photograph—the woman downstairs—was beautiful. Grown up, sophisticated, self-assured.

He sighed. If his family were kicked out of Florena, living in Paris, being near Simone, would have its benefits.

He should stop moping and do some work. He was still the trade envoy to North America—for the time being at least.

CHAPTER SEVEN

ED WAS WAITING when she got to the top of the stairs. He was wearing the fedora and the silly glasses. 'Do you have dinner plans?' he asked.

'I thought we could order something in,' Simone replied.

'How about ordering something out?'

'Go out? But, Ed…'

'Not to a restaurant…maybe just have a walk. It's dark. We can go along the quieter streets.'

Her heart leapt. She'd love to go out with Ed, and could tell he was bursting to leave the apartment.

'Are you sure?'

'If you can bear to be seen with me?'

He did look slightly ridiculous. In addition to the hat, glasses and bow tie, he'd found an old black coat of hers.

'In that get-up? I wouldn't miss it.'

He smiled.

Simone bought a bottle of Burgundy with a screw top from the shop across the road and they picked up a box of pizza from her favourite place down the street. They made their way to the Seine. The light had gone and they found a section of the bank with no one around and sat, with their legs dangling over the edge, taking turns to drink the wine straight out of the bottle.

Ed seemed relaxed, but Simone kept looking around.

'Relax. There's no one. I have a sixth sense for photographers. Besides, we look like students down here, with our wine in a brown paper bag.'

'I am surprised you came to me,' she confessed, taking a sip of the wine.

'I was in Paris. You're my person in Paris.'

Of course. That was all. She was convenient. The nearest warm body.

'I was just wondering…' The wine had loosened her tongue. But he'd probably be gone in the morning, so she might as well ask her question now. 'Are they pressuring you at all?'

'What about?'

'To find someone. Get married. Produce an heir and all that.'

Her mouth was dry when she asked. She'd never been quite so direct with him. They talked about other things, not relationships.

'Always.'

'Is there someone?'

'Are you asking if I'm dating someone?'

'Well, I suppose so. Yes.'

He laughed. 'No, Sim. I'm not dating anyone. I would've told you long before this if I was.'

He leant towards her, close enough that she could see the crinkles around his eyes through his fake glasses when he smiled, and said, 'Simone, I'd always tell you something like that.'

'You would?'

'You're my person.'

'Your person *in Paris*,' she clarified.

'No. My person. Full stop.'

The muscles in her chest tightened. 'Really?'

'Yes.'

Despite the cool air, her face was warm. His eyes were too serious. She closed the lid to the pizza box and brushed invisible crumbs from her lap.

He just means you're his friend—that's all. You've always known that. It's not a surprise.

But the way her heart was beating so fast at his declaration was a surprise.

They were best friends. It should be enough. But one day Ed would marry a beautiful princess. Or a movie star. And Simone would be back to being his person in Paris.

'But if they're pressuring you? Your parents?'

'They've been throwing heiresses in my direction for the past decade.'

'And?'

'I keep ignoring them. Delaying. It's not something I plan on doing. I told you this, didn't I?'

'Yes, when you were twelve.'

'It's still the plan.'

She'd never have to stand in the royal cathedral in Florena and watch him get married to someone else. It was something at least.

'But what about the monarchy. Having an heir?'

'Not you too!' He pushed himself back, making to stand.

'No. I don't care. Honestly.' That was a big fat lie. This was one of the most significant conversations she'd had in years. 'I'm just curious. Your parents must have said something?'

'Yeah, well, I try to avoid their questions. It only leads to arguments. But now that I'm going to have a sibling it's worked out great. I'm about to have a younger brother or sister. They can inherit after me. As far as I'm concerned it's the one good thing to come out of this mess. They'll have to stop hassling me for an heir. Father's done that for me.'

'You can't be serious?'

'Why can't I be?'

They sat in silence, watching the lights reflecting in the river and the boats slowly passing by.

After a while she couldn't help herself. 'Can I ask why? As a disinterested bystander not as your parent.'

He looked at her again, his eyes narrowed in sharp focus. That look of his made something inside her flip.

'Sorry. It's personal. You don't have to tell me,' she said quickly.

'I'm happy to tell you. It's not a secret.'

She held her breath.

'I'm a playboy looking for the nearest warm body. Everyone knows that.'

Something inside her twisted. 'But that's not true. Not really.'

'It's what the tabloids say.'

'But…it's all exaggeration? Lies to sell papers?' She held her breath, and her heart seemed to stop as she waited for his answer. She knew Ed's reputation, but she also knew Ed. He wasn't a womaniser. Or was he?

'Yes, it's lies…mostly. But…'

'But what?' Simone felt sick, waiting for his answer. What wasn't he telling her? Had he really slept with half the models in Europe?

'I don't think I have what it takes. Besides, I don't believe that love lasts. Certainly not long enough to sustain a long marriage. If anything, the events of this week just prove it. My parents hate one another. They've made one another miserable. Mine wasn't a happy childhood home. You know that.'

It had been barely a home. Ed's parents had often been away, and when they'd been around, Ed had just seemed unhappier.

'But not every couple is like that. My parents were happy.'

He looked as though he were considering his next words carefully. 'Everyone falls out of love eventually.'

Her heart cracked. If only that were the case…

'You didn't know my parents together,' she said.

'Did *you*, though?'

He probably meant that she must have only vague memories of her parents together, but you only had to see how Alea still spoke about her husband to know that love could last years and years—even beyond death.

'Your parents might be unhappy. That doesn't mean every couple is. Have you ever been in love?' The question was out before she realised she didn't actually want to know the answer.

'No.'

She exhaled. Of course he hadn't been in love. If he'd really felt the exquisite pull and pain of true love he wouldn't be saying this.

'Have you?' he asked.

If her face hadn't been red before, by now it would be setting off fire alarms.

She looked at her plate and considered her answer.

'That's a yes,' he said.

'I didn't say that.'

'It's a yes—otherwise you wouldn't look like that.'

'Like what?' she squawked.

'Like you don't want to answer the question. And it ended badly, didn't it?'

It didn't even begin.

She pressed her fingers to her burning cheeks to cool them.

Ed raised an eyebrow, but he must have noticed her discomfort because he didn't ask anything further.

They watched the boats a while longer, and when they had finished the wine Ed stood and offered Simone his hand to help her stand. She took it hesitantly, anticipating the jolt that would race through her. Yep—there it was. As predictable and inconvenient as ever.

They walked along the bank, up the river and then climbed the stone stairs to cross the Pont d'Austerlitz.

Halfway along Ed stopped.

The middle of a Parisian bridge looking up the Seine must surely be one of the most romantic places on the planet. Why was he doing this to her?

Ed turned his face to the sky, giving her a moment to steal a glance at his beautiful torso and then his face. Free to study him, she let her gaze follow the line of his strong jawbone, move over his cheekbones and rest on his soft brown eyelashes. Even in the silly glasses he was still heart-stopping.

'Have you been in touch with your mother?' he asked.

'Yes. She doesn't know much.'

'Has she seen my father?'

'Apparently no one has apart from his private secretary. And Laurent.'

'Laurent's been at the palace?'

Simone nodded. 'At least once a day, apparently.'

'Checking the joint out?'

'Meeting with your father, they say.'

'Did she say what the mood's like?'

'Tense. Sad.'

She didn't want to tell him everything her mother had said. It would just make him worry. Everyone was very concerned about their jobs, about Florena, but also about the royal family.

'Mum knows you're here. I couldn't lie to her. But she hasn't told anyone except to let them know you're somewhere safe and loving.'

Loving? She couldn't believe that word had come out of her mouth. It was the word her mother had used, but Simone hadn't expected to repeat it.

Ed studied her through narrowed eyes. It was that new, strange look she had seen a bit lately. As if he was puzzled by her.

Great.

He wasn't attracted to her. He was puzzled. It was a step up from 'I think of you as a friend', at least.

'Do you remember we used to play pretend?' he asked.

'Of course. Detectives and superheroes.'

'You always wanted to play kings and queens.'

'Yeah, but we had to play superheroes because you said, "Kings and queens isn't pretending." Even though I was definitely not a queen. And we had a palace to pretend in and everything. But no, we had to investigate who had taken Suzette's dog toys. I knew all along that you had hidden them.'

Ed laughed. 'I'd forgotten that.' He looked thoughtful for a moment. His green soulful eyes stared, unfocused, over the water.

'We did play kings and queens once.'

A memory long forgotten, dreamlike, surfaced into her consciousness. They'd been in the palace, had sneaked into the throne room one evening when his parents had been away and the staff distracted. Ed, who'd felt comfortable in the room, had run around with Suzette. Simone, who had not shared his ease at being in the throne room, had entered the room carefully and with awe. It was lined with gilded mirrors and portraits of past kings and queens of Florena, and they had looked down at them with disapproval as Ed had chased the dog until she barked.

Her chest warmed—as much from the memory as from the fact that he had remembered.

No one knew her like he did.

'You told me to sit on the throne,' she said.

'And I crowned you with my baseball hat.'

She laughed. 'Why?'

'Because you wanted to be crowned and that was all we had.'

'I was eight. I probably did.'

The baseball hat had felt precious and serious while they were pretending. Now she shuddered. A crown would be an impossible weight to bear.

Which was fine, since Ed was never getting married and didn't believe in love. And since she was never going to return to Florena.

A boat full of drunken revellers passed underneath them. They were waving, as boat passengers often did. Ed waved back and she laughed.

'What if they recognise you?'

'In my brilliant disguise?'

'Even in that. Those glasses are ridiculous.'

She reached for them, as if to pull them off, but her hand froze. Ed's hand had wrapped around hers, preventing her revealing his disguise to the world. He was meant to be incognito. But she wanted to see his face without them.

They were so close. She knew she should let go, but it was like trying to separate magnets. He pulled her hand away from his glasses, but far from letting it go he drew their clasped hands into his chest.

They mustn't be seen. It would be bad if he were recognised—worse if she were seen with him. But still she was stuck. Ed didn't let her go and she didn't pull herself free.

She could hardly breathe. Tonight the rest of the world had fallen away. Tonight the only thing stopping her standing on her toes and kissing him was the wall she had built around her heart. And that wall was starting to feel less like stone and more like paper.

Thin tissue paper.

That could be blown away with the merest breeze.

Like the air that escaped Ed's lips as he sighed. 'Simone...'

He didn't sound hesitant. He sounded tortured. He sounded like her heart felt.

Just as she was about to step back his lips were on hers. It was quick. Even though Simone had been thinking of kissing Ed, the surprise nearly brought her knees out from under her. It might also have been the perfect way Ed's lips fitted against hers. The way his fingers tilted her head to the precise angle needed to send blissful sparks shooting through her.

She pulled herself back. What was he thinking? This was madness.

'I'm sorry... I thought you wanted... I misread.' He looked at the ground.

This was ridiculous. He wasn't to blame any more than she was.

'No, you didn't misread.'

He lifted his gaze back to hers. Through the clear lenses of the glasses she could feel the gravity in his next question. 'You wanted to kiss me?'

'Want. Present tense.'

She lifted herself up onto her toes, feeling his body rub against hers as she brought her lips to his mouth.

The sensation of his hard body pressing against hers only blew that wall further into oblivion. Had she gone too far?

Would they be seen? No. They wouldn't be identified out of all the other couples making out on all of Paris's beautiful bridges.

His broad hands slid up her back and into her hair. He gently held her head in place while he covered her with kisses. From her lips to her neck. Behind her ears and back again.

Ed is kissing you. His tongue is currently in your mouth. You can feel him. All of him. What does it mean? He doesn't believe in love, so what is this?

She ordered the voices in her head that were telling her to be careful to stop. Not to ruin what could be the most perfect moment of her life. She wanted to live in the moment. Savour each kiss, each caress, each heartbeat.

His tongue, tasting of red wine and hope, slid past hers. His muscles slackened and then tensed under her hands, which for the first time had the freedom to roam where they wanted to over Ed. She slid one hand over his shoulders, around the soft nape of his neck into his thick hair.

It was something she'd only dreamt of. The feel of his skin. The taste of his mouth. She'd rehearsed it in her head so often as a teenager, but the sensations coasting through her body still caught her off guard. There was no way she could have prepared herself for the way her muscles shivered when he slid his hand down her back, rested it on her bottom and pulled her firmly against him.

When the desire pooling inside her was about to overflow, the voice of reason became louder and she pulled her mouth back from his. She caught her breath and saw he was doing the same.

His face was flushed and his breath shallow, and it took every last ounce of her sanity to ask, 'What's going on?'

CHAPTER EIGHT

SHE EXHALED WITH a half-sigh, half-groan, and Ed trembled as he answered.

'I don't know. Maybe we could make it up as we go along.'

His lips travelled past her ear, down her neck to the low neckline of her dress and she wobbled on her stilettos. He held her tight and steadied her. He checked that she was all right, then he closed his eyes and kissed her again.

'Is that okay?' he murmured into her neck.

There was no roadmap where he was going. This was uncharted territory. Off-road into the unknown.

But what if he got hopelessly lost?

You're already lost. You may as well see where this leads.

This was a far better way to be spending his time than fretting about his future. Simone's kisses were sweet and soft, and after trying just one he was completely, hopelessly addicted.

That's probably why you never kissed her before. You knew it would be impossible to stop.

'Are you sure this is a good idea?' she asked.

He couldn't remember being more certain of anything. Kissing her. Wanting her. It was like gravity. The sun, the moon and the tides.

There were probably good reasons why they shouldn't be doing this, but with Simone in his arms they paled into insignificance.

'For starters we're friends,' she said.

That was the very reason he wanted to kiss her and slip this dress off her gorgeous body. To feel every inch of her. Because she was Simone. His oldest friend. His beautiful, amazing friend.

He guessed that must be what she meant. Friends sometimes didn't want to sleep together because they were afraid it would ruin their friendship. The thought hadn't occurred to him. This would only deepen their relationship. Make it even more special.

'Our friendship won't change. It's too old for that and too strong.'

He layered kisses along her low neckline, nudging the fabric down even further as he went. Maybe she did have a point. If he lowered his mouth much further maybe everything would change between them. The taste of her skin and the warmth of her pressed against him caused another thought. Their relationship might change, but only for the better. He'd never felt so close to her. That had to be a good thing, didn't it?

He'd never slept with his best friend before. He'd never slept with a friend before. So how did he really know?

You know that Simone will always be in your life. You know that losing her isn't an option.

He felt her body lean into him, her desire matching his, letting him know she agreed. The skin of her hand was unspeakably soft. He had to keep going back over it with his fingertip to see if it really was as beautiful as if felt. Soft and warm. Alive.

'But not here,' she said, thankfully being sensible enough for both of them.

It was dangerous enough for him to be out and about, let alone losing himself like this in public.

He wanted her. All of her. And it was threatening to overwhelm everything else.

He grabbed her hand and pulled her in the direction of her apartment. They walked fast, but each time they had to stop to cross a road they would kiss again, and inevitably fall back into the kisses. He wanted to get back to the apartment, but he was enjoying the lingering and anticipation nearly as much.

They stopped to kiss on every street. They stopped to kiss in front of the bookshop. On the stairs, on the landing. And finally they were inside her apartment, jackets being pulled off and shoes kicked away.

He trailed kisses along her collarbone and felt her shiver.

Then a buzzing startled them both, and Simone's limbs froze beneath his hands.

'Is that your phone?'

Leave it, he was about to say. But he knew it was hopeless. He couldn't give his whole self to her while he wondered what the call was about. Who it was.

'Check it. You have to check it.' Simone untangled herself from him.

He wasn't sure if his decision to leave his phone behind had been accidental or deliberate, but it had been serendipitous. Because there were many missed calls.

Calls that would have disrupted his evening with Simone.

Calls that he needed to return.

'My father,' he said.

'Should I leave you?'

'No. Stay. Please.'

Ed didn't bother listening to the messages. He wanted the news straight from his father. He sat on the couch and motioned for Simone to sit next to him.

He dialled his father and placed the phone on speaker. Simone's eyes widened, but he simply picked up her hand and squeezed it.

'Ed. You took your time.'

'Sorry, Father. I was caught up.' Ed squeezed Simone's hand again and she squeezed back.

'I've made a decision. It is mine alone to make. I've abdicated the throne. I signed the papers just over an hour ago.'

'You're abdicating?' The words felt strange on his tongue.

'I have already—Your Majesty.'

It sounded like a joke. A cruel, cruel joke. Made all the worse by the timing. He could hardly bear to look at Simone, sitting next to him. She rested her head on his shoulder.

'There should be a car arriving for you shortly. It will take you straight to the airport. We can talk more when you get here. I'm about to speak to the press.'

Ed couldn't answer—not even to argue. He knew, as well as his father did, that there was no point. It was done.

His father ended the call.

Don't make any decisions without me.

Ed wanted to throw up. He was now the King of Florena. King Edouard the Fourth of Florena.

He focused on his breathing, hoping the news would start to sink in if he did.

Another day, another night, and they might have a chance to figure out what was happening between them.

'That's all? It's done?'

Simone was as shocked as he was at the swiftness of the King's actions. At the brevity of the phone call.

Ed laughed. 'He didn't even ask how I was.'

'You're not even there. He didn't wait for you to get back.'

'That's been the point all along.' He could taste the bitterness in his voice. 'That's why I had to stay—so that I wouldn't be standing next to him now. So that I wouldn't talk him out of it. So that I wouldn't have a choice.'

She nodded. 'He should have talked to you. Should've involved you.'

'But that would have been too hard for him. Over these past few days my father's hardly proved himself to be a man of courage or honour.'

Simone stood to get them both a drink. She pulled a dusty bottle of Scotch down from her top cupboard and poured them both generous glasses. Then she turned on the small television and they waited. The tickertape announced that the King of Florena would be giving a live address at any moment.

Ed wondered how long they had before the knock at the door came and he was taken away.

The screen changed to a shot of the palace of Villeneuve and then to the King.

Except he's not the King any more. You are.

His father looked tired as he sat behind a desk and looked down the camera.

'Thank you all for joining me this evening. It has become apparent over the past few days that I am not the best person to be serving this country. I have allowed my personal life to distract me from my duties and I have not been the King you deserve or the man I want to be.'

The Scotch burnt Ed's throat on the way down, but he still took another large sip.

'The most appropriate person to be serving our beautiful country is my son, Edouard, who as of one hour ago became your sovereign. Edouard is devoted to this country, and I know he will dedicate his entire life to your service.'

'He was talking about you like you aren't a real person,' Simone whispered, once the King had finished.

'But from now on I'm not. Not really. I'm the sovereign. The head of state. The embodiment of Florena.'

He had to go back to Florena and save his country.

Simone clenched her fists and paced the room. It only took four steps in each direction, so she was pretty much going in circles.

How would he get through the next few days without her? How would he get through the nights? Less than half an hour ago they'd been undressing one another. Now…? Now he was lost.

'Come with me.'

If he couldn't stay, she could come.

She shook her head and kept shaking it. As if she was convincing herself it was the right decision.

He knew what she should do. 'You could come with me—please.'

'I can't leave the bookshop.'

'I'll pay for someone to look after the bookshop. Please.'

'Oh, no, no, no. That's not how things are going to work.'

'What do you mean?'

'I mean… I just can't.'

'Is it about the money?'

'It's the whole damn thing! Ed, this is happening so fast.'

She didn't need to tell *him* that. He'd been the monarch for ninety minutes and hadn't even known for most of that time.

He needed her. Couldn't imagine going back to Florena and getting through the next period without her. He didn't want to return without her by his side.

The realisation was almost as overwhelming as the news his father had just delivered.

He wanted Simone.

He needed her. As he needed air.

What had happened between them on the bridge hadn't been an aberration.

'Come with me. Please.'

He stood and went to her, grasping her shoulders with his hands and stopping her pacing.

She looked up at him, but her expression was pained. 'Ed… What would I be?'

'What do you mean?'

'You know what I mean. If I came with you, what would I be?'

Ah, right…

Why couldn't they just be Simone and Ed? Best friends? Surely not everything had to change at once.

'You would be my friend.'

She grimaced. 'And I'd just sit in the palace all day as your *friend*?'

Would that be so bad? She was his best friend, and now they were exploring whether she might be something more.

She looked at him, as if waiting for him to catch up. Would she be his *girlfriend*? Did kings even *have* girlfriends? He knew the answer to that. Kings had wives. And they had mistresses. And Simone would be neither his wife nor his mistress.

Bringing a new, unsteady relationship into the mix at this point would make things in Florena go from bad to worse. There was no room for exploring their new relationship now he was the new king. There was no room for missteps, break-ups, gossip or rumours. There was no room for them to see how this new side of their relationship developed naturally. Privately.

She was ten steps ahead of him. She'd already seen the problems that he wanted to ignore.

'The absolute last thing you need is gossip and speculation about your personal life,' she told him.

'I see what you mean. It's complicated.'

But how was he going to get through this without her?

Simone couldn't be more than his best friend because he didn't believe in love. And throwing a nascent relationship into the mess that was the current saga of the Florenan royal family...

He couldn't do that to her. And he couldn't do it to his people. *His people.*

'Ed, I want to be with you. Please know that. You are one of the most important people in the world to me. And I want to help you. But do you really think me going with you...as things are now...is that the best thing for Florena? For you?'

He picked up her hand and turned it over in his, steadying his breath and his thoughts. Her skin was soft. Her nails short and clean. He wanted to know these hands as well as he knew his own.

Damn, why could he taste salt in the back of his nose?

Because you're going to miss her. Because standing up and walking out of this room is going to be the hardest thing you've done in your life.

He looked at her and almost broke—but didn't. He wasn't being fair on Simone. It wouldn't be fair to drag her into the circus of which he was now the ringmaster.

This is what you always knew, isn't it?

It wouldn't be fair to subject a woman to the scrutiny of the

Florenan royal family. He couldn't do it to anyone he really cared about. Least of all Simone.

He choked out a rueful laugh. It was either that or cry.

'Is there nothing I can say to make you come with me?' he asked, though he already knew the answer.

'You know as well as I do that having me there will just make it worse for you. And my life is here. I can't just abandon it for a few months.'

'A few months?'

'Well, yes… Until you find your feet. Until…'

She didn't need to finish the sentence. *Until we break up.*

Because he didn't believe in love. Or marriage.

He looked back down at her hands, still wrapped around his. Keeping him anchored. He was afraid to let them go. Afraid that when he did she would float away from him.

There was nothing else to do but say goodbye.

He cupped her chin in his palm and tilted her mouth towards his. He opened his mouth and pulled her in, making sure that every taste, every shiver, every sigh was marked indelibly onto his memory. But as he did so he felt his eyes fill with water.

He pulled back and saw his own tears glistening on her cheeks. He brushed one away with the back of his thumb. She jumped back as though she'd been scolded.

'Goodbye,' she squeaked, before pulling away and moving to the door. 'Good luck.'

She grabbed her coat and closed the door behind her before he could catch his breath to reply.

CHAPTER NINE

THE ENGRAVED INVITATION arrived for her just before Christmas.

The presence of
Simone Auclair
is requested
at the coronation of
King Edouard the Fourth of Florena
on 31st January at 11 a.m.
Dress: full morning dress.
The coronation will be followed by
a state dinner and ball.
Further instructions will be provided upon your acceptance
of this invitation.

With the invitation, or summons—she wasn't sure which—was a handwritten note.

Dearest Sim,
I know it might be hard for you to come back to Florena,
but I can't imagine getting through this day without my
best friend.
All my love, Ed.

She turned the card over and slipped it under a book on her desk. Go back to Florena? Not just for a quick flying visit to her mother but to go to the coronation? And a ball? To be seen and photographed?

You don't have to go.

It was true. No one would tie her up and force her to attend. And once the coronation was over she would be free to leave.

She didn't have a choice. Not really.

I can't imagine getting through this day without my best friend.

My best friend. After everything, he was still her best friend, and this was probably the most important day of his life. As hard as it would be for her, it would be unforgivable not to be there for him.

To go as his friend.

He'd said that on that wonderful and horrible evening two months ago, before he'd been whisked away to assume his duties. He might as well have asked her to go as his sister.

'Friend' was something, though. It wasn't nothing.

But even after their kisses he was still thinking of her as just his friend.

That time on the bridge had nearly ripped her in two. There was no doubt in her mind that if the phone call from his father had come later they would have made love and their relationship would have changed for ever.

She sighed. It didn't matter what either of them had thought or felt on the bridge that night.

She couldn't have gone to Florena as anything *but* his friend. Now that he was King there was really no possibility of them being together. Friendship would be all they were allowed to have. No matter how much their bodies might wish otherwise. Ed knew that. Her heart just had to realise too.

To be fair to Ed, he hadn't meant to hurt her or insult her by asking her to go to Florena as his friend. He really did want his friend there by his side. And she wanted to be there for him too—as his friend, apart from anything else.

She ached when she thought of him in Florena on his own, facing his new life. Alone.

Once it's over you will leave.

CHAPTER TEN

SIMONE HADN'T BEEN back to Florena for over two years. Her mother always joined her in Paris for a week over Christmas, so Simone did not have to leave the bookshop. It had been a decade since Simone had called the kingdom home, and now she could see the country as any visitor might.

The palace sat on a high peak, keeping watch over the city and the great valley of Florena. In summer the valley was green and lush. Now, in midwinter, the slopes were covered in their famous powdery snow.

The small country was picturesque.

Her heart began to soar when she saw it, but she caught it and pushed it back down again. Florena might look as if it had been ripped from the pages of a fairy tale, but she knew better. She knew that looks were deceiving and fairy tales were most definitely not real.

The apartment where Simone had grown up was two storeys above the palace kitchen. The building was nearly as old as the main palace, but in the last century the upper levels had been converted into comfortable and spacious apartments for the senior staff.

Their living room overlooked the ancient cobblestoned courtyard that palace staff criss-crossed all day, going about their lives much as they had for centuries. Doing laundry, gardening and cooking. Simone's old bedroom had a view of one of the palace's private walled gardens. The manicured grass where Ed and Simone had once played with Suzette was now covered in snow.

She was privileged to have grown up there and to be able to return when she wanted to visit Alea, who had now been given the security of a lifetime tenancy in her apartment—one of the last things the former King had done before abdicating.

The old King Edouard might have deeply hurt his son in the way he'd abandoned the crown without consultation, but Simone could not help being grateful for the way he'd thought about his loyal staff at the end—especially with everything else on his mind.

Simone understood that the King—that was the former King, now styled as the Duke of Armiel—was living in southern France with Celine, awaiting the birth of their daughter in the coming May.

The Queen, who still held that title, had only returned to Florena briefly and quietly, and was now dividing her time between the Caribbean and New York. She had agreed to a divorce, but the negotiations over property were fraught. Simone understood from her mother and from general rumour that the Queen would keep half her fortune, leaving the remaining half with Ed. Ed had some money his maternal grandfather had left directly to him, but the Queen's fortune was so large that even half of it still left both of them on most rich lists. The new Duke of Armiel would have to rely on his own funds, which were believed to be small, along with generosity from Ed.

Ed… She sighed.

He had been in touch since he'd left Paris, with occasional messages and phone calls that were memorable for all the wrong reasons. There'd been either long pauses or they'd spoken over one another. Even their messages had been polite and perfunctory. Neither of them had dared to mention that night in Paris.

The morning after her arrival back in the palace, Simone sat looking out of the window at the activity in the courtyard with a cup of hot coffee warming her hands.

'What are you doing today?' her mother asked as she ate her breakfast.

'Relaxing here, I think.'

'Do you have plans to see Ed?'

Simone shook her head. Ed knew Simone had accepted her invitation to the coronation, but she hadn't told him exactly when she would arrive. He'd be busy with preparations and with being King. He wouldn't have time for her.

'I think he'd like to see you. He'd appreciate seeing a friendly face.'

Simone wanted to pump her mother for further information, but didn't want to risk giving anything away. She wasn't even mentally prepared to answer questions about Ed, let alone to see him.

They'd kissed. Made out as they'd wound their way across Paris like teenagers or tourists. And if that phone call hadn't come from Ed's father they would, she was ninety-nine per cent sure, have ended up in bed. Any reservations she might have had had been shattered as he'd held her and she'd felt how much he'd wanted her too.

'Never mind,' her mother said. 'Do you have an outfit for the coronation?'

Simone nodded. 'An advantage of living in Paris.'

She'd spent some of her precious savings on it, but she was determined to look amazing.

'And for the ball?'

'I don't think I'll go.'

'What? You must come. All the long-standing staff have been invited.'

Simone winced. She knew she couldn't miss the coronation…but the ball? It was a social event and she would feel completely out of place. Besides, her mother's comment confirmed what Simone had expected. All the long-term staff of the palace were invited. Simone's invitation was by virtue of her mother's position only.

'So I take it you don't have a dress?'

'No. So, you see, I can't go.' She shrugged.

'Not so fast, *mademoiselle*. I may have something… It might need taking in, but we're a similar size.'

Alea disappeared into her room and returned with a large white box. She lifted the lid and Simone gasped. The box was overflowing with raw silver silk. Her mother lifted miles of fabric out of the box, revealing a bodice with a sweetheart neckline. The bodice was embroidered with intricate flowers and swirls.

It was a work of art.

'When did you get this?'

Simone had thought she was aware of most of the formal wear in her mother's wardrobe, and was sure she would not have missed something like this.

'Oh, I'm not sure.' Alea waved the question away. 'Try it on.'

Even without make-up or her hair done, Simone was transformed. She wouldn't be inconspicuous if she wore this dress. Her plan for her stay in Florena was to fly under the radar. She wanted to avoid press attention at all costs.

'It's a statement piece,' her mother said.

'But what sort of statement would I be making?' Simone mumbled, mostly to herself.

'It says that you belong. It says you are regal.'

'But I'm not regal—and I don't think I should pretend I am.' She had no intention of pretending to be royal.

'Regal is a state of mind,' Alea said.

'I'm not sure I can back up whatever this dress is saying.'

'Why not?'

Simone shook her head. Any answer would only invite more questions.

Since arriving back in her childhood home, she had been struggling to supress her sixteen-year-old self. The naïve, uncertain parts of herself. In Paris she was confident, worldly and strong. Back here she was constantly expecting someone to remember her as the girl who had tried to serenade the Prince.

Paris, she realised, was also a state of mind. She needed to channel some of her inner Parisienne to make it through the next week.

'But you'll wear it?' her mother asked.

Simone nodded only to placate her. She would decide later if she really could subject herself to the scrutiny of a public ball.

'Great.'

Her mother kissed her and left for work, leaving Simone standing in the dress in front of the mirror. She swayed her hips and watched the fabric swirl around her legs.

Make-believe.

It wasn't real.

Just as what had happened between her and Ed wasn't real.

Oh, it had happened. She hadn't dreamt it. They had really kissed and spent an amazing evening wandering the streets of Paris together.

But her feelings were pointless, hopefully temporary, and maddening. She'd fallen for Ed once—a childhood crush, certainly, but still devastating in the way only first love could be. She wasn't going to make the mistake of falling in love with him as an adult. She'd worked too hard to overcome her heartache the first time.

And Ed's feelings for her…? They were fleeting at best. Most likely already non-existent. She'd caught Ed at a vulnerable moment. He'd been under stress because of his family problems. Trapped in her apartment. In the ordinary course of things he would never have kissed her. Much less said he wanted to sleep with her. Simone *knew* that.

Fairy tales were not real.

What *was* real were internet trolls, threats on social media and online harassment. She'd already had a taste of that, thank you very much. Now that Ed was the King, the scrutiny on anyone he dated would be intense. She wasn't up for that, emotionally or psychologically. It was part of the package Ed came with, so she needed to keep a firm lid on any feelings that threatened to rise up in her again. Like they had when she was a teenager.

So she wasn't about to drop in on him today or any other day she was here. She wasn't going to bombard him with messages that would only distract him from his duties. Or, worse, make him feel that he had to come down here and explain to her that what had happened between them in Paris had been a mistake.

Two days after the coronation she'd leave. The next time she returned to Florena would be next Christmas, and by that point the time she and Ed had spent together in Paris would be a vague memory. Something that had happened in the crazy time before the old King's abdication.

André had offered to run the bookshop while she was away and she had gratefully accepted. In the meantime, she would stay in her mother's apartment and catch up on some screen time. Watch some movies by the fire. She might help her mother out in the kitchen, but she was unlikely to cross Ed's path.

She probably wouldn't even see him. He was the King now. He'd be too busy to see her, much less anything else.

She unzipped the dress, climbed out of it, and went for a shower.

Ed hadn't thought it would be easy leaving Simone in Paris, but he hadn't expected it to be as hard as it had been. He'd walked away from women before, and even though Simone was different from the others he hadn't expected this.

Constantly looking around for her.

Starting to speak to her.

Reaching for her and always finding she wasn't there.

He hadn't expected to go to bed hoping to dream about her.

He hadn't expected to feel so devastated each time he woke to find she wasn't next to him. That he had to face another long day alone.

The past few months had been the most stressful in his life. The abdication, defending the country against pressure from Laurent and now preparing for the coronation... It had been enough to push even the most resilient person to the brink.

Was it any wonder his feelings for Simone were so confusing? She was his oldest friend, and now a woman he'd kissed and been minutes away from sleeping with. That didn't have to mean anything, did it? The dreams? Talking to her when she wasn't there? The longing that rippled through his body when he thought of her? That was all just because of the stress, wasn't it?

The one thing he knew for certain was that she was back in Florena today.

Last night, to be precise. Alea had told him she would arrive late. He'd figured she needed some time with her mother, but it was now the morning and Alea would have left for work. He couldn't wait another moment.

He'd wanted to call Simone every day, and each time had had to stop himself. Partly because hearing her voice wasn't the balm he'd hoped it would be. Only a further reminder of what was missing from his life. And also because what if she got the wrong idea and thought that his intentions towards her were more than they could be?

Because they couldn't be together. She lived in Paris, had a life there—a life she was rightly proud of—and he couldn't ask her to give that up. Besides, since his father's abdication, the very future of his country depended upon Ed staying out of the tabloids.

A relationship wasn't in itself a problem…but a break-up? A scandal? That would be just the sort of thing that would send his people to the polls and end the independence of his country.

That was not going to happen while Ed was King. He'd devoted his whole life to this country and he wasn't about to see it swallowed up to fulfil the political ambitions of Pierre Laurent. His role might be largely ceremonial, but that wasn't nothing. His job description stretched from diplomat to charity worker and many things in between. The monarchy gave Florenans pride in their country and in their history. It gave them stability.

It was a lot to put on one person's shoulders. Which was probably why sometimes—after the dreams, after he spoke to her when she wasn't there—he forgot all the reasons why they couldn't be together. Because he wanted her. It was self-ish, but he needed her.

She should be here with him. She belonged here. She should be with him. Should share his bed and share his life.

Then he'd remember.

Duty. Fidelity. The future of Florena. The fact that no King Edouard had ever managed to stay faithful to his wife. The fact that one more scandal might spell the end of the entire country.

Ed drew a deep breath and knocked on Simone's apartment door.

Duty. Fidelity. Florena.

Simone threw open the door and said, 'Did you forget your key—? Ooh!'

Ed forgot all those things. At that moment he wasn't even capable of remembering his own name. Simone was wearing only a white towel, her skin still bright and glistening from a recent shower, her hair tied messily on her head.

Ooh! indeed.

He wanted to reply with a witty retort, but he'd forgotten every word he'd ever known.

'Ed, I'm sorry. I thought you were my mother.'

Ed. She'd called him by his shortened name. His nickname. She was the first person in three months not to call him 'Your Majesty' and he wanted to kiss her for it.

He wanted to kiss her for many reasons.

When he still couldn't respond, she said, 'You'd better come in, just in case anyone comes past.'

He followed her inside and as she reached behind him to close the door he caught her scent. Flowers. Summer.

'I'll just get dressed,' she said.

'No,' he said.

The first word out of his mouth since he'd walked in and his voice felt strange.

She gave him a questioning look.

'It's good to see you, Simone.'

He stepped towards her and leant down to kiss her cheek,

breathing her in. The scent of her bodywash mixed with the steam from the shower and swirled around him. His knees weakened.

He felt a sweet sigh escape Simone's mouth—and that was the end of him. He pulled her into his arms, wet towel and all, and kissed her lips. Properly. Without hesitation or restraint. Picking up exactly where they had left off before the phone call telling him about the abdication had come.

She melted into the kiss. Paris came back to him in flashbacks: her smiles, her soft skin, their bodies pressed against one another's. His body remembered hers as if it had been yesterday. And hadn't it? Hadn't everything else in the world stopped when she hadn't been around?

'Ed!' she gasped as she pulled away. 'Is this…? Should…?'

'You're having trouble with your words too,' he said.

Her brow furrowed.

'Your mother's downstairs.'

'My mother's the least of our worries.'

'I'm not worried.'

And he wasn't. They were in private, and he trusted Simone with his life. For once his feelings were completely certain. He wanted her. As soon as possible.

'I am!'

He reluctantly let her go. As he stepped back her towel dropped, exposing a beautiful bare breast and a very erect pink nipple. He grinned, and Simone pulled the towel to her. Muscles inside him that had been inert for the past few months suddenly woke up.

'They don't deserve to be covered up,' he said.

Her flushed face turned ever redder. 'I'm only here for a week,' she said.

'Do you mean, *I'm only here for a week so I shouldn't let that towel drop*? or do you mean, *I'm only here for a week so I may as well let the towel drop*?'

His throat went stone-dry as he waited for her answer. Just

when he thought he might crack, the shadow of a grin appeared across her beautiful face.

'Maybe the latter?'

'Maybe?'

He stepped towards her. Ready to pull the towel away. Ready to rip his own shirt off his back as soon as she told him she was sure.

'What if someone finds out?' she said.

'I'm not cheating on anyone. We're two single consenting adults. We're not doing anything wrong.'

'I don't want to do anything that will jeopardise your job… the country.'

'It's unlikely anyone will ever find out. No one knows about Paris.'

He reached out and rubbed the back of his thumb over her bare shoulder. There was no one in the world he trusted more.

'Is that all you're worried about or is there something else? Say the word and I'll walk away now.'

She swallowed hard.

'Okay. I won't walk away. I'll leave the room while you get changed, and then I'll ask you to come and have a coffee with me and a walk around the garden. Which was, by the way, my original plan. You greeting me warm from the shower and wearing only a towel that doesn't seem to be able to stay up was a happy accident, but not part of my plan.'

She laughed, and he knew it would all be okay. Whatever happened.

In a rush she moved towards him and lifted herself to his lips. The surge of relief and emotion that ripped through him made him groan. Simone was in his arms. Warm, soft, wet. Smelling like soap and heaven. Tasting like coffee and home. Their lips pressed together. Their muscle memory from Paris knew exactly how to angle their heads to mesh their mouths perfectly.

She slipped her arms around his neck and pushed her fingers through his hair. His knees almost gave way. This woman was magnificent. Her sighs asked him for more and he was only too happy to give it. It was more wonderful and more satisfying than anything he'd felt since the last time he'd held her in his arms.

The towel dropped away again, this time to the floor. Simone was utterly naked, utterly gorgeous, and utterly in his arms. Suddenly his own clothing was too hot and way too tight. He shrugged off his jacket and it landed with her towel. Simone's pretty fingers dug his shirt out of his waistband and the sensation of her fingertips stroking his stomach made every muscle south of his waist tighten. She kissed him passionately as she undid his shirt buttons, one by one. He wanted to help, but his fingers were currently busy trailing their way down the smooth skin of her back to her perfect bottom.

It was a dilemma. Every second he spent undressing himself was a second he couldn't hold Simone, and he was quite sure he never wanted to let her go.

She tugged his shirt away from his body and threw it to the floor with a force that suggested she was as pleased as he was to see it gone.

Skin on skin was magical. The feeling of her bare body against his brought every sensation in his body to the surface.

'You have no idea how much I've missed you,' he murmured against her neck.

'I have some idea.'

'I've thought of you every hour… I've missed you every minute…'

Simone pulled back and looked at him. Her expression was dumbstruck. Her eyes were open wide and her jaw slack. He'd said too much and was in danger of saying even more. He didn't know how he felt about Simone. His feelings were confusing. Overwhelming. He didn't know how to describe them to himself, let alone how to explain them to her.

Except to say that he'd missed her so much that it had ached. A physical pain in his body that wasn't relieved by exercise or work, sleep or alcohol.

Her mouth found his, again and again. All his words left him. There was only Simone and skin and warmth and this room.

Coronation? What coronation?

Constitutional crisis? What constitutional crisis?

Her fingers were at his waistband again, expertly undoing his belt and his trousers.

Manoeuvring his trousers at this stage of his arousal needed a gentle touch, and when her fingers touched him he reached down and held her hand.

He'd been waiting so long he knew that if she touched him there he might just come apart.

'Is everything all right?' she asked.

'Everything's wonderful.'

He wriggled his way out of his underpants and then pulled her back to him. For a brief second he thought about slowing down and taking their time. This was the first time they'd made love. They should be savouring, lingering… But maybe she felt, like him, that they were already making up for lost time. This hadn't been five minutes in the making. It had been three months. Their lives had been on pause since their last kiss.

Things were building inside him…sweet and, oh, so strong.

He felt himself being nudged in the direction of her bedroom, but her mouth didn't leave his. They were having a new type of conversation with their lips. No less meaningful than any they had had with actual words in the past.

I want you. I need you. Don't stop. Yes. There. Please.

She kicked the bedroom door closed with a satisfying bang and they tumbled onto her bed. His lips sought out her breasts and took a hard nipple into his mouth. She moaned, and he could feel her sighing. She was barely holding herself together, just like him. His tongue and her nipples were a magical, combustible combination.

Her hips bucked beneath him and the sheets bunched in her hands. She was as ready as he was, and it made him feel more powerful than any title they might bestow upon him.

'Ed... Ed, for the sake of your kingdom, please tell me you've got protection.'

Her question momentarily snapped him back to reality. The royal family already had one unexpected child on the way—they did not need another.

'Yes,' he panted, and dragged his body away from hers. 'Wallet.'

He hadn't come to see her with the intention of seducing her, but a part of him clearly hadn't ruled it out entirely.

Simone sat up on her bed with her blonde hair tousled around her flushed face. She grinned at him, temporarily halting his mission. He knelt back on the bed and kissed her again. He couldn't get enough.

A low murmur escaped her lips and she pushed him away. 'Have you forgotten what you were doing?' she asked.

He climbed off the bed and opened the door, hearing Simone whistle as she watched him from behind. With relief he saw that the living room was still unoccupied. He grabbed his trousers and went back to the bedroom. He found his wallet and the protection it contained. Ripped the packet as he rushed back to her.

She took his hand and the packet. 'Let me...' she murmured.

He had to bite back a moan as he watched her delicate fingers sheath him, trying his hardest not to come apart in her hands.

'I want you...' She nuzzled his neck.

'I want you.'

All of you. Always.

But he didn't say that to her. He barely acknowledged the thought to himself. It was too big, too much, considering the task that now lay before him. Not falling apart before she did. Not making a right royal mess of their first time together.

He must have paused too long with the thought, because Simone tugged at him, took his face in her hands and looked him straight in the eye. Then she adjusted herself, guiding him into her.

Her eyes half-closed, mouth half-open, she surrendered herself completely to him. There was a thin sheen of perspiration on her forehead. Her lips were swollen as he brought her to the brink.

Once they were as one, he didn't want it to end. This was his true destiny.

The rest of the world stopped and it was just them. Nothing else mattered. Not duty. Time. Nothing but Simone. They wound each other so perfectly tight and reached a perfect peak before they both found release. They held each other as they tumbled, fell, and came completely undone.

CHAPTER ELEVEN

IT WAS AS if she'd just woken up from an erotic dream. Disorientated, breathless, hot. And very confused.

Because this wasn't a dream.

It was a very real encounter.

Ed was next to her, also catching his breath, warm and trembling.

She rested her head against his chest and he pulled her against him, each anchoring the other as the waves of pleasure continued to wash through them.

She brought her breath in time with his and enjoyed the feeling of his firm chest against her cheek.

You've just made love with the King, a little voice whispered in her head.

But she dismissed it easily. He might be the King, but he was still just Ed too.

You've just made love with Ed.

She was incapable of moving even an inch because of the happy chemicals still thumping through her body.

And the shock.

And Ed's arm, flung across her, trapping her where she'd fallen.

His breathing was heavy, his face sweaty. His head tipped back and he looked up at the ceiling as he groaned.

'Oh, Sim. I can't believe we've only just realised we could do that.'

She was in real trouble.

Over the years Simone had often sought solace in the thought that maybe Ed wasn't very good in bed. That maybe they weren't physically compatible. It hadn't been a silly thought. They were relaxed in one another's company, and ease in public didn't always translate into heat in the bedroom. It might just as easily lead to something very bland. Maybe Ed, under his suits and underwear, was really not that much…

How wrong she had been.

Not only was Ed really all that and more under his clothes, he had also been at constant pains to please her. She shouldn't be surprised. He was her kind and caring friend. But, strangely, she had expected him to be more selfish in bed than he was. And Ed had most definitely been generous. Over and over again.

Her heart was in more danger than ever.

Ed isn't going to marry, and you aren't going to marry a prince.

No one, least of all Ed, was talking about marriage. This was just a one-off. Completing what they had started in Paris. That was all. A fling.

Can you really have an emotion-free fling with Ed?

She was about to find out.

'You know what I said in Paris?' he murmured.

He'd said so many things in Paris, but she knew what he meant.

'Do you think we've just ruined our friendship?'

'No, I don't feel differently about you,' she said honestly.

So many things had changed between them in the past few months. She cared for him as much as ever, but her emotions were closer to the surface, instead of being safely locked away.

He made a face. 'Really? Then I needed to try harder. Can I have another go?'

She laughed, but he didn't. His face was still calm and serious.

'Do you…feel differently about me?' she asked.

'I've felt differently since Paris,' he replied.

Her stomach swooped. 'What do you mean?'

She was afraid she wouldn't hear his answer over the roar of blood rushing past her ears.

'We haven't seen much of one another over the years.' His gaze fell on her bare shoulder and on his thumb, stroking it. 'I forgot…or rather…maybe I'm seeing you for the first time.'

She couldn't speak. They were words she'd dreamt of him saying. Ever since she was sixteen and had stood up in front of a room of people to sing to him. To tell him she loved him without saying the words.

'And for you? Was this too much of a surprise?' he asked.

'Definitely a surprise.' *You have no idea.* 'But a good one,' she added quickly.

A surprise. In the same way that winning the lottery was a surprise. Something you dreamt of, but never expected to actually happen.

'I'm glad to hear it.'

Ed tipped his head towards her and pressed his lips to hers. Pleasure slid down her spine. Not just because it felt wonderful, but because of the ease with which he did it. As if it was the most natural thing in the world to be kissing one another. Lying here, with him, placing languid kisses on one another was like a dream. Literally. She'd had this dream several, sweaty, discombobulating times in the past few months.

'What's it like?' she asked.

'Being with you? Wonderful.'

She swatted him gently.

'I meant being the King.'

'Oh, that. Not nearly as fun as what we just did.'

She smiled against his chest. For a moment he was hers. Just hers.

'I'm serious, though. Now I'm here you can tell me. How's it been? Really?'

'Busy. Stressful. Lonely.'

She tightened her embrace around him. For this moment at

least he wouldn't be lonely. At this moment everything was as it should be.

They lay like that for a while. Talking, laughing, touching one another. The distant sound of a trumpet playing somewhere in the palace reminded her.

'Don't you have a kingdom to run?' she asked.

'Do I? I'd forgotten.'

His joking was sweet, and for a few precious moments she felt like the most important thing in the world to him.

But they both knew it couldn't last.

'You can't forget,' she said.

'I know, but it would be nice, wouldn't it?'

She propped herself up and looked at him. 'Yes, but it's just a fantasy. We both know it's fun to think about from time to time, but you have your life and I have mine.'

Ed's eyes darkened as he held her gaze. 'How long are you here for?'

'A week. I leave two days after your coronation.'

He grimaced, as if she'd reminded him of an execution and not of what should be one of the proudest days of his life.

'I'd like to see you again,' he said.

Again. The word shocked her back to the present and the reality they had forgotten for the past few hours.

Simone spun her legs off the edge of the bed and grabbed the nearest piece of clothing—her pyjama top, discarded hours earlier—and pulled it to her. The happy hormones had worn off and she'd hit the cold wall of reality with a thud.

She tugged the top over her head.

It was all very well to let herself get swept away with Ed and how wonderful it felt being with him, but they had to return to the real world. The one where he was the King of a country in crisis and she had built her own life and her own business in Paris.

Ed sat up. His gorgeous bare torso taunted her from her messed-up bed. Begging her to slide her hands over it and feel its hard magnificence.

'What's the matter?' he asked.

'It can't happen again.'

She searched her bedroom floor for some other clothes. Something to cover her bottom half. Suddenly she was feeling too naked. It was all very well to walk around the apartment naked when they were in the throes of passion, but now that they had to redraw the lines of their relationship she was feeling too exposed.

Protecting her heart was now her first priority.

'As wonderful as this was, you know we can't do this again.'

For a heartbeat, part of her hoped he'd argue with her, but he didn't.

'Can we see each other as friends?'

'I don't know.'

It was an honest answer. She didn't know how she could possibly sit across a table from him or on a sofa and talk to him while not thinking about what they had just done. She could still feel his mouth on her most sensitive parts. Her mind was still full of the memory of him moving so strongly and beautifully inside her. Her muscles were still trembling.

The answer on her lips was, *No. We can't. Because if we do I won't be able to push these feelings back down again. You are so close to breaking me completely.*

It hurt to even think it.

'Simone, I'm not just going to walk out of here without a plan to see you again. I don't want us to do the awkward silence thing again. The last few months…not knowing if I should call you or not…have been awful.'

She put her face in her hands so she wouldn't have to look him in the eyes and see the pain written across them.

Could they be friends?

Can you imagine not being friends with Ed?

And that was it, wasn't it? She couldn't really conceive of a future that he wasn't part of in some way.

'Tonight?' she said.

'Tonight I have an official government dinner.'

And there it was. It wasn't his fault, but his duty would always come first. As it should. She hung her head.

'Tomorrow, though. I can cancel my plans tomorrow night.'

She shook her head. 'Ed, this is hard enough as it is. We both know this is impossible. *We're* impossible. I don't think we should make things any harder than they already are.'

'I have a few hours tomorrow afternoon, I think.'

She laughed. 'Ed, face it. Your life isn't yours any more. I don't want to make things harder for you.'

Or for me.

'You don't even want to spend time with me?' he asked.

It was so hard to explain that she did want to be with him, but she also didn't. It sounded foolish, but there it was. She was torn in two.

'Of course I want to spend time with you. But things just got complicated, didn't they?'

She looked down. She was wearing only her pyjama top and her panties from yesterday. She couldn't even dress herself, she was in such a state.

'You said nothing had changed,' he said.

'What?'

'A moment ago, you said your feelings hadn't changed.'

A moment ago her body had still been flooded with endorphins. Now reality had broken through.

'I spoke too quickly. Besides, it doesn't matter how I feel. The world has changed. The situation is different. You're the King.'

'I'm still me.'

His voice was small. Not at all regal. And it broke her heart.

How could she reconcile this monarch, the figurehead of his country, with the boy she'd always known?

It didn't matter if she could or not. She simply had to. They both had to.

And they both had to realise that this thing between them—whatever it was—belonged to their old lives and not their new futures.

'I know.' She knelt on the bed and took his face in her hands, cradling it. God, he was beautiful. 'I know. But we can't change what's happened. You have your duty and I won't let you jeopardise that for me. Besides, we both know I don't belong here.'

'Sim…'

His words petered out and they both knew there was nothing left to say. She left the bedroom and him to go and get dressed.

A few minutes later he emerged from the room, fully dressed and ready for a day of official duties. Looking as if nothing had just happened.

He kissed her quickly on the cheek. 'We'll figure something out. I promise.'

She nodded, but didn't believe him.

It was late morning—not even lunchtime—but to her body clock it felt like the middle of the night. She felt as if she'd lived a thousand hours, yet in real life it was no more than four.

That was the effect Ed had on her.

She wandered around the apartment, looking at her mother's things. Ceramic figurines that had belonged to Simone's grandmother, a framed photograph of Simone's mother and father on their wedding day.

She picked it up and held it closer to study it. It was slightly yellow, older than Simone herself. They looked happy. They had loved each other. And if cancer hadn't taken her father too soon they would still be together. Simone was sure of it. After all, Alea had never remarried. Until the last two or three years Alea hadn't even considered dating anyone.

Simone put down the frame and picked up the next photograph. It was of her and Ed, posing with Suzette. They couldn't have been older than ten. She didn't remember the photo being taken, but she remembered the jeans and bright stripy sweater she'd been wearing.

This was why she didn't come back here. It felt and smelt like her childhood, and those memories were overwhelming. Because they were all memories of Ed.

Happy memories, to be sure. Her happiest. Of waiting for Ed to come by. Of playing in the garden with him. Of sitting on her couch—this very couch—watching television with him. Of playing video games. Of playing with Suzette.

Suzette the cocker spaniel. She'd been a deep golden brown that had faded as she'd got older. She had been one of the first beings to meet her here when Simone had first arrived, still reeling and confused after her father's death. Not quite understanding the enormity and significance of their move, she'd been excited to be moving to an actual palace. She'd loved her new bedroom at first sight, and then she had seen the garden from her window.

She'd rushed down and found Suzette.

A puppy! She'd always wanted a dog.

The palace really had seemed like a fairy tale. And then the boy had come along. She hadn't known he was the Prince at first. In fact, she hadn't realised that for a while. He'd just been Ed. A boy about her own age who had told her where the balls were, to throw to Suzette, and shown her all the secrets of the garden.

Simone fell asleep on the sofa. But even her dreams were about her childhood.

Another memory. She was fourteen. The last day of the school year. She'd come home from school, sad to be saying goodbye to her friends for the summer, but glad that Ed was returning from boarding school. And there he'd been, in the palace kitchen, talking to her mother. And eating. Because that was what fifteen-year-old boys did.

And no wonder. When he'd stood up she'd seen that he was nearly a foot taller than he'd been in the winter. Clean, soft face. A jawline that was starting to firm up. Shoulders that were broader and straighter than when she'd seen him last. But still the same deep green eyes that reminded her of the evergreen trees that grew in the garden. When he'd smiled her stomach had flipped. A new and strange sensation.

I love him, her fourteen-year-old self had thought.

She might have been young, but she'd *known*. She'd known in her heart that she loved this boy like her own soul, and would never stop loving him.

And then suddenly they were in the summer house, and everyone was laughing and pointing at her. Mocking her singing. She tried to get out of the room, but people kept blocking her way. And laughing. Laughing. Laughing…

CHAPTER TWELVE

ED HAD HIS dinner with the French Ambassador moved to lunch, and then cancelled some other appointments, saying he needed to preserve his energy for coronation day. It wasn't a lie, exactly. He was doing something for his own mental health by seeing Simone that night.

She didn't want them to sleep together again, and he not only respected that decision but reluctantly agreed that she was right. She was stronger than him. She was saving him from himself. Making sure that this thing between them—he didn't know what to call it—didn't get any more difficult than it already was.

He had to put his job first.

Duty first.

Wasn't that what being the King was really all about?

His father had spoken to him throughout his life about sacrifice—sacrifice for his country, his people, the greater good—and Ed had never understood. Being King would be an honour and even a pleasure, he'd thought. He wouldn't be giving up anything. Anonymity? He'd never had that anyway.

Now he understood. Now, not only did he understand in his head, but he felt it in his chest—the true meaning of sacrifice.

Simone would leave Florena after the coronation. Things would return to how they had been and it would get easier. It always did. Any time he said goodbye to a woman it hurt for a while and then it got better.

Simone's been the last thing you think of each night and the first each morning since you got back from Paris.

He conceded that might be true, but that was just due to their unfinished business in Paris. The rude interruption of his father's abdication. Now that they had scratched that itch—so to speak—things would return to the way they had been. Simone had made it clear there was no other choice.

And as usual she was right.

This brought him to Sara. His stylist, hairdresser and some-time make-up artist. Because, yes, he occasionally wore make up. For television appearances, mostly. Or official photographs. A light dusting of power to stop the glare of stage lights. Or some concealer to hide the effects of a big night.

He was a figurehead. If he didn't look healthy people talked. If he looked hungover they talked even more.

But now Sara paused when he made his request. 'Are you sure?'

He nodded and she set to work. In fact he was shocked with the enthusiasm with which she tackled her assignment. A few times she even laughed. She was enjoying herself way too much. And when he asked for recommendations as to where he could take an old friend for a night out she was equally obliging.

When she'd completed her handiwork, she even helped him choose an outfit and pad out his shoulders to complete the look.

When he stood in front of the mirror she cackled, patted him on the shoulder and wished him luck. 'I'll be keeping an eye on social media.'

'What?'

'Kidding. I'll resign if someone identifies you. I'd consider it a professional failure.'

Ed turned from side to side in front of the mirror. He was quite proud of his new nose. It was large. Any larger and it would be too distinctive. But it was balanced out by the wrinkles she'd given him. And the wart. He was less keen on the wart, but Sara had insisted.

She'd definitely got too much pleasure from making him look

as if he was forty years older than he was, but he had been pre-pared to let her. She was doing him a favour. He wanted to show Simone that even after yesterday morning they were friends, first and foremost. No funny business. He wasn't taking her out to seduce her, but so they could have a friendly night together.

Simone would not be attracted to him looking as he did now. Like a seventy-year-old man with a gigantic nose and a wart on his chin. When he arrived at her door looking like this she would know that he was serious about their friendship. That he could accept that friends were all they would ever be.

Either that or she'd laugh.

It was very strange, walking through the palace made up as he was. No one bowed, but they did give him puzzled looks. Still, no one stopped him to ask who he was and what he was doing. Something he ought to bring up with his head of security.

Simone opened the door to the apartment and didn't speak for a long time. He didn't want to be recognised, but this was Simone! If she didn't recognise him he'd know that he was safe to go out in public.

But he'd also be strangely disappointed.

A few heartbeats passed before a smile crept over her face. 'Your Majesty.'

'What gave me away?'

'What do you mean? You look exactly like you did yesterday morning. Only now you look like you had a good night's sleep.'

'Ha-ha.'

'What on earth are you doing?'

'I've come to ask if you would like to go out for a drink with me.'

She laughed. 'With you looking like that?'

'It's my disguise. The glasses might have worked in Paris, but here I need something a bit more.'

'That's definitely *more*. Who did you get to do it? Jim Henson?'

'Again, you're hilarious. My stylist—Sara. She was surpris-ingly happy to do it for me.'

Alea poked her head around the door, did a double-take, then laughed.

He stepped into the room and did a spin. 'What do you think?'

Alea was kinder than her daughter. 'It's only your voice that gives you away. If you don't speak, no one will know who you are.'

'Thank you.' He turned back to Simone. 'So, will you come with me?'

Simone turned to her mother, said they'd been planning on spending the evening together, but Alea waved her out through the door.

'Go—have fun. You've been hanging out here all day. Go and have a good night.'

'I'm in my pyjamas,' Simone said.

Ed recognised the lovely curve-skimming silk set from Paris. He swallowed.

'So go and change!' Ed and Alea said in unison.

Simone pulled on some fitted black trousers and a soft, loose white sweater. She examined herself in the mirror. It was just a casual night out. There was no need to go overboard. But then she remembered the last time she'd gone to one of Florena's bars and she pulled down a box from the top of her wardrobe.

It was her old dressing up box. Full of odd but fun items that she and Alea had collected over the years. She took out the short dark wig she had worn to a fancy dress party when she had gone as Lois Lane. She tucked her long blonde hair up inside it and put on some lipstick.

She hardly recognised herself.

'Hey, why do *you* need a disguise?' Ed said when she emerged from her room.

'It's hardly the same as yours,' she said, as they made their way to the back door of the palace.

'But still… Why?'

She should be honest with him. This was still Ed.

'Once, a few years ago, I went out in the old town with Mum. I was photographed. And…well, they linked photos of me with that video and piled on the abuse. I know it isn't anything like what you have to endure, but I'd rather wear the wig.'

And if Ed was recognised her name might be published next to his.

She didn't tell him that, though, because it would sound as if she was ashamed to be with him. Which she wasn't.

She was protecting them both.

Ed frowned, but picked up her gloved hand and squeezed it. Simone looked around the quiet street. There was no one around. For a few minutes they walked along the road like any normal couple.

The moment ended when they reached the old town. Despite the cold and the late hour, the cobblestoned streets were still full of people and Simone dropped Ed's hand. The Christmas decorations had been taken down and replaced with bunting for the coronation. Flags of red and white—Florena's national colours—hung in strings across the streets. Fairy lights adorned half the houses. The other half were strung with garlands of evergreen branches.

The shopfronts were decorated too. A string of bejewelled paper crowns hung in the window of an old sweet shop. The next shop was a cake shop, with a large cake shaped like a crown in its window and a display of cupcakes making up the Florenan flag. It seemed every shopfront on the cobblestoned street was preparing for the coronation.

'It's amazing,' Simone said.

Ed nodded.

'This is all for you,' she whispered. 'Can you get your head around it? I'm not sure that I can.'

'No, I can't. It's like there are two of me,' he said. 'The King and Ed.'

She nodded and turned. 'Duty first.'

He reached for her hand again and drew her to him. Even that small, innocent gesture felt risky, standing where they were.

'Don't forget, Simone. I'm still Ed. I'm still your Ed.'

She nodded, though she didn't agree.

Ed showed her into a nearby old-style pub. It was small, with low ceilings and a roaring fire. Simone ordered their drinks, both judging it best if Ed did as little speaking to others as possible, and they found a quiet table near the back.

Candles lit the table, but even in the low light she could still make out the sparkle in Ed's eyes.

Even with the make-up he was still handsome.

You will still adore him when he's old. There will never be a time when you are not attracted to him.

She shook her head.

'What are you thinking?' he asked.

She sighed. 'I'm thinking how unfair it is that you will probably still be handsome when you're seventy.'

Ed smiled, but then looked down. 'Do I look like my father? I'm worried I look like him.'

'Honestly, no. You don't. You look like your mother.'

He grinned. 'I'm sure she'd love to hear you say that right now.'

'Not now, silly, but in general. You have her eyes and her hair.'

'I feel I'm destined to be like him.' Ed's words were soft.

'You aren't like him.'

'Edouard the Fourth. Philanderer. Cheater. Playboy.'

'You aren't any of those things.'

Simone wanted to reach over the table and pick up his hand, and for a moment it felt as though she could, but she kept her hands tightly in her lap.

'You are your own person. A good person. And you will show everyone that. You will do your duty. You won't make your father's mistakes.'

You will not get involved with the palace crooner.

Simone continued. 'And your plan is the best one. Stay single. Stay loyal to your country. You will be like Elizabeth the First of England!'

Ed looked sombre. 'I really didn't ask you out tonight to talk about that. I simply wanted to have a night out with my best friend. Truly.'

They ordered another drink each and he told her about his parents and feeling trapped between them and their lawyers. He asked about the bookshop and about Paris. She told him about the TV shows she'd been bingeing, the books she'd come across. Everyday mundane things. For a moment she forgot where she was and why she was there. They drank, they laughed, and they pretended for a few precious hours to be just Simone and Ed.

But soon they made their way back through the streets and to the private gate of the palace. Entering without being noticed, they walked along an ancient colonnade that bounded one side of a small quadrangle at the side of the palace.

'Thank you for this evening,' he said.

'You don't have to thank me.'

'I do. Thank you for giving me a few hours of normality. For letting me pretend.'

'Oh Ed…'

A wave of emotion rushed through her. She wanted to make everything all right for him. She wanted to spend many evenings with him as they just had.

Before she could say anything he had slipped his arm around her waist and pulled her towards him. Their lips, cold at first from the walk, quickly warmed one another on the outside and from within. Her knees wobbled and he pushed her gently against the nearest wall for support.

It was exquisite.

It was tender.

It was too much.

'We shouldn't be doing this. Not here!'

His lips tugged on her lower lip and he let out a tortured groan. 'I know…but it feels so good.'

She felt so good.

Complete.

Home.

She dipped her head. *No.* Home was in Paris.

'Stay,' he said.

The word hung in the air. She was waiting for him to take it back. He was waiting for her answer.

'Not for ever,' he said.

She exhaled.

'Just a little longer…'

'I have to get back to the bookshop. To Paris. I can't come back here. You know that. Nothing's changed. If anything, it would be harder for me to stay here.'

'Why not just try it for a while? A month or two? That's all. Your mother would love it.'

The mention of her mother and the look in his pleading eyes made her chest ache.

'You know I don't feel at home here.'

'But this *is* your home.'

She sighed. She hated having to talk about that video. The mockery and the trolling.

'Ed, please, you're not being fair. Not to me. Or to yourself.'

He couldn't promise her for ever and she respected that—because she couldn't promise it either.

'Is it really about the video?'

'Yes, partly.'

'You shouldn't be worried about that.'

She cringed and stepped away from him. 'Stop joking. It isn't funny.'

'I'm not joking. You sounded fine. It's a difficult song and you weren't awful…'

'Wow, thanks.'

'Sim, you looked lovely. Beautiful. It was really sweet.'

A horrible uncomfortable thought crept over her. 'When was the last time you watched it?'

He bowed his head. 'Recently…'

She narrowed her eyes.

'Okay, maybe yesterday.'

'Yesterday! Why? It was the most embarrassing moment of my life and you're still watching it?'

She set off along the colonnade.

'Simone, I love watching it. I'm sorry, but I do. I love looking at any photo or video of you. I'm quite addicted.'

She stopped and looked across the courtyard at the towers of the palace. He liked her singing. It had taken thirteen years, but she'd finally charmed him. She let out a rueful laugh.

'Have *you* seen it lately?' he asked.

She shook her head.

'You should watch it. I think you might find that it isn't as embarrassing as you remember.'

But whether it was good or bad wasn't the point. The fact that it had made its way to the smartphone screens of everyone in Florena was mortifying. The fact that the photo of her clutching the microphone, mouth wide open and eyes half closed, had launched a thousand memes was enough to make anyone want to emigrate.

And then the online abuse… It had come right off social media and into her own inbox. Trolls, going out of their way to tell her how ugly she was. How stupid she was. How pathetic she was for throwing herself at the Prince. How she should probably end her own life.

'So it was embarrassing?' said Ed. 'We've all done drunk karaoke. We've all had embarrassing photos of us published. Join the club. Remember those photos of me with the Spanish models?'

She nodded. She remembered those photos all too well. 'It looked like you were enjoying yourself.'

'I'd had too much to drink, and I *was* enjoying myself, but the photos were out of context. It made it look like I was a second away from ripping their bikinis off with my teeth.'

She raised an eyebrow 'And were you?'

'No. Someone just took the photo at the wrong moment.'

She didn't want to think about Ed and the trio of Spanish

models he'd been partying with. She also didn't want to think about the video. And what had followed.

She pulled her coat tight against the cold. 'They hate me here.'

'No, they don't.'

'They mocked me. Laughed at me. Some of them told me…'

Some of them had told her to die. She couldn't even say it aloud.

The messages had continued for weeks. At first she'd changed her email address, and then her phone number. But the trolls had still found her. She'd eventually given up all social media. For a sixteen-year-old away from home that had been hard.

It had been weeks before she'd been able to sleep properly again. And all she'd done was to sing a song at a party. If people knew she had slept with the King… Then what? What sort of attacks would await her?

Even if she wanted to stay and put herself through that kind of humiliation again, she wasn't sure she physically could.

'I'm constantly worried that someone will make fun of me, but I've had to learn to rise above it or I'd be paralysed,' Ed said.

'It's different for you. You're the King.'

He blinked. A long, confused blink.

'I'm nobody,' she clarified.

'You're not nobody.'

'But I'm not your Queen. Or even your girlfriend.'

She held her breath while she waited for him to answer. Half hoping and half dreading that he'd contradict her.

You could be my girlfriend. You could be my Queen.

But he didn't.

'I could protect you,' he said.

She sighed deeply. 'You couldn't the last time I hit the front page. No one could. I was sent away. Banished!'

Ed frowned. 'I was a kid then. I didn't know what had gone on. This time I'll protect you.'

'I was sent away. I was such an embarrassment to the palace that I was *sent away*.'

She was one more word away from breaking down.

'Is that what you think?' he asked.

'It's what I *know*. And you even think your father paid my school fees. That's how much they wanted to get rid of me.'

He groaned. 'That's not why you were sent away.'

'Then why?'

He looked at her for a long while before saying, 'I can't tell you why.'

She tugged on her gloves and tightened her scarf, which had been dislodged by their kiss. 'Because that *is* why. I was sent away in disgrace. Even though your father isn't around now, having me here would just give Laurent more ammunition. I have to leave for your sake.'

Ed laughed loudly. 'Bad karaoke singing is not scandalous enough to destroy the country. Even yours.'

Rage built inside her and it took every ounce of control not to scream at him. *Hysterical woman screams at King!* She could write the headline herself.

'The country turned on me—'

'It wasn't the entire country.'

'I wasn't welcome and...'

Her throat closed over. The things they'd said to her... She didn't want to stay and be abused again. Even for Ed.

They reached the door that led up to her apartment.

Ed stepped towards her with his hands out. Perfectly earnest. 'Simone, I'll protect you. It wouldn't be like last time.'

'It doesn't matter. My life's in Paris.'

It was lovely that he wanted to try, but they both knew that her fear of the spotlight was only one of their problems.

'I just wish you'd feel comfortable spending more time here. I don't want to upset you, but I want to keep talking about this. I understand there are many reasons why you wouldn't want to come back, but I don't want you to think that banishment is one of them.'

He leant down and kissed her cheek. His lips lingered and they breathed in each other's scent, as if to carry the memory away with them. Every time she had to say goodbye to him her heart broke a little more.

She turned and began to climb the stairs before she could change her mind.

Back in her room, she tugged off the wig and rubbed her itchy scalp.

He didn't understand what it was like for her. He was the King. He had people to check his social media. He had an army sworn to defend his honour. She'd been kicked out of the country the first time she'd done something wrong.

Even if she wasn't about to be deported again, would she be able to withstand the scrutiny and criticism that was sure to come her way if anyone got wind of the fact that she had slept with the King?

Did she even want to? Was it worth it?

You have to have a strong sense of yourself.

She did have a strong sense of herself. Much more so than when she was sixteen. She was Simone Auclair. She ran a second-hand bookshop in Paris. She loved books and reading and her mother. She loved her friends, Julia and André. She *knew* who she was.

And if she didn't have Paris and her bookshop then who was she? Her mother's daughter? Ed's friend?

She didn't want to be defined by being Ed's girlfriend. Once upon a time that might have been a dream come true, but if that was how she defined herself and then it was taken away from her…? Then who would she be?

Because if she didn't even know who she was, she certainly wouldn't be able to withstand the trolls.

CHAPTER THIRTEEN

AFTER A MEETING to decide on the final details of the coronation, and when he'd finished signing the box of papers for the
day, his staff left him alone. Ed took out his phone and brought
up the video of Simone singing. He watched it more regularly
than he'd like to admit to anyone.

Remembering her words from last night, he didn't click on
the link. To her, it was a betrayal for him to watch the video.

Simone in his arms was everything he'd never known he
wanted—no, needed. All the dreams he'd been too afraid to
picture.

*She's your best friend, and for a precious morning was your
lover.*

His overwhelming thought after making love with Simone
had been that she was the only person in the world he should
be doing it with. That everything else in his life up to that point
had been not quite right.

He'd put Simone into a mental box. Childhood best friend.
And for years he'd kept her there, convinced that that was the
only place for her.

Until Paris.

Until he'd finally seen her as the woman she was.

And now there was no going back.

Not that he wanted to. This Simone—this woman who'd lain
with him the other morning—was magnificent. Soft and firm
in all the right places. Warm and loving and everything he'd
never even let himself imagine a lover could be.

Now when he clicked on the video he did feel he was betraying her by doing so. She had been genuinely traumatised by the fallout. She had been young. She'd had to deal with it alone. Worst of all, she genuinely believed that she had been banished from Florena because of it.

What a mess. If only she understood that she'd been sent away to boarding school because of the affair between his father and her mother and that it had nothing to do with the video. If only he could make her understand that… Clearly Alea had not divulged that secret.

For the first time Ed did more than glance at the comments below the video. There were thousands of them. Some complimentary, but most were vile. He'd dealt with online bullies in his time, but the vitriol reserved for women was on a different level entirely. And aimed at a sixteen-year-old girl?

Thank goodness he'd never have a daughter of his own. He didn't have the slightest idea how he'd prepare her for what she was likely to face from the trolls of the world as Princess of Florena.

Still, he didn't put his phone away and considered rewatching the video. Because Simone was gorgeous, and lovely, and her voice played on his heart strings like a maestro. Her singing was heartfelt…as if she was singing to someone.

Maybe he was a little obsessed.

But he was also curious.

Why had she been she singing? Why *that* song? Karaoke had been her idea. But something didn't feel right. It didn't feel like Simone. She wasn't a show-off. She wasn't shy, but usually she took a little persuading to put herself forward in a group where she didn't know many people. She must have had a well thought-out reason for singing.

You've been asking the wrong question. The right question is who was she singing to?

She hadn't known anyone at the party apart from her mother and the senior staff who had always been invited to those events. The rest of the guests had been either his friends or his parents' friends. Simone hadn't known most of those people. Ed hadn't even known many of those people.

Which meant…

His veins turned to ice and he froze.

He was such an idiot.

A special kind of stupid.

Seventeen-year-old boy stupid.

He couldn't believe he'd assumed that Simone's feelings for him had been running parallel with his. That they had only begun seriously in Paris, when his own feelings had.

But what if she had loved him…for ever?

When she'd declined his invitation to come back to Florena with him after the abdication he'd assumed it was because she didn't have feelings for him. Or that any feelings she did have were not strong enough.

But what if it wasn't that at all?

All this time he'd been thinking he'd just been reckless with his own feelings. Risking his own heart. That was one thing, but he realised shamefully that he'd been careless with hers too. He had assumed that he was the only one in danger of being hurt.

You don't know how she feels about you. You don't know anything for sure.

But it might explain why she'd been so upset about the fall-out from the video. It might explain why she'd been so reluctant to come back to Florena. He knew she'd been upset by the trolls and didn't want to risk further humiliation. And she thought she'd been banished once before. Those were all real fears and concerns.

But all this time he'd been assuming that her feelings for him were not strong enough to help her overcome those fears.

But what if he was wrong? What if it was the complete opposite and she didn't want to return precisely because she had feelings for him?

He took off his tie and jacket and threw on his casual sweater.

Even if he was a monarch, he could still be diabolically stupid.

* * *

Simone spent the afternoon in the kitchen, helping chop vegetables, cut pastry and wash dishes. Anything the kitchen staff would let her do to keep her mind off what had been happening between her and Ed.

Her mother had hired additional hands to handle the influx of guests over the coronation weekend and to cover for her. As the manager of the kitchen Alea was invited to the coronation and the ball, but she still had to co-ordinate the catering.

The kitchen work might not have kept her mind completely away from Ed. Or his hands. Or the things he could do with his tongue. But at least it had kept her from doing anything stupid. Like calling up André and asking him to run the bookshop on a permanent basis while she lived the rest of her life locked away in the palace as the King's secret mistress.

Of course she'd never do that.

Like everything else it was a silly fantasy. But now she was elbow-deep in grimy water, reminding herself that being with Ed in the long term and keeping her sanity were two diametrically opposed outcomes.

The large kitchen, which had been filled with laughter and chatter, suddenly fell silent behind her. She looked around to see what the problem was. Ed was walking towards her through a wave of bows and mutterings of 'Your Majesty'.

As he approached her he grinned, almost shyly.

But that couldn't be right.

He was never shy around anyone—least of all her.

When he reached her, she bowed too.

'Simone, would you like to have a walk with me?'

'I'm…' She was about to tell him she was busy and refuse his invitation, but then she saw all the eyes trained on her. 'Certainly, Your Majesty.'

He raised an eyebrow.

Simone dried her hands and followed him out of the kitchen. When they were out of earshot he said, 'What was all that about? The bowing…the "Your Majesty"?'

'In case you've forgotten, you're the King. If I don't bow people will want to know why. If I don't call you "Your Majesty" people will pretty much assume we're sleeping together.'

'They know we're friends.'

'The old staff do. But not the temporary staff here for the coronation.'

'They've all signed NDAs.'

'That's not the point, Ed.'

He stopped walking and grabbed her arm, so she stopped too.

'What *is* the point? Do you not want to see me?'

She sighed. 'We just need to be careful. And you know that more than anyone.'

He nodded. 'I don't know what I'd do without you,' he said.

She laughed wryly. 'You'll be just fine.'

Future tense. His life would go on perfectly smoothly and scandal-free once she'd left.

Hers, on the other hand…? She would be the one piecing her broken heart back together.

They reached the door to the garden and looked out. It had begun to snow. She looked down at her outfit. A long dress, tights and a long cardigan. He wasn't suitably attired either, with his dress shoes and only a thin sweater.

'It's too cold outside. Will you come to my room?'

This had now progressed from a casual walk and talk to a visit to his private rooms.

'Ed. I… I thought we'd talked about this. I'm not going to be the nearest warm body,' she whispered.

'What? You think I want to be with you just because you are close and warm?'

She glanced at the butler coming towards him and motioned for him to lower his voice.

'We're *definitely* going to my room for this conversation.'

He took her hand and pulled her in the direction of the royal apartments. She shook his hand away—but followed him anyway.

They walked quickly in silence to his room, greeting each person they passed with an overly friendly hello.

His apartment had a spacious sitting room, an office space, and an oversized bedroom. It was the same one he'd had for ever.

'Will you move into the King's apartments?' she asked.

He glared at her. 'Not the time, Simone. What did you mean, you don't want to be the nearest warm body?'

'Well… I didn't mean exactly that. But Paris…? The other morning…? And now you've brought me to your apartments.'

My heart may not be as important as a country, but I need it to live and breathe.

'I kissed you in Paris because I wanted to. I slept with you the other day because I've been dreaming about it since I left Paris. And because I wanted to—very much. Because after having you as my friend for so long…after so many years of taking you for granted as my friend… I finally see what an amazing and beautiful woman you are. I know I was slow on that account, but there you go.'

She could only stare. Amazing and beautiful woman?

'And, for the record, I don't just go around sleeping with women because they are close and warm. Do you actually believe what they print about me?'

She bit her lip. 'I don't…'

His look challenged her. She might as well get all her insecurities out into the open.

'But I know you've been with a lot of women, that's all.'

He let out a cynical guffaw.

'That's what you think of me? After everything you know about royal life, you still believe the headlines?'

'I don't need a number, Ed, but I see the photographs. I try my best not to see *all* the photographs, but I see them. And even if you only slept with a fraction of them, then…'

What? She'd run out of words. And she'd said too much.

He moved back to her. 'You try not to see the photographs? What do you mean by that?'

His voice was kind, and he raised a gentle eyebrow.

'Because…because I care about you, Ed.'

He encircled her in his arms and she pressed her face to his chest, so he wouldn't see the colour in her cheeks.

'Now we're getting somewhere. "Care…"?'

'Care is as much as you're getting now. We're friends. I like to know what you're up to.'

He pulled back to look at her with a broad smile. 'Again, for the record, it's not even a fraction of what the press would have you believe. And I do like it that you are close. And do I like that you are warm. But even if you weren't I'd still want to do this.'

He brushed his lips across hers.

She closed her eyes and breathed him in. There was no denying he was close…and very, very warm.

She let his speech run through her head a few more times, conscious that his hands were sliding up her back, sliding over the sensitive skin on her neck. Making her shiver.

'I've been dreaming about it since I left Paris… I finally see what a beautiful and amazing woman you are…'

She opened her eyes and sought out his lips.

CHAPTER FOURTEEN

THE KISS GREW deeper as they both fell into it. Fingers in each other's hair. Hands under one another's clothes. Tongues encircling one another's.

All the air left Simone's body and with it all her inhibitions.

She grabbed at the hem of Ed's sweater. Tugging. Pulling it out of the way. And he did the same with the buttons down the front of the dress she was wearing. He lifted her backside onto the nearest desk and she finally got his sweater over his head.

Ed pushed her lacy bra down, lifting and exposing one swollen, tender breast and taking it into his mouth. He kissed her painfully hard nipple and the room spun around her. He slid his hand up her thigh. Higher and higher.

Desperate need pooled inside her and came close to overflowing. She pushed him away. Very conscious of the fact they were in his apartment, not hers. And on his desk, no less.

'What if someone comes in?'

'They won't.'

'But...'

'Come.' He took her hand and led her to the other room. His bedroom. He shut the door behind him. 'I'm still just Ed. This is still my room.'

Simone swallowed hard. He was right. Ed was in front of her. Pulling her towards his bed and everything she'd always wanted. She just had to find the courage to take it.

He stepped back to her, shirt awry. She reached out and undid the last of his buttons, ran her hand over his chest and slipped the shirt over his magnificent shoulders. She threw it to the ground and reached for his belt buckle.

'Don't rush. I want to savour every second of this.'

The subtext was that this might be the last time. It might not have been what he meant, but it was what she heard.

And he was right. If this was to be the last time she would commit every second to memory. Every caress, every stroke, every sensuous lick.

Ed kissed her all over as he slid her dress away, coaxed her bra off and eased her panties down. Waves and waves of pleasure washed through her.

She slowly divested him of the rest of his clothes. Committing each inch of his body to memory and each inch to her lips. She consumed his addictive scent, surrendered her body to him and was worshipped in return.

He trembled as he said her name.

'Yes. Yes…' she replied.

Protected and on the brink, they finally came together.

She closed her eyes and let go. Desire gathering, tightening, hardening…finally breaking apart. All her being seemed to concentrate on this one moment of perfect, terrifying clarity. She'd love him no matter who he was. She'd love him until the end of time.

She broke and so did he.

They lay in one another's arms, spent and satiated. For the first time since the other morning Ed felt normal and content. Like himself. And that was all because of Simone.

'I have a question for you,' he said after a while.

He felt her body tense in his arms. She knew him well enough to know that his question was going to be serious.

'Why were you singing? At my party?'

'Oh, that… I don't remember.'

'I don't believe that for a second.' He said it gently, but felt her body stay frozen nonetheless.

'We went over this before. You've got to get back to work and I'd better get back to Mum.'

'What are you not telling me? It wasn't like you to put yourself out there in front of a whole lot of people you didn't know. Why did you?'

He stroked her hair and felt her shift under him.

'I had a crush on you,' she mumbled into his chest.

He'd guessed as much, but to hear her say it still stirred up many emotions. Surprise, delight, worry...

'You *had* a crush on me? Past tense?'

She groaned, as if it was something to be ashamed of.

'Because *my* crush is very much in the present tense. Just so you know. And I'm not embarrassed in the slightest,' he said.

She giggled, and lifted herself up to look at him. Her blonde hair was tossed around her shoulders. Her lips still red and swollen from their kissing. She took his breath away. She was beautiful and she was Simone. *His* Simone.

'Yes, I had a teenage crush on you. Along with every other girl. Except it was mortifying because you were my best friend. You knew me and didn't share my feelings. Everyone knew how pathetic I was. That's why they sent me away.'

He couldn't believe that she believed everything she was saying.

He took her chin in his fingers. 'Simone, no. That's not why you were sent away at all. No one knows you had a crush on me!'

'They mocked me for singing to you.'

He rubbed his head. Was that really true? How could her recollections be so different from his?

'I think they were just laughing at the video. I don't think anyone thought you were singing to me.'

'Hashtag *palaceserenade*? That's pretty clear to me.'

'But...' It hadn't been clear to him. He sighed and bit his lip. He'd failed to notice a lot of things. 'Simone, I'm sorry I didn't notice.'

'You weren't meant to. I mean, you were only meant to realise if you shared my feelings. And I thought it worked, and you hadn't realised, and it all would have been fine except that then someone posted the video and made fun of it and everyone saw.'

The way she was talking in the past tense was starting to worry him. Was she over him? Had her feelings dissipated over the years, just as his were growing?

'Does any of it remain? Your teenage crush?'

She grinned. 'Ah, I don't know. My teenage crush was very...chaste.'

He laughed.

'This is something new.'

She trailed a finger down his chest and slid her hand under the covers. Just the thought of her fingers encircling him was enough to make his body react.

His fingers slid into her thick hair. He cradled her head and tilted her face towards him.

Something new.

But what?

It was powerful. And wonderful. But also dangerous.

This wasn't a chaste teenage crush or even an unchaste one. This was real life—both their lives—not to mention the future of his country.

He knew that. He knew that by continuing to be with Simone like this he could be putting all his carefully laid plans at risk.

Stay away from any hint of scandal. Be a monarch above all reproach. Beyond any criticism at all.

But this was Simone. She was next to him now and he needed her more than he needed air. No one needed to know. This would just be between them. She'd go back to Paris. He'd vowed to fulfil his royal duties alone. She didn't want to stay in Florena, and he accepted that, but that didn't mean they couldn't both make the most of this brief interlude in their lives.

Ed took a deep breath and knocked on the familiar apartment door. He heard movement inside and the door opened.

Alea smiled when she saw him. 'Eddie, sweetheart, come on in.'

He was instantly grateful that she had greeted him as usual, and hadn't curtsied or called him by his new title.

'It's lovely to see you,' she said.

'You too.'

'I'm afraid you've missed Simone. She's out having her dress fitted.'

'I confess I knew that. It's you I've come to see.'

Ed's throat was dry. Alea was one of the people in the world he felt most comfortable with, but what he'd come to ask was… delicate. He'd thought about coming weeks ago, before Simone had returned, and every day since then. But he wasn't sure what Simone had told her mother about the developments in their relationship. And he wasn't sure how she was going to react to his impertinent request.

'That sounds slightly ominous… Eddie, you know you're welcome here any time. Do you have time for a coffee?' she asked.

He nodded. They made small talk until the coffee was brewed, placed on the table with milk and sugar.

The coffee was sweet and robust, as always. Alea was a magnificent cook. But he was delaying. None of his etiquette lessons had ever taught him the art of raising one of his father's affairs with one of his old mistresses.

'I was wondering…that is… I don't think Simone knows about your affair with my father.'

There. No going back now.

Alea placed her cup down. 'I don't think she does either.'

'I was wondering if you had planned to tell her.'

'I hadn't really thought about it.' She crossed her arms.

'I wonder if you would like to think about it, now she's older.'

'Honestly, I'm not sure I planned to keep it a secret from her for ever, but it's in the past. You know that. Your father and I haven't been together for years. I don't think there's any need to dredge up the past. Particularly not now, with Celine and everything.'

'I know that. But I think maybe Simone deserves to know.'

'Eddie, I don't regret being with your father. You know it ended amicably between us. No harm done. You're an adult now. Old enough to know that people need company. People need touch. Companionship.'

Ed ran his hand over his head. This wasn't what he'd come to hear from Simone's mother.

'Alea, please, *please* don't think for a moment I'm judging you. I do understand. That's not it.'

'Then why raise it now?'

'Ordinarily I wouldn't, but Simone and I have…'

This was dangerous ground too.

Alea narrowed her eyes.

'Simone and I are close.'

'You always have been.'

'Yes, but recently I've realised we have this secret between us.'

'You've always kept this from her—what's changed now?'

No. Simone clearly hadn't discussed their relationship with her mother. Alea was smart, and she had probably guessed, but she was wanting confirmation. This was harder than he'd thought it would be.

'It's important to me that there aren't any secrets between Simone and I.'

That explanation would have to do. He wasn't about to tell Alea that he was sleeping with her daughter—especially as Simone hadn't.

Besides, she might ask him about his intentions, and he wasn't sure that he could use the 'we're both consenting adults' speech back to her.

'It isn't your secret. It's mine and your father's.'

'I know. Which is why I'm coming to you and not Simone. The thing is, she believes she was sent away from the palace because of that video of her singing.'

'What video?' Alea asked.

'The one of her singing karaoke at my seventeenth birthday.'

'Where she sang *I Will Always Love You*?'

'Yes.'

'But that's absurd.'

'Yes, that's what I thought. But the clip went viral and she got a lot of horrible online abuse because of it.'

'But that wasn't why she was sent to school. The events were not connected.'

'I know that. But the timing was close and she never knew about the affair. It's what she believes, and I can see why she might. Rightly or wrongly, the abuse she received because of that video is one of the reasons she doesn't like coming back here.'

Alea paled. 'Really?'

'Yes—and it's why she plans on going back to Paris as soon as the coronation is over.'

Alea waved his suggestion away. 'She has a bookshop to manage. She always has to go back.'

'I want her to stay,' he said. 'Don't you?'

Alea held her face in her hands. 'Of course I do. And you're right. She should know the full story.'

Ed nodded, but then Alea shook her head and stood. She began to pace.

'But it isn't as simple as you suggest. We've all put it behind us. Your father, me, your mother... Even you. I know you and your mother accepted it as the way things were, but I don't know if Simone will.'

Ed hadn't been happy about the affair, but as his mother had accepted the relationship he hadn't felt it was his place to rock the boat.

'I'm not sure we should dig up the past. It's over,' Alea continued.

But not for Simone. And not for him.

'Please talk to her. If you won't do it for me, maybe you should do it for you.'

Alea frowned.

'I thought you should know,' Ed said, before downing the last of his coffee and taking his leave.

CHAPTER FIFTEEN

SHE WAS GOING to go to the ball.

If only because if she didn't Ed, her mother, the dressmaker and the Queen's assistants wouldn't forgive her.

The Queen had only returned to Florena briefly since her divorce had been announced. However, Ed wanted his mother to continue to be called the Queen, and to maintain a presence in Florena to support him if necessary.

Queen Isabella was not returning for the coronation. She had told Ed she didn't want to overshadow him. Simone suspected the real reason was that the Queen didn't want to see the former King Edouard, who would have to be at the coronation.

With the Queen so often away, her staff were at a loose end—and the thread they had latched on to was Simone. Simone was getting her hair and make-up done twice on the day of the coronation, which felt absurdly excessive.

'They want something to do. They *need* something to do,' her mother had insisted. 'They're helping me as well—and any of the other staff who would like their services.'

Simone carried the cardboard box back with her from the dress fitting. Her mother's old dress hadn't needed much work. The waist had been taken in and the bust taken out a little.

Her mother wouldn't tell her when or why she'd bought the dress in the first place, but the whispers she'd heard between the Queen's assistants had been curious.

'It's not ready-to-wear. It's bespoke. Looks like the aesthetic from a decade ago,' they'd murmured.

That would make it too recent for it to be a dress Alea might have worn when she was dating Simone's father. What had her mother been doing ten years ago, wearing a designer dress much less owning one?

When Simone opened the door to the apartment her mother was pacing the room, but she smiled when Simone entered.

'Do you have time for a drink?' she asked. 'I feel like I've hardly seen you at all since you got back.'

Simone took a seat. Alea was right to heap guilt on her. She had been seeing Ed every spare moment he had—which meant she hadn't seen as much of her mother as either of them expected.

'I'm sorry, Mum.'

'There's no need to be sorry. I know you've been busy. I just thought it might be nice to have bit of time together. Catch up with no one else around. Do you have plans?'

Simone shook her head. Her mother knew she had been spending time with Ed, but if she realised that their relationship had changed she hadn't let on. Maybe that was the point of this conversation? Would she approve or caution Simone against it? She had no idea.

You're too suspicious. She just wants to spend some time with you.

'Wine?'

'Yes, please.'

Alea poured them both a glass and joined Simone by the fire.

'You've been spending a lot of time with Eddie, I understand?'

Ah. So this wasn't just a casual chat.

'He's my friend, and it's a stressful time for him.'

'I know that—and I'm not judging.'

Judging? The word hung between them. Her mother saying she wasn't judging felt very much like…judgement.

Her mother played with the stem of her wine glass for a long time.

She knows about Ed and me. She wants me to tell her.

But Simone didn't know what to tell her mother. She didn't know what was going on herself.

'You and Eddie have been friends for a long time,' said her mother, but I wonder if lately you've become closer?'

Simone dropped her head. She wasn't going to lie to her mother. 'I'm not really sure what's going on between us,' she confessed. 'It's new, and difficult, but for the time being we're taking it day by day.'

That was what she was telling herself as well. Taking each day as it came. Enjoying it while it lasted. Definitely not analysing her feelings in any depth at all.

'I'm not asking you to tell me, but I want you to know that you can.' Alea's voice was warm.

'Of course I know that I can, Mum. I can tell you anything.'

Alea reached over, took Simone's hand and squeezed it. 'That isn't what I wanted to talk about. I'm sorry this has come out all wrong...'

'Oh?' Simone was as confused as Alea looked.

'There's something I need to tell *you*,' her mother began. 'Something I never told you before.'

Alea's expression was pained, and Simone's mind instantly jumped to a million conclusions. Her mother was sick. Ed was sick...

'It's about the King. That is...the former King.'

Simone sat upright. Was King Edouard sick?

'It's about Edouard and I...'

It was funny how you could know something the second before you were actually told it.

Suddenly Simone just *knew*.

Was she a good guesser or was she simply remembering something she had forgotten from years ago?

Suddenly some of the cryptic things Ed had said in Paris became clear.

'You had an affair,' Simone said.

'You knew?'

Simone shook her head. 'Not until this second. Is it true?'

Alea nodded. 'Yes. Yes, we had an affair. You were a teenager, and your father had been gone a long while. Edouard is charming. You know that.'

Simone nodded. Like father, like son.

'And I was lonely and flattered. The King and Queen had ended their intimate relationship years before, and sometimes two people...'

Simone held up her hand. She was in shock, and surprised, but she wasn't angry. She was just processing.

'It's okay, Mum. I get it.'

There were many things that were not okay. The fact that the King had been cheating on his wife. The fact that her mother had kept this secret from her all this time. But she did understand that sometimes these things happened. And if the former King had been as hard to resist as his son, then Simone really didn't blame her mother.

'Did you love him?'

'No, I don't think so. But I was terribly fond of him and we had a lovely time. He made me feel good about myself.'

Simone grimaced. Why had her mother not felt good about herself?

'I knew there was no future in it, and I didn't want there to be one. Heavens, I didn't want him to leave the Queen! We tried our hardest to be discreet. But there is one thing I feel bad about. One regret.'

'The Queen?' Simone guessed.

'Isabella knew. She told Edouard that at least I was age-appropriate and would be discreet.' Alea smiled, as if remembering something.

'The Queen knew?'

'Yes. It was all very adult.'

Simone wanted to be mature, but her stomach lurched at the thought of King Edouard—the philandering King—Alea and the Queen, all sharing this secret. The three of them might have been able to be calm about it, but Simone didn't think she would ever be able to treat such a situation in the same way the three of them seemed to have.

Perhaps she was just naive. Unsophisticated. Clueless.

'Why are you telling me now?' Simone asked, but she suspected she knew the answer. Ed had played a part in this.

'I regret agreeing to send you away to boarding school.'

'"Agreeing"? It wasn't your idea?'

'It was partly my idea. I did want you to get the best education you could. And I wanted you to have the opportunity to see life somewhere away from the palace. But it was Edouard who arranged it and paid for it. That is the part of the relationship I look back on with regret. It was only meant to be for a term or two. I thought you would come back. I always made it clear I wanted you to.'

It was as though her mother was telling her that the sky was green and always had been.

'I wasn't sent away because of the singing.' Her voice was soft.

'No. *No.* I can't believe you ever thought that.'

Simone had thought that the timing proved it. She'd made a fool of herself. She'd been asked if she wanted to go away and, feeling ashamed, she had agreed to go.

I was sixteen.

'It was to get me out of the way?'

'No, not as such… I thought it would be the best thing for your education. But I suppose that having you out of the palace may have been Edouard's intention.'

'I thought it was because of the singing… The video…' The contents of her stomach rose.

'I realise that now. And I'm sorry you thought you were being punished. That wasn't what it was about at all.'

'I wasn't in trouble?'

'Heavens, no, sweetheart. If I'd known how much that video had affected you I would never have sent you away to school to deal with it on your own. I'm so sorry.'

Simone took a sip of wine, but it tasted wrong in her mouth. 'Why didn't you tell me before?'

'I figured it was in the past.' Alea shrugged.

It was in the past.

The King had spectacularly moved on.

It was in the past for them—but Simone and Ed were still very much in the present.

And Ed knew. He had known all along.

The walls of the apartment closed in on her. Breathing became an effort.

They had all lied to her.

There was a lot to take in, and she couldn't do it here, in the warm apartment, with her mother looking on.

'I need a moment,' Simone said as she stood.

She had to get out.

She had to breathe.

'Simone, I had no idea the fallout from you singing that song had affected you so much. If I had I would have told you sooner.'

Simone nodded, but couldn't speak.

'Get some air. I'll be here when you get back if you want to talk some more.'

Alea looked stricken, but Simone couldn't worry about that now.

Everything she'd always believed had been turned on its head.

She grabbed her coat and left the apartment.

In summer the palace garden was the perfect place to sit and think. With its thick green grass, shady trees and a riot of coloured blooms, it was a calm oasis from the bustle and formalities of the palace. In winter it was the only place to go without actually leaving the palace walls.

The snow had stopped, but the cloud cover remained so the air was not frigid. Simone had on proper boots and a thick coat. She walked around the frozen pond to the small playground. She'd expected to find it dilapidated—it had been years since any children had lived permanently in the palace—but she was delighted to find it well maintained.

She brushed the snow off one of the swings and sat. It was smaller than she remembered, but she could still fit on the seat and gently swing.

It's not smaller...you're bigger.

Yeah? Well, memory was a fickle thing.

With one conversation half the things she remembered about her childhood had been flipped on their heads. Her mother? Ed's father?

What did that make her and Ed?

The sensible voice in her head said, *Nothing. It changes nothing between you and Ed.*

But another voice, the confused, lonely voice screamed, *Everyone knew but me. They let me think I was sent away because of the drama with the song.*

They had all let her down. Even Ed. Though as the dark settled in and her emotions stilled she realised he'd thought she already knew.

And, as upset as Simone was with her mother, she realised she was right. Alea was always asking her to come back. The first term at boarding school had been Alea's idea. But every term after that, and then Paris, had all been Simone's idea.

Even now she knew she would go back to Paris. Florena was not her home.

The evening wore on and the cold seeped into her fingers, but she wasn't going back inside. She didn't know these people any more. She didn't know her own mother.

Why had Alea had stayed working at the palace even after the affair was over? That didn't make much sense. Who would want to stay around to see their former lover every day once the affair was over?

'It was all very adult.'

Maybe she should just go back to Paris. It was her true home. Paris had never lied to her. She'd miss the coronation, but so what? Florena wasn't really her home. It hadn't been for years.

It was then that Ed found her, mentally booking her return flight to Charles de Gaulle.

'Hey,' he said gently, as if starting a conversation.

She had no time for niceties. 'You knew about the affair, didn't you?'

He took the swing next to her. 'Yes.'

'What I'm trying to understand is why she's told me now.'

'I asked her to,' he said simply.

Simone had guessed as much. 'Why?' she asked.

'Because I thought you needed to know. Not so much about the affair, but you needed to know why you were really sent to boarding school. It wasn't because of the singing or the video.'

'What on earth did you say to her?'

Oh, to have been a fly on the wall during that conversation...

He laughed. 'I was polite. So was she. I'm glad she understood where I was coming from.'

Simone rocked. The swinging was strangely calming.

'I felt bad that I knew and you didn't,' he said. 'But most of all I hate that you don't feel welcome here. I hate that you think you were banished.'

She could see his breath. He was wrapped up in a heavy coat and a thick grey scarf. His hair was slightly ruffled by the breeze. He looked as edible as ever.

Would there ever be a time when the sight of him didn't make her heart stop?

She might not have been banished because of the singing, but she'd still been sent away. They'd wanted to hide the affair from her.

'My mother and your father... Together.'

'My father and I have good taste in women. What can I say?'

'Stop! Ed, this changes everything. Between us.'

He got off his swing and stepped into her path, holding her swing still.

'No. It changes nothing between us. So what if our parents had an affair? It was ages ago. It's over.

She couldn't meet his eye. 'It changes the way I see my life. It changes things I thought about myself.'

It was also mildly uncomfortable to know that their parents had once shared a bed. But it was more than that.

Simone's mother was palace staff. She might live in the palace, but she lived in the servants' apartments. Simone and her mother were the type of woman Kings had affairs with. Nothing more.

Yet you don't expect anything more from Ed. You don't want anything more. You don't want to be the Queen.

Her chest ached. She didn't want to be the Queen, but that didn't stop her wanting to be with Ed. And not as his mistress, but for ever. She'd tried to push those feelings aside, but they were overwhelming her. They were too strong to overcome.

Now, even in the crisp open air, she felt the world closing in on her again.

'Ed, I'm not sure I want to talk now. This is a lot to think about.'

I want to be with you. For ever.

'I understand, but please don't mind if I stay here, to make sure you don't die of exposure. Your mother said you've been out here for at least an hour. Can you still feel your feet?'

'I can neither confirm nor deny.'

'At least come in somewhere warm. You can pace the Great Hall if you want.'

'No, I can't; it's set up for the ball.'

She kept swinging.

Swing back, breathe in…swing forward, breathe out, she told herself.

They both swung back and forth for a while, but thankfully he swung in silence and let her process her thoughts.

'Did it go on for long?' she asked after a while.

'I don't know. A year, maybe.'

'Do you think they loved one another?'

'You'd have to ask her that.'

She had, and her mother had denied it.

'Do you think he loved her?'

Ed scoffed. 'You know my father. I don't think he's ever loved anyone.'

Alea understood what Simone's heart couldn't. Loving a king was hopeless.

She looked across at Ed. Swinging as if he was a kid again. He'd spoken to her mother, asked her to divulge her greatest secret, and done it in such a way as to get her to agree.

Ed really was a world-class diplomat. And he'd done it for her.

So she wouldn't think she'd been banished. So she might stay in Florena.

But for what? So she could remain his secret mistress? Simone loved Ed, but she was never going to agree to that.

'I still have to go back,' she told him. 'You know that.'

Ed paused and took a few swings before he replied. 'I would like you stay, but I understand that it's not simple.'

'Ed, I'm not going to stay here as your secret mistress. My mother might have been happy with that kind of arrangement, but—'

'Oh, Simone! No! That was not my intent. I don't want you to be my secret mistress,' he blurted.

'But that's all I'd ever be.' She picked up his hand. 'This week has been lovely, but we both know that's all it can be.'

For a brief moment she let herself hope that he would contradict her. Tell her that not only did he love her, but that he wanted to marry her. Despite his vow. Despite his country. Despite everything, he loved her and would love her for ever.

But he didn't say any of that. He simply said, 'If we only have a few more days we'd better make the most of it.'

She nodded. A few days. They had only that interlude before life would go back to normal.

Ed stood up and came to her swing, lifted her from it. His green eyes sparkled in the moonlight and he pulled her to him. His lips were warm and she leant into the kiss, but even as she did so he pulled back.

'Sim, you're freezing. Let's go inside.'

'I can't go in. You can keep me warm.' She tugged him closer.

'And have us both get frostbite? Do you want them to find our frozen corpses out here?'

Despite herself, she laughed. 'Think of the memes on that!'

He laughed too.

CHAPTER SIXTEEN

'YOUR FATHER WOULD like to talk to you,' Ed's assistant said.

Ed stood before the full-length mirror in his dressing room. The suit was itchy. Its fabric stiff and weighed down with medals and embellishments. Coronation outfits were definitely not made for lounging in on the couch. And he was still expected to get a cloak over this. Not to mention a five-pound crown on his head.

'Great. Please send him in,' Ed said, desperate for some pointers about how to get through today.

His assistant looked at his shoes. 'No, sir. He's on a video call at your desk.'

Ed's heart sank. His father should be at the palace by now, in time for the coronation.

He sat at his desk and opened the call. His father had a white wall behind him. He could've been anywhere in the world.

'Father, what's going on?'

His father smiled sadly. 'You're dressed. You look wonderful. Very regal.'

Despite his status, Ed felt himself blush. 'Thank you. Where are you?'

'That's what I wanted to talk to you about. I've decided not to come.'

Not come? This was the most important day of Ed's life—how could he not be there? It was obviously unorthodox for a former king to be at his successor's coronation, but they had talked about it and Ed had decided he wanted his father to be there. No matter how unusual it might be.

'How can you not be here? We agreed.'

'I know we did, but I've thought long and hard about it. I know how important it is to you—which is why I can't be there.'

Ed had never seen his father look so uncomfortable. So not regal.

He isn't the King any more. You are.

'It isn't right for a former king to be at the new King's coronation. As much as I want to support you, I think I will serve you best by giving you space. If I'm there the focus will be on me, and that wouldn't be fair to you. They need to see you as the one and only King.'

'But you're still my father—not my former father.'

'A coronation isn't a family affair. It's about you and the country.'

His father had never intended to come. He'd just agreed so that they wouldn't have this conversation until it was too late.

Now he'd have to do it all. The diplomacy. The outmanoeuvring of Laurent. Everything.

It hit him, almost as if for the first time, that his country's future was on his shoulders and his alone. He'd have to please and placate Laurent and his cronies on his own.

'We'd be stronger and more united together, not apart.'

'I can't leave Celine.'

Having his father at the coronation would be a good thing—having Celine there would most definitely not be. She was a lovely person, but if she was at the ceremony the media would have a field day.

'Not even for a couple of days?' he asked his father.

'Not even for a couple of days.'

Was he serious? His father had changed dramatically since meeting this woman.

Another thought occurred to Ed. 'Is she well? Is the baby okay?'

'Yes, she's well, and so is the baby.' His father smiled.

'Then why can't you leave her for a few days?'

'Because I don't want to.'

'I don't understand...'

'Because I love her.'

Ed laughed. 'Oh, don't be ridiculous.'

His father didn't know the meaning of the word.

'I'm not being ridiculous. I love her with all my heart.'

'Like you loved Mother? Like you loved Alea? Like you loved every other one of them?'

'I like your mother—don't get me wrong. And I adored Alea. But I didn't love them.'

Ed shook his head. 'You didn't even love Mother when you got married?'

'No—and I don't think she loved me either. It was a fortuitous, diplomatic and financial match. I tried to love her. I wish I had loved her. But I didn't. If I had, our lives would've been very different.'

'You would have been faithful, you mean?' Ed knew he sounded like a kid, and yet he was about to be crowned.

'Yes, that's exactly what I mean. I'm not proud of the way I've lived my life, but from now on things will be different.'

Ed scoffed. 'Yeah, right. I don't think the Berringer men are capable of love.'

Countless generations of men before them had proven the Berringer bloodline to be fickle and disloyal.

'I thought that too once, but I just hadn't met the right woman.'

'And you have now?'

Ed knew his voice was laced with sarcasm, but he didn't care. His father had let him down. *Again.* First, by abdicating without even a discussion and now by leaving him to get through this day alone.

'Yes. I was a little slow to the game, and my meeting with Celine was a little unusual. But I love her deeply, truly and for ever.'

For ever? How could he even know that?

'For ever? Seriously? You're a Florenan King. Not one of our ancestors has managed to stay with one woman.'

His father laughed. 'You've read too many fairy tales. See them for what they are. Morality tales, at best. Propaganda from those in power, at worst. Laurent and his like use stories like that to their advantage.'

'Laurent didn't write the Florenan fairy tales. They've been around for years.'

'Yes. But he's using that story now, about the Cursed Kingdom, to try to persuade the people to get rid of us. It's a story. That's all. It has nothing to do with you.'

But Ed did know his family. His father. His uncle. His grandfather. And all who had come before them. He shook his head.

'Ed, son, you know as well as anyone that the stories the media tell about our family aren't true. Most of what they print about you is a lie. So why don't you see that story for what it is? A children's story. Marry the woman you love and you will not have any of the problems I had.'

His father ended the call shortly afterwards.

Ed stood and ran his hands through his hair, and squeezed his scalp for good measure. His father wasn't coming. His father was halfway across the world with his young girlfriend. He wasn't coming to the coronation—the most important day of Ed's life—because he wanted to be with her.

If he cared about you he wouldn't have got Celine pregnant in the first place.

If he truly cared for Ed he wouldn't have abdicated.

Objectively, from a public relations point of view, it did make sense for his father to stay away. But Ed had reasoned that having his father there would show the family was still united. And by seeming united they would appear stronger.

Although his father had a point as well. If he was there they would be sending a message to the world that his father was still around. It would look as if Ed was his father's puppet rather than his true successor.

If things had been different you wouldn't have expected your father to be at your coronation.

His death would have been the reason for his absence. But

if things had been different Ed would probably have had many more years to prepare for this day. Not mere months.

No. He had to concede that his father had sound reasons for staying away. His absence was irritating, but it wasn't what was really bothering him. It wasn't the reason Ed wanted to run ten miles. Or scream until his lungs hurt. It wasn't the reason for this growing uncontrollable sensation in his chest.

He let out a cry and felt foolish. It was the other things his father had said. About Celine. About not wanting to leave her for a moment. About the fact that his father had never loved his mother.

'Marry someone you love and you won't have any of these problems.'

But how could he marry the woman he loved? It wouldn't work. There were too many things keeping them apart.

The fact that he hadn't told her he loved her was just the first...

Simone had chosen her coronation day outfit in Paris. White and red—the Florenan national colours—it was a knee-length white shift dress paired with a red jacket and red pumps. Her hair was down, styled into gentle waves and completed with a small white hat.

Simone wasn't used to dressing so formally—long cardigans and floral dresses were her usual look—so she felt self-conscious when she stepped out of her room to find her mother.

Alea had also chosen white and red—a white suit and a red hat.

'You'll steal the show,' her mother said.

'I'm hoping to blend into the background.'

'As if you ever could. Besides, we're up front.'

Simone was horrified. 'At the cathedral?'

'Who else would be?'

'The Prime Minister, for starters. Other heads of state. All the important people!'

'We *are* the important people. Eddie has seated us with his close friends and family.'

'How do you know this?'

'He discussed the seating plan with me weeks ago. We're seated in the first row. Not in the centre—that's reserved for his cousins and their families—but to one side.'

'How can we be at the front?'

On the screen. Photographed. Where her every move could be scrutinised. Her stomach rolled.

'What about the King?'

'If you mean the former King, I understand he hasn't returned.'

'What?

'It's hardly appropriate—'

'I need to speak to Ed.'

As soon as possible. He'd be devastated. When they'd spoken last night Ed had told her that the only good thing about the abdication would be his father being there to see his coronation.

Her mother gave her a quizzical look. 'Now?'

Simone didn't care what her mother thought. What any of them thought. This was between her and her best friend.

'Excuse me a moment.'

She went to her room and pressed Ed's number into her phone.

What was she thinking? He would be too busy preparing to get crowned to take her call.

But the phone clicked and he said in a whisper, 'Hello?'

'Ed, I just heard about your father.'

'Yeah, he called to tell me the good news.'

Simone heard muffled noises, a door closing, and then Ed said, 'Dropped it on me when it was too late to do anything about it.'

'I'm so sorry.'

'Don't be. I see why. He can't be seen to be supporting me. His presence will detract from me and it should be my day. Former kings don't usually go to their successor's coronations.'

'Except as ghosts,' she said.

'Except as ghosts.' He laughed. 'I guess I just thought he would be there…and Mother too.'

It hit her. He really was alone now. Left by both his parents. That was why Simone and Alea were in the front row. She'd have to sit there now. For Ed.

'If it helps, I'm sure he'll be watching—and your mother too. I know they're both proud, even if they can't show it. And I am too,' she said.

'I hope you won't chicken out.' His voice was tinged with uncertainty.

'I wouldn't miss it. I'll be there with bells on.'

'Bells? Really? Don't ring them. That'll only draw attention to yourself.'

She laughed. 'I'd better let you go. See you out there. Good luck—and remember to take the crown, not the baseball hat.'

He laughed.

It was so strange, sitting in the front pew at Florena's royal cathedral. She'd been in the cathedral before, but it looked remarkably different now, decorated with red and white flags and banners interspersed with evergreen branches from Florena's famous pine trees.

The place was packed—literally to the rafters—with guests. Special seating had been erected for the occasion, to allow even more people to attend. But the ceremony itself was to be traditional and austere.

Ed had donated the money that would have been spent on processions and lavish feasts for the select few to charities in the city itself. Tonight's ball would be the only official celebration. Though the coronation would still show the world that Florena was as strong and independent as ever. So much more than a crown rested on Ed's head and shoulders. It was the fate of the whole country.

Simone no longer marvelled that she'd had an invitation. It seemed as though half the country was there. Though she did have literally a front row seat. Just below the high altar, so that when Ed walked in and took his position he was directly in front of her. Despite her earlier reservations, she knew she wouldn't have missed it for the world. Laurent and Morgane were on the opposite pew, but once Ed arrived they blurred into the background and all she saw was him.

He's the King. Your Ed is the King.

For as long as she lived it would be hard to explain her emotions that day. But there was one in particular that stayed with her, and that was the way her heart had felt as the crown had been placed on Ed's head. He'd turned briefly to her, smiled and winked.

She'd resisted the urge to giggle, but her heart had never felt so full.

Because after everything he was still her Ed. And that realisation had been comforting and terrifying at the same time.

She'd hoped that maybe once the crown was on his head something would change. That *he* would change and become more distant and regal. She'd hoped that at the very least she would look at him differently. That it would make it easier for her to leave in two days' time.

But she still saw her Ed.

Only he wasn't her Ed any more.

He belonged to Florena now and would never belong to her.

After the ceremony was complete, and Ed had left the cathedral for photographs, Simone and Alea returned to their apartment to get ready for the ball.

'Stay.'

She sat on her bed with the silk of her dress spread out around her and put on her shoes.

What if she could do what Ed suggested and rise above her fears and stay? Learn to drown out the noise from the trolls? Trust that Ed and the palace would be able to shield her?

She had sat in the front row at his coronation and she had

felt fine. More than that, she wouldn't have missed seeing that special moment for anything.

She'd miss out on so many experiences with Ed if she returned to Paris.

Wasn't he worth it?

Yes, but it wasn't that simple. She had a life in Paris, and she wasn't about to give that up to skulk around the palace with Ed until their affair ran its course.

Because it would. Ed wasn't going to marry—her or anyone else—so a secret affair was all it ever could be.

There was a knock at her bedroom door.

'Is everything all right?' asked her mother. 'We'll be late.'

Simone took a deep breath and emerged from her room. Alea brushed a tear from her eyes and sniffed another away.

'I knew that dress would look wonderful on you. You look spectacular.'

She carried her mother's compliment like a shield as they walked across the palace to the great hall. Did she imagine it or was everyone looking at her? It was probably because she was self-conscious, wearing such a magnificent dress. When she climbed the grand staircase up to the ballroom, she had to lift the voluminous skirt so she didn't trip.

Yeah, that would make a great photo. Her falling face-down on the palace stairs tangled in her dress.

But Simone made it to the top of the stairs without incident and more people turned. She walked through the doors. No, she wasn't imagining it. People *were* turning to look at her— but they weren't laughing. They were smiling.

Still, Simone's heart hammered behind the corset of the dress as she and Alea walked along the short receiving line.

She recognised Ed's closest relatives, his cousins the Dukes of Linden and Clichy, accompanied by their wives. And after them stood Ed. He was shaking someone's hand as Simone approached, but he stopped, paused for far too long.

Simone felt heat rise in her cheeks, but she focused on the two dukes. They greeted her warmly, though showed no sign of knowing who she was. There was no reason why they should, she reminded herself. They'd only met her as children. The last time she'd seen either of them had been Ed's seventeenth birthday, and they clearly wouldn't connect her to the teenager who had embarrassed herself in front of the world.

Maybe no one else would either.

Then she reached Ed. He kissed her mother on both cheeks first, and then swallowed hard. Simone was next. She held out her hand and curtsied, knees wobbling, unused to executing the movement in high heels. Once she'd risen he pulled her in for a kiss on the cheek, just like he had her mother. Only on the second kiss he held her shoulders and kept her close.

'Not only are you the most beautiful woman here tonight,' he whispered. 'But you're also the most beautiful woman I've seen in my entire life. If you dance with anyone else I think I'm going to have them sent to the dungeon.'

She laughed. 'Do you even have a dungeon?'

'I'm not sure. Just…' He pulled her close again. 'Please, save a dance for me.'

Simone floated into the ballroom.

CHAPTER SEVENTEEN

IF THEY HAD handed out dance cards Simone's would have been full. Particularly after Ed had singled her out for the second dance, after his obligatory one with the highest-ranking woman at the ball, the Duchess of Linden.

Simone had been worried she'd be standing next to her mother all night, like a spare part, as her mother spoke to her colleagues and friends, but Simone had met many people. Women she didn't know had come up to her and asked about her dress, and men had asked her to dance. They'd all been friendly and not at all intrusive. Conversation had come easily. Particularly when she'd divulged that she had grown up in the palace and now lived in Paris. People found her life story delightful and asked about her bookshop.

Not one of them thought she didn't deserve to be there.

Not one of them recognised her as the hashtag *palaceserenade* girl.

Later in the night, when her feet ached, she went to find her mother. She sat and reacquainted herself with some of the palace staff, past and present, whom she hadn't seen in years.

Then she and Ed snatched a brief moment together, as she was on her way to the bathroom. They stood, respectably apart, and spoke briefly.

'Thank you for coming,' he said.

'Of course.'

'Not just for tonight. Thank you for being here this week. I don't know what I'd have done without you. I couldn't have got through today without you here.'

She smiled at him, unsure of what to say. She wanted to reach over and hug him, but knew that was out of the question with everyone looking on.

'If it were up to me I'd just dance with you all night,' he whispered.

'But you have to mingle.'

'I do have to mingle, and I fear that if I keep dancing with you then more than one person is bound to notice that I can't keep my eyes off you.'

Simone's body came alive at his words, and she wanted to slip her arms around him and press her body against his. But she knew he was right, so they parted. Ed brushed his hand against hers, sending sparks right up her arm. Two hands touching had never felt so exciting. She turned quickly, so no one would notice the blush in her cheeks.

She glimpsed Laurent and Morgane once or twice, but they didn't come close to where she was. She felt surrounded and protected by friendly people all night long.

When it was all over she and her mother returned, exhausted, to their apartment. Alea helped her undress and Simone went to the bathroom to wash off the make-up and brush out the styling.

She had survived the ball! Not only that—she had thrived. Her mind was dizzy with thoughts of the evening. She'd laughed and talked with so many interesting people. None of whom had thought she was out of place.

She heard soft voices and when she emerged in her pyjamas she saw Ed, standing in the living room. Like her, he'd changed out of his stiff uniform and formal clothes, and was wearing grey track pants and a soft blue sweater. Her fingers itched to stroke him.

'I'll bid you both good evening. Or is it good morning?' Alea said, leaving them alone.

He came straight to her and wrapped her in his arms.

'Should you be here?' she asked.

'It's my palace now.'

She swatted him. 'Here? Now?'

'Do you want me to leave?'

'Of course not.' They only had two more nights together. 'But my mother—'

'Knows you've been sneaking out to my apartment.'

Simone had suspected as much, and found she didn't mind her mother knowing about her and Ed. After all, if she ever needed to go to someone for advice about navigating a secret affair with a king she could think of no better person.

'I just want to hold you,' he said. 'I've never been so exhausted in my life and I just want to be with you.'

They fell into her bed and held one another. With her last ounce of energy she picked up his hand and entwined her fingers with his.

'Do you feel different?' she asked.

'I think maybe I do. But that isn't because of my new hat. I think it's because I now feel that my father really has left.'

Oh, Ed.

'But I realised something today. I'm actually lucky. I could've become King at any moment if he had passed away. But I'm lucky because I can still go to him for advice. He isn't dead. Just living somewhere else. Not many kings are that lucky.'

'I'd say hardly any at all,' Simone said.

'I just have a new job. And it's a job that I've been trained for. It's a job I think I can do.'

She squeezed him. 'I'm really glad to hear that.'

'But it's a job that would be much easier if I had someone else here with me.'

'Your mother?'

'No, Sim. You.'

'Oh, Ed. We've talked about this.'

'But have we really? We've skirted around it, but we've never really talked about it.'

They had, hadn't they? He wasn't going to marry anyone and she wasn't moving back here.

'What would happen?' she asked softly.

'You would move back here and be my girlfriend.'

Did kings even have girlfriends? And was that enough? Was a title and a ring important to her? Maybe not. They were Simone and Ed. Maybe it didn't matter what anyone called them or how their relationship was defined. Because they would always be Simone and Ed. Best friends. And nothing, no one in the world, could change that.

You'd have to move back to Florena.

For the first time she didn't panic at the thought. People had been so friendly and welcoming to her tonight. She'd had a marvellous time.

What was more, after Alea's revelation she understood that she hadn't been sent away to boarding school because she was an embarrassment, someone to be banished from Florena, but because of something that had nothing to do with her at all.

The people didn't think she was a disgrace.

Some of her own fears began to dissolve. Maybe she could start by returning to Florena more often and see how that went? And surely Ed would have to make some diplomatic trips to Paris?

'What would I do?' she asked. 'I couldn't work.'

'You could if you wanted to. You could do anything you want. I'd see to it. I am the King.'

Was he right? Or was he daydreaming?

'Do we have to decide now?'

Exhaustion was overwhelming her. Pushing her lids over her eyes. Maybe she could stay...? Maybe her fears were all unfounded...?

'No, we don't. I just want you to know that I want to be with you.'

Simone fell asleep in his arms and knew that.

Simone laughed, glowed, and looked as though she was having a wonderful time. He loved seeing her like this. Not just enjoying herself, but relaxed and thriving at the ball.

He tried to go her, but someone stopped him. He was stuck, listening to a boring conversation about the crown jewels.

He finally extricated himself as politely as he could, took two steps, but Laurent blocked his way.

Simone disappeared into the crowd. He pushed after her, but again his way was blocked—this time by two men who looked like Laurent.

He caught a glimpse of silver in the next room, but knew he could never reach her. She kept slipping further and further away...

Ed woke up drenched in sweat and shaking.

Simone had not slipped away. She lay next to him now, still fast asleep. Her golden hair was spread around her on the pillow. She looked so peaceful he had to stop himself leaning over and pressing his lips to her cheek in case he woke her.

It was still dark, but a glance at his watch told him it was after six and the palace would soon be waking. He should get back to his apartment as quickly as he could. He trusted his staff, but rumours had a way of leaking out, and the last thing he wanted was any undue attention being drawn to Simone. He could handle any bad press about himself—after yesterday he somehow felt more confident that he could beat Laurent at that game—but if Simone was spooked by internet trolls again she might never return.

As he walked back to his apartments he thought about which rooms were empty and where Simone might be comfortable. Somewhere as close as possible to him. Maybe she could visit more often, or even divide her time between here and Paris. If she was going to do that she'd need her own space.

And then what?

The palace looked different this morning. The sun was slowly rising, and though he had already been King for three months, his being crowned officially had shifted something. Now his father really couldn't come back.

He'd meant what he'd said to Simone last night. He had made his peace with his new position and yesterday had been invigorating. He was going to be the best King Florena had ever had. He would make the Florenans proud of their country and its independence and make sure they put any idea of a union with France behind them as soon as possible.

'If you marry the woman you love then it will all be okay.'

His father was a lovesick fool, and probably rewriting history. He was sure his parents had loved one another once. Even if only for a short time.

What Ed and Simone had was stronger than anything his forebears had felt. Ed and Simone were old friends. Best friends. And amazing together in bed. Surely the odds of a long and happy relationship were stacked in their favour?

As he approached his apartments a staff member passed him and gave him a knowing wink. Why would the King be entering his apartments at six a.m. unless he hadn't slept there all night?

But what if Ed was just as weak as his father? What if he was the unreliable player everyone said he was?

The Playboy Prince? No. He had to block out those voices. They did not speak the truth. He wasn't a playboy. Or a womaniser, like the tabloids said. He was just Ed. A regular guy. Simone Auclair's best friend.

He couldn't imagine cheating on Simone. But if what one day, after those first heady days disappeared, that changed? What if he was as fickle as his father? And his grandfather? And every other King Edouard who had come before him?

What if he played right into Laurent's hands and showed him that the royal family was the disgrace he'd said they were?

He pushed open the door to his rooms.

No. He had to get Laurent out of his head. He would never cheat on Simone. She was his best friend. The person he felt closest to in the entire world.

In his suite, breakfast was laid out for him, and his valet stood by the table, holding the newspapers.

'Sir, there is something you need to see.'

Ed took one look at the front pages and knew that today was not going to go as planned. There was no way Simone would agree to stay now. She'd probably get on the first plane back to Paris.

CHAPTER EIGHTEEN

IT WAS LATE when Simone emerged from her room. Ed had left early. She hadn't expected him to stay. It was another work day for him. So she was surprised to see him in the kitchen, talking to her mother. He was wearing a suit and tie and she stopped. He looked handsome, but she decided she much preferred him wearing nothing at all.

They both turned to look at her when she entered.

'Don't you have a country to run? To save?'

She smiled as she said it, so he'd know she was joking. The truth was she was delighted to wake up and see her two most favourite people in the world.

Neither smiled back.

'Sim, darling, sit down. I'll get you a coffee.'

This wasn't good.

'What's the matter?' she asked as she pulled out a chair, her legs suddenly unsteady.

Ed sat next to her. 'There's been some media coverage.'

She pulled a face. Of course there was media coverage. It had been his coronation.

'Of you?'

They both shook their heads and it hit her.

'Oh… Me?'

But she hadn't done anything! She'd been one of hundreds of guests at the coronation. She and Ed had only danced once, as they had planned, and had only spoken to one another that brief time. They had been so careful not to do or say anything too intimate, in case they were filmed or overheard. Besides, everyone had liked her! No one had recognised her or known she was in that video.

'Can I see?'

Ed and his mother conferred with a look, and then Ed slid an open tablet across the table to her.

The King and the Crooner was the headline, and below it was a photo of the two of them dancing. But Simone's focus was immediately drawn to the next image. A still of the video taken at Ed's seventeenth birthday party.

Bile rose in her empty stomach and she scrolled down to the article itself.

Back to embarrass the Crown: the servant's daughter who managed to manipulate her way into the coronation and the celebratory ball. It seems Simone Auclair won't give up her ambitions with the King.

Simone even managed to trap the King into a dance. But we all know the newly crowned King is vulnerable to a pretty girl. It's no secret that he's known all over the world as the Playboy Prince.

Our sources tell us she is currently running a dusty bookshop in Paris, and it is still unclear how or why she managed to connive her way back into the palace after causing so much disgrace fourteen years ago.

A spokesperson from the Prime Minister's department has said they are looking into the matter and assessing any security risks.'

'Wow… This is…'

'Lies,' Ed said.

How did they know all this stuff? Only someone who knew her would be able to spin it this way.

'Yes, but not entirely. There's just enough truth in it, isn't there? That's what so awful. It isn't lies. Half-truths, maybe.

But I *am* the daughter of a member of palace staff. I *do* run a dusty bookshop. I *have* been hiding in Paris.'

Simone opened up her own social media. She kept it very private, and her settings were as secure as they could be. She didn't even use her own name, for crying out loud, but went by *BookGirl*.

And yet there were many messages about the coronation and the ball. And they were all vile.

Her eyes went to a particular person.

MAL17. The thumbnail was an avatar, different from last time, but the words were similar.

Bad singer, bad dancer...why hasn't she died from embarrassment?

Her hand shook and Ed took the phone from her. He frowned.

'*MAL17.* That was one of the trolls from before,' she said.

The one who had told her to die.

'From when? The video?'

'Yes. I recognise the name. Or rather I recognise the comments. The words are the same. This is the same person.'

'I'll get Home Affairs to look into it.'

Home Affairs. The government.

If they couldn't trust Laurent, they couldn't trust his government. Ed was only a figurehead. He didn't control the government. Laurent did.

She felt even more exposed.

'No. Not them.'

'Why not?'

'Because...because Laurent is after you. Is there someone else you can ask?'

'Laurent wouldn't risk getting involved in something like this. It's too tawdry. Surely it's beneath him?'

'By attacking me he's attacking you. It sounds like his *modus operandi*.'

Ed and his mother shared a look. They thought she was overreacting.

Maybe it wasn't Laurent. But she knew who else it might be. And once it occurred to her she wondered why she hadn't realised it before. It was so obvious.

'Morgane. His girlfriend. Morgane Lavigne.'

She saw their faces turn from incredulity to understanding.

'It's a long shot… Would she risk it?'

'*MAL*. Morgane Lavigne. I bet her middle name begins with an A.'

Ed and her mother were staring at her with open mouths.

'Oh, God. Am I paranoid? It sounds crazy when I say it aloud.'

'You're not crazy or paranoid. You've been viciously and unfairly attacked.'

'Do you want me to go back to Paris?' she said.

'No!' they shouted in unison.

She didn't want to be here, but even Paris might not be the sanctuary she thought it was. If this *MAL17* knew about her bookshop then she might be followed there.

She shivered. Where could she go? Canada? Australia? The middle of the Pacific Ocean wouldn't be far enough.

'Let's look at it before you go anywhere,' said Ed.

She opened a browser on her phone and typed 'Morgane Lavigne' into the search engine. The page opened with lots of glamorous shots of Morgane with Laurent, and also some from years ago, with Ed. Simone swallowed down bile and clicked on one of the links.

Morgane Adrianna Lavigne.

She passed it to Ed.

'I might be paranoid. I might be wrong. But I have this feeling…'

Ed nodded, and then pulled her into an embrace. He held her as if he was trying to protect her and give her strength all at once. She appreciated it, but knew that even he couldn't protect her completely.

No one could.

'I'll get someone to look into it.'

'But not anyone connected to Laurent. Promise?'

'I promise.'

He kissed her on the forehead and left.

'I hope you're right,' said Alea, passing her a coffee and a plate of warm pastries.

'Why?'

'If it's her they'll expose her. It'll all be over.'

Simone shook her head. 'I don't think it will ever be over. I know these things go on and on. She's just one of many.'

'But she's not a nobody. She knows the royal family and she's dating Laurent. She isn't a random person.'

Alea gripped Simone's hand. She started to speak again and then stopped.

Finally, just as Simone was losing sensation in her hand, her mother said, 'Simone, I'm so sorry again you had to deal with all this alone last time. I had no idea.'

Simone nodded. She had forgiven her mother. It was no one's fault except the internet trolls'. 'I know Mum. I know.'

'Can I cook you something?'

Simone couldn't drink the coffee, let alone eat anything. 'I think I want to go back to bed for a while. It was a late night.'

'Do you want to talk?'

Alea's eyes pleaded with her. But Simone didn't want to talk. She didn't want to be awake.

She shook her head. 'I just want to bury myself in my bed.'

And she did.

Simone woke a few hours later, not at all refreshed, and feeling just as beaten as she'd felt earlier that morning.

It was just like last time.

She'd been in this same room. The same bed. Looking at the same snowy view out of her window.

It was as though she'd been transported back fourteen years.

Nothing had changed. Including her sense of suffocation and the desire to get out of there.

Her flight wasn't until tomorrow, but that was less than twenty-four hours to go, and she had no intention of leaving the apartment. She still wasn't hungry, but her mouth was parched. She went to get a glass of water, but as she entered the kitchen Alea sat up, alert and concerned.

'Did you sleep?'

'A little.'

'Do you feel better?'

Simone frowned. 'I think I will when I get back to Paris.'

'Oh, Sim. No. Please at least stay and see how this all plays out.'

'There's no point. No matter what happens, I have to leave.'

'But why? If they find out who spoke to the paper... If they find out who wrote those things...'

'That won't change anything. Not really. Another troll will pop up in their place. You know that. And they will always dig up that video.'

Alea brewed new coffee and this time Simone accepted it, and curled up on the couch.

'The sooner I get back to Paris the sooner I'll be able to get away from all this embarrassment.'

'Why are you embarrassed?' Alea asked. 'You've done nothing wrong.'

But she knew she must have. Half the world was saying so.

'Mum, the comments are horrible. Some of them are telling me to die.'

Alea picked up her hand and squeezed. 'The comments *are* awful. Inexcusable. Criminal. But Eddie is getting someone to look into them.'

Simone nodded. She was out of words. She knew that no matter what Ed found these people would continue. Trolls always found a way. Being in the spotlight made you a target.

Alea scratched her head. 'How does Eddie do it, I wonder?'

'Ed? He was born into it.'

Ed didn't love the scrutiny, but he knew it was part and parcel of the job.

Simone sighed. 'He has a thick skin. He doesn't let things get to him.'

'Doesn't he?'

It wasn't a rhetorical question. Alea put her hands on her hips, as though waiting for Simone to think carefully about her answer.

'I don't know what I would have done without you.'

'I couldn't have got through today without you there.'

They weren't just the platitudes Simone had assumed them to be. Ed managed because he had supportive friends and colleagues around him. When the video of her singing had gone viral Simone had been alone. She'd had no one to help her deal with it. They had sent her away. Maybe things would have been easier if she hadn't had to go through it by herself.

'It does bother him, but he draws strength from the people he loves. Including you,' Alea said, echoing her daughter's thoughts.

Simone nodded. Then shook her head. 'I don't think I'm strong enough.'

'But you wouldn't be alone. You would have me. And Ed.'

'Oh, Mum, if I stay here it'll get worse. And if the government gets wind of the fact that Ed and I are more than friends then they'll use it as more ammunition. *The Playboy Prince strikes again*. I couldn't do that to him.'

'Then here's a crazy idea… Why don't you marry him?'

Simone nearly spat out the last of her coffee. 'He's not going to marry me.'

'Why not?'

'Because he's Ed. He doesn't believe in marriage. He's the Playboy Prince.'

Alea laughed. 'You know him. You know that's all nonsense, don't you? It's all made up by the press. Eddie hasn't slept with any more women than the average thirty-year-old.'

'How do you know?'

'Because I know Eddie. I live here. I see him. I know that pictures of him with pretty women sell papers. I know most of what's published in the press is lies.'

That was what Ed had said the other day, wasn't it? He hadn't slept with even a fraction of the women everyone thought he had.

But it was more than that. 'He's too worried about Florena. He thinks if he doesn't marry then there won't be any further scandal. He thinks not getting married is the way to save the royal family's reputation.'

Alea laughed. 'Really? That's nonsense. Being married—to the right woman—would do wonders for his reputation. And for the monarchy. Who doesn't love a royal wedding?'

'Everyone loves a royal wedding…until the inevitable royal divorce.'

Alea frowned. 'Oh, you two are impossible. What makes you think you and Eddie wouldn't last the distance? You do love him, don't you?'

Don't fall. Don't fall.

'He's my oldest friend.'

Alea raised an eyebrow. 'Sounds like a pretty good foundation for a marriage.'

'Ed hasn't asked me—and he won't.'

It was a ridiculous idea. Besides, she could never be with him. Being married to the King would draw even more trolls in her direction and make things worse than they already were.

Simone went back to bed. Just like last time, sleep was the only thing that stopped the thoughts in her head. Though she never stayed asleep for long.

The next time she woke it was nearly dark outside. She pulled on her dressing gown and went into the living room. Alea was sitting by the fire, still looking concerned.

'How are you doing?' she asked.

Simone shrugged.

'Eddie called while you were sleeping, but he asked me not

to wake you. He has some meetings, and an official dinner, but said he will come by once he's finished.'

Simone longed to see him, but at the same time she knew it was the last thing either of them needed.

'He said to tell you he's working on it. He seems to think that your theory about Morgane may not be out of left field.'

Simone sighed. She should be happy to be right, but she wasn't. Knowing who it was didn't make it any easier to accept.

'I wouldn't be at all surprised if she was behind the video of Eddie's birthday party too.'

'Why on earth would she do such a thing? Why film me and then post it?'

'Because she was jealous.'

'Of me? Why? She was the one he was with at the birthday party.'

Simone could still remember how close Ed and Morgane had been. Their legs tangled in one another's on a sofa.

'Because Eddie loves you.'

Simone grimaced. 'He doesn't. And he certainly didn't then.'

'Oh, Simone. He always has. You're the love of his life. His best friend. He's always loved you. Just for a while he was too young to realise.'

Alea put an old movie on the TV and left Simone staring blankly at it while she prepared some food in the kitchen. A hearty chicken soup with fresh bread. Simone didn't feel like eating, but when the smell hit her she began to salivate.

They ate slowly in front of the television.

'Mum, where did you get that dress? The one I wore last night?'

'I was wondering when you would ask that. Edouard gave it to me.'

That made sense.

'When did you wear it?'

'I didn't.'

'Then why did he give it to you?'

'He wanted me to accompany him to a dinner. I thought about it, but refused. It wouldn't have been right.'

'So you broke up with him?'

'I suppose so. But these things are rarely one-sided. We couldn't give each other what the other needed.'

'Just like Ed and I.'

'No, Simone, not like that at all. You and Eddie are very different. You could find a way through if you wanted to.'

But her mother was wrong. There was no path forward for her and Ed, just as there had been none for Alea and Edouard.

Ed didn't love her. And even if he did he wasn't going to risk his country's future for her.

Besides, she'd never let him.

CHAPTER NINETEEN

As soon as he'd cancelled his remaining appointments for the evening, Ed pulled off his tie and exited his office by the back door. He knew the quickest route to the apartment above the kitchens and took it, finding himself unable to stop smiling at every single person he passed.

He'd decided.

He laughed when he thought of how it had taken him so long when it was really the simplest and most natural thing in the world.

Alea let him in. Simone was reclining on the couch, tousled and gorgeous.

She sat up quickly when she saw him. 'I thought you had a dinner.'

Ed walked in slowly. He was suddenly more nervous now than he'd been entering the cathedral yesterday.

'I cancelled it. I had something more important to do.'

'What?'

'Talk to you.'

Alea cleared her throat. 'I have plans to meet a friend this evening. Have a good night.'

Simone looked at her mother, watching her leave. They both knew Alea had no such plans.

Ed glanced at the other armchairs, but chose the sofa, where Simone was ensconced in a pile of blankets. Guilt tightened around his heart. She wouldn't have to go through this again. He'd make sure of it. No matter how long it took, he would find out who was behind these attacks on her and make it stop.

Simone cleared away the blankets and he sat next to her. He moved to pick up one of her hands, but she put both in her lap before he could.

'I came as soon as I could,' he said.

'It's okay. You're busy. You didn't have to come.'

'Of course I did.'

'Mum said you might be able to trace the article to Morgane?'

'Possibly. We may not know for a few days. Would you…? Simone, why don't you stay until we know?'

She looked down and his heart crashed.

'I have to go back to Paris. My life is there.'

'What if your life was here? Your mother's here. And I'm here,' he said slowly, cautiously.

He had once thought that he would never marry, because marriage had only brought unhappiness and scandal to his family. But now he had figured out the way to stop that. The way to stop scandal wasn't to avoid marriage. It wasn't to avoid commitment. The way to avoid scandal was to make sure you married the right person and committed to them totally. Completely. And the right person—the only person—was sitting right next to him.

'I love you, Simone.'

She swallowed. 'I know you do. We're friends.'

'No. Not as a friend, but as my lover, my soulmate, my life partner. I love you in every sense of the word—body and soul. You are my match. And I want you to be my queen.'

She tilted her face back and closed her eyes. She drew in a deep breath and said, 'Love doesn't last. You said that.'

'That was before I knew what it was,' he said softly.

She shook her head. 'I know how you feel about marriage. I know that it's the last thing you want.'

'No. I've changed my mind. It was after I spoke to my father yesterday, actually. I've realised that the best way to avoid scandal is to marry the right woman. Marry the woman I love. Hiding from commitment won't help.'

Simone opened her eyes and faced him. 'I wish I could believe you.'

His heart thudded to the floor. He dragged both hands through his hair, gripping his skull. 'Why can't you?'

'You just said you want to marry me to avoid scandal. After everything you've told me, that doesn't make any sense.'

'Of course it makes sense! I love you. I'd never cheat on you. I'd never leave you.'

'It's been less than a week. Our relationship has barely begun.'

'It hasn't been a week. It's been a lifetime! I know you and you know me.'

Simone raised one perfect eyebrow and shook her head. 'I don't know that I do. Four months ago we sat by the Seine and you told me that you would never marry. That love didn't exist. And now you want me to upend my entire life? Ed, I care for you deeply. But this isn't the way to get me to stay here for longer.'

Why was she arguing?

Why didn't she believe him?

Because you've spent your entire life telling her you don't believe in marriage. You've spent your entire life actively avoiding marriage.

'Don't you…?'

At the last moment he thought better of asking the question. *Don't you love me too?*

She'd loved him once. Loved him enough to stand up in front of everyone he knew and sing to him.

No. She had a crush on you when she was sixteen. Like every other girl her age in the country at the time. She's smart enough to know that the fantasy of dating a prince is far removed from the reality of marrying a king.

He wasn't Ed, telling Simone that he loved her. He was a king, asking the woman he loved to turn her life upside down for him. Simone was spooked by the press and not without reason. She hated the spotlight. He'd been a fool to ever think she'd say yes.

It felt as though his five-hundred-year-old palace was crumbling around him. Everything he'd ever told himself had been wrong. Everything he believed his whole life had been wrong. And now he was adrift. Alone.

'No. Never mind.'

He shook his head. It didn't matter. Even if a part of her did love him, it wasn't fair of him to ask her what he was asking.

Duty would be his to fulfil alone.

'I love you.'

He'd said it. And Ed didn't lie to her.

He loved her as a friend…but big love? Everlasting love? He'd told her that didn't exist.

'I'll go. I'm sorry.'

He stood and walked to the door.

Simone moved to get up from the sofa, but he waved her back.

'Ed, I'm sorry…'

'Don't be.'

He shook his head, but wouldn't meet her eyes. Was he crying?

No. He couldn't be.

And he was out through the door before she could reach him.

'I love you.'

The floor felt unsteady. But that was probably just her entire reality being tipped upside down. And shaken for good measure.

'I love you.'

She'd made the right decision.

The last thing Ed needed—the last thing the country needed—was someone like her in a relationship with the King. Rightly or wrongly, she brought controversy with her. Ed's main focus needed to be on improving the reputation of the monarchy, not defending her. She was a liability.

Ed's scheme to get married to avoid scandal was so bizarre that he'd wake up tomorrow and change his mind. He was panicked. Not thinking straight. That was all.

Because why would he want to marry her?

He loves you.

And you love him.

Simone buried her face in her hands. Of course she loved him! She'd never stopped. Not since that fourteen-year-old boy had arrived home from school that summer with broad shoulders and a whole new foot of height.

She'd loved him when she'd sung to him at his seventeenth birthday party. Promising that she'd always love him.

And she'd loved him when he'd arrived on her doorstep in Paris. And when they'd kissed by the Seine. She'd loved him then and she would always love him.

In fact, she loved him too much to tell him how much she loved him.

She loved him, she wanted him, she needed him to breathe. *I ache for you. I adore you. I yearn for you.*

But it didn't matter what she felt. Love wasn't always enough, and she had to start protecting her heart.

Simone's phone pinged and she picked up her phone from where she had thrown it earlier. There was a message from Julia. She opened it, but her chest constricted when she saw that Julia had sent a photo from the ball. The one from the article Ed had showed her earlier.

OMG you two are adorable. This pic has made my heart melt! xo

Simone enlarged the photo on her screen and studied it properly.

The photo wasn't bad—that was part of the problem. They both looked lovely. They really did look adorable. She studied the way Ed was looking at her in a way that was impossible to do when he was actually looking at her. His eyes were soft. The skin around them creased. Any outsider who looked at this photo would know that the two of them were very much into one another.

They had both tried not to be obvious. Tried to be discreet all evening. But the photographer had managed to capture a moment between them when their gazes had been locked and slightly dreamy. It had just been one moment, she remembered, but it had been enough.

Was that how the world saw her?

Her hand shook as she opened her social media.

She was tagged in so many posts she couldn't count them. A quick glance showed her that while many were telling her how lovely she looked, most were less complimentary. They called her an upstart. A gold-digger. Ugly. Fat.

She threw her phone on to the couch and clutched a pillow.

If she stayed in Florena…if she stayed with Ed…it would always be like this.

She could ignore social media. She could stop reading the papers. But she couldn't divorce herself from reality entirely.

Even if Morgane turned out to be this particular troll and could be stopped, others would pop up in her place. The palace could protect her to some extent, but it was still up to her. Was she strong enough?

And then she did something she hadn't done in years. She clicked on the link to the video of her singing at Ed's seventeenth birthday party. Her hands trembled.

The opening bars of the song played and her muscles gave the familiar involuntary reaction they always did when she heard them. But this time the rest of the song was unfamiliar. Because *she* was singing.

She was so young…but also so beautiful and sweet. Why had no one told her how gorgeous she was?

She wanted to reach into the screen and shake that sixteen-year-old, tell her how beautiful she was. She was wobbly on her high heels, and she kept tugging at her dress, but her face was gorgeous. Young and bright and hopeful. Untouched by worry and strain.

There was also nothing particularly bad about her singing. She wasn't ever going to win a recording contract, but she held the tune.

She hadn't made a fool of herself. Not really.

No one should have posted that video. No one should even have been taking photos at that party. It had been in the palace, and the guests had all signed non-disclosure agreements.

She should have been safe.

None of this was her fault.

It was someone else's.

And the article published this morning had been lies.

She'd believed the trolls. She didn't blame herself for that. She'd been a teenager and all alone.

But not once had Simone done anything wrong or embarrassing.

And even if she had that was still no reason to attack someone on social media.

She wasn't being weak by leaving. She was being strong. She was leaving the man she loved because it was for the best. She was being strong for him, and she had to keep being strong.

She flicked through the posts until she finally fell asleep on the couch.

Ed would have been lying if he'd said that sitting across the desk watching Pierre Laurent sign his resignation letter wasn't deeply, deeply satisfying. A caretaker Prime Minister had been appointed, and would form a new government as soon as possible.

Ed understood that Laurent and Morgane planned to leave the country later that day. Their reputations were irretrievably ruined in Florena. But he hoped they wouldn't inflict themselves upon another unsuspecting nation.

Laurent looked at him and smirked as he pushed the paper across Ed's desk. Ed smiled back broadly and honestly.

Good riddance.

It turned out the French government had been keeping a close eye on Laurent for a while, given his declared ambitions. They had traced a lot of unusual social media activity to Morgane's PR firm. Simone was not their only victim. Morgane's firm had created a network of fake accounts to attack all kinds of people—especially Laurent's political opponents.

After that it hadn't taken long to also determine that Morgane was the source of the leaked video from Ed's seventeenth birthday party.

The fact that the PM and his girlfriend's private PR firm were leaking material to the press and running so many private social media accounts had caused the newspapers to publish many follow-up articles, and Laurent's resignation had come faster than anyone had guessed it would after his cabinet told him he had lost their confidence.

Laurent might be gone, but it was two days too late. If Ed had done something about Simone's trolls earlier he might have stopped this latest attack on her. Simone might have agreed to stay.

Now...? Now there was no way. How could he convince her to embark on a public life with him when he knew as well as she did that he'd failed to protect her? And there was no guarantee he'd be able to stop other attacks in the future.

The fact was he couldn't offer her his love and promise to protect her at the same time.

Ed had been right all along. It was best to remain single. To dedicate himself to his country and his duty and forget about love. Love was not his destiny.

He might have seen off Laurent and secured Florena's future for the time being. But it had come at the cost of his heart.

'Your Majesty?'

One of his aides had come in.

'Yes?'

'You have an unexpected visitor. It isn't in your calendar but...'

Ed sighed. He wanted to go to his room. Perhaps drown his sorrows in a few glasses of Scotch and take his frustration out on some video games. Not engage with lobbyists.

'No. Tomorrow. Or the next day. I've had enough.'

He stood.

'It's Mademoiselle Auclair.'

CHAPTER TWENTY

THE LAST PERSON Simone had expected to see as she waited outside the King's offices was the Prime Minister. She'd come to say goodbye. To see Ed one final time before she flew back to Paris.

A part of her—a very large part—wanted to leave without having to go through the hurt of a proper goodbye. But he was still her friend and she owed it to him.

And he loved her.

Or thought he did.

Because Ed didn't believe in love. Or marriage. Yet last night he'd claimed to have changed his mind.

Simone didn't have an appointment. She had no right to be rocking up unannounced at his office. Thankfully one of Ed's staff—a woman who had worked in the palace for years—had recognised her and hadn't sent her away at a glance.

'Mademoiselle Auclair, it's lovely to see you. What can I do for you?'

Temporarily shocked at this formal greeting from a woman who had known her since she was a child, Simone had told her that she would like to have a few minutes with the King, if at all possible.

'He is busy at the moment, but if you can wait I will let him know you are here.' She'd smiled and motioned for Simone to sit on the large sofa in the waiting room. 'Can I get you a coffee while you wait?'

Simone had shaken her head. Her nerves were jangling

enough as it was, without adding another coffee into the jit-
tery mix.

The door to Ed's private offices opened shortly afterwards
and Simone stood, expecting Ed to walk out. Instead, she came
nose to nose with Pierre Laurent.

The Prime Minister froze when he saw her, and Simone saw
the exact moment he recognised her. His expression hardened.

But he couldn't hurt her. Nor could his girlfriend.

She met Laurent's gaze, held it, and straightened her back.
She did not need to bow to this man. She certainly didn't need
to smile. This man was trying to destroy her country—not to
mention Ed's life.

And your life.

She held his eyes and dared him to look away first. He
couldn't hurt her. She wouldn't let him.

Laurent lowered his eyes, nodded curtly, and left the room
without acknowledging anyone else.

Wow.

Endorphins rushed through her. She'd looked him in the eye
and nothing had happened.

Except…not nothing. There had been a rush. Exhilaration.
Victory!

The double doors opened fully and there was Ed. Wearing a
bespoke suit and filling it out like…like a king. He stood with
a posture that was intended to say he was ready for anything,
but the paleness of his face belied his confident pose.

She wanted to run to him and pull him to her. But she'd
come to say goodbye.

Hadn't she?

'Simone. Would you like to come in? Have they offered
you a drink?'

'Yes—and yes.'

She stepped into the offices and the large doors were closed
behind them.

She looked around, took it all in. Ed's new offices. The
King's offices.

'Welcome.' Ed waved his hand around the room. 'Have you been in here before?'

She shook her head. The King's offices were not open to children. Even a prince's playmate. In the centre of the room sat a large and imposing desk. The type that would have furniture movers balking. The walls were crammed with Old Masters and portraits of Ed's ancestors.

He led her to a circle of leather armchairs, in the most comfortable-looking part of the room, and motioned for her to sit.

'Unless you'd rather go somewhere less formal?'

She shook her head. Formal was good. Formal would remind her why she'd come to say goodbye.

'I thought about doing some redecorating. But this is an official reception room and when I'm in it I am the King. Having all this around me reminds me of that.'

'Duty first,' she said.

'Not always,' he replied.

Ed met her gaze and held it. The muscles in her chest tightened. Why was this so hard?

'I just saw Laurent.'

'Ah, yes.' Ed's face brightened. 'Good news…great news, actually. He's just resigned.'

'He's what?'

'Yes—just now. I suspect he's off to announce it.'

'Wow…' She saw her recent interaction with him through a new lens. 'Why?'

'Because his girlfriend was using her PR company and various fake social media accounts to harass people. Not only you. Also members of the media. Members of the opposition. And she was doing it at his behest. He's finished.'

Simone frowned. 'I'm glad. Really glad.'

'All talk of Florena being incorporated into France should end. For the time being. I don't expect it to stop for ever. And…' He leant forward. 'I can't promise that there won't be other trolls.'

She nodded.

No wonder Laurent had scurried away when he saw her. Laurent and Morgane had been exposed and it did make her feel slightly better. But there would always be another Laurent, waiting to find a weakness in the royal family. And there would always be another Morgane waiting to humiliate one or the other of them.

But you stared him down. You looked him in the eye and you didn't know he'd resigned. You stood in front of a powerful man, a man who had hurt you, and you didn't hide.

'Sim, why are you here?'

'I came to say…'

Goodbye.

Hadn't she?

Ed reached over and picked up her hand. He clutched it between his and her body flooded with warmth.

She never wanted to let him go.

'I meant everything I said last night. I love you, Simone,' he said. 'Not just as a friend. But as my lover, my partner, my other half. I want to spend my life with you.'

He made it sound so simple—but it wasn't.

'What if the country turns against you?

'Why would they?'

'What if they don't like me?'

'Sim, is that what you're worried about?'

'I'm worried about so many things.'

'There's only one thing you need to worry about. Only one thing we can't get through together. Do you love me?'

She opened her mouth to answer, but the words caught in her throat…behind the tears that had suddenly materialised.

She nodded. Swallowed her tears and said, 'I've always loved you. I never stopped. I tried and tried, but…'

And Ed was next to her, pulling him to her, crushing her against his chest, wiping her tears away.

'Oh, Simone… Oh, Simone… Thank goodness. We can do this. I promise. I love you so much. The people will love you when they get to know you. Besides…their King marrying his oldest friend? How can that be a bad thing?'

He was right. At least he should be. But their world would be filled with so many lies and half-truths. She'd spent fourteen years believing that she'd been sent away for embarrassing the palace, when in truth it had been for a different reason entirely. What if one of them stopped seeing the truth?

'But you're the Playboy Prince and I'm the palace crooner. What if…?'

'What if what? I don't believe any of those headlines and nor should you. You know as well as I do that they are all lies. All that matters is that you and I know what the truth is.'

He clasped her hands tighter.

'Ed, I love you,' she told him. 'With all my heart. More than anything in the world.'

It was such a relief to admit it.

He exhaled and smiled, pulling her to her feet and into his arms.

'So stay. And if the people don't like you we'll leave. I want you as my queen. But more than that I want you as my wife. I want you as my partner. Whether we're living in an attic in Paris, or in a boat on the Seine, or in a caravan in the Alps. I want you as my best friend…my soul mate.'

'Yes!' she sobbed into his chest.

'Yes to what? Living in Paris?'

'No. Yes to staying here with you.'

'Are you sure?'

'Yes. Neither of us have done anything wrong. And we will be stronger together. I've loved you all my life, and I'm not going to let what other people do or say stop us being together.'

They *were* stronger together. Together they would keep one another safe and grounded. Together they would know each other's true selves. She wouldn't be complete without him.

'Then you and I will do this together. I don't want to be apart from you for a single day.'

And he wasn't.

EPILOGUE

THE LITTLE GIRL attempted her first steps in the lush palace garden. Her father held out his hands a metre away from her mother, who gently let her go. The girl took three steps before falling into her father's arms. Both parents hugged their daughter proudly.

'It's so lovely to see children in this garden again,' said the girl's father Edouard, Duke of Armiel.

Celine, the new Duchess, kissed his cheek and steadied their daughter, Alexandria, before letting her try walking again.

'I hope that there are more children soon.' The Duke winked.

'Hang on!' Simone said. 'We'll get there one day.'

Edouard and Celine laughed.

'We've only been married a few months. Give us a chance,' Ed added.

Children would come one day, but there was no rush. Simone was getting used to one new role already: Queen of Florena.

Ed was loving having her by his side every day, but was determined she would have her own projects as well. Things that had nothing to do with her walking three steps behind him.

Her choice had been to focus on charities concerned with teenage mental health, fighting against online abuse and bullying. She had also taken a place on the board for Florena's public libraries. Both positions into which she had thrown herself with passion and gusto.

She did still, on occasion, accompany Ed on his official duties as well. Which he loved. Because every moment she was by his side was easier and more pleasurable.

All the days.

And the nights.

Children would come in time. Children who would not be neglected or ignored. But for the time being he was enjoying having Simone to himself.

She was extremely popular everywhere they went. Any fears she'd had of being rejected by the Florenans had evaporated as soon as their relationship and then their engagement had been announced. The public had lapped up the story of two childhood friends falling in love. Furthermore, the new government had made it clear that personal and vicious abuse and threats to any member of the royal family—or indeed anyone in Florena—would not be tolerated.

Ed's father and Celine now lived in Paris, in a house much larger than Simone's attic.

Julia and André were now living in the attic, and André was running the bookshop full-time.

However, André's new landlord was a bit more relaxed than Mr Grant.

Ed had purchased the bookshop and the attic apartment for Simone as a wedding present.

She'd been horrified, but he had told her, 'I want you to always feel that you have somewhere to run away to. I don't want you to feel trapped here.'

Simone didn't feel trapped in Florina.

She felt at home.

Queen Isabella had been back for some visits as well. In fact both the former King and Queen had attended Ed and Simone's wedding, in a feat of diplomatic gymnastics that Simone still wasn't sure how they had managed to pull off.

But they had. Because together they were much stronger than they had been apart.

The wedding had been wonderful and the press commentary all positive, although neither of them had lingered too long in following it. Their trusted aides had told them what they needed to know. Besides, after the wedding they had enjoyed a very private honeymoon in a location no one had managed to discover—Tahiti—but they kept that to themselves.

'Your son will be King Edouard the Fifth,' said Ed's father.

'No. I am the last Edouard. The fourth King.'

The curse—if there really ever had been one—was lifted. By him marrying the right woman. By him making the woman he loved his queen. The kingdom would be cursed no more.

* * * * *

COMING SOON!

We really hope you enjoyed reading this book.
If you're looking for more romance
be sure to head to the shops when
new books are available on

Thursday 1st February

To see which titles are coming soon, please visit

millsandboon.co.uk/nextmonth

MILLS & BOON

MILLS & BOON®

Coming next month

CINDERELLA IN THE SPOTLIGHT
Sophie Pembroke

He tried not to let his mouth fall open at the sight of her, but he honestly wasn't sure if he'd succeeded or not.

If he'd been blown away by the dresses she'd worn on previous nights, nothing had prepared him for tonight's gown.

It was black and white, fell all the way to the floor, and—crucially—was strapless. In fact, Eli assumed the thing was only staying up from sheer force of will. Or perhaps because it fitted so closely to her torso, before flaring out into a wide skirt with a slit that ran... oh, God. It ran all the way up to her mid-thigh.

She looked stunning - a point that was lost on none of the people she walked past.

She looked... she looked like she always did in the photos in magazines. The ones where she was on Ben's arm, going to some flashy event or another.

That thought brought him back down to the ground, fast. And when she reached him, he struggled to return her smile.

"Everything okay?" she asked, looking concerned.

"Everything's fine." *Except I've fallen for my brother's ex, who he probably expects to get back together with any moment. And she's so far out of my reach I shouldn't even be able to see her.*

But he could. And that fact was doing things to him.

"Is it the dress?" Willow looked down at herself, dismayed. "I was worried it was too much. But when I sent Kelly a photo, she said it was perfect."

"It is perfect." His voice sounded gravelly, even to his own ears. "You look perfect."

Perfect for Ben. Not for him.

"Okay. Good." Willow was still eyeing him sideways, like she was trying to figure out what was wrong with him.

But it wasn't like he could tell her, was it?

Kelly came to his rescue, thankfully, although she shot him an accusatory look as she did it. "Willow, you're here!"

The two women appreciated each other's dresses, and then Kelly whisked her off to chat to some of the kids she'd met at the Castaway Cafe the other week. But not before she paused to whisper at him, "That was lame, boss. Very, very lame."

And the worst part was, Eli knew she was right.

Continue reading
CINDERELLA IN THE SPOTLIGHT
Sophie Pembroke

Available next month
millsandboon.co.uk

Copyright © 2024 Sophie Pembroke

Introducing our newest series, Afterglow.

From showing up to glowing up, Afterglow characters are
on the path to leading their best lives and finding romance
along the way – with plenty of sizzling spice!

OUT NOW

Two stories published every month, find them at:

millsandboon.co.uk

OUT NOW!

Available at
millsandboon.co.uk

MILLS & BOON

OUT NOW!

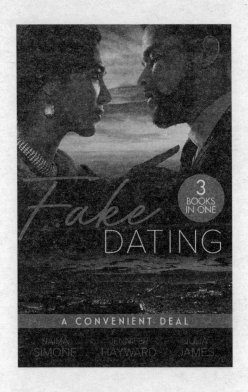

3
BOOKS
IN ONE

Fake
DATING

A CONVENIENT DEAL

NAIMA
SIMONE

JENNIFER
HAYWARD

JULIA
JAMES

Available at
millsandboon.co.uk

MILLS & BOON

OUT NOW!

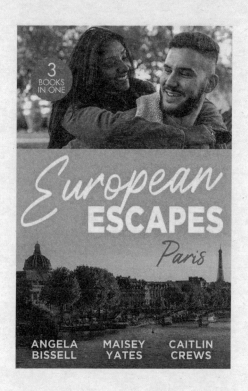

Available at
millsandboon.co.uk

MILLS & BOON

LET'S TALK

Romance

For exclusive extracts, competitions and special offers, find us online:

- **f** MillsandBoon
- **X** @MillsandBoon
- **◎** @MillsandBoonUK
- **♪** @MillsandBoonUK

Get in touch on 01413 063 232

For all the latest titles coming soon, visit
millsandboon.co.uk/nextmonth

MILLS & BOON
A ROMANCE FOR EVERY READER

- **FREE** delivery direct to your door
- **EXCLUSIVE** offers every month
- **SAVE** up to 30% on pre-paid subscriptions

SUBSCRIBE AND SAVE

millsandboon.co.uk/Subscribe